PASSION'S FLAME

"Scott O'Roarke! What are you doing here?" Angelique's thick black lashes fluttered, the way they always did when she was excited.

"I had to see you," Scott said. "I'm just a fisherman, but I understand the ways of your people. Your father . . ."

"And what is wrong with being a fisherman, Scott?" she whispered, aware that he had taken her hand and was holding it gently in his. Was this the night she would receive her first kiss? Her heart pounded.

"You are the most beautiful girl I've ever seen, Angelique Dupree," he murmured into her hair. "I lost my heart the moment I saw you." Powerless to resist any longer, he took her in his arms and kissed her gently. He knew that he was the first man to kiss those rosebud lips!

A flame of passion rushed through her and she nearly swooned. Instinctively, her arms went up to encircle his neck and she pressed her body against his, wanton with desire.

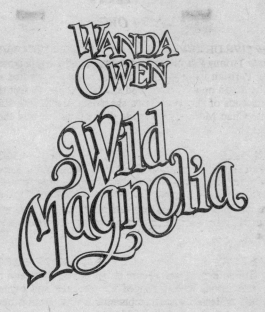

WANDA OWEN

Wild Magnolia

ZEBRA BOOKS
KENSINGTON PUBLISHING CORP.

This book is for you, Ann LaFarge. It's been a pleasure to have you as my editor and I also feel that you are a very dear friend.

ZEBRA BOOKS

are published by

Kensington Publishing Corp.
475 Park Avenue South
New York, NY 10016

Copyright © 1992 by Wanda Owen

First printing: February, 1992

Printed in the United States of America

Part One

The Splendor of Springtime

Chapter One

Maurice and Simone Dupree had always felt that since they were to be blessed with only one child, they'd surely been sent an angel from heaven. So they named her Angelique.

She was a beautiful baby with delicate, perfect features and a little rosebud mouth. Her head was covered with silky black ringlets. As she grew older, Simone could never bring herself to cut the beautiful tresses.

She was raised in the strictest traditions of her French Creole parents. The slightest childhood illness would demand that the doting Maurice and Simone sit by her bed throughout the night to assure themselves that she was breathing properly or her fever wasn't soaring too high.

All their friends knew how the couple pampered and adored their only daughter. It amazed them that the child was not an obnoxious, precocious little brat, which was not to say that Angelique did not show spirit. She was a happy little girl with a soft, infectious laugh. Everyone adored her.

Wherever the Duprees went with her, she always drew stares as people admired the long black curls that fell almost to her waist by the time she was ten years old.

Angelique found nothing annoying about the smothering love of her parents until she reached her fourteenth birthday, when she began to wish for the freedom her friends had.

Maurice and Simone were perplexed by her sudden pouts and sullen face when they refused her a request. Maurice wisely remarked to his wife one evening after Angelique had haughtily marched off to her room in a temper. "She's growing up, Simone, and I guess we were stupid not to know that she would not remain our little girl forever."

"But I had to refuse her tonight, Maurice. It's different for the Gervais girls, for they have older brothers to look out for them."

"Ah, ma cherie — I understand exactly but our Angelique doesn't."

This particular scene was repeated over and over in the next year. Simone saw traits in her beautiful daughter that reminded her more and more of her own grandmother. She recalled how her mother had spoken of *her* mother, Delphine, who'd come to New Orleans in 1763 from France and was put in the care of the Ursuline nuns. She and her fellow emigrants were called "cassette girls," for each brought a casket or dowry, hoping to marry one of the settlers.

From the tales her mother had told, Simone knew that her sixteen-year-old grandmother had been a very adventuresome belle.

Now that Angelique was suddenly struggling against the tight reins, Simone began to wonder what the next six months would bring.

Finally, she and Maurice decided that Angelique would feel she had more freedom if they allowed her to visit friends and go for rides in the carriage without her mother. They informed their driver, Zachariah, that he was responsible for her safety and the black man took their orders very seriously.

Monsieur Maurice Dupree was a very important man and a very wealthy one, and Zachariah was proud to wear the livery as the driver of the Dupree family. He always noticed how people seemed to be impressed as he guided the fancy carriage down the streets of New Orleans when he took members of the family around the city.

He felt it a very special trust to be asked by Monsieur Dupree to perform the duty of protector to the beautiful Mademoiselle Angelique. He would do just that, no matter what was required of him.

Old Zachariah had lived long enough to know that a stunning little French Creole beauty like Angelique Dupree could demand that a man lay down his life for her. Fancy ladies in New Orleans had often sparked duels between amorous suitors.

She had not reached her sixteenth birthday Zachariah knew, but his eyes had already seen the blossoming of the very sensuous lady she would soon become.

Zachariah started taking Angelique to shops and to friends' homes to spend the afternoon. He was constantly aware of the stares from gentlemen as his carriage rolled down the streets.

He saw the pleased look on Angelique's pretty face as she emerged from shopping in the salons and boutiques. She was enjoying her freedom! An amused smile creased his shining ebony face. He understood the sweet taste of freedom.

He watched her come out of the houses of wealthy families who were close friends of the Duprees and she would be gaily laughing with the young girls.

Zachariah always felt satisfied as he guided the carriage back to the grounds of the Dupree estate. He had seen Mademoiselle Angelique home safely.

She was always gracious and rewarded him with one

of her lovely smiles when she left the carriage to rush to the house. There wasn't a haughty bone in her body.

Zachariah considered his duty of taking Mademoiselle Angelique around New Orleans a delightful pleasure. But he could not know that in the short period he'd been taking her to various places in the city, he had been trailed by a most ardent admirer. From the first moment Francois LaTour had seen the beguiling beauty sitting in the carriage, he was determined to find out who she was, for he'd never seen a more enchanting beauty in New Orleans.

While the dapper Francois LaTour was welcomed into many of the homes of the wealthy families, certain French Creoles did not accept him, for there was the rumor that he was a friend of Jean Lafitte. Others accepted his story that he'd broken with Lafitte before he ever settled in New Orleans. He projected the image of a respectable businessman.

He had obviously been very prosperous, for he owned a secluded estate out at Pointe a la Hache, west of Black Bay and Breton Sound.

After trailing the Dupree carriage for several weeks, Francois learned that the lady he admired was Angelique Dupree, the young daughter of Maurice Dupree. It was more than just an attraction. Francois was beguiled by her breathtaking beauty.

He became obsessed, thinking about that lovely face day and night. He had to possess her and it mattered not what he had to do to accomplish it.

Another man had chanced to see the lovely Angelique in her carriage as it traveled along Lake Pontchartrain one afternoon. It had been a good day for Scott O'Roarke, for he'd caught a bounty of fish that spring day. He couldn't think of a better way to be rewarded than by the sight he saw on the road along the lake! He was ready to dock and get in his canoe to go home, back in the bayou, when his eyes caught sight of Angelique in the carriage. He turned to his friend, Justin. "Look at that. Just look at that! Now that's one lovely lady. That beautiful hair! Makes a man want to run his fingers through it, wouldn't you say?"

"Can't deny that, Scott! But damn you, don't you ever tell my Mimi I said that because I'll call you a liar," Justin laughed.

"A man can look, Justin. The sin is when he touches." Scott knew that Justin and Mimi were devout Catholics, as his mother and father were. Scott had always sensed that a lot of the French in the area had resented the Irish who'd sought to settle there. But Justin and Mimi had been the exception. They lived back on the bayou like Scott's family.

Bad health had forced Scott's father to turn the helm over to him a year ago. He worked the bays for fish every day to support his family and the only time he took off was when bad weather moved in.

Scott was glad to have a man like Justin, who worked the last five years for his father. When Scott had taken charge, he'd found the experienced Justin a tremendous help.

Justin was a hard worker, as Scott knew from his father. He was back attending to the nets after he and Scott had taken a moment to admire the lovely lady in the carriage. Justin had already forgotten about her but his younger friend obviously had not.

"She was a beauty, wasn't she? Wonder who she is."

"I have no idea, Scott," Justin mumbled as he shrugged his robust shoulders, his tanned hands busily untangling the net.

He turned around to glance over at the handsome young Irishman staring up at the road where the carriage had lingered. An amused grin came to his face. Young Scott had a lovestruck look. He would not have dared voice his thoughts, but a poor fisherman didn't have a chance with a wealthy young miss like that. If Justin were wagering he'd say she was the daughter of a wealthy French Creole family.

Justin was right, for Scott could not forget that lovely face with the wide-brimmed straw hat and long black hair. He'd had an eye for pretty girls since he was fifteen. This lady was exceptional! She possessed the grace and elegance of a queen!

By the time the fishing boat had traveled down the bayou to the pier where Scott let Justin off to go up to his cottage, he told Justin, "I'm going to meet that girl. Can't get her off my mind!"

Justin smiled. Scott could not read his thoughts, but there was a feeling inside him that it was inevitable they'd meet.

It didn't matter that she was probably the daughter of a wealthy New Orleans family because the cocky Irish fisherman was rich, too — in the confidence that he could make it happen.

He was determined to find out who she was!

Chapter Two

A week later Scott O'Roarke was still thinking about the beautiful Angelique Dupree as he and Justin were moving around the deck of their boat barechested in faded blue pants, as the warm Louisiana sun shone down at mid-afternoon.

On one of her outings, Angelique requested that Zachariah stop the carriage so she might observe the boats in the cove of the lake. There were three other boats there besides O'Roarke's *Bayou Queen,* but it was this one Angelique's dark eyes were drawn to for she spotted the bronzed figure of a very handsome young man sauntering across the deck. His black hair curled around the back of his neck and a long, unruly wisp fell over his forehead. She found herself entranced as she watched him move, unaware of her gaze.

She saw the broad tanned shoulders and chest and the trim waistline. His firm hips seemed to be molded to the faded blue pants that were rolled up halfway to his knees. He wore no shoes.

To Angelique, he was the handsomest man she had ever seen. None of the sons of the French Creole families were this dashing or good looking despite their fine attire.

Zachariah turned around to see the intense look on her lovely face and assumed that she was just intrigued by the sight of the fishing boats which she'd probably never seen before. Being with the Dupree family as long as he had, he knew the cloistered life Mademoiselle Angelique had led up to a few months ago. Many young girls were married by the time they were Mademoiselle Angelique's age. This pretty young girl had never been allowed a suitor yet, as far as Zachariah knew.

When Scott's eyes were drawn to the place where the carriage had halted before and the same lovely enchantress was staring directly at him, a smile brightened his face. He knew she was looking at him and he held up his hand to wave. His heart pounded wildly when her gloved hand waved back.

Zachariah saw this and quickly responded. "I think it's time we start for home, mademoiselle."

"I guess so, Zachariah," she replied halfheartedly. But she was not looking at the black man when she spoke, for her eyes were still on the young fisherman. When he'd waved and smiled, Angelique knew he was handsome even though quite a distance separated them.

As Zachariah guided the carriage back to the Dupree estate, he knew his job might not prove to be as easy as he'd first thought. Like bees are drawn to honey, men were going to be drawn to the honey-sweet lips of mademoiselle. For all his power and wealth Monsieur Maurice Dupree could not keep it from happening.

Francois LaTour had left New Orleans late in the afternoon for his estate at Pointe a la Hache to spend the next few days. There was nothing unusual about

14

this routine, for Francois spent time at both of his homes. The one in New Orleans was not as lavish as his mansion at Point a la Hache, but he found it necessary to conduct business affairs in New Orleans, so he needed a home in the city.

His old friend and cohort, Jean Claude, accompanied him down the river to his fortress estate some thirty miles south of New Orleans. Knowing Francois so well, Jean Claude knew he was preoccupied as they traveled down the muddy Mississippi. Would he take him into his confidence as he often did? Francois sometimes frightened him with his daring, adventuresome nature. Jean Claude wanted no problems with the authorities but he also had to admit that he lived quite well on the fees he earned from Francois for his counsel.

Jean Claude considered it lucky that he was a bachelor, for no wife would have tolerated these sudden jaunts he was asked to make with Francois.

It was dark when they docked at the wharf at Pointe a la Hache, but the glowing light of torches brightened the area as they went ashore. One of Francois' men had a buggy to take them from the wharf to the nearby mansion. His devoted servant, Darius, was at the door to greet them as he always was when Jean Claude had come with him to Pointe a la Hache.

It was not until the two of them had enjoyed their dinner and were relaxing in Francois' elegant parlor that Jean Claude was given a hint about what was on Francois' mind. In the last week he had managed to find out the name of the beautiful young lady with hair as black as a raven's wing.

"Tell me, Jean Claude, about the Dupree family. What do you know?"

"You speak of Maurice Dupree?" Jean Claude inquired. He assumed that Francois had been invited to the soiree Madame Dupree was giving for her husband's birthday. He had not received an invitation, but one of his wealthy clients had, and had mentioned it to him.

"The same. I've heard of them but I've never met them at any social affairs in New Orleans."

"From what I've heard, I don't think they attend many social affairs. Maurice is a very private person who is completely devoted to his family and his land. Doesn't often come in to the city from his country estate."

"Large family, eh?"

"Not at all. There is only one daughter, as a matter of fact. A very beautiful daughter she is! She has a lot of young men eager to court her but I understand that Maurice has not allowed that yet. In fact he and his wife, Simone, rarely let her out of their sight."

Francois could see why old Dupree was so protective.

"Were you invited to the Dupree's party, Francois?"

"Party?"

"Guess you weren't. Nor was I. I suppose only a chosen few got an invitation," Jean Claude remarked, taking the last sip of his brandy.

"No, I did not receive an invitation," Francois confessed as he rose from his chair to pour himself another a brandy and refill Jean Claude's glass.

Jean Claude was curious about Francois' interest in the Dupree family. He felt sure it had nothing to do with business.

In a lighthearted, jesting mood, Jean Claude taunted him. "It couldn't be the beautiful Angelique who interests you could it, Francois?" He threw his head back and laughed.

Francois' black eyes flashed with a brief moment of fire until he gained control of his emotions and started to laugh, too. Forcing a smile, he retorted, "Now what

16

would be wrong with that, mon ami?"

"Because it would never work, Francois. They stay within a small, select circle of French Creole friends. The young man allowed to court Angelique Dupree will be the son of one of the dozen families of that group. It's as simple as that, Francois."

What he did not add was that certain of Francois' dealings over at Grand Terre with LaFitte would have been frowned upon by Monsieur Dupree. Jean Claude knew that many of the lavish treasures in both of Francois' homes were purchased from LaFitte's warehouses. Pirate's bounty would leave a foul taste in Maurice's mouth.

But Jean Claude realized that Francois was a welcome guest in some wealthy businessmen's homes. As a young lawyer, Jean Claude welcomed the generous fees Francois paid him for his legal advice and service, but he could be a very demanding, overbearing individual.

Jean Claude was weary from the trip down the river and more than ready to go to his room. It was good to hear Francois say he was ready to get some sleep. Jean Claude wasted no time finishing the brandy so he could get on upstairs.

The next morning he slept very late. He figured that since he would be away from the routine of his office he might as well take it easy. Pointe a la Hache was an incredibly beautiful and restful setting.

It was noon when he finally made it downstairs and Darius informed him that Francois would not be back until late afternoon.

Jean Claude speculated that Francois was paying a visit to Jean Lafitte, since he would be gone until late afternoon. Knowing his habit of getting up at dawn, Francois would have had time to go to Grand Terre Island. But he did not ask Darius where his master was.

He ate a light lunch and went for a roam down by the beach at the back of the vast estate. The property was bordered on the east by the bay and on the west was the river. This was a marvelous place to relax because there were no crowds milling down busy streets and no noise. He drank in the beauty of colorful exotic flowers and tall majestic palms lining the beach. There always seemed to be a breeze blowing in over the bay.

Jean Claude walked a long way down the beach and sat down to rest before he started the stroll back to the house. He couldn't resist taking his shoes off to let his feet burrow into the sandy beach.

In fact, he didn't put them on again until he reached the flagstone path leading to the house. When he arrived he was surprised to find that Francois had returned.

He was also surprised to hear him announce that they would return to New Orleans the next morning, cutting short their stay by one day. That was just as well, as far as Jean Claude was concerned, but he wondered why Francois had urged him to come, for they had not discussed any business matters yet.

They dined together that evening and played cards later, but Francois mentioned nothing that required Jean Claude's opinion. Instead, they shared casual conversation. Yet, he knew Francois had some reason for bringing him here.

The young lawyer felt that something was very much on his companion's mind. Francois could be a very complex man at times.

When they arrived back in New Orleans, Francois' carriage was there to meet them. Jean Claude wondered how that could have happened. But when they arrived at Jean Claude's house and he was getting out of the carriage, Francois told him, "Enjoyed your company, Jean Claude. We'll have lunch next week."

Jean Claude gave him a nod as he prepared to mount the steps to his house, perplexed as he went inside. Francois LaTour was one of the most puzzling clients he had. It was impossible to get to know the man, though he'd done work for him for two years.

As Francois traveled on toward his own house, he sensed that his young friend was slightly frustrated about the jaunt. But he had accomplished what he'd set out to do — and sooner than he'd expected.

Now he was ready to proceed with his plan to possess the lovely Angelique Dupree and he was more aware of the tedious task it was going to be to do it.

The first day a basket of roses arrived at the Dupree home for Angelique, she was excitedly surprised. "Who would have sent them, Mother?"

Simone tried to seem casual as she smiled at her daughter. "As the card states, my darling, from a secret admirer."

She wondered how Maurice would take this and if he would be disturbed that Angelique had met someone on her recent rides around the city.

"Have you met someone, Angelique?" Simone asked.

"No, mother — I haven't. That's why I'm so puzzled."

But when another basket of roses arrived the next day, Angelique immediately was struck by the thought that the handsome young man she'd seen on the fishing boat might have sent the flowers.

Her romantic young heart wanted to believe this, for she had never seen a more handsome man. It never dawned on her that a young fisherman like Scott O'Roarke could not afford such gifts, especially two days in a row.

Maurice Dupree was irate when his wife told him that Angelique had received another basket of roses from a mysterious admirer.

"I don't like this at all, Simone. There's something wrong when a young man does not sign his name. He is not the proper young man for our daughter. We have to keep a sharper eye on her until this is cleared up."

Chapter Three

Simone Dupree was usually a calm, organized lady but the last few days she'd been anything but that! She found it impossible to get on with her plans for the birthday dinner she was having as a surprise for Maurice when she had to keep soothing his agitation about this mysterious admirer. She also felt sorry for Angelique because she did not understand her father's attitude. He was making her feel guilty and she swore to her mother she had no idea who it might be.

"I don't think Papa believes me, Mother. But I've never lied to either of you. It isn't a thrill to get them now for they've caused too much trouble here," she said as she turned to leave the parlor and go up to her bedroom.

It pained Simone to see the sad look on her daughter's face. Tonight after dinner she would have a talk with Maurice. He was being very unfair to Angelique and this was not like him at all. But it suddenly dawned on her why he could be acting as he was and this made her feel sorry for him, too. Maurice was dealing with something he was not in charge of and he didn't like it. He was not prepared

21

for any young man to come into Angelique's life just yet.

Perhaps it was a shame that they could not have had more than one child upon whom to lavish all their affection and attention.

After dinner she carried out her plans to speak to him about Angelique. "She can't help this, Maurice, and she should not be treated as if she is guilty. You aren't being fair with her and she's hurt."

He was certainly aware that his devoted Simone was running out of patience with him and her sympathy was with Angelique. "Well, Simone—I think for her own good we should not allow her these little jaunts she's been taking for a week or two until we can get to the bottom of all this."

"And how do you suppose we'll do this, Maurice?"

"We could find out from the delivery man where they're being sent from," he pointed out.

"Maurice! Maurice, I can't sit by the front door all day. They arrive at various times and it's the servants who accept them. All I know is some young man is spending a fortune buying our Angelique flowers so he'll make himself known to her."

Maurice had to accept the fact that Simone was not as disturbed by all this as he. Perhaps he had overreacted, he thought.

But baskets of roses continued to arrive and by now it had been a week since all this had begun. But Simone and Angelique had both been grateful for Maurice's mellowed manner.

Simone had continued with her plans for the dinner party. Her elaborate menu had been turned over to her cook and the wines and champagne had also been selected. She and Angelique had gone into New Orleans for the final fitting of their gowns. The mood had been light and gay as the driver loaded their packages into the carriage before they stopped at Simone's favorite little tearoom for lunch. Andrea's was crowded.

But as they began dining, Angelique's dark eyes chanced to glance across the room at a gentleman staring at her intensely. He gave her a warm smile and she returned her eyes to her plate. But she could not resist looking back and each time he was still staring.

He was finely attired with a debonair manner. She saw that he knew some of the people sitting near him, as she saw them engaged in conversation.

His hair was as black as hers and he wore long sideburns. His thin-lined mustache enhanced his features, she thought. A mustache on a man was usually not that attractive to her, but there was something about the way his black eyes held her that made her want to turn away. She was glad when they had finished their lunch and Simone announced that they must be leaving.

Still in a happy mood, she told Angelique, "We must get our parcels in the house before your father arrives. So far, he has no idea about the party but he would certainly suspect something if he knew I'd bought a new gown."

As they left Angelique could not resist glancing back over her shoulder. The man was standing up watching them prepare to board their carriage.

By the time they pulled away, he was leaving the tearoom. He was a trim-figured gentleman and much taller than she'd suspected. Never would she have imagined that this was the admirer who'd sent her seven baskets of roses.

Francois was certainly a man obsessed. He had to have this little temptress now that he'd observed her

23

in the tearoom. Previously he had seen her only for brief, fleeting moments but today he'd had a chance to study that lovely face and savor it. It was like no face he'd ever seen.

He had watched her and her mother leave the tearoom, her petite figure moving with such grace. He watched the swaying flounces of her gown; her glorious crown of jet black hair seemed to sway in the same tempo as she moved out of the tearoom.

When he went to board his carriage he was aflame with impatience to claim her. Perhaps the perfect time to do it would be on the night of the party her mother was planning.

Francois had been a very busy man this last week, for he met and spoke with several influential businessmen in the city. In the course of conversations, he had learned the date and time of the party. In some social circles of New Orleans' elite families, Francois could have managed to get invited to the soiree. But this time he would never have managed to manipulate an invitation.

Francois was not adverse to doing anything he had to do to get what he wanted. If he had been he would not have acquired the wealth and riches he possessed. There had been a time when he did not wear the finely-tailored clothing he wore now, and he had never lived in a grand home like the one he now owned.

Few people knew the truth about Francois LaTour. He had established himself in New Orleans some six years earlier as a young businessman and purchased a house, which he still lived in when he wasn't at Point a la Hache.

There had been a time when his attire was a pair of baggy pants and a loose-fitting tunic when he sailed out of the gulf flying the flag of a pirate ship. He was one of Jean Lafitte's best captains, but Francois had seen that era coming to an end. Jean was a fair man, for he gave Francois his freedom to pursue the life he wanted.

Jean knew that the day would come when he could no longer do battle with the authorities in New Orleans or defend his fortress on Grand Terre Island. All the influential businessmen who eagerly did business with him, just as Francois did, would not lift a finger to help him against the law.

Francois was the first to admit that the few years of adventure he'd shared with LaFitte would never be matched in his lifetime but the idea of being thrown in jail was not for him. When he'd said a fond adieu to his friends on Grand Terre, he turned his back and assumed a new life and a new name. He'd never regretted that decision.

But if he had to return to his days as a reckless young pirate to get the beautiful lady he idolized then he'd do it by taking her captive and keeping her at his remote estate at Pointe a la Hache. While she might protest as a lot of the young lovelies had when they were taken captive by the pirate crews most became the lovers of the men they'd fought so desperately at first.

Perhaps it would be that way with the beautiful Angelique, he thought to himself, and soon she would become his willing mistress and he would be her ardent lover. He fantasized that after that she would not wish to leave him to go back to her parents.

This was the magnificent obsession that consumed him from the first moment he'd seen her.

It was Friday and the day that the fishermen pulled in along the wharf to sell their fish to the passersby and servants from the fine houses. Zachariah was one of these servants whose carriages had pulled up by the dock. Against his better judgment he'd finally agreed to let Mademoiselle Angelique go with him when she'd given him one of her prettiest pouts, saying, "How could I be a problem, Zachariah? I'd just like to sit in the carriage and watch all the people on the wharf. That would be fun."

He'd not had the heart to turn her down, for it did seem like a little thing.

When he arrived at the wharf and got down from the driver's perch to seek out the boat where he usually bought fish for Madame Dupree, he urged her to be sure to stay inside the carriage.

"Oh, I will, Zachariah It's a sight to see, isn't it? So many people milling around! These fishermen must make a lot of money on these days," she declared excitedly as her black eyes danced back and forth over the crowd.

"Fresh fish is mighty fine eatin', miss," he declared as he prepared to leave the carriage to seek out the *Bayou Queen* or the *Swamp Angel* which he considered brought the best catch.

Angelique leaned out the window of the carriage with her dainty hands cradling her chin as she watched the sea of faces all around her.

Her gorgeous face was immediately recognized by Scott O'Roarke as he jauntily walked down the wharf. His happy-go-lucky Irish nature swore that destiny had arranged it — he could see as he got closer that she was alone.

Old Mindy, the flower vendor, was selling her

26

flowers to the passersby on the wharf and Scott gave her a wink as he plucked one of the perfect white rosebuds from her bucket. She gave him no fuss for she knew he would bring her a fine fish for supper tonight. But she could not resist playfully admonishing the cocky young Irishman.

"Behave yourself, lad!"

"Oh, always!" he grinned, walking on toward the carriage where he saw the long-haired miss looking out the window. Angelique did not know he was approaching until he stood smiling by the door, the white rose in his tanned hand.

"Good day, mademoiselle. A beautiful rose for a beautiful lady."

She looked at him, recognizing him immediately, and her hand hesitated to take the rose for one brief moment but he insisted so she could not refuse.

"May I ask your name? I'm Scott O'Roarke."

"Angelique—Angelique Dupree," she declared in a faltering voice. She was thinking he had to be the one sending the baskets of roses. It could not possibly be anyone else.

"Angelique Dupree—a beautiful name for a beautiful lady. Forgive me for being so bold when I say you are so beautiful, Angelique Dupree, that you take this Irishman's breath away." He laughed infectiously saying, "My mother is always telling me I'm too bold for saying exactly what's on my mind. So forgive me if I've offended you."

Angelique smiled, for she could have hardly been offended. In truth, she was quite pleased. "I think it's rather nice that someone can say what they feel Honesty is to be admired." A teasing glint came to her black eyes as she grinned, "But I wouldn't wish to take your breath away."

Both of then broke into a gale of lighthearted laughter. Angelique found herself feeling relaxed and at ease with this handsome stranger who had come by her carriage.

Scott's bright blue eyes danced adoringly over her face. He asked if she had come here for her servant to purchase fish, for he had no doubt that she came from one of the wealthy New Orleans families.

"As a matter of fact that *is* what Zachariah is doing. My mother sent him to buy twenty pounds."

"Twenty pounds, eh? That's a lot of fish, Angelique! I hope he buys it from the *Bayou Queen,*" he grinned.

Before she could reply, Zachariah hastily walked up to the carriage with the huge package of fish swung over his shoulder. His black face wore a stern look, as he inquired in a gruff tone, "You all right, mademoiselle?"

"I'm just fine, Zachariah. This is Scott O'Roarke," she quickly added. He had only to look at her to see that she was just fine. In fact, she seemed very cheerful and happy.

"I'd say you got a good twenty pounds of fish for mother."

"Yes, ma'am. I did that." His black eyes turned to Scott O'Roarke. "A pleasure to meet you, monsieur."

"My pleasure, too, Zachariah, and I hope you found some nice fish."

"Always find my best buy on the *Bayou Queen,*" Zachariah declared as he prepared to lay the huge bundle under the driver's perch at the front of the carriage.

"Well, it's good to hear you say that, Zachariah, for that's my boat. I'm the captain of the *Bayou Queen.* Guess I should really say it's my father's boat but I'm running it for him since he's ill."

Zachariah took his seat and grabbed the reins. "A good day to you, monsieur, and a pleasure to meet you. I must get these fish to Madame Dupree."

Scott grinned and nodded as his eyes darted back to Angelique. He saw the white rose in her small hands. It was only necessary for them to exchange smiles as the carriage began to roll away — they both knew they were destined to meet again.

No one had to tell old Zachariah that something had sparked between those two young people in that brief interlude. Zachariah had to say he was a very likeable young man and very handsome. He'd never seen Mademoiselle Angelique's face so radiant.

It was inevitable that something like this would happen when a young lady like the mademoiselle blossomed as she had the last year. Monsieur Maurice Dupree was powerless to stop it. Zachariah knew the force of it after living so long. The years taught a person many things about life that youth could not know.

This was the thing that made Zachariah feel sorry for this hard-working young fisherman and the pampered beautiful daughter of Maurice Dupree. There was no future for the two of them unless they sought to defy the traditions of the French Creole families.

Being around the young lady more the last few weeks, the old black man had seen something that set her apart from her parents. She was curious about life and everything around her. There was something else old Zachariah had seen in her manner and in those flashing black eyes. She was more daring and spirited than he'd suspected. She was not the shy, demure young girl that Maurice Dupree thought her to be.

She was ready to break those chains binding her to that cloistered existence. Mademoiselle Angelique was ready to taste the sweetness of romance and young love and Zachariah knew that when he saw the rosy flush on her cheeks just now.

That young captain of the *Bayou Queen* was handsome enough to make any young girl's heart flutter!

Chapter Four

Scott and Justin went back to their bayou very happy men as the sun was setting across Lake Pontchartrain. Their take for the day had been a good one and before they'd left the docks, Justin bought some flowers from the old vendor for his wife, Mimi, and Scott had taken her enough fish for two fine meals. He had also purchased an armful of flowers to take to his mother.

The sun was low in the western sky as their boat left the lake and headed into one of the channels of the bayou streams. Once they entered the particular channel they were to follow home it was a different world. Huge rooted cypress trees flourished, profuse sprays of Spanish moss hanging from the branches.

"I never cease to love this place, Scott. Don't think I'd ever want to live anywhere else," Justin declared as he gazed at the banks of the bayou. The little creatures of the swamp scampered around on the banks and herons waited on fallen logs to catch an evening meal. From the thick underbrush came the calling of birds—their songs could be sad or happy. But Justin knew that this paradise also

31

held the dangers of poisonous snakes and alligators. He'd had close encounters with both.

Twilight was high by the time Scott made for the small dock on the bayou where Justin would leave him for his little cottage where his wife and two sons greeted him as they did every evening. He understood why Justin was such a happy man. He had a loving wife and two fine boys and they lived in a cozy cottage. Mimi worked tirelessly every day to prepare delicious meals and keep her little cottage a pleasant place for Justin to come after his hard day on the boat. What else could any man ask of life?

Scott wanted no more than that. He doubted that some of the very wealthy people he sold his fish to in New Orleans were as happy as Justin and his family back there in the bayou even though they lived in fancy houses with servants.

As he approached the little plank dock he'd watched his father build years ago, he saw smoke circling upward and he knew his mother's cookstove was producing something delicious.

They might not be wealthy, but Scott could never remember a time when Kate O'Roarke had not put a feast on their supper table. It was probably why both he and his father were so robust. He'd never known a man who could put out more work than his father—up to a few months ago when his health began to fail.

He hastened his pace to get up the path, anticipating the happiness on his mother's face when she saw the colorful bouquet. He swore by the time he reached the porch that he could smell the pork roast and kettle of boiling cabbage which she always seasoned generously with pepper.

When he entered the door, his father saw the proud smile on Scott's face and knew he had good news to report from his day at the dock. It was a great pride to Timothy O'Roarke that he had a hard-working son like Scott. Some were not so blessed as he and Kate.

"Mighty pretty posies you've got there—for your mother, no doubt, eh?" A broad grin was on his apple-cheeked face. There had been a day when his hair was as thick and black as Scott's. Now it had thinned and turned grey.

"Thought momma would like them. Had a good day for us today, Poppa," he declared as he went over to the chair where his father sat smoking his pipe. Scott handed him the pouch of money.

By now, Kate had heard her son's voice and came scurrying into the parlor. She immediately saw the bouquet Scott cradled in his arms and thought she had to have the dearest son a mother could have. He was always so thoughtful about her and his father.

He caught the image of his mother's plump figure and jumped up to hand her the flowers. With a twinkle in his blue eyes, he declared, "To the prettiest lady I know."

"Go on with you, Scott O'Roarke!" she laughed. "I taught you not to lie and you know it. Mercy, these are pretty!" She thanked him for them as she turned to get the largest vase she had. Scott's flowers lent a festive air to Kate's kitchen that night as the three of them dined. Scott had been right, for there was a huge crock of boiled cabbage and a pork roast with little new potatoes. And large flaky biscuits, so delicious with jam spread on them.

He ate so much he felt very lazy after the meal, so he decided not to fight the urge to go to bed.

His sleep was not deep and he found himself waking up four hours after he'd gone to bed. At first, he blamed the heavy meal for his restlessness but it was not a matter of digestion—it was the lovely face of Angelique Dupree haunting his dreams.

He thought about walking down the wharf at just the right moment. Had it been an hour later or an hour earlier they would not have met as they did. His Irish nature convinced him that it was deemed that this should happen.

But it was also his nature to be an impulsive, impatient young man so he decided that he could not allow everything to remain in the hands of fate. He must make it possible for the two of them to meet. As his head lay on the pillow, he pondered all the various ways that he might do this.

He was not fool enough to think that Angelique's wealthy French Creole family would allow her to be courted by a lowly fisherman. But he also knew that this wasn't going to stop him.

He smiled when he finally thought of a way that he might be able to have a rendezvous with the beautiful Angelique. He'd ruled out an encounter when she was on her rides with the eagle-eyed Zachariah, for he never left her side for long.

No, the meeting he desired was a very private one when they could be alone. He thought about how wonderful it would be to walk with her in the moonlight. He could also envision taking her for a canoe ride along the bayou, that lovely long hair of hers cascading over her shoulders. What a sight that would be! Somehow he just knew that she'd like the strange sounds and sights of his bayou, if only he could bring her here.

When he did finally fall asleep it was almost dawn so he had very little sleep when he had to get up to start a new day. But this didn't bother Scott, for his head was whirling with all kind of ideas by the time he left to pick up Justin and head out to the lake.

Justin was also happy when he leaped aboard the fishing boat this early morning and Scott knew that his wife must have been as happy as his mother had been to receive flowers. Knowing the very affectionate Mimi as he did, Scott could figure that it was a night of passion and romance that was bringing a smile to Justin's face this morning. They were still very much in love after several years of marriage. Scott had great admiration for both of them.

After they had worked through the morning and into the mid-afternoon, Scott guided his boat toward the dock. "I've some business to talk over with Kirby, Justin. I'm going to let you take the *Bayou Queen* on home. Tell my folks I'll be getting home late so they won't wait supper for me."

"Sure Scott, I'll be glad to." He always figured when Scott sought out his young friend, Kirby, it was time he did a little carousing in New Orleans. He could hardly fault him for that as he was a handsome young rooster and it would not be natural if he didn't want to have a little fun once in a while. As Scott was taking over his father's fishing boat, Kirby Murphy had taken over his father's blacksmith shop near the riverbank.

By five in the afternoon, Scott said goodbye to Justin as he jauntily walked down the wharf toward the blacksmith shop.

Kirby was delighted to see his old friend as Scott came through the open doors of the smitty shop. He was ready to go out and kick up his heels, which he assumed was what O'Roarke had in mind.

The red-headed Kirby threw up his huge hand and greeted Scott, "Hey, bucko — hope it's a little fun you're seeking! I'm ready to go if you are."

Scott knew this was what Kirby would be thinking when he showed up and figured he could share a few drinks and some of those huge sandwiches always on the trays at the bar over at River's Inn. But what Scott really wanted from Kirby was the loan of a mare and a place to sleep after he'd gone to seek out the lovely Angelique.

If he failed to find her, he wanted to use Kirby's canoe to get back to the bayou. But Scott never doubted that he'd find her before this night was over.

"I'm ready, Kirby. You going to be working much longer?" Scott sat down on an old wooden crate while Kirby finished the new shoe he was putting on the horse's hoof.

"Give me another minute and we'll shut this place up for the night," his friend assured him.

A few minutes later, he and Scott were walking down the road toward the Murphys' cottage. An hour later, Kirby had cleaned up and dressed in a fresh pair of pants and shirt.

The two cocky young Irishmen were on their way to the River's Inn. When they took seats back in the corner and ordered their favorite Irish whiskey, Scott asked if he might have the use of Kirby's old mare.

"Sure, but you mean you're going to desert me to go spark some gal? Damn, Scott—I was planning on a long night," Kirby grumbled.

Scott roared with laughter. "Couldn't be too long a night anyway, Kirby. I got to get up early to make my catch for the day—remember? And you got a smitty shop to open."

"Guess you're right. Too bad we weren't born wealthy instead of being so damned good-looking." Kirby had quickly regained his fun-loving air as he took a hefty gulp of his whiskey and a generous bite of the thick roast beef sandwich.

Scott ate his sandwich as eagerly but it was nothing like the meal he was missing back home. However, tonight he didn't exactly have his mind on food.

The two of them enjoyed the usual camaraderie and told each other what had been going on since the last time they'd seen each other. Finally, Scott got around to asking him if he happened to know where the Dupree family lived.

"Sure. I've got work for old Maurice from time to time. You got some kind of business with him?"

Scott grinned. "No, Kirby—I've no business with Maurice Dupree." The devious expression on Scott's face was enough to cause a questioning look from Kirby. "God Almighty, tell me I'm wrong, Scott! You ain't crazy enough to try to mess around with Angelique Dupree, are you? I knew you were always a reckless rascal but never figured you for a fool!"

"I'll remember that you gave me a warning, Kirby, but I have to try to see her. She's like no other girl I've ever laid eyes on. She acts like she likes me, too, so I'd be a fool not to try to see her, I figure."

"You're telling me that you've been with her and talked with her?"

"One brief moment but it was all I needed to know I've got to see her again. I won't be satisfied if I don't," Scott declared and Kirby knew that there was nothing he could say to stop Scott. He directed him to the Dupree estate out on Old Cypress Road. "Just about half a mile out of New Orleans," he told his friend.

Another sandwich and some more whiskey was all Scott wanted before he was ready to leave. Kirby accompanied him back to his house and wished him good luck as Scott rode away on the mare, heading for the Old Cypress Road.

Dressed in black twill pants and shirt on Kirby's black mare, Scott blended into the black night. He arrived at the Dupree place quickly. Emerging from the darkness was the large two-story house with its many white columns lining the long front entrance and supporting the roof. Scott did not seek to enter the long drive leading up to the house for fear he might be seen, so he circled around slowly to the back of the property. Everything seemed deserted and dark but he could see the servants milling about in the kitchen. Obviously, the Duprees had finished their evening meal.

He leaped off the mare to move the rest of the way on foot. Lights from the house gleamed out over the large veranda at the side and beyond that was a garden area with beds of flowers and shrubs. At the back of the garden was a gazebo. This was where Scott sought to take refuge so he might catch sight of Angelique should she chance to come out on the veranda or walk in the garden. She just had to, he kept telling himself as he sat down on one of the little benches.

He knew it was foolish to think he'd get a chance to see her. Impatience set in after a while. Each minute seemed like an hour to Scott as he sat in the gazebo. When he was just about ready to give it up he came alive as he saw a lovely vision in pink come out on the veranda. Trailing at her heels was a black cocker spaniel pup.

He heard her lilting laughter as she called out. "Oh, Cuddles—you little imp!" He watched her dash down the two steps to the grounds below to follow the feisty pup, who seemed to be coming directly to the gazebo.

Scott stood with a pleased expression on his face as he watched the little spaniel, its ears almost touching the ground, dash directly toward him.

That little pup was bringing the lovely Angelique right to the spot where he was waiting!

Chapter Five

Scott watched her rush directly toward him with her lovely long hair flowing and her pink gown swishing to and fro. He waited anxiously as the pup suddenly stopped to sniff at one of the shrubs.

Quietly, he coaxed the pup to come to him and she did, with her tail wagging. He whispered that she was certainly a pretty little thing as he gave her head some generous strokes which was all it took to win her over.

By the time Angelique came into the gazebo, Scott and her pup, Cuddles, were buddies. She gasped with surprise at the sight of him sitting there with the dog happily snuggled at his feet. He playfully teased her. "We thought you'd never get here, didn't we, Cuddles?"

"Scott O'Roarke! What are you doing here?" She smiled as her thick black lashes fluttered.

"I hoped to see you—and I have, Angelique. You aren't angry, are you?" He stood up to take her hand.

"Why would I be angry?" she asked him in a hesitating voice as his hand urged her to come sit on the bench with him.

"I hoped you wouldn't but I wanted to see you again so much and knew that I could not come calling at the front door as I would have liked. I'm just a fisherman, Angelique, but I understand the ways of your people. My family has lived in New Orleans for a long time."

"And what's wrong with being a fisherman, Scott? It's honest work and very hard work, I would imagine," she responded.

"I'm not making any apologies for it. It's a happy good life my family has and there's a lot of love."

"Well, that's all that's important," she replied, aware that his hand was still holding hers. It was obvious that Cuddles liked him for she'd not barked once. Sitting here in the moonlight with such a handsome young man was exactly what her romantic heart had imagined lately and now it was actually happening.

"Could—could I come here again to meet you, Angelique, since I know without asking that your parents would not approve of me?"

"Of course you could, Scott. I usually take Cuddles for a walk in the gardens after dinner every night," she told him for she would welcome having these little private rendezvous with the handsome O'Roarke. Angelique had suddenly reached a point in her life when she realized she had been more restrained than her friends. Her best friend, Nicole Benoit, was always telling her about the young men she'd allow to kiss her. Angelique had never known what it was to be kissed and she was anxious to find out.

Scott suddenly realized he was still holding her hand and it was so dainty and soft. His blue eyes devoured the loveliness of her face as the two of them sat close. He found himself overcome with the urge to kiss her, for he could not know that this precious moment would ever come again.

He spoke from his heart: "You're the most beautiful girl I've ever seen, Angelique Dupree. I think I lost my heart the moment I saw you."

He was powerless to fight the urge to take her in his arms and kiss her as he so fervently wanted to do. The sweet nectar he found there was exactly what he'd expected and he knew he was the first man to kiss those rosebud lips. This was enough to make him swell with pride and exultation.

The sensations Angelique experienced as Scott's sensuous mouth claimed hers were far more titillating than she imagined. The flame of his passion rushed through her. Instinctively, her arms rose to encircle his neck as she softly murmured his name when his lips finally released hers.

Scott O'Roarke was shaken by the impact of that first kiss and he could not deny it. He'd kissed many a girl in his lifetime and bedded a fair share but nothing had compared to this. "Oh, Angelique! Angelique, I adore you!" His eyes devoured her as he looked down at her and she stared up at him with the same radiance.

Their rapture was shattered by a deep masculine voice calling out to Angelique. It was her father.

"I must go, Scott," she said urgently as she broke from his arms. But as she and Cuddles rushed out of the gazebo, he called softly to her that he would meet her again.

She called back, "I shall watch for you, Scott!"

Going back to fetch his horse he was in the highest of spirits. Dame Destiny had been very generous tonight. Now he knew beyond any shadow of a doubt that he and Angelique Dupree were destined to be lovers.

He was certain of that after tonight!

When his daughter came rushing up breathlessly with her pup at her heels, Maurice gave her a warm smile. "It's getting late, my dear, for you to be out here in the dark. It's probably not wise," he gently cautioned.

For the first time in her life, she dared to voice a hint of resentment as she walked beside him up to the veranda. "Poppa, I'm not a child and after all I was walking in our own gardens."

"Well, Angelique—that doesn't exactly assure you of security," he sternly pointed out as they entered the house.

"I realize that but I can't be a prisoner all my life," she retorted.

Angelique's outspoken manner took Maurice by surprise and by the time he gained his wits, she and Cuddles were dashing up the stairway as she bid him a hasty goodnight. A quiet air fell on Maurice Dupree as he walked to the parlor to join his wife.

When he sat down in the chair and lit up his pipe, he asked Simone if she'd noticed a change in Angelique lately. She told him she had not but she knew her husband well enough to know he had a reason for asking.

"Just a little more flippant and independent than she was a few weeks ago, it seems to me," he told her.

Simone laughed. "Well, I think this is something we must expect from Angelique. She's quickly becoming a young lady. She's not our little girl anymore, Maurice."

He could certainly not deny that but he sometimes wished he could have kept her a little girl forever.

More than anyone in the house Angelique knew she was no longer a little girl. Tonight, she had been kissed by a handsome young man and she was still stirred by the ecstasy he ignited as he held her tenderly and his lips had touched hers.

Had her father not called out when he had he suspected that Scott would have kissed her again.

There was certainly no doubt in Scott's mind that he would have kissed her again but for the fact that he had to make a hasty exit. Nevertheless, his impossible dream had come true for he had seen Angelique Dupree tonight and he had held her in his arms and kissed her honey-sweet lips. That was enough to make him feel he was soaring in the starlit sky as he rode back into New Orleans.

The hour was not so late that he felt the need to stay over in the city as long as Kirby would lend him his canoe. He could have it back at the docks the next morning.

When he rode up to the Murphy cottage and led the mare up to the picket fence, he saw that Kirby was sitting on the porch in the wooden swing. He called out to Scott as he was leaping off the horse, "Bet you didn't see her, did you, Scottie?"

"Bet I did," Scott laughed as he sauntered jauntily up the path to the front steps. That was enough to get his friend's attention and he stopped the swing. "Now you don't try to fool me, O'Roarke? You sure weren't gone all that long."

But the pleased, smug look on Scott's tanned face was enough to convince Kirby he wasn't lying. "Well, it was time well spent, shall I say. It wasn't Angelique's or my fault that my stay was so short. It was old Maurice who broke it up by yelling at her to come into the house." Shrugging his shoulders, he told Kirby, "Well, there will be another time."

After they'd talked for awhile longer, Scott asked Kirby about the canoe to get back to the bayou. Kirby made a deal with him, jesting that his canoe should be worth a nice fish for his supper tomorrow night.

"You got it, old friend. You'll have your canoe back in the morning and I'll drop off your fish before I start for home tomorrow evening," Scott assured him as he prepared to leave.

"I'm going to beat you to bed by a good half hour so you take on out to go home. I wouldn't want to be going down that bayou after dark. Ain't no gal that would make me travel there this late. Sure you don't want to sleep here tonight, Scott?"

Scott laughed and shook his head. The bayou did not frighten him as he knew it did a lot of people like Kirby.

Some found the bayou a remote, lonely place but Scott always found it like a world apart. He entered the narrow little waterway he traveled down to go to his home.

He listened to the calling of the night birds as he paddled down the stream. Up in the sky there was a full bright moon which seemed to light the many turns along the bayou. He wondered why anyone would feel fear to be here in his place.

True, he would not like to find himself in the waters should the canoe flip with him and he was bitten by one of the many poisonous snakes swimming around nor would he like to be a meal for one of the alligators. But Scott never worried about this and he wouldn't until it happened.

Lights were gleaming from the small windows of the cottage and Scott smiled as he was thinking that his mother was still up. The minute he walked through the door the first question she was going to ask him was why he was so late.

He wasn't going to lie to her—not really, for he was with Kirby a part of the evening and she knew that he and Kirby had been friends for a long time.

Often he'd thought that Irish mothers had to be the most inquisitive souls in the whole world!

46

When he tied up the canoe and walked up the pathway leading to the small house he could not help comparing it to the huge estate he'd visited. There was quite a difference in the grand surroundings Angelique Dupree lived in when he compared it to his humble home here on the bayou.

Maybe he was being quite foolhardy ever to expect that a girl like Angelique could fall in love with a fellow like him. What could he offer her but all the love in his heart and soul? Would that be enough to satisfy a beautiful young lady?

Only Angelique could answer that!

Chapter Six

Scott could never become too vexed by his dear mother and her questions when he saw that she had been sitting stitching him a new shirt by the lamplight. And after she'd worked all day at chores around her cottage and tended her ailing husband, who'd probably been in bed for three or four hours!

"Momma, why aren't you getting your rest?" he gently admonished as he came into the parlor.

"Didn't want to until I saw you safely in tho door, Scott O'Roarke! You should know that by now. Besides, I've your shirt to finish tonight. Pretty, isn't it?" she asked as she put her needle down and held the light weight cotton fabric of white and blue up for him to see.

"Sure is, Momma. Why, the girls will go crazy when they see me in that," he teased her as he walked over to plant an affectionate kiss on her cheek.

She laughed, "Well, I hope so, Scott O'Roarke, because I'd like to have some grandchildren running around this house before I die. I certainly hope some pretty little thing does capture your heart."

"Oh, Momma, you'll see that time, I assure you. Just be patient!"

Now that her son was home, she was ready to dim the lamp in the parlor and go to bed and Scott was certainly ready to do the same.

When he was alone in his bedroom, Scott thought about what his mother had said about wishing for grandchildren. He could not imagine more beautiful children than the ones he could have if Angelique were his wife.

But the sweet dreams he had that night about him and the girl he adored with all his heart would have become a nightmare if he'd known the devious plots already in the making to destroy all his fantasies and hopes.

Like Scott O'Roarke, Francois LaTour was enamored with Angelique and just as determined to possess her. Like Scott, he was an impatient and impulsive man.

In a far more sophisticated manner, Francois was very charming with a winning way about him.

Francois was ready to carry out the next step in his scheme he'd so carefully plotted in the late night hours as he'd sat alone in the darkness of his bedroom at Pointe a la Hache.

He found himself constantly haunted by her lovely face day and night. Lately, he'd found himself distracted from his business dealings by thoughts of her.

He knew that he must not delay much longer for he would not be satisfied until he'd known and experienced the pleasure of loving the beautiful Angelique. There was really no reason why he shouldn't go forward with his plans, he thought to himself.

Luck seemed to be on his side as he guided his buggy down the bustling New Orleans street the next afternoon and chanced to spot the Dupree carriage coming to a halt in front of a little boutique. He saw that Angelique was traveling with only the driver of the carriage. So he turned his buggy down the next side street to drive to the back of the shop so he might pull up behind her carriage.

When Francois peered through the front glass window he saw that she was there to pick up a parcel so she was not going to linger long. He casually ambled back and forth in front of the shop, for the old black man seemed to be taking a short nap.

Zachariah was not asleep and he was well aware of the dapper young dandy prancing back and forth and he was wondering if he had not seen Mademoiselle Angelique. Zachariah had seen his kind before on the streets of the city.

Angelique had only to pick up the satin slippers she would wear for the party her mother was giving tomorrow night. The only other stop she had to make while she and Zachariah were out this afternoon was at the tobacco shop for the pipe her mother had ordered for her father, along with a pouch for a special blend of tobacco he liked.

But as she stepped out the door of the shop two young lads were rushing down the street to get away from a merchant in pursuit of them for stealing something. They slammed into her and Francois happened to be in the perfect spot to catch her before she was knocked to the street. Ah, there was no doubt that Lady Luck was with him today! His arms were actually holding her and she was so close that he could smell the intoxicating fragrance of her gardenia toilet water.

"Are you all right, mademoiselle?" he asked as he continued to hold her even though she had gained her balance.

"Yes, thank you, monsieur," she stammered, feeling a little embarrassed as she recognized him as the man who'd stared so intensely at the tearoom recently.

"I am Francois La Tour, mademoiselle," he informed her, but before she could tell him who she was Zachariah was by her side. But it did not matter that she had no chance to tell him her name for he was well aware of who she was.

"You all right, Mademoiselle Angelique?" the driver asked, his black eyes darting to Francois. There was something about this tall, reed-thin man with his thin black mustache and long sideburns that hit the old man with instant dislike. That overprotective attitude he had toward the little mademoiselle made him scrutinize the man carefully. He didn't like seeing the man's hands still clinging around her waist so he offered his wrinkled hands and she took them. The man was forced to release her, and old Zachariah saw the disapproving glint in his eyes as he glared at him.

"Shall we go, mademoiselle?" Zachariah asked

as he glared back at the young man. She nodded but paused long enough to thank the gentleman. "Thank you, monsieur. I fear I would have landed on the street if you hadn't caught me."

Francois gave her a gallant bow. "It was my pleasure, Mademoiselle Dupree." He turned to go to his buggy as the two of them mounted the carriage.

It was not until they were traveling to the tobacco shop that it dawned on her that he'd addressed her as Mademoiselle Dupree. How had he known her name? Zachariah always called her Mademoiselle Angelique as he had just a few minutes ago.

This continued to puzzle her after they had made their stop at the tobacco shop and were heading for home.

Old Zachariah was also puzzled about the man but in a different way. Why had he just happened to be there as if he had been stalking the beautiful daughter of Maurice Dupree? He, too, had pondered how he knew that she was Mademoiselle Dupree. She did not know this man — he was certain of that.

Knowing how the Dupree family had been disturbed about those constant basket of flowers, Zachariah wondered if he should inform Angelique's father about this incident.

But somehow the right moment did not come for Zachariah to speak with Maurice Dupree privately. Suddenly, it was the day of the grand celebration Madame Dupree had been planning for weeks so Zachariah would not have dared to spoil this time for him by mentioning anything which would have upset him. This was Monsieur Dupree's fiftieth birthday—a very special affair for the family.

The spacious house was like a beehive with activity all day long. Simone could not believe that everything was going so smoothly and Maurice did not seem to suspect a thing. It was perfect that he had spent the entire day in New Orleans taking care of business matters with his banker and lawyer. He and his good friend, Edmund Villere, were going to have lunch together. Edmund had promised that he would keep Maurice occupied until late afternoon.

When he did arrive at five-thirty to find his wife looking most fetching in her new gown, she gave him a smile and said, "Well, I wanted to have a new gown as it's a special evening, Maurice. Angelique and I bought new dresses for your birthday." She quickly excused herself from the bedroom, urging him to rest awhile before he dressed for dinner. "I've some things to attend to downstairs. I shall meet you in the parlor in an hour, my darling."

Her pretty mauve frock rustled as she left the room. Maurice thought to himself that he had not seen his wife look so attractive in a long, long time. It had been a very active day so he sought the comfort of the overstuffed chair for awhile to refresh himself before going downstairs for dinner which he knew would be a feast. Simone had surely had the cook prepare all his special dishes.

For a leisurely half-hour Maurice laid his head back on the chair and closed his eyes to relax. He knew nothing about the activity downstairs. His wife scurried busily around to see that everything was just perfect when her guests arrived and Maurice came down.

When Simone saw her daughter coming down the stairs, her loveliness took her breath away and she had to ask herself how she and Maurice had ever produced such a beautiful child. She was no beauty and Maurice was certainly not the most handsome man. But she recalled an old faded picture of her grandmother, Delphine, and it was she Angelique resembled. Those very delicate features of Angelique's were like Delphine's.

The pale pink silk gown Angelique wore was so attractive with her jet black hair and dark eyes. Simone thought she was as beautiful as the pale pink rose buds filling the cut crystal vases in her parlor.

"Angelique. I don't think that I've ever seen you look more beautiful than you do tonight," Simone declared as her daughter joined her at the base of the stairs. Her pretty pink satin slippers peeked out as Angelique lifted her full skirt to descend the stairs. Simone wondered if Angelique had any inkling of just how breathtakingly beautiful she was.

"And you look very pretty tonight, Momma. Is Father still in the dark about everything?"

"I think so, cherie. He had a very busy day and I've Edmund to thank for that."

Simone and Angelique sat in the parlor aglow

with candlelight and fragrant pink and white flowers. They enjoyed a glass of chilled white wine while awaiting their guests' arrival.

"Momma, I think this is going to be a night we'll remember for a long time," Angelique said.

"Oh, I hope so, Angelique."

Neither of them said more for the first of their guests began to arrive. The select list of twelve French Creole families began to arrive. Simone and her daughter greeted them at the entrance to their home, and by the time Maurice descended the stairs the parlor was filled with all his dearest friends.

Knowing her husband so well, Simone was convinced that he was absolutely taken by surprise as she saw the stunned expression on his face.

He was surrounded by all the guests who wanted to give him their best wishes but he also spotted his attractive wife and daughter across the room exchanging smiles. What a devious pair they'd been the last few weeks planning all this behind his back!

He finally made his way across the room to give Simone an affectionate hug and kiss. "I thank you, my dear, for such a nice gesture." He turned to his daughter. "And you were most likely a part of this, eh?"

She laughed gaily and leaned over to kiss his cheek. "Happy birthday, Father, and may you have many more."

The guests enjoyed the fine wines from Maurice's cellar for the next hour before they gathered around the long dining table in the spacious dining room to enjoy a scrumptious feast. Maurice was toasted as the guests raised their glasses of champagne.

The young man waiting out in the gardens for Angelique listened to the gay laughter inside the house. He knew he had come on the wrong night.

He was preparing to leave the grounds the same way he'd entered when he spied two husky ruffians jumping over the walled garden. He wondered what they were up to for they were certainly uninvited, Scott thought as he watched them moving cautiously through the flowering shrubs.

He moved in their direction with the only weapon he had with him. Gripping the scaling knife in his hand he boldly approached them.

His firm, muscled body with the wicked looking knife in his hand made Scott O'Roarke look like a most formidable foe to the two men when they spied him coming toward them.

Chapter Seven

The two men creeping around the shrubs did not expect the threatening figure with the knife in his hand as he demanded to know what they were doing in the garden. It caught them unprepared as they froze in their tracks.

Scott's tall, powerfully built body was impressive. As trim as his waistline was, he had a massive broad chest and a pair of very strong, firm-muscled arms. The two of them knew they had encountered a forceful man as he inquired, "Have you business here? If so, why were you entering like thieves in the cover of darkness?"

"We meant no harm, mister! Just curious to see about the shindig going on in a big house like that," one of the men said as the other backed toward the garden wall.

"Well, I think you better just forget it and save yourselves a lot of trouble. Monsieur Dupree wouldn't take too kindly to this. The authorities would have the two of you in jail quite hastily. I'll be generous and allow you a minute to climb that wall."

Neither of them sought to argue with him as

they swiftly scampered up the wall.

Scott watched them go before he turned to the spot where he'd secured Kirby's horse. He had borrowed it again to ride out on Old Cypress Road.

He soothed his disappointment by telling himself that he would come again tomorrow night.

As he mounted the horse to ride back to New Orleans, he gazed up at the sky to see that it promised rain by morning.

He didn't like to think about losing a day's work but the signs were there and he saw them. He wasn't in the mood for Kirby's cajoling about the trip being futile because he didn't get to see the pretty Angelique.

So he didn't linger long before he made for the docks to get the canoe and paddle toward the bayou and his home. When he arrived home he noted the questioning look on his mother's face and he knew that his absences were whetting her curiosity. He took no time to explain where he'd been or what he'd been doing.

He gave her a hasty goodnight kiss and went directly to his room, leaving her in the parlor. There was an amused smile on his face as he closed his bedroom door for he knew she was going to lie in her bed pondering his whereabouts for a long time before she finally dropped off to sleep.

But Scott also knew he was a dutiful son who had always been respectful of his parents. He was well past the age when he had to account to a father or mother about his activities but he'd pampered them more than most young men did once they reached his age.

Maybe it was time he started making some changes, he thought as he began to undress.

It was a very irate Francois LaTour the two hired hoodlums encountered at the late night hour when they met with him in his parlor to tell him they'd failed in their mission.

"You idiots! You let one man stop you? I was told that you two were tough. Holy Christ—you sound like pussycats to me. Get out of here and I won't pay you one cent for you earned nothing," Francois yelled.

The fierce look in Francois' black eyes was enough to cause them to rush into the darkened hallway and out the front door.

As the two ran out of the parlor, Francois gave way to the rage churning within him and flung his glass of brandy across the room. Next time, he would hire his own men, he told himself as he angrily marched upstairs. The men remaining back on Grand Terre Island with his old friend, Jean Lafitte, were not the same calibre or breed that were his cohorts a few years ago. He had to wonder if Jean's henchmen were slowly deserting him as Francois had decided to do some years ago. He knew Lafitte was not the powerful figure he once was.

Francois had never regretted his decision to pull away from Grand Terre and seek his fortune in New Orleans as a businessman.

He knew from all the gossip from time to time that his old friend was losing his battle with the authorities in New Orleans. There would come that day when he'd have to flee Grand Terre or land in jail in New Orleans.

Tomorrow, Francois promised himself, he would find the men to carry out his plan. This time it would work. He would pick and hire the men himself instead of leaving that to someone else as he'd done this time.

Angelique knew that the party had put her father in a very grand mood when her mother informed her the next morning that he had given permission for her to spend the weekend with their old friends, the Benoits. Their daughter, Nicole, was the same age as Angelique and this was the first time Maurice had finally agreed to allow his daughter to have this liberty.

Her black eyes twinkled with delight as she asked her mother, "And he really said I could spend the whole weekend with Nicole?"

The two young girls had tried to arrange this for so long that Angelique was still a little dazzled by her mother's announcement.

"He would not have had the heart to turn down Celeste Benoit when she told him what they'd planned for the two of you." It would have been difficult for Maurice to refuse her most anything when he was so happy.

"Well, young lady, since the Benoit carriage will get here this afternoon I would say you better think about what you'll want to take." Simone smiled, so happy to see the excited look on Angelique's face. It was due time she be given more a freedom like the rest of their friends' daughters.

Nicole had already been allowed to have some of the young French Creoles call on her; her aunt had chaperoned when the young gentlemen had taken Nicole for a ride in their buggy or gone horseback riding at her father's country place.

Poor Angelique was at least a year behind all the girls her age and that was why she'd finally urged Maurice to allow her to go on rides with Zachariah. She knew Angelique was in good hands, for Zachariah was a devoted, loyal servant.

Her daughter didn't have to be told twice to pack as she swiftly dashed out of the room and up the stairs. One of the first things she took from the armoire was her bright green riding ensemble, for she knew Nicole would want to go riding on the fine thoroughbreds in their stable.

She had to include the lovely lavender organza she felt was one of her most attractive gowns.

She laid two of her simpler afternoon gowns on the bed. Then she couldn't resist flinging one more fancy gown with them, knowing she would be at the Benoits two evenings and they were constantly entertaining guests.

Antoine and Celeste Benoit were not a quiet, reserved couple like her parents. Angelique could see why Nicole was such a vivacious little creature and perhaps that was why she had been drawn to her more than to the other daughters of the families she knew.

There was no denying that she wished her parents were more like Nicole's, especially her father. The last year or two, as she'd grown older, Angelique felt that her mother would have been more fun-loving if she'd had her own way about things.

She also took down the frock she would wear to the Benoits this afternoon which she thought would be perfect with her new wide-brimmed white straw with its black velvet band and streamers. The top of the gown was white batiste and sleeveless. With a huge ruffle edging the scooped neckline. The skirt was a black challis with little clusters of white flowers dotting it. It was perfect for this warm summer day.

Later when she was dressed and had placed the wide-brimmed hat at just the right angle, she was very pleased with her reflection in the mirror.

She found herself thinking about a certain handsome young man and it dawned on her that if he did come to the gardens to keep the rendezvous they talked about a few nights ago she would not be there. She was not exactly happy about that but if he really wanted to see her he would surely return, she thought, trying to comfort herself.

She wondered if he might have been out there in the dark gardens last night. She had not ventured beyond the veranda the entire evening as there was too much going on with that many people around. But she had not forgotten about Scott O'Roarke and now she would have something to tell Nicole who was always talking about some dashing young man.

The Benoit carriage arrived promptly at three and Simone saw her daughter off. One would have thought she was staying for a week instead of a weekend, Simone thought to herself, even though she didn't say anything to Angelique about how much she was taking.

How grownup she looked as she stepped inside the carriage, Simone thought as she stood on the front steps until the carriage rolled down the drive lined with magnolia trees. With a thoughtful expression, she walked slowly back into the house and once inside, she felt lonely because for a whole weekend Angelique would not be there. Simone knew it was because this was the first time she'd been away for so long.

The golden-haired Nicole was on the porch anxiously awaiting Angelique's arrival. When the carriage came to a halt, she rushed down the steps to greet her friend as she emerged. With a girlish giggle, she hugged Angelique.

"We finally got our way, didn't we? I thought your papa would never say yes."

"I know. I was stunned when Momma told me this morning. I think maybe I'm still dreaming it." She laughed as Nicole took her by the arm and they went up the steps to the house.

They went directly to Nicole's room, chattering like two magpies, while one of the servants placed Angelique's luggage in the room across the hall.

Nicole told her about all the plans she had made. As Angelique was sure she would want to do, they were going for a ride tomorrow. Nicole wasted no time telling her about the new young man in her life.

"He's not of the gentry, if you get my meaning, Angelique?"

"What do your parents think about that?"

"They don't and I don't want them to know. You know what is expected of us, Angelique. We've got to fall in love and marry a nice French Creole man but I may not do that."

Angelique's interest was whetted. "Well, who is he and where did you meet him, Nicole?" She was suddenly thinking about what Nicole had said, knowing that Scott O'Roarke would not be an acceptable suitor for her either.

"His name is Mark Terherne and he's from Natchez. He came to the Beaudeaus' to train the race horses he's bought."

Angelique listened as Nicole told her how they'd chanced to meet as he was running one of the thoroughbreds on the trail and she was out on one of her rides. Giggling, she told Angelique, "Needless to say, I'm riding more often than I was."

"He must be much older than you, Nicole."

"I'm going on seventeen as you are and he's almost twenty-four, which appeals to me much more than silly fellows about twenty. Don't you find the sons of our families' friends to be a bore?"

Angelique had to admit that she did. She was

64

ready to tell Nicole about the dashing young fisherman.

Now it was Nicole's turn to be curious. "How did you meet him? How in the world have you managed to be alone with him, as strict as your papa is with you?"

Angelique told her about the trip to the wharf for Zachariah to purchase fish for her mother's party and how she shared a few brief moments with Scott. But Nicole got very excited when Angelique told her about their nocturnal rendezvous in the gardens and how he'd held her in his arms and kissed her.

Nicole laughed deviously. "Why, Angelique Dupree! You're no more an angel than I am. My parents are always telling me that I should be an angel like you are."

Angelique laughed. "I'd never want to be an angel, Nicole. That night I was with Scott convinced me of that."

Nicole Benoit saw her friend in a different light. There was a little of the coquette in Angelique Dupree, too!

Chapter Eight

Angelique was to realize what a conniving little minx Nicole Benoit could be the next morning when she decided to make a quick change of plans and go for a ride in the countryside. It also made her realize Nicole was not prevented from doing as she wished as she was by her strict parents.

"Shall we take a jaunt into the city and go down by the wharf in hopes you might see your handsome Scott O'Roarke? If you did you could invite him to go for a ride with us this afternoon. I can always manage to send Mark a message if I change my plans. I worked that out a few days ago."

For a moment Angelique hesitated but the idea of seeing him again swept away any hesitation. "We might not see him, Nicole. It might be all for nothing. But if you're willing, then so am I."

"Let's do it!" she declared exuberantly. The two of them dashed excitedly up the stairs to change into something more suitable for the city. Nicole had taken the time to write her little message and summon a young servant to run her errand before she met with Angelique to board the carriage.

In less than a half-hour, the carriage was taking them to the wharf. Angelique suddenly remembered it was Friday so it was quite likely that the *Bayou Queen* would be docked to sell fish.

It did not take O'Roarke long to spot the two lovely young ladies on the wharf as they emerged from the carriage. He instantly recognized the black-haired beauty with the wide-brimmed straw hat. He did not know who the pretty golden-haired lady was but she didn't interest him.

"Hey, Justin—look up there! Ever see anything more beautiful? She's the one I was telling you about. Think you could do without me for a minute while I go say hello?" Scott was already preparing to depart before Justin could answer—nothing would have stopped him.

Justin laughed and shook his head. Young O'Roarke was truly lovestruck!

Nicole was very impressed when Scott came rushing up to Angelique with a big grin on his handsome, tanned face. He took her dainty hand to his lips. "Angelique, this is a wonderful surprise!"

Nicole's eyes were busy darting from her friend to the good-looking fisherman. Dear Lord, he *was* something! She could certainly understand why Angelique was overwhelmed when they first met.

Angelique confessed she was as pleased to see him and suddenly remembered to introduce Nicole. "The truth is, it was Nicole's idea to come to the wharf."

"Well, I'm glad, Nicole," Scott declared.

"Angelique is spending the weekend with me and we're taking a tour around the city. The wharves are always an interesting sight, I find. I had forgotten that this is what they call 'fish day.' "

"That's right, mademoiselle. This is the day that we fishermen hope to make some money." He spoke to Nicole but his eyes were devouring Angelique, a fact not lost on Nicole.

But since Angelique seemed mesmerized by his forceful presence, Nicole took charge. "Well, monsieur, I trust it will be a good day for you. Perhaps you could reward yourself by taking tomorrow off and joining Angelique and me for a picnic and ride around the countryside."

Angelique found Nicole's boldness amazing. But she also admired her, wishing she was more like her. "The Benoits live just south of us, Scott. Do you think you might arrange it?"

A broad grin crossed his face. "I'll make a point to make it, Angelique." She knew he was more than pleased by Nicole's invitation.

"Would the Benoits like some of the finest fish caught in these Louisiana waters," he inquired cockily.

"Why, monsieur, we would be most grateful," she laughed. "Shall we say about noon then?"

"I'll be there." His hand had never let go of Angelique's, Nicole noticed. He took one last lingering look at Angelique before he turned to leave and jauntily walk down the wharf.

Nicole gasped, "God, Angelique—he *is* handsome! It's obvious that he adores you. His eyes never left you the whole time.

A smug grin was on Angelique's face, for she had been aware of it, but she still found herself amazed at Nicole. She wondered how her parents would respond to their daughter's plans for a picnic with a local fisherman!

But Nicole quite casually had an explanation. "It's very simple, my dear Angelique. My parents and my Tante Colette are going over for a luncheon at Madame Lemercier's and they won't be back until the late afternoon. Is this all not perfect?"

Angelique laughed, "Oh, Nicole—I never knew how clever you were. It's no wonder you manage to manipulate things the way you want them."

Nicole promised that before this weekend was over she would teach her a few tricks to use in the future. "You think my parents weren't as strict as yours at first? I can assure you they were but I found myself a champion in my Tante Colette and she's come to my rescue many times since she's been living with us. God bless Tante Colette!"

When they returned home, Nicole excused herself to request the picnic basket she wished their cook to prepare for tomorrow.

With an impish grin, Nicole explained, "If I waited until the morning then she would run and complain to my mother but I always work her this way and she does anything I want her to do. She thinks I'm a very considerate young lady."

Angelique just smiled and shook her head in amazement. She had no doubt that she would be much wiser by the time she returned home on Sunday.

Removing her hat, she sat down on the bed to slide her feet out of her slippers. Lying back on the bed, she was filled with happiness that she was actually going on a picnic and Scott was joining them. Oh, she'd just die if he didn't show up as he'd promised! He just had to come!

But she did not lie there long in her private reverie, for Nicole came bursting through the door. "Lord, Angelique—I didn't know until I talked to my mother just now that we've got guests coming over tonight. The Calmeils, along with their son, Andre. He's just returned from France and he's absolutely gorgeous! Dress in the prettiest gown you brought."

"Thank goodness I did bring two. You think I should wear the lavender one, Nicole?"

"Oh, yes—that's the prettiest one. Andre might just want to paint a portrait of you. That's why he's been in Paris. He hopes to become an artist." She told Angelique she had to check her own gowns to see which one she wanted to wear. "I'll see you in a couple of hours, Angelique," she said as she hastily dashed out the door.

Angelique found herself feeling weary as she watched Nicole's spirited vivaciousness!

She had plenty of time to indulge herself in a leisurely perfume-scented bath and afterwards she stretched out on the bed for a while. Angelique had decided that fancy hairdos were not for her, so she never had to spend a long time on it as Nicole did with her shorter hair.

70

When the clock revealed that it was time to get dressed she got up from the bed to brush her black hair until it looked like glossy satin. She always wore it parted down the middle to fall in its soft, flowing waves or she tucked it behind her ears with jeweled combs.

Tonight she pulled one side back with a little cluster of lavender velvet flowers, allowing the other side to flow free. By the time she'd stepped into the lavender gown to stand in front of the cheval glass, she was very pleased with the way she looked.

From Nicole's reaction when she came to join her so they could go downstairs together, it was obvious that she did look very attractive.

"Well, I guess I know who Andre Cameil will have his eyes on tonight," she declared flippantly.

"Nicole, you look beautiful in that yellow gown," Angelique whispered as they moved out into the carpeted hallway.

"I guess I could say I look pretty but you, Angelique — you have that breathtaking beauty few girls have. Lord, don't tell me you can't look in a mirror and see it!"

"Guess I just never saw it that way, Nicole," she replied as they started to descend the steps.

"Well, let me tell you this for your own good since I have to be a little smarter about men. Your kind of beauty can drive a man crazy with desire."

As young as she was Nicole Benoit had certainly spoken some words of wisdom that would prove to be true sooner than she could realize.

Angelique Dupree heard the words but she could not take them seriously.

Antoine and his wife were already in the parlor and so was Celeste's sister, Colette, when the two pretty girls made their appearance.

Colette absorbed the beauty of Nicole's young friend as she thought to herself how Nicole paled walking by her side.

Antoine greeted both of them with an affectionate kiss on the forehead. "My, what beauties we have here tonight, *oui*, Celeste and Colette?"

Both ladies wholeheartedly agreed as he served them a glass of wine. The two had taken a seat, enjoying a sip of wine when the Calmeil family arrived.

Angelique and Colette were the only ones who did not know the Calmeils so Antoine introduced them before they were served their wine.

The conversation was instantly directed to Andre about his sojourn in Paris to pursue his talents as an artist. Being a very egotistical young man of twenty-five, he was pleased to be the center of attention. His artist's eye could already envision a portrait painted of the enchantress in the lavender gown, her black hair falling around her shoulders. Such thick lashes he'd never seen before—and her dark eyes were just as entrancing.

Once dinner was over and the families had moved back into the parlor, Andre made a point of moving over to join Angelique and Nicole as the older couples became engrossed in conversation.

It came as no shock to Nicole that Andre

seemed so completely hypnotized by Angelique. She had expected it. But even she was taken by surprise at his haste in asking her friend if she would consider posing for him. "I see a most exquisite portrait and I know what I should call it, mademoiselle. It would be "The Lady In Lavender."

Angelique found herself flustered by his unabashed adoration and she'd sensed that his eyes had been on her the entire evening. "I could not possibly give you an answer tonight, monsieur. My parents might not approve," she added stammering.

"And would you agree, mademoiselle?"

"I am not even sure of that, monsieur," she responded.

Nicole sat listening, applauding Angelique for the way she was handling this sophisticated, worldy-wise man who had assumed that Angelique would have eagerly accepted his offer.

Nicole could tell by the look on Andre's finely-chiseled face that he had not received the response he'd expected. His offer had not changed the expression on Angelique's face and he had to be crushed that she didn't show more enthusiasm.

It also told Nicole something else: Angelique was more like her than she'd realized. Regardless of what their families might expect Angelique would not be ruled by the traditions of their families either. She would follow her heart's desire.

At the moment, Scott O'Roarke was Angelique's passion and Nicole could certainly see why!

Chapter Nine

Angelique had to admit it was certainly a far more exciting scene here at the Benoit's than it was back home. She could not deny that she felt flattered when Andre Calmeil was so impressed with her beauty that he wanted to capture it on canvas. Any young lady would have.

She found herself so excited about the promise of the next day and seeing Scott again that sleep escaped her. She tossed and turned and finally fell asleep from sheer exhaustion. She slept until Nicole came dashing through her bedroom door the next morning to announce that her parents and aunt had just left for most of the day.

"Ah, Angelique—we're going to have a most glorious day!" she declared, flopping down on the bed beside her.

Angelique believed her as she dressed in her riding ensemble and pulled her long hair back with a green ribbon. She prayed that Scott would not disappoint her—she would be shattered.

She and Nicole sat on the veranda awaiting his arrival. The cook had their picnic basket packed and ready.

Astraddle Kirby's horse, Scott came galloping

up the drive and both Nicole and Angelique saw him. Angelique's heart seemed to pound hard as she thought that he had to be the most handsome man she'd ever seen. Her outspoken friend sighed, "God, he's one fine figure of a man—fisherman or not!"

Angelique giggled in amusement. She'd never known anyone like Nicole. Nicole called out to Scott to let him know they were on the veranda. "Over here, Scott!" Scott turned in their direction.

Leaping off the horse, he walked around the corner of the house. He carried a package of fish he and Justin had caught the day before.

"With the compliments of the *Bayou Queen,* Mademoiselle Benoit. I hope you and your family will enjoy this." He turned his bright blue eyes in Angelique's direction to tell her how fetching she looked in her green riding ensemble. As his eyes danced over her face he declared, "A perfect day for a picnic."

Nicole took the package to the cook and in exchange got the picnic basket so they could be on their way. She was more than anxious for this meeting with Mark Terherne after not seeing him for the last two days. It had seemed like forever and she hoped he was feeling the same way.

Bouncing back out on the veranda, she asked, "Well, shall we be on our way?"

"I'm ready," Angelique declared gaily. She told Scott they would meet him in the drive and he urged Nicole to allow him to take the basket.

Angelique and Nicole left to go in one direction as Scott took the basket and went toward the front drive where he'd left his horse.

His busy eyes surrounded the vast grounds. It was all very impressive. He realized as never before what people were talking about when they said that the French Creole families controlled the wealth of New Orleans. In the last few weeks he'd seen where Angelique lived and now he was seeing the Benoit's lavish estate.

But Scott O'Roarke also knew that it did not take all this luxury to be a happy man or woman for he had witnessed the love and devotion of his mother and father. No kid could have had a happier childhood, so he had no complaints.

What a damned lucky guy he had to be, he thought as the two pretty young girls rode up to him. Talk about the luck of the Irish!

The only thing he wished for was a young man to keep the feisty Nicole occupied so he would not have to be shared. This wish was soon to be granted when Nicole informed him they would be joined by a young man she'd invited. At least, she was hoping he'd be able to make it.

When she mentioned his name, Scott had laughed. "Ah, another Irishman, eh?"

"I truly can't say about that," Nicole remarked.

"Well, I can. It's a fine Irish name."

Nicole laughed delightedly. "Oh, I can believe it! There's a bit of devilment in him which all you Irishmen seem to have. Beware, Angelique."

It was a very carefree, jolly trio that rode down the country trail to the shade of the woods which Nicole thought would be perfect on this summer day. Besides, it lay about half-way between the Benoit property and the Beaudeau estate.

Angelique and Scott knew when they encountered a tousle-haired gent sitting atop a fine black stallion that this had to be the Mark Terherne that Nicole had told them about. They had only ridden a short distance into the woods when they met him.

As soon as they all dismounted and introductions were made, Angelique could sense the very intimate way Nicole and Mark Terherne responded to one another. He was a striking-looking man with hair as golden as Nicole's and eyes as bright and blue as Scott's. He wasn't as tall as Scott but just as stoutly built with firm, muscled arms and legs.

The four of them were together only a brief time before it was apparent to Angelique that Scott and Mark liked one another. They were talking and jesting as if they were old friends. Nicole winked at Angelique.

As Nicole had known she would, the cook had prepared a delicious basket. Fresh baked bread, crispy golden fried chicken and slices of her poppa's smoke ham were there to enjoy. A jar of the green tomato relish that Nicole liked so much had been included along with a mountain of little fried fruit pies.

Both young men ate their fill and since Nicole had slipped in a couple of bottles of her father's best white wine, everyone was divinely sated.

"Your mother's cook beats the heck out of the

Beaudeau's cook, I can tell you, Nicole" Mark declared with a lazy sigh. "Everything was delicious."

"Well, that will please Maggie very much, Mark. However, I don't think I'll tell her for she's cocky enough as it is," Nicole smiled up at him and he playfully tousled her hair.

Mark extended his hand to Nicole and invited her to take a walk. "I find myself in the need of walking after eating so much."

But when they were a short distance away from Scott and Angelique, he confessed that he wanted a few brief moments alone with her since he could not linger too long. "I've missed you the last two days, little imp," he declared in a deep husky voice.

"Angelique leaves tomorrow to go home, Mark. I'll be able to meet you as we've been doing," she promised.

Back at the spot where they'd sat to enjoy their picnic, Scott was as delighted to find a moment alone with Angelique. He wasted no time telling her he was sorry he had missed seeing her.

"I came but it was the wrong night. It was the night of the grand party your folks were having."

"I'm sorry I missed you. I never ventured into the garden that night. It was too hectic—such a huge crowd," she told him, suddenly realizing that his hand had reached over to take hers.

"It doesn't matter, Angelique, for we're together now. That's all that matters. Shall we take a stroll?"

"It's a beautiful spot Nicole picked out for our

picnic, isn't it?" Angelique remarked as she allowed him to support her as she stood up.

"Any place is beautiful for me if you're there, Angelique Dupree. You've haunted my dreams since the first day I laid eyes on you, do you know that?"

Her black eyes glanced up at him and there was a twinkle of mischief as she boldly declared, "Good, I'm glad!" She later wondered if her friend Nicole's flippant ways were rubbing off.

"Now, are you? And why would you want that, eh? Can I dare to hope that you think of me once in a while when we're apart?"

In a soft sincere murmur, she said, "I think about you, Scott."

He stopped and his arms encircled her tiny waist. "Do you really, my little angel? Nothing under God's good green earth would make me happier!" For one fleeting moment his eyes searched the deep pools of hers before he lowered his head so their lips could meet. She responded with the eagerness he prayed for.

Slowly, he lowered her petite body to the thick carpet of grass. With very gentle and unhurried strokes, he smoothed out her glorious long hair to the side. "I've never in my whole life seen such hair as yours. But then I've never seen a beauty like you, Angelique."

Before she could have said a word his anxious lips were greedily seeking her lips. Even though she had never been kissed as Scott was now kissing her, she was so stirred that she did not refuse him as his tongue pressed against her lips. It was

79

as if her arms and her body had a will of their own as they moved instinctively to draw him closer. Her arms reached up to encircle his neck and her body longed to feel more of the heat of his firm male body pressing against her.

Scott was aflame with a passion that he knew was completely out of control. He was helpless to stop this frenzied desire to possess her. She seemed to want him as much as he wanted her.

His hands caressed the round mounds of her breasts and he felt the exciting quake of her body. His lips sought the jutting, pulsing tips of her breasts and she made soft, kittenlike sounds of pleasure. He relieved her of the soft cotton tunic and slowly his strong hands lowered the divided skirt. As the two of them lay together, their bodies touching and pressing, Scott knew that nothing was going to stop their rapture. He was sure of it when he pulled away only long enough to remove his shirt and pants and the impassioned look on her lovely face seemed to beckon him to hurry back.

Covering her with his powerful male body, he sank down in the velvety softness of her. The sensation was enough to make Angelique arch against him. His forceful thrust caused on brief moment of pain but this was swiftly swept away by ecstatic pleasure. Breathlessly, she clung to him, soaring to an unknown world that she never even imagined.

Together they shared that sweet, sweet interlude of paradise that only lovers can know. Afterward, they lay on the grassy carpet in each other's arms. Somehow, Scott wanted to let her know just how much he loved her—he never wanted her to be sorry she'd surrendered. He was well aware of her strict upbringing and he knew beyond a shadow of a doubt that he was the first man to make love to her. She had been a virgin.

What could he say? What could he promise? He was not a wealthy man. What would mean something to her and let her know how deep his love was?

His tanned hands gently stroked the damp ringlets away from her face. She lay so still in his arms that he had to wonder what she was thinking.

"Oh, Angelique," he whispered in her ear. "I have nothing to give you for what you gave me just now, but all the love in my heart and soul."

He felt her stir in his arms. When her eyes met his, she murmured softly, "I couldn't ask for more than that, Scott. You must know how I feel or this wouldn't have happened."

There was no man happier than Scott O'Roarke that wonderful summer day, but neither of them could know how their love would be tested in the days to come.

Angelique could not imagine how she would be forced to prove how strong and spirited she could be.

It was a strange, wonderful world she'd entered with him this afternoon but there was another world she was to be swept into that was nothing like the bliss she'd found in Scott O'Roarke's tender, loving arms.

Chapter Ten

When they were ready to get back to the picnic spot to join Mark and Nicole, Angelique voiced the fear that her friend would know what had happened between them. But Scott embraced her affectionately, realizing how naive and sweet she really was as he assured her, "Angelique, you look exactly like the same beautiful girl Nicole last saw and she will know nothing. This is our private little secret. Believe me, I'm telling the truth."

Those trusting black eyes looked up at him as she asked, "Are you sure, Scott? Are you really sure?"

"Wouldn't say it if I wasn't, little Angel!" he grinned as he urged her to follow him back through the woods.

When they had reached the edge of the clearing, Angelique stopped and Scott halted to see why. She spoke in a soft stammer. "What we did wasn't wrong, was it, Scott?"

His blue eyes warmed with compassion. "Did it feel like it was wrong, Angelique?"

Her voice rang wtih sincerity as she confessed, "No, I thought it seemed right at the time. If I

82

hadn't, I would not have allowed you to make love to me."

He kissed the top of her head. "I think you've answered your own question, my darling. I didn't think it wrong. I thought it was wonderful!"

Her pleased smile was enough for Scott to know he'd eased any qualms she might have had. Both of them had happy expressions on their faces as they returned to find Nicole sitting on the blanket alone.

"Well, I was about ready to send a searching party for the two of you," she teased. "Mark had to get back so he left a few minutes ago." She got up and suggested that they'd better be getting back to the house. Scott lifted the basket off the blanket as the two girls began to fold it up.

When they'd ridden down the trail to the Benoit estate, Scott decided he would say his farewell at the road before they traveled up the long winding drive to the house. Something told him that this would be wiser. It was probably why Terherne had met Nicole in the woods instead of coming to her home for he, like Scott, was probably not an acceptable suitor to this French Creole family.

So this was what he did, telling Nicole how much he appreciated her gracious invitation. "It was the nicest day I can ever remember." Then his eyes turned to Angelique. "I shall be seeing you, Angelique."

The look she saw there was a promise that she knew he would keep!

As the two young girls rode on toward the house, it was Nicole who remarked, "I think your Scott O'Roarke is very nice, Angelique, and it's apparent he's in love with you."

"So is your Mark Terherne and I got the feeling that he's rather taken with you."

The two of them exchanged smiles and broke into peals of girlish laughter. The impish Nicole told her friend, "I think both of our parents are going to be very put out with us because of the young men we seek to marry, Angelique."

Still feeling the flush of Scott's ardent lovemaking, Angelique could not imagine herself feeling about any other man as she did about her handsome young fisherman.

By the time the Benoit carriage took her back home, Angelique was thinking about the weekend she'd spent with Nicole and all the excitement she'd enjoyed. She knew that this one weekend had forever changed her life. She was not the same young girl who'd left her home on Thursday.

Scott had not lied to her. She had not looked any different when they joined Nicole and he had casually commented that they had wandered farther into the woods than they'd realized and that was why they were gone so long.

Knowing that Angelique was not as promiscuous as she was, Nicole never doubted his story for a minute. She was too engrossed with her own private thoughts about the very amorous Mark Terherne whom she considered to be the most magnificent lover. The feisty little Nicole had lost her virginity almost two years ago. It had been with one of those nice little French Creole gentlemen of whom her parents heartily approved. Charles Garonne's awkward attempts had left her disillusioned and disgusted by the time he was finished.

She'd never seen him alone again after that.

Anything her mother and father had encouraged where Charles was concerned was quickly and firmly refused by Nicole. "I find him an absolute bore and I'd rather be by myself!" she had told them.

Monsieur and Madame Benoit had only to look at their daughter's face to know she meant every word, so they pursued it no further.

It was a very quiet and peaceful weekend that the Duprees had spent and Simone found that she was enjoying the time to be lazy after all the preparing for Maurice's birthday celebration. Perhaps it was the same for Maurice, for he seemed content just to relax.

Since the baskets of flowers to Angelique had stopped arriving, the stress of that mystery was over. It had been very disturbing to him during those seven days.

But there was no denying that both of them were anxiously anticipating Angelique's arrival this Sunday afternoon. When she emerged from the carriage, they were at the front door to greet her with open arms.

They knew she had thoroughly enjoyed herself at the Benoits when she told them about the various things she and Nicole had done like taking a jaunt around New Orleans and going on a picnic. She spoke about the Cameil family and how their son, Andre, who'd just returned from Paris, had asked that she allow him to paint her portrait. "He's an artist, you know," she'd informed them.

But Maurice was not impressed and quickly shrugged the suggestion aside. "I heard the gossip that he was studying in Paris but I doubt that he could be considered an artist yet. He's not paid his dues."

His attitude did not matter to Angelique but his instant disapproval told her something that she had been suspecting secretly for many months. He wanted no young man entering her life but he was going to have to accept the fact that a young man had done so. His little girl was all grown up and she certainly realized that after this last weekend. If he knew about Scott O'Roarke he would surely suffer apoplexy.

It was like Nicole had said—they had to keep their meetings with men like Scott and Mark a secret. It was the only way.

But as soon as the evening meal was over, Angelique excused herself to go to her room so she could be alone. To linger in the parlor after dinner would be boring. She had told them all she intended to about her stay at the Benoit's. The rest was her own private secret, and she wanted to be alone to think about it.

Maurice Dupree did not notice the change in his daughter but Simone did. She did not mention it to her husband for she knew what a fury he could get in where Angelique was concerned. She knew it was not her imagination—she observed something different about her daughter.

Simone watched Angelique when she was not aware that her mother's scrutinizing eyes were upon her. She saw a thoughtful young lady completely absorbed in something and Simone wondered just what it was.

Was it this young artist, Andre? Did Angelique honestly wish to sit for him, knowing that her father would never agree?

It was very interesting to Simone that before the week was over, they received an invitation for dinner at the Cameil's in New Orleans. The invitation included Angelique.

At first, Maurice had been very adamant that they would not attend but Simone had quickly pointed out to him, "They're friends of our good friends, the Benoits. Maurice, I think you should give this some thought." Simone wanted to say much more for she was seeing that her husband had been too overprotective of their daughter and perhaps she had been, too. But she was ready to change all this.

All week she had allowed her daughter to attend to certain errands that she normally assumed herself. This seemed to please Angelique.

But as she'd taken on the extra errands for her mother around New Orleans, Angelique found herself encountering the gentleman she'd seen ogling her that day in the tearoom and who just happened to be outside the boutique the day the two young scamps came rushing down the street, almost causing her to fall. He seemed to be everywhere she went. Was she only imagining it? Was she only imagining that he could be following her? If this were true, then why?

There was no doubt in Francois LaTour's mind that the black man who was constantly with Angelique Dupree would have to be taken care of before his men could kidnap the beautiful young lady.

Let him follow her and look, she concluded. He did not interest her for her heart belonged to another. She knew that the weekend spent with Nicole had sparked a new boldness in her so when she went with Zachariah to buy fish on Friday at the wharf, she sweet-talked him into allowing her to purchase the fish.

Zachariah was reluctant at first. "What could possibly go wrong, Zachariah? You can see me at all times. It would be fun!"

When that pretty face of hers looked up at him that way he couldn't resist. And it was true what she said—he could see her at all times, so he finally agreed.

Angelique found herself very excited about stepping aboard the *Bayou Queen*. She sashayed down to the wharf and Scott saw her coming. His chest swelled with excitement—he couldn't imagine how she'd managed it. He nudged his partner, Justin, and told him, "This is the girl I'm going to marry, Justin. This is Angelique. Isn't she a beauty?"

Justin had to agree as he watched her approach the boat dressed in her pale yellow gown, the matching yellow chapeau framing her face. But it was that lovely waist-long hair that took Justin's admiring eye for he'd never seen more glorious tresses on any lady.

She was certainly a saucy little miss, Justin thought. He had only to look at Scott's face to know that he was one happy man to be greeted by such a wonderful surprise. Justin thought that he wished he could buy his Mimi such a pretty frock and hat.

Scott took great pride in introducing Angelique

to Justin. He could not suppress his curiosity any longer and asked her how she had managed to get Zachariah to allow her to come down to the boat.

With a pert look she explained, "I used my silken tongue, Scott, and it worked."

He wanted desperately to take her in his arms and kiss those inviting lips but he knew old Zachariah was surely watching so he restrained himself.

But as he gathered up her order and wrapped it in paper, he told her he would come to her tonight. "I'll be there in the gardens tonight, Angelique. Meet me there."

She promised she would as she paid him for the fish and took the wrapped bundle. "I must go before Zachariah comes here wondering what's taking me so long."

"Tonight," he murmured as she turned to walk away. At the other end of the boat Justin had been watching the young couple. He had made a point of moving to give them privacy.

There was no doubt she was a very fancy little lady but Justin also knew that this could cause a lot of problems for his friend.

But he was still young enough to know why Scott could not resist her!

Chapter Eleven

Angelique came back to the carriage and handed the package to Zachariah. "See there, Zachariah, I purchased the fish and everything went just fine," she announced.

He gave her a big, broad smile. "It sure did, mademoiselle. Guess we better be heading for home now, shouldn't we?"

"I'm ready," she replied as she took his hand to be assisted into the carriage.

She was in the highest spirits as the carriage made for the outskirts of the city for she had Scott's visit to anticipate all afternoon.

Angelique was not the only one in high spirits. So were Scott and Justin, for they sold all their fish by early afternoon. They felt it was a reason for the two of them to go to one of the nearby taverns by the riverbank and enjoy a couple of drinks before they returned to the bayou.

As early as it was, Scott figured that he and Justin could give themselves the luxury of a little fun and he'd go home to share supper with his folks before he paddled back upstream to New Orleans to keep his rendezvous with Angelique.

Both of them were in a happy-go-lucky mood

when they sauntered into the tavern and found an unoccupied table. It seemed a lot of other fishermen and dockworkers had had the same idea and Justin and Scott knew some of the fellows they saw there, laughing with one another.

They did not know the two burly-looking characters sitting at the table next to them. Scott had no inkling that every word he was saying to Justin was being heard by them. But neither could Scott know that the last week he had been stalked just like Angelique Dupree. Since the day he had been observed talking to her on the docks when Zachariah had been down on the wharf buying the fish for Madame Dupree's party, Francois LaTour had been curious about his association with Mademoiselle Dupree.

When his hired thugs had failed in their mission to abduct Angelique from the gardens the night of the party, Francois had concluded from the description of the man who'd chased his men away that it had to be this Scott O'Roarke. So Francois had a score to settle with him as well.

Before Justin and Scott paid for their drinks and took their leave, the two men at the other table exchanged smiles. They could not wait to get to Francois LaTour to report what they'd overheard.

They also went from the tavern directly to Francois' house. Their news was enough to bring a very pleased look to his face. This time it would work out, Francois was sure. He was so elated that he went to his desk to take out some money as a bonus for a job well done.

"Now, I think maybe this might be just the right night to pull off this little plot. Sit down, Bill and Mack." He ambled over to his liquor chest and poured each of them a glass of whiskey. "So this fisherman is to have his little tryst with the mademoiselle in the garden tonight, you said?"

"That's right, Monsieur LaTour," Mack told him. "That's what he was telling his friend."

"Well, it would be perfect if she came into the garden expecting to find him and found the two of you, eh?"

The two of them exchanged grins. Francois smirked as he asked, "I'd think that you could handle one tiny little minx who doesn't even reach your shoulders."

"You don't worry about that, Monsieur LaTour. We'll get her, won't we Bill?" The one named Mack seemed to do all the talking.

"But after we take her what do you want us to do with her?" Mack wanted to know.

"You'll bring her here and I want her to be blindfolded so she will not know where she's going. That's very important. Do you understand me?"

"Yes, sir. We'll tie a kerchief over her eyes."

"All right, Mack. Carry this out tonight and when you arrive here with her there will be five hundred dollars for each of you. But mind you, the lady is not to be roughed up or you'll get nothing. This is most important to me. Should that happen there would be a price on your heads." The look in Francois' black eyes was enough to convince Mack he meant every word.

"She'll be here before the midnight hour, Monsieur LaTour," Mack told him as he rose out of the chair.

Bill followed him. Francois remained in the chair behind his desk. He figured that they could see themselves out as other thoughts were occupying his mind. The idea that he would have Angelique Dupree under his roof before the night was over was enough to put him in a state of rapture.

The next few hours Francois paced nervously through the house before Bill and Mack arrived with his enchanting captive. He was taken back to yesteryear when he and his pirate crew took lovely ladies as their spoils when they plundered ships on the high seas before returning to port at Grand Terre Island. A part of his past would always be with him!

His plan was to keep her here overnight and wait until the early morning hours to go down the Mississippi to Point a la Hache. But he made a change — he would leave with her tonight to make the journey. For his own interest and safety, that would be best.

He found himself constantly looking at the clock on the mantel as he continued to sip his brandy.

Francois LaTour was not the only one watching a clock. Scott had arrived back at his cottage and enjoyed a hot bath after his long day on the wharf. He put on his black pants and the new shirt his mother had sewn. When she saw him come to the table looking so handsome, she smiled proudly.

"Thanks to you, Momma, and this nice shirt."

"Well, it was worth it to see you looking so grand, my son. It was one fine day from what your father told me. It's proud of you we are, Scott — I'm sure you must know how grateful we are."

"And why wouldn't I be when I had such loving, generous parents?" He kissed her cheek as she busily stirred the food she was cooking.

Timothy O'Roarke enjoyed a smoke from the new pouch of tobacco Scott had purchased before he'd come home tonight. There was also a bottle of the good Irish whiskey that Timothy enjoyed every now and then. Scott had bought that at the tavern before he and Justin had left this afternoon.

His mother was delighted with the three wicker baskets he'd picked up for her as he and Justin had gone back to the wharf to start for home.

It was a pleasant meal for the O'Roarkes but Timothy and his wife were taken by surprise when Scott got up from the table and announced he was leaving.

"You're leaving?" his mother asked.

"Got myself a girl, Mom. I'm going to see her tonight," he declared with a grin.

"So that's why you're wearing your new shirt, eh?"

"That's right, Mom."

"And may we ask who this young lady is, Scott?"

"Her name is Angelique and she *is* an angel."

It was enough to tell Timothy that the girl wasn't the daughter of their Irish friends. This young miss was a French Creole, which caused him concern for he knew how they looked down their aristocratic noses about Irish settlers.

"And shall we be meeting your Angelique?" his father inquired.

"I sure hope so, Poppa," Scott replied as he hastily left the kitchen table and went to the front door. He rushed down the path to the little wharf built out over the stream where a canoe was tied to the post. There was a bright full moon to guide him.

Once he was seated in the canoe, he paddled the little boat toward New Orleans, thinking about meeting with Angelique in the dark, secluded gardens.

It was a lover's moon shining up there tonight, Scott thought as he secured the canoe and prepared to go up the wharf to Kirby's house to get the horse.

Kirby jested when he prepared to ride away. "Damn, Scott, I got to find you a good bargain on a horse so you'll give old Sally a rest."

"You start looking, Kirby," Scott called back.

Kirby laughed and nodded as he turned to walk back up on the front porch. Scott urged the mare into a fast pace as he was anxious to get to the Dupree's house.

Mack and Bill had already climbed over the wall and found a dark spot where they could see all around the garden. Ironically, Scott had entered at the exact same spot.

Bill started to move but Mack stopped him. "Not yet, Bill," he whispered. "Let's see where he goes to wait for his ladylove. Then we take care of him and you sit there. The little lady will rush there thinking it's her young man and I'll grab her from behind. You put a gag in her mouth and we'll tie a kerchief around her eyes as Monsieur LaTour told us to do."

They watched Scott go directly to one of the many wooden benches around the spacious garden. It was some distance from the house and in a dark area which was perfect as far as Bill and Mack were concerned.

"What's it to be—my knife or your pistol, Mack?" Bill asked his partner.

"Neither, you fool! We weren't hired to kill him. We just get rid of him for the time we need to grab the girl," Mack declared with a disgusted look. It was a miracle that Bill hadn't swung from a noose a long time ago. Five hundred dollars wasn't worth taking that chance but that stupid Bill would probably do it for so little.

Slowly, the two of them began to sneak over the grounds, separating them from the spot where Scott

95

sat fidgeting on the bench. Mack had his pistol ready as he was going to slam it against Scott's head to render him unconscious.

But Scott's keen ears picked up a sound that made him turn around just in time to see the two huge figures directly behind him. But it was not enough time to protect himself from two strong hands, but it kept him from taking a swing at either of the fellows.

At the same moment he felt the vise-like grip on his arms, his head received a sharp, brutal blow causing him to sink into a black abyss.

The two dragged Scott's limp body to the far corner of the garden where the flowering shrubs were thick and large. When that was done, Mack told Bill, "Take a seat on the bench and I'll be right behind that bush. By the time she sees you aren't the fellow I'm going to be on that little gal like a mountain cat. Just be ready with that gag to muzzle any screams. You got it straight, Bill?"

"I got it, Mack. Got the gag right here in my hand," he said as he sat down. Both of them were in position, so they could only wait.

Angelique rushed to finish dessert — all she could think about during the meal was excusing herself to go to the garden. Scott would be waiting for her.

She'd dressed with special care and picked out a pretty soft pastel green gown. Both her mother and father had remarked about how lovely she looked in that particular gown as they'd dined together.

"Why, we should be having a party tonight," Simone laughed softly. "You look so lovely, my dear."

"Thank you, Momma."

"Your mother is right, Angelique. You do look awfully pretty tonight."

She hoped she was not showing how eager she was

to leave the table, but she could not restrain herself from fidgeting in the chair.

Giving them one of her prettiest smiles, she excused herself. "Going to take a walk in the garden with Cuddles. I'm sure she must have missed me while I was away at Nicole's."

She had no fear that Cuddles would cause any problem for her and Scott. He had won her over the first time they met.

Quickly, she called out to the pup and the two of them hurried out the door. Her heart was pounding wildly at the idea of secretly meeting him in the dark garden.

Chapter Twelve

The bright full moon seemed to focus on Angelique as she left the veranda — Bill and Mack saw her at the same instant. The vision was enough to make Bill gasp, "God Almighty, Mack — do you see what I see?"

"I saw! Shut up!" Mack muttered. But he was thinking the same as his pal that he'd never seen a prettier gal and he knew why Francois LaTour had warned them about no rough treatment getting her to him.

Angelique made directly for the particular bench where she knew Scott would be waiting.

Cuddles trotted right at her feet as they moved farther into the garden where numerous trees blotted out the light of the moon. As she came closer to the spot she could make out the outline of a man on the bench, so she hastened her step. Scott was there!

Suddenly, Cuddles halted as if she sensed danger, but Angelique continued on. It was only Cuddles's growls that made her hesitate for a moment to gently admonish the pup. "It's just Scott, Cuddles and you like him — remember?"

But when she was less than ten feet away, Angelique realized it wasn't Scott. It was too late to run or scream for one strong hand was over her mouth and the other encircled her waist. So many things happened in that next minute of madness. She felt something being stuffed into her mouth as the hand slowly released its hold over her face. Something was being spread over the front of her head and tied at the back. She had enough sanity left to know that there were more than one pair of hands restraining her. She couldn't see her assailants nor could she yell for help. She felt her hands being tied together and a few minutes later she felt a strap around her ankles.

There was the complete and utter feeling of helplessness as she felt herself being carried by a foul-smelling man. A million thoughts paraded through her head as to what fate had in store.

The next thing she realized was that she'd apparently been placed in the bed of a wagon that was away from her home. Why would anyone abduct her like this?

She felt her body being jarred as they traveled over the rutted dirt road at a fast pace. During all the crazy melee, she had heard two different men's voices. She heard one of them damning her dog for nipping him on the ankles. She prayed that they'd done no harm to poor little Cuddles — she didn't think that they had for she'd heard no yelps.

It seemed that they'd traveled for hours before the wagon came to a halt, but it had actually been less than a half-hour before the wagon pulled up to the back of Francois LaTour's huge two-story house.

Still addled and dazed, Scott caught sight of the two men with Angelique swung over one of their shoulders. He could only manage a weak moan of protest as he tried to struggle up from the ground. The next thing he felt after he collapsed back on the ground was Cuddles licking his face.

He made an attempt to pet the pup and slowly managed to sit up and rub the side of his throbbing head. His hand knew the dampness was blood dripping down the side of his face and on his new shirt. He also knew that he had to get out of there fast before Maurice Dupree came out and found him like this. He'd never believe he was innocent.

Giving Cuddles a couple of pats he told her he had to go. "Hate to leave you like this but there's nothing more I can do here. Our Angelique is gone," he told the pup as he grabbed the shrubs for support. His legs wobbled as he tried to walk. Climbing the wall proved to be quite a feat but he managed it. Once he straddled the mare and spurred her into motion, he moved away from the Dupree estate trying to figure out all the strange things that had just happened. His heart was heavy with concern about Angelique but he didn't know what to do. It was a nightmare but he was not asleep.

By the time he got back to the city he was more alert. Like Angelique, he felt it had been an endless night. Actually it was still very early and Kirby was prepared to tease Scott as he saw him riding up. He'd not been gone two hours.

But by the time Kirby saw his friend staggering through the gate and observed the bloodstain on his shirt, Kirby was in no jesting mood.

"Damn, Scott! What the hell happened to you?" he asked as he rushed to take his arm.

"Get me up to the swing and I'll tell you." Once Kirby got him seated he told Scott he could use a stiff shot of whiskey and dashed into the house. Hastily he returned and handed the glass to him.

"I'm damned if I know, Kirby. Climbed the garden wall and went to the bench to wait for Angelique like we'd planned. First thing I know two bastards jump me and give me a hell of a slam on the head."

"Think maybe old Dupree had these two do it 'cause he disapproved of you seeing his daughter?" Kirby asked.

"No, Kirby, that wasn't it — the two guys that did this carried his daughter off. I came to just enough to see them leaving with her but I couldn't do a damned thing to stop it. Couldn't do a damned thing!" he declared dejectedly.

"You couldn't help that, my friend. You can't go home tonight as I see it. You better just stay here."

"We'll see. What time is it?"

"Almost ten."

"Help me get cleaned up, will you, Kirby?" Scott made an attempt to move out of the swing. Perhaps it was the shot of whiskey or just the time he'd rested but he felt stronger.

"Sure, pal, and I'll loan you one of my shirts. We need to get that one soaking or your momma's gonna have your hide," he said with a chuckle.

They went to the kitchen and Scott took the cloth Kirby gave him and dampened it in a basin of water. After holding it to the side of his face Scott squeezed the cloth out and pressed it to the part of his head he knew had taken the fierce blow.

"Sit down over there by the lamp, Scott, and let me see about your head," Kirby urged. Scott did as he suggested and Kirby parted his thick hair to get a look. "Ain't bad, Scott. The cuts are small compared to all the damned bleeding you did. You're lucky, I guess."

"Guess I am. If you pour me one more shot of that whiskey, Kirby, I'm going to feel pretty much up to par." Scott placed the wet cloth back to his head as Kirby took the glass from his hand.

"Still think you ought to spend the night here even if you're feeling better, Scott."

"Appreciate your offer, Kirby, but it would be best if

101

I get on home. My mom will stay up all night and worry her head off if I'm gone all night. I'll have to tell her one way or the other what happened. Tonight or tomorrow, it would have to come out. I'm going to head for home in a few more minutes but I'll take you up on a shirt to borrow — I'll come by here tomorrow to get mine and bring yours back."

Kirby couldn't argue with him. He knew Mrs. O'Roarke and there wasn't much chance that Scott could lie to her for long tonight or tomorrow. She was a sharp-eyed old dame who doted on her one and only son.

"Well, as long as you think your head is clear enough to navigate that bayou," Kirby told him.

"Couldn't have done it an hour ago but I can now, I think, or I wouldn't try it."

But Kirby wanted to assure himself so he walked down to the dock with him when Scott decided to leave. He was satisfied that his pal was all right from the way he was walking. He stood there in the moonlight on the docks until Scott boarded the canoe and paddled away.

Only then did Kirby turn back to his cottage, promising himself that sooner or later he and Scott would take care of those two bastards. Kirby had a very volatile temper — a rugged, stout Irishman who never shied away from a fight.

Since the time he and Scott were little tadpoles they'd stood up for one another. His huge fists itched to slam the heads of the men who'd done this to Scott for no apparent reason. Poor old Scott had just been in the wrong place at the wrong time.

The bright full moon guided Scott's canoe into the bayou and around the turns and bends of the stream.

As he paddled, his thoughts were about his beautiful Angelique—never had he felt such a pain in his heart. His tormented mind pondered what could be happening to her at this moment. How wrong he'd been when he'd thought it was a lovers' moon in the sky as he rode toward her house tonight. It was a devil's moon!

Even the night birds' songs were a soulful screech, Scott thought, as he moved farther and farther into the dense bayou. For a while he felt he was the only person in the vast darkness until the lights of the first bayou cottage came into view. After a while, there was another one along the stream. He heard an occasional splash and knew it was a huge fish or an alligator slithering over the banks into the water.

Finally, he rowed past Justin's cottage—the next one would be his father's small dock jutting out over the stream. He paddled faster as his head was beginning to pound again. A cool cloth would feel good, he told himself.

He never doubted that there would be a light burning in the window as he secured the canoe and walked to the path leading to the cottage.

He ran his long fingers through his hair, hoping to conceal as much of the tangle on the right side of his head. But he was not about to lie to his mother because he saw no reason to do so.

He was not guilty of anything but if he lied to her then he would have felt guilt. It was not the O'Roarke way to be anything but straightforward and honest.

When he stepped through the door, she did not notice the blood in his thick hair in the dim lamplight but she quickly saw that he was not wearing his new shirt. Indignantly, she inquired, "And where is the fine shirt you left here wearing? Why are you wearing this old faded blue one."

Scott managed a weak grin for he was well aware of

her spitfire Irish temper. "That's a long story and I'll tell you as soon as I sit down."

He felt those piercing eyes on him as he moved to take the chair his father usually sat in.

She placed her needlepoint to the side and folded her hands in her lap. "I'm waiting, Scott."

"And I'm going to tell you, Momma."

Part Two

Summer's Fury and Folly

Chapter Thirteen

As Scott had told Kirby what had happened, he told his mother and saw the various expressions etching her face as he related each and every thing that took place. When he had finished, she shook her head in the deepest despair. "Oh, mercy, Scott—how grateful I am that you were not harmed worse than you were, but my heartfelt sympathy goes out to that sweet child and what her fate could be this night. Glory be, I feel like crying!"

"I know, Momma. I feel exactly the same way."

"Well, we shall both pray for her, Scott, for I know of nothing else we could do. I'm sure you wish you could have done more for I suspect that this little Angelique means very much to you."

"She means everything to me. I love her!" Scott confessed.

With an understanding smile she looked at her sober-faced son. She knew the agony he must be enduring knowing that the pretty girl he loved was in the hands of these unsavory characters.

"We'll just hope that God puts his protective arms around her, son. Somehow—someway, you'll find her, Scott. You have to have faith."

"Oh, I know. Thank you, Momma for your kind,

understanding heart. I — I needed to talk to you to-night."

"I'm always here, dear. I always will be. Now, I know it's foolish to tell you to try to go to bed and get some sleep but go ahead anyway, eh?"

"I will and you do the same — all right?" The two of them left the parlor to go to their bedrooms.

There was no sleep for Scott for many reasons and his mother found herself restless for a long time after she went to bed. Her heart was so heavy with feeling for Scott and this little Angelique whom she'd never met. But exhausion finally overtook her and sleep did come.

Scott got only a few moments of sleep. When the first rays of dawn came through his window, he rose and went to get a pail of the rainwater his mother always gathered to wash her hair so he might do the same.

Afterwards, he dressed in his usual work clothes for the day on his fishing boat. But all the time he dressed, he thought about Angelique and the Dupree family. By now, they had to know their daugther was mysteriously missing and had informed the authorities.

Knowing the influence that Maurice Dupree had in New Orleans, Scott had no doubt that nothing would be spared to find his daughter. If only he had any information that would help! What could he have told him except that there were two fellows who took her over the garden wall? Scott could not even have described them.

In his overwrought state, he wondered how Maurice Dupree would have reacted to him. The news that he was in the garden to meet his daughter with her approval could never have been accepted by Monsieur Dupree. He could have found himself in a jail cell. Scott was not about to put himself in that position —

he had his parents to think about. He provided their livelihood by running the *Bayou Queen* six days a week. He could not afford to be in a jail cell.

With that thought in mind, he left the cottage to row toward Justin's little wharf where the *Bayou Queen* was waiting for them to go out for the day's catch.

Mack and Bill delivered their precious cargo to the two-story house on St. Charles Street. With the awful gag in her mouth and the blindfold over her eyes, Angelique had no idea where she was being taken but she could hear.

There was no way to free herself during the ride for her ankles and hands were bound. But she could listen to the two men talking and she knew their names. She would never forget it was two men named Mack and Bill who'd abducted her from the garden.

As she was led into Francois LaTour's house she listened very intensely to the men they addressed.

When they guided her somewhere in the house she noted the gruff tone of the new man's voice when one of the men was about to utter his name.

Suddenly she found herself dismissed from the trio and she was led up a stairway by some unknown person. At least, the leather strap was removed from her ankles.

It was a woman's voice she heard next. "I'm going to remove the gag, mademoiselle, for no screams will do you any good. The rest of the bonds will remain but I shall sit you here on the bed so you will not harm yourself unless you're foolish enough to move around."

Angelique felt herself being lowered onto a bed. But at least, it was nice to have the terrible cloth from her mouth. She felt herself being inspected around her face and arms. She felt the woman's hands lift her long

109

hair off her neck and sensed a stronger light from a lamp being moved nearer. Francois' trusted quadroon servant was carefully checking the young beauty's neck and looking over the hint of cleavage exposed at her low-scooped neckline. Monsieur LaTour was not going to be happy about her report. She left the young girl to return to his study to tell him that the gag had been placed too roughly in her mouth and her lips were swollen. There were angry red marks on the delicate flesh of her arms.

"Please, mam'selle—do as I ask and sit where you are. I shall return shortly," the servant, Gabriella, told her. Angelique heard the door close and she knew she was alone.

Gabriella went directly to Francois' study where she knew she would find the three. There was something about the tall dignity of the quadroon in her scarlet frock, her head covered with a matching turban, that impressed Bill and Mack. It was evident that she held an exalted place in Francois' home. They were nervous the minute she entered the room.

Her almond-shaped eyes glanced briefly at them before she walked around the desk to whisper something in Francois' ear.

"Thank you, Gabriella. You can return upstairs now," he said, dismissing her. Both men sat there curious about what the quadroon had told him.

Francois made no attempt to speak until she left the room. But as soon as she had closed the door, it opened again and a huge man came striding into the room. Francois invited him to take a seat. "I'll be with you in just a minute." Then he turned his attention to Bill and Mack. "Be at my warehouse tomorrow at four and I'll pay the fee you've earned tonight."

Bill and Mack did not give him any argument, though their fee was due tonight according to their agreement. But the air around the room and in this house had made them nervous. This giant who'd just come into the room had a very threatening manner. It was evident that he was one of LaTour's men and neither of them wanted to tangle with him.

Mack was the first to leave his chair and Bill followed him. "We'll see you tomorrow at four then," Mack replied as he headed for the door.

As soon as they left the study and moved down the hallway, Francois gave Desmond a nod and he wasted no time going out a side door.

The two stupid bastards would receive no more money after what Gabriella had told him about the harsh way they'd slammed the gag in Angelique's mouth and made the marks on her arms.

He was leaving their payment in the hands of Desmond and his friend. In the meanwhile, he poured himself a brandy to try to calm his rage before he went upstairs. He knew that Gabriella would be tending to the girl in her usually capable way. Her special ointment would perform its fast healing before morning.

He had been sitting there only a few minutes when there was a soft rap on the door and Gabriella's voice called out, "Monsieur, may I speak with you, please?"

"Of course, Gabriella—come in."

"I thought you would be pleased to know that the girl has calmed down and I have tended to her lip and arms. I left her hands bound, monsieur, but her poor ankles needed the ointment so I released them. The door is locked so she cannot leave. Is that all right?"

"Exactly right."

"There is something else I think you should know, monsieur. Joseph just returned from the wharf and it seems the city is already buzzing about what happened tonight. The authorities are scouring the city and patrols are being put on the wharf, so Captain Andrews

111

told him. I thought you should know this."

"Did Joseph know how soon patrols would be sent there?"

"By midnight, monsieur," Gabriella told him, for she knew of his plans to take the mademoiselle to Pointe a la Hache.

"Mon Dieu, it isn't far from that now. That means we must leave immediately. Tell Joseph of my plans and get mademoiselle downstairs while I inform Sarah that she is to take charge as I'll be gone for a few weeks," he ordered anxiously. Hastily, he moved away from his desk and out of the room with Gabriella behind him.

Once again, Angelique found herself being moved elsewhere but at least the touch was more gentle and the voice kinder. Angelique was grateful for that, so she did as the woman told her to do. She realized she was going down steps — a stairway, and heard the woman tell a man that they were ready.

"So are we. Let us not tarry any longer then," Francois declared as he, Gabriella, Joseph, and his little captive went out the back door to board the carriage. They traveled up the dark streets swiftly as the hands of the clock approached the midnight hour.

As quickly as they had boarded the carriage, the four got into Francois' boat. Joseph went into immediate action to get it away from the dock while Francois took charge of his captive. Luckily for him the crew was ready for an early morning departure or they never could have left New Orleans so quickly.

He took Angelique to the small cabin he occupied when he made his trips back and forth from New Orleans to Pointe a la Hache. Gabriella went to the one across the small passageway to stay until she was summoned again.

For the first time, Angelique dared to speak to this

112

unknown stranger. She knew that the woman was not the one holding her arm but it was still a gentler touch than she'd experienced from the two ruffians who'd abducted her.

"Please, monsieur, may I sit down before I faint?" she pleaded, her voice trembling. "I — I don't feel well."

"You may, mademoiselle. Here, sit down on the bunk," he urged. His hands released her arm once she was on the bunk and he fluffed up the pillows. With a tender motion, he lifted her legs from the floor to suggest that she lie back and rest. "There will be no harm to you, mademoiselle, so you can relax. Soon, all this will be explained, Mademoiselle Angelique."

He knew her. He knew her name and now she was more perplexed than ever. "Who are you, monsieur?"

"That you will find out soon but for now just rest."

She was too tired to protest so she slowly moved back on the bunk but she sensed that he was still in the cabin even though there was complete silence.

She was obviously exhausted and did fall asleep; only then did he leave the cabin to go check with Joseph. After they were far enough away from New Orleans there was no reason he could not take the blindfold from her lovely face.

She was his now and there would come a time when she'd grow to love him even though it might take some convincing, he realized.

Chapter Fourteen

Joseph was as relieved as Francois that they were getting farther and farther from New Orleans. He wore a weak smile as he told his boss they'd passed by Chalmette a few minutes earlier and had made the turn in the river, heading for Dalcour.

"You're making good time then, Joseph," Francois said, giving him a comradely pat on the shoulders.

Francois left to check on some other matters before he sought out Gabriella. It was his intention for her to stay in the cabin with Angelique for the rest of the night. He would try to get a little sleep later in the other cabin.

The bright full moon was shining down on the muddy Mississippi, guiding Francois' boat as it had Scott's through the bayou. By the time the first rays of dawn were lighting up the Louisiana countryside, Francois' boat was within ten miles of Pointe a la Hache. Francois, Gabriella, and Angelique were sleeping.

Back in New Orleans, the authorities as well as a number of Maurice Dupree's friends had been making a search for Angelique but not a single shred of evidence had turned up. It was as though the earth had suddenly swallowed her up.

Two close friends had come to the house to console Simone as soon as they found out what had happened. There had been no sleep at the Dupree home all night.

Angelique's little pup, Cuddles, had whined as though grieving for her mistress. Simone held the pup to console her, wishing she could speak and tell them what had happened.

One of the Duprees' first friends to arrive at the house were the Benoits and their daughter, Nicole. All of them were in a state of shock. The first thing to cross Nicole's mind as she sat listening to Simon Dupree was Scott O'Roarke. She had to let him know about Angelique. As soon as she returned home, she told her parents she was going for a ride. They gave her no argument for they knew how upset she was about her little friend. But her mother could not resist urging her to be careful and not ride too far. "If this could happen to Angelique, it could happen to you, *ma petite*," Madame Benoit pointed out.

"I'll be careful, Mother," Nicole promised.

Nicole quickly rushed to the stable to get her horse so she could ride back toward the city. She would take the road that led around Lake Pontchartrain in hopes of spotting Scott's fishing boat.

But her hope of seeing the *Bayou Queen* was in vain. She knew she could do no more searching this afternoon or her parents would be in a panic so she reined the thoroughbred homeward. But tomorrow she would try again to find him, she vowed, as she put the horse into a fast gallop.

Had Scott and Justin not called it a day an hour earlier than usual, she would have seen his *Bayou Queen* as she rode along the lake road.

It had been Justin's idea that they quit a little early since Scott had told him everything that had happened the night before. He'd insisted on going along with

Scott to Kirby's smitty shop to get his shirt and return Kirby's.

"Then we're heading for that bayou. You need one of your momma's suppers and a good night's sleep, my friend," Justin told him. "That's the best way you can help this lady you love, Scott. You need a clear head."

"You're right, Justin. I've not been worth a damn today for you or myself. I'll be better tomorrow," he said with a hint of a smile.

" 'Course you will, Scott. I know that," Justin told him, as they left the dock for the smitty shop.

Kirby had Scott's shirt in case he came by and it had been cleansed of the blood stains. "These hands did that job for you, buddy," the happy-go-lucky smitty laughed as he handed him the shirt. Scott could not make the same claim, for he'd not laundered Kirby's shirt.

"This place is like a beehive about what happened to your lady, Scott. They're turning the place inside out from the rumors I've head all day. Maurice Dupree has offered quite a handsome reward for any information."

"So she's still missing then?" Scott asked.

"Last I heard," Kirby told him.

Kirby saw a customer approach the shop so Scott and Justin departed.

Scott could not deny that it would be good to get back to the bayou before the sun set. "And Mimi will be pleased to have her husband home an hour earlier, I know."

"That she will!"

"Well, you're a lucky fellow, Justin, 'cause you got yourself a wonderful woman," Scott remarked.

"Tell myself that every day and every night." As they traveled down the bayou Justin thought he noticed that Scott seemed a little more relaxed like his old self.

116

He hoped that the worst pangs of anguish were easing for his younger friend.

Scott felt better when he left Justin at his wharf. There was a special peace about the swamps and the bayou that he found nowhere else. There was still enough daylight so he could enjoy the sight of the blue herons on the bank and the beautiful water hyacinths in full bloom. He wondered how anyone could not think of this place as paradise. There was beauty everywhere, and a tranquility for him.

He found the old trunks of the cypress trees jutting out of the water a fascinating sight with the long sprays of Spanish moss cascading from their branches. A couple of raccoons rolled and tumbled over each other on the bank. For a moment his thoughts were distracted from Angelique Dupree.

But it only lasted a brief moment as his thoughts drifted back. He knew he needed some sleep and a good meal before he could think straight.

When Scott got home he enjoyed a good supper and a deep sleep. The next morning he was thinking more clearly about everything.

Justin could tell the difference when he arrived to pick him up and was glad. "You look much better, my friend."

"I feel much better, too," Scott declared as they set out to make their catch.

They had a good catch by the noon hour. They lingered by the lake to eat the food Mimi had packed for Justin before he left for work.

It was then that Scott spied a familiar figure astride her horse on the banks of the lake. Nicole was waving frantically and calling out. He waved back. He also interpreted her gestures to mean that she wanted to meet him at the dock so he wasted no time moving his fishing boat through the waters. He was hoping she might have some news of Angelique.

As soon as he got to the dock he rushed to meet her. "Nicole, it's good to see you again."

"Good to see you, too, Scott, but I wish it was a happier time. I had to come for I didn't know if you'd heard about Angelique. I tried to find you yesterday on the lake but I didn't see you."

She sensed from his sober look that he did know. "I know, Nicole, but I appreciate your thoughtfulness. I was there when it happened."

He watched her gasp. It took her a moment or two to speak. "You were — what are you saying, Scott?"

"I'd gone to meet Angelique in the garden that night as we'd planned. I was sitting on the bench waiting for her when I was suddenly jumped by two guys. I was hit on the head by God knows what. I was out of it — blacked out. I think Angelique came and they grabbed her. When I came out of the fog, I saw them taking her over the wall but my legs were so weak and I was so dazed I couldn't move."

"Dear Lord, did you tell Monsieur Dupree this, Scott?"

"No, I didn't. I managed to get myself over the wall and get the hell out of there — that was all I was interested in. I knew there was nothing I could do for her at that point. Monsieur Dupree doesn't know me or that his daughter knows me, Nicole. If he did he would certainly not approve. I'm just a lowly Irish fisherman and certainly not worthy to be courting his daughter as far as he's concerned."

"But I know how you feel about Angelique and how she feels about you, Scott. You must go to him and tell him all this," Nicole insisted.

"Now, wait a minute, honey. In the state he would have been in had I gone to him and told him the truth he might not have believed me and I could have ended up in jail. This would not have helped Angelique and I cannot afford to land in jail. I've a mother and father to support. My parents aren't wealthy like yours and Angelique's. You must understand!"

Compassion warmed Nicole as she saw the pain and worry on Scott's face. "Oh, I can understand, Scott — truly I can."

"I want you to since you and Angelique are such good friends. But I couldn't see how this would help Angelique and she is my only concern. I had nothing of real value to tell Maurice Dupree. I doubt that I could identify the two men who jumped on me. It was dark and it all happened too fast."

For a moment Nicole did not say anything and then Scott noticed the spark in her eyes. "Perhaps, Scott, this is the time for the Duprees to meet you. If I took you there and stood behind you as you told them what you've told me maybe it might help in some way that you or I can't know now."

"Oh, I don't know about that, Nicole," he told her in a hesitating voice.

"Scott, I assure you that the Duprees honor my family too much not to respect the fact that I brought you them. They would know that I would not bring you there if I didn't think of you as an honorable man. I know the ways of the French Creole as you know the ways of your Irish family. Trust me!"

He had only to look at her face to know that it was her spirit he'd liked from the moment he'd met her. He grinned, "Then maybe we Irish and you French Creoles aren't so different after all. I'll go with you, Nicole."

She smiled as she declared, "Well, I'm ready when you are."

He told her that he had to tell Justin what he was going to do and then he'd be ready to join her. He hesitated for a moment. "I have no horse, Nicole."

She laughed. "This big guy can carry the two of us." Scott had to admit that the strongly-built thoroughbred put Kirby's mare to shame.

He rushed down to the boat to tell Justin. As quickly he dashed back to the dock to mount the fine stallion behind Nicole. It wasn't until the two of them were riding down Old Cypress Road that he thought about his fisherman's garb.

He could imagine what a sight he would present to Angelique's parents in his old dark blue twill pants and faded blue shirt. His thick black hair was tousled from the morning's work he'd put in.

He had to hope that Nicole was right — he was putting his trust in her where the Duprees were concerned.

If she was wrong then he could be walking into a maelstrom of trouble and danger.

Chapter Fifteen

Simone happened to be looking out the window when she observed Nicole Benoit riding up their winding drive on the fine black stallion with a strange young man behind her. Looking out the window was something she'd done quite often lately in hopes that she would see her dear Angelique. Oh, she was beginning to realize that it was wishful thinking and Angelique was not coming home as soon as she might have hoped. But she could not bear to think that she would never return.

She rushed to the front door to greet Nicole and the young man. No one had to tell Simone that Nicole was sharing their sorrow for she knew her love for Angelique.

Opening the door, Simone greeted her guests. "Nicole, it's so good to see you."

"Good to see you, Madame Dupree. May I introduce you to my friend, Scott O'Roarke."

Simone surveyed the young man for a fleeting moment before she responded. "Nice to meet any friend of Nicole's. My pleasure, Monsieur O'Roarke."

"Nice to meet you, Madame Dupree," Scott replied.

She ushered the two of them into the hallway and

guided them toward the parlor. When they were seated, it was Nicole who wasted no time in telling Simone that Scott also knew Angelique.

"You know my Angelique?" Simone sat up in her chair.

"Yes, ma'am. I'm the owner of the *Bayou Queen*. It is from my boat that your man Zachariah buys your fish when he comes to the wharf on Friday. Angelique has been with him and we met. We were attracted to one another and knowing that you and her father would not approve of me we've met secretly in the garden a couple of times."

Simone could certainly see why her daughter would be attracted to this bronzed, firm-muscled fisherman. He was a very good looking young man. She liked his honest, open manner.

"The night all this happened I had come to the garden to meet her as we'd planned. But as I sat on the bench waiting for her, two hooligans jumped on me and knocked me out. I have the scar here on the right side of my head. By the time I roused, Cuddles was licking my face and I saw Angelique being taken over the garden wall by the two men."

Simone listened intently for she at last was learning something about what had happened that horrible night. Until now she had nothing to go on. It was obvious he had been with Angelique before because he knew the name of her pup.

"I was too weak and dazed to do anything to help her and I lingered only long enough to gain enough strength to get over the wall myself. As I told Nicole, you did not know me and I did not wish to be thrown in jail. My parents rely on me to run our fishing boat."

Angelique's little pup chose that moment to wan-

122

der into the parlor and, wagging her tail, made an eager dash toward Scott. A smile crossed his face as he stopped talking to greet her. "Well, hello, Cuddles." His hand went out to gently pat her head as she jumped on his leg.

It was enough to convince Simone that this young man was telling the truth. Cuddles was too fond of him for it to be otherwise.

"I'm very grateful to you, monsieur, for everything you've told me. What was a mystery has now had some light shed on it. I shall certainly tell my husband all this, and we are beholden to you."

Simone Dupree could not take it lightly when his honest blue eyes looked at her so intensely. "I care very deeply for Angelique, madame. I won't rest until I find her. Right now, I don't know where to start looking."

She gave him an understanding smile and nod. "Nor do we, monsieur."

His next words completely mellowed Simone's heart and endeared him to her because she saw the agony in his eyes. "My mother says we must have faith that God will put his protective arms around her. She's Irish, madame, and she always says this when she's concerned about someone."

"You must have a most wonderful mother, Scott O'Roarke. Maybe I'll meet her someday. I think my Angelique was lucky to have met such a nice young man as you. I thank you for coming to see me today."

Later, as Nicole was taking him back to the dock, she could not resist taunting him. "You see, Scott— we French Creoles are not all snobs. Your visit with Madame Dupree did her a lot of good. She will forever be grateful."

Scott smiled, "You were right, Nicole. I'll admit it. I was wrong. I'm glad I went and I thank you for insisting that I accompany you."

"I'm glad, too, Scott," Nicole said as she turned back to look at him as the black stallion galloped back toward the docks.

Nicole waited only long enough at the dock for Scott to dismount and then she spurred the horse homeward for she had been gone a long time. She knew that her parents were apprehensive after what had happened to Angelique.

Justin was glad their catch was good during the morning hours for the afternoon was going to be short. He was glad to see Scott finally sauntering across the wharf. There were a good three more hours that they could work the lake.

Whatever had been Scott's mission when he left with the young lady, Justin knew that his spirits were high when he leaped on deck. He did not question him about what he'd been doing. If Scott wanted him to know he would tell him.

The last two days and nights had been like two months to Angelique Dupree. She now knew who her captor was and that she was in some strange place a long way from New Orleans. She also knew that the quadroon who'd been her constant companion since she'd arrived at this place was called Gabriella.

But what she could not know was that for the first time since Gabriella had been brought into the house of Francois LaTour and dutifully done his bidding, she did not approve of what he was doing to this innocent young girl.

Angelique had Gabriella to thank that Francois had cooled his amorous desires. The other women he'd brought here over the years had not disturbed her but this one drew her sympathy. All she knew was that she didn't want him to use this girl.

Gabriella knew the awful chance she was taking; if Francois LaTour ever found out she had been lying about the young girl's condition and that she was not truly ailing he would be furious.

But when Angelique had looked up and thanked her for being so kind, Gabriella felt a wave of guilt that she'd been a part of this wicked plot.

"Monsieur will be coming in to see you before the day is over. I know not when but come he will. Pretend you are ailing—sick in your stomach and I shall swear it is so, too, mademoiselle. I will say that you can't keep your food down." It was the only thing Gabriella could think of that might spare her for another day and night. He could not stand the sight of anyone sick. There was something about someone being ill that turned Francois very cold and he wished to get away immediately.

"Thank you for being my friend, Gabriella. I hope I can return the favor for you someday," Angelique declared.

"You can by not giving me away to the monsieur. He would be furious as I am his servant. I shall try to help you when I can but that is all I can promise," she said as she took the tray from Angelique's lap. There was no food left as Angelique had been famished.

Managing a weak smile she told Gabriella, "You have a wonderful cook in the kitchen and I hope I keep it all down."

Gabriella smiled back as she started to leave. "You

125

will but it will be our little secret. I am going downstairs to report that you have a very upset stomach."

Angelique tossed the covers aside and wandered over to the window to survey this strange place. But she quickly dashed back to pull the covers over her when she thought she heard heavy footsteps out in the hallway.

The door did not open and she heaved a deep sigh of relief. What she'd seen outside the window was grounds with no beautiful gardens but just majestic palm trees surrounded by a tall, ugly, grey stone fence. It made her feel even more like she was in prison.

She quickly threw the coverlet off and sat back on the side of the bed. It had taken only one fleeting glance to recognize the man she'd seen at various places recently. But he'd said not a word as their eyes locked for that one second.

Oh, yes, she remembered his face with his trim, thin-lined mustache and his tall, reed-like body. Dressed in his usual finely-tailored attire, he'd held her for a moment when the two young scamps had almost knocked her down when she'd come out of the boutique. Now, she had to wonder if he'd been stalking her that day as well as the day when she and her mother had been having lunch in the tearoom and she'd caught him staring. But why would he abduct her like this? Was it for the ransom that her father would pay? That had been her first thought. Now, something was troubling her that made her very nervous. From the things Gabriella had suggested it made her feel that she must pretend to be ill to keep the man from having his way with her. But if a man wanted to make love to a woman it was not necessary to go to this extreme, she reasoned.

Gabriella came rushing into the room. "Quick, mademoiselle, put the wrapper on and lie back on the bed with a most distraught look on your face. He is going to come up to see for himself that you are feeling so poorly."

Angelique quickly stood up to put the coral-colored silk wrapper over the sheer gown which displayed the lovely curves of her body. Just as quickly she got back into the bed and struck a pose.

Gabriella whispered, "Perfect!" She had barely managed to turn around when the door opened and Francois LaTour came marching in. There was an intense look on his sharp-featured face as he ambled over to the bed to look down at Angelique. There was a crisp tone in his voice as he addressed her. "I'm sorry to hear you're ailing, Mademoiselle Angelique."

Angelique uttered a soft moan of discomfort and slowly turned her head on the pillow to look at him.

"I see that you recognize me so I'll introduce myself. I am Francois LaTour and we are not exactly strangers."

"I recognize you, monsieur, but I know not why you've done this to me," she told him in a faltering voice, turning back on her side.

"You will know, *ma petite,* but later. Gabriella, come with me," he said, turning away.

Obediently, Gabriella rose from the chair. Once the two of them were outside the door, he told her, "I see you are right as usual. Use your magic healing powers on her for I am not a patient man, as you well know. That's the trouble with beauties like Angelique Dupree. They're such delicate females. As you said, it's probably a good case of nerves."

"Oui, Monsieur LaTour. I will do all I can for

her," Gabriella assured him, nodding her kerchief-covered head.

She stood in the hallway to see that he descended the winding stairway before she went back into the room. Once Angelique saw it was Gabriella she leaped out of the bed to ask, "Did it work?"

Gabriella laughed softly. "You are a grand little actress, *ma petite*."

Angelique laughed, too, for the first time since this whole horrible nightmare started. "Oh, thank goodness!"

But their levity did not last for Gabriella had to tell her that Francois LaTour would not be put off for long. "You must have suspected his intentions, mademoiselle?"

"I think I know, Gabriella."

"And I can do nothing to stop it."

"I understand that, Gabriella. And please call me Angelique."

Gabriella gave her a warm smile. "I shall if you wish."

"But why me, Gabriella? Why would he hire men to abduct me?"

Gabriella walked over to the bed and spoke in a low voice. "Monsieur LaTour can be a very strange man, Angelique. He obviously saw you and he became obsessed by your beauty. You are a stunning lady, Angelique. You surely know that. Many men must stare at you anywhere you go."

"I did recognize him as a man I've seen often who just happened to be passing my way," Angelique told her.

Gabriella shook her head and smiled, "Oh, no, Angelique it was not by chance. It was planned. I've been with Monsieur LaTour for a few years and I've come to know many things about him. That is why I tell you that you became an obsession. What Monsieur LaTour wants, he takes!"

"Well, he'll never possess me. There is another man I love. I could never care for a man like Francois LaTour. The fact that he had me abducted makes him disgusting to me."

Gabriella was having many private thoughts that she could not voice to this young girl. However, she did tell her something she felt might help in the days to come. "It will not matter to monsieur about your feelings. What he desires is all that matters to him, Angelique. Always remember this when I will not be around."

Angelique could not dismiss her words lightly. They continued to haunt her during the rest of the day and that night.

Chapter Sixteen

The next morning when Gabriella came to her room, Angelique was out of bed and dressed in the lovely green gown she had been wearing the night she was kidnapped.

"Angelique, you hardly look like the ailing belle this morning! We'll never fool him with you dressed in that gown."

"I'm tired of this one miserable room and I'll not play the coward! As you yourself said it's only a delay. Well, I intend to face this despicable man and demand that he take me back to New Orleans immediately."

Gabriella's almond-shaped eyes widened. "Mon Dieu, Angelique! Are you sure?"

There was fire in her eyes and determination in her voice. "I'm absolutely sure, Gabriella. I'll do him no good if I'm dead and I shall fight him to the death before he'll have me. I thought about what you said yesterday. I thought about it very seriously the rest of the day and last night after we said goodnight. I decided to face him today and I will."

Gabriella had to admire her bold spirit and the truth of it was one more day would have been the most it could have been delayed anyway. But she could not deny that she was filled with concern.

"Where is Monsieur LaTour, Gabriella?"

"He is downstairs having his breakfast."

"Take me to him."

"If this is what you wish."

"It is," Angelique declared as she started for the door. Gabriella motioned to her to follow. She was beginning to realize that Angelique Dupree was a headstrong young lady. Behind that beautiful face with its delicate features was no fragile flower. This girl could be brave and strong.

The two of them went down the stairway and as they reached the base, Gabriella hesitated a moment before ushering her into the dining room. "You're sure, Angelique?"

Angelique gave her a firm nod, so Gabriella led her into the lavishly furnished room where Francois was sitting in one of the velvet-covered chairs, enjoying his breakfast. But when he looked up to see Gabriella and Angelique, he almost dropped his fork.

Angelique was a vision of loveliness in her pastel green gown with her glossy black hair around her shoulders. He admired her arrogant air as she stood looking at him.

"Well, mademoiselle—this is a delightful surprise. Please join me for some breakfast. I have to believe that Gabriella worked her miracles and you're feeling better. You look better than you did yesterday."

"I am much better, monsieur," she told him as she allowed him to assist her into the chair directly across the table. She looked as regal as a queen.

131

Reluctantly, Gabriella forced herself to leave the room as she knew she must do. Angelique was on her own.

Angelique ate the food and enjoyed the coffee the tall black manservant served her.

When the meal was finished Francois invited her to take a stroll with him around the grounds. "It's really a beautiful place as you will see for yourself. Part of the estate is bordered along the river and the back has a sandy shore on the bay."

Angelique tried to stay calm and in control for this was the only way she could stand up to Francois LaTour and she knew it. "And what is this place called, monsieur?"

"Pointe a la Hache." It was only after he'd so easily allowed her to work her wiles on him that he knew he should never have told her that. He wondered if that angel face of hers was as pure and innocent as it seemed.

He quickly offered her his arm as the two of them left the dining room and went out to the terrace. The grounds were much more beautiful than the ones Angelique had looked down on from her bedroom window.

Huge palms flourished with all kind of exotic flowers. It was shaded and cool as they strolled along this pathway. Angelique noticed that the same tall stone fence surrounded these grounds, too, only here it was partially hidden by growth.

Francois was aware that she was quiet, making no comments about his lovely paradise. The few times he glanced her way she showed no interest in any of the beautiful areas. The look on her face was thoughtful—she might have been a large stuffed doll. Most young women he'd brought to his gardens were demonstrative about the glorious atmosphere he'd created.

His fountain had come from Italy and the elaborate fish pond was filled with gold fish and built with careful detail. Water lilies floated at the edges.

He found himself becoming vexed and a tenseness was reflected in his face and voice. "You're certainly not a talkative young lady, Angelique."

"I've nothing to speak to you about, monsieur, except to tell you that I request that you take me back to my home. I have no wish to be here!"

"But I have no wish to take you home!"

"Well, you might as well for I shall prove to be no source of entertainment or pleasure, I assure you!" Her hand fell from his arm.

"Well, that remains to be seen, mademoiselle," he smirked. The look on his face infuriated Angelique and she stopped. With her hands placed firmly at her waist and her dark eyes sparking with fire, she hissed at him in a fury that surprised Francois. "And I assure you of this, monsieur, and hear me well! There's no pleasure you'll get from me! I'll fight you to the end before I'd allow you to have your way with me! I'd die first!"

"Why, you little hellcat! What ever made me think you were worth all I did to get you here?" he snapped.

"You were very presumptuous and you made a very costly mistake. My father will have your head for what you've done."

Francois would never have suspected this young girl to rattle him this way. He'd expected her to be intimidated by him and everything that had happened. It was completely against his plan and his fantasy to use force to possess her. This was not the way he'd dreamed about this romantic interlude.

"You dare to fault a man who fell hopelessly in love the first time he saw you and wanted to show his love and adoration. But circumstances would never have allowed that, so I sent the baskets of flowers."

"So you were the one?"

"I was the one," Francois declared, thinking that this would have impressed her favorably.

"Once again, I must tell you that you were most presumptuous to do what you did."

Francois was so furious that he felt tempted to slap that pretty face instead of kiss it as he'd hoped to do for so long. "So I guess you just don't like me — oui?"

"Oui, I do not like you! You are disgusting to have abducted me. I find it very debasing and that I would never forgive! The pain you've caused my parents and me has nothing to do with the love a man has for a woman, monsieur. It has to do with greed and lust!"

She turned to go back toward the house. He called out to her, wanting to know where she was going. She called, "I don't care to be here any longer. I find you very offensive."

Francois was so befuddled he just stood and watched her sashay up the pathway. Suddenly he heard a loud roar of laughter back by the gate of his garden. He knew who it was who'd been privy to the scene between him and Angelique Dupree. It was his old friend, Jean Lafitte.

"Mon ami, you've got yourself a little hellcat there," Jean declared as he sauntered up. "Who is this little enchantress?"

Jean Lafitte was a true connoisseur where beautiful women were concerned for he'd squired and courted some of New Orleans' most beautiful ladies for years. But the one who'd truly captured Jean's heart was a lady he could never claim for she was married and in love with her handsome English husband. But everyone in New Orleans knew it was Elise Edwards whom Jean had idolized from the first moment he saw her. Today, the beautiful green-eyed Frenchwoman haunted him even though he'd taken many mistresses to ease his yearning.

Francois told Jean that her name was Angelique. With a deep, husky laugh, he said, "Well, there's a little bit of devil in that angel, I'd say. But she's a gorgeous little devil!" To know her name was not enough so Lafitte implored Francois to tell him more.

Francois invited him to the terrace to enjoy some coffee while they talked. After the servant had left, Francois told him it was Angelique Dupree in the gardens.

"You're not telling me she is the daughter of Maurice Dupree, are you, Francois?" He knew most of the wealthy families in New Orleans and the name Dupree immediately alerted Lafitte. Her stunning beauty matched the rumors and gossip he'd heard.

"She is," Francois told him with a pleased grin.

"Oh, mon ami — I know she's not at Pointe a la Hache with Dupree's approval so you want to tell me how she happens to be here?"

Francois saw no reason to conceal the truth from Jean, so he told him and immediately saw the frown on Lafitte's face. "That's all I need, Francois—the authorities swarming around Grand Terre or Pointe a la Hache. Some of them know of our association in years past. You've done something very foolish, mon ami."

Francois grinned, "Oh, Jean—we go back a long way. Don't tell me you've forgotten those days? We took anything we wanted."

Jean's dark eyes were sober. "You're right, Francois, and I don't deny the bounty I took from ships—but I never took a lady and kept her against her will. I never had to. Francois, if a woman isn't willing, you'll not get a damned bit of pleasure."

"She's like a goddess, Jean. Damn it, I couldn't eat or sleep until I took her. I know I can make her realize how much I adore her."

Jean shook his head and took a sip of coffee. "That's going to take more time than you've got, Francois. I don't think you checked out Maurice Dupree as you should have before you attempted this folly of yours. He'll turn all of Louisiana upside down to find his only daughter."

These words were enough to make Francois a little apprehensive. "Guess I should have talked with you instead of my lawyer and another cohort—they were supposed to know most of the influential people in the city."

"Only wish you had, mon ami. I didn't realize that the old pirate fever was still in your blood. I'd had the impression you'd left that all behind you."

"I was convinced of it myself until the day I first saw Angelique. I knew that I could not court her

136

as I would have if she'd been someone else so I took her captive, Jean."

Before Lafitte took his leave, he gave Francois one last word of warning and told him he better be prepared to pay one hell of a high price.

Respecting the formidable Lafitte as he did, he sat on the terrace for a long time to do some very serious thinking.

Then he went to Joseph to tell him to prepare the boat. He was returning to New Orleans to check out just what was going on. Angelique would not get away from Pointe a la Hache just because he would be away for a couple of days. After all, he could always depend on Gabriella to keep an eye on her. And there were four other trusted, loyal servants to carry out his orders while he was away, he reasoned.

Lafitte had planted seeds of trepidation and he was alarmed about his welfare!

Chapter Seventeen

Simone Dupree told her husband about the visit she'd had in the afternoon while he was away. "Nicole Benoit brought a young man here who knows our Angelique, Maurice. While we were not aware of it, it is obvious that the two of them met and were attracted to one another."

Maurice bristled and snapped, "Are you saying she was slipping around to see some young man we didn't know, Simone?"

In a calm voice she replied, "I guess that's exactly what I'm saying. If you will just shut up, Maurice, and listen for a change I shall try to enlighten you about what I learned from Nicole as well as this young man, Scott O'Roarke."

He was not accustomed to his wife using such a brusque tone and it caused him to shut his mouth and sink back in the chair. When he did, Simone told him everything Scott had told her and also what Nicole had said.

"Why under God's green earth didn't he come to us that night?"

"He was addled, as I told you, and probably in a foggy state. As he admitted to me, Maurice, we didn't know him and he was afraid of what our reaction would be. I believed him, Maurice. I saw the sorrow in his eyes when he told me how he was too dazed to do anything when he saw the two men carrying Angelique over the fence."

"Oh, dear God, Simone—it drives me crazy not knowing where she is or what is happening to her," Maurice moaned.

"I know, dear, but at least we know more than we did. I've thought about something ever since Nicole and Scott left. I've wondered if you have any enemies who would have hired men to kidnap our daughter in revenge?"

"Not a one that I know of, Simone. And this young man—did you learn what he does or where he works?"

"As a matter of fact, I did. He runs a fishing boat and supports a mother and an ailing father. That was another reason he told me that he feared coming to us. He wasn't afraid for himself but he could not afford to be thrown in jail and be unable to work his fishing boat. He seemed like a very honest, straightforward young man."

"Well, it's apparent that he impressed you, my dear. Nicole Benoit must feel the same way to have brought him here in the first place," Maurice admitted.

Simone had to agree as they went into their dining room to have their evening meal but it was difficult to see Angelique's empty chair.

But they went through the ritual and afterwards retired to the parlor where their conversation was once again centered around Angelique.

Maurice told his wife that he would make a

point of talking to this young fisherman, Scott O'Roarke. "He has shed some light on this whole thing. Obviously the two men who knocked him out were hired by someone. It was certainly planned — of this I'm sure. I've got to talk to Scott O'Roarke. He's the only chance we've got to find Angelique, Simone."

Knowing that Kirby's smitty shop was a good place to hear gossip, Scott decided to stop there before he left the lake to go back to his bayou.

It was the end of the day for Kirby, too, when Scott walked through the open back doors. He greeted his friend with an anxious look. "Damn, Scott, I was hoping you would come by. Heard a lot of rumors today and I don't know whether anything I've heard will mean anything to you."

"I won't know until you tell me," Scott declared with a grin. Kirby was a sight to behold with dark smudges all over his face and his body gleaming with sweat.

Leading the horse he'd been working on over to an empty stall, Kirby closed the gate. He came back to sit down on the old wooden bench.

"Well, here's the rumor as I've heard it about a half dozen times today. The night your pretty lady got abducted, or I should say the next morning early, the patrol checking the wharf down around the riverbank found these two burly-looking fellows. One was killed and the other one was beaten to a pulp, left for dead, but he wasn't. Now, the thing that's stirred the gossip this morning is that in the dead fellow's shirt pocket was a slip of paper with the name of 'Dupree' on it."

Scott was churning with intense curiosity, wondering if they could have been the two he'd seen carrying Angelique away that night.

"And the other one?"

"Well, he died a few hours later but he kept mumbling about some dirty sonofabitch. Kept saying it over and over that he and his pal, Mack, had been betrayed. Called him a rich sonofabitch by the name of 'La-something' but he never managed to get it all out before he died." Kirby waited for Scott to absorb all he'd told him before he asked if any of this made sense.

"Damn, it might, Kirby. It just might. Too bad that the guy could not reveal that rich gent's name."

"Yeah, isn't it? Now, you know me and some of my wild and crazy Irish thinking. You gotta know, as long as the two of us have been friends. There may not be a thing to it but one of the fellows I know that works on the docks told me that a boat left the pier in a great big hurry that night. Said he saw the group boarding the boat and it was a very interesting entourage. There was this tall gent and a young lady. Then he said he saw this little hump-shouldered man walking with a tall woman of color with one of those bright kerchiefs tied around her head."

"There was a young woman with them?"

"That's what he said but what got me to thinking, since I've never seen Mademoiselle Dupree, was I recalled you telling me about the lady's extremely long hair. Well, this was a thing that had caught old Dick's eyes. He kept talking about this girl's hair."

This whetted Scott's interest even more than Kirby's other gossip. "By any chance, did he happen to see the name of the boat?"

"Yeah, he did! It was the *Mississippi Belle*. You think maybe they could have been the ones taking your lady somewhere, Scott?"

"There's only one lady who has hair like Angelique's. I'm very grateful for your information, Kirby—now I've got something to go on. I have no doubt it was Angelique your friend saw, no doubt at all!"

He gave Kirby a hasty farewell for he had some plans to make. At last he felt he could do something to help his beloved Angelique, so there was no time to waste.

He rushed back down to the pier where Justin was waiting. Justin could tell by the look on his face as he boarded the boat that something had happened.

In an excited voice he asked Justin if he would mind handling the boat alone tomorrow. "I've got some checking to do." He told him everything Kirby had said.

The Acadian fisherman assured him he would be happy to do that if he could track down his pretty lady. "It sounds like you may have stumbled on something important, Scott."

"It's a feeling in my gut, Justin. I know it must have been Angelique. I've got to find out who owns the *Mississippi Belle*."

"Then you get on it in the morning and let me tend to the fishing," Justin assured him.

The next morning, Scott left the boat to go into the city. It didn't take him long to find out the information he was seeking. The *Mississippi Belle* was owned by one Francois LaTour.

Once he found that out, he went back to the smitty shop to ask Kirby for the loan of his mare so he might ride out to the Dupree's estate.

It was old Zachariah he encountered first when he galloped down the drive. As he quickly dismounted and told the elderly black man he was sure he'd heard some news about Mademoiselle Angelique, he saw tears misting in the old man's eyes as he sighed, "Oh, I pray so. My heart is so heavy for her, monsieur."

Scott gave his shoulder a consoling pat. "So is mine, Zachariah. We'll get her back. Believe me!"

"If anyone could, I have faith that it would be you, monsieur. I know a good man when I see him. You are a good man," Zachariah declared.

"I thank you for that and hope I shall not disappoint you or Angelique. I love her very much."

"I know this, monsieur. I knew this when I saw the two of you together the day I'd been down to buy the fish." A sly grin crossed his ebony face.

"Guess I sorta had that figured out, too, Zachariah. Would you know if Monsieur and Madame Dupree are home?"

"Madame Simone is but I don't know about Monsieur Dupree," the black servant told him. At that moment Maurice came around the corner.

143

"I'm home, Zachariah," Maurice called as he walked up to Scott and Zachariah. Turning his attention toward Scott, he introduced himself. "And I figure that you must be Scott O'Roarke. My wife told me about your visit to see us."

"Yes, sir, I'm Scott O'Roarke. I've come again because I heard something this morning you'll be interested to learn."

Maurice anxiously invited Scott to accompany him into the house while Zachariah moved back toward the stable. As they entered, Maurice led Scott into his study. "Would it be best if I heard it first or should I summon Simone?"

"I think Madame Dupree could hear everything I have to say, sir. I'm very encouraged—it's the best lead I've had."

Maurice asked Simone to join them and she did so with a look of excited expectation. Scott wasted no time telling them everything he'd learned at Kirby's smitty shop. With the name of the boat, *Mississippi Belle,* he was able to trace the owner and told the Duprees the name.

"I've heard this name. Oh, yes, Simone, I've heard about this man but I've never had any dealings with him. I do know of a few businessmen in the city who have. Somehow, what I'd heard left me with the impression he was a shady character, but he has no grudge against me that I know about." Maurice was grateful to Scott for he had found out more than the firm he'd hired to investigate the whereabouts of his daughter. He would certainly look into this latest development.

When Scott prepared to take his leave to return

to the dock, Simone gave him a grateful hand-shake. "We shall never forget your efforts to help us find our Angelique, Monsieur O'Roarke."

Maurice echoed his wife's sentiments and Scott thanked them for their kind words. With a look of sincerity he declared, "I can't rest until I know she's safe."

They both nodded to agree with that!

Chapter Eighteen

From an upstairs window Gabriella had witnessed the episode that took place between Angelique and Francois in the garden. She saw them from the time they'd left the terrace and Angelique's hand was lightly holding his arm until the moment she'd stopped on the flagstone path and started unleashing her fury.

Gabriella stood in the window with an amused grin as she watched the spirited miss tell Francois off. She had never seen anyone do that since she'd been under his roof. She applauded this spunky young girl!

As she watched Angelique rush back toward the terrace, she saw the familiar handsome figure of a man come into the garden. He was laughing heartily as he walked up to Francois. She continued to linger at the window until the two moved to the terrace—then she went to look for Angelique.

When she entered the room she found the young girl crying and rushed over to comfort her. She told her how bravely she'd stood up to Francois LaTour. "I was watching out the window, *ma petite*. You were *magnifique!* I've never seen anyone dare to talk back to the monsieur like that!"

Angelique's tear-stained face looked up at her as

she stammered, "I—I did stand up to him, didn't I, Gabriella?"

"That you surely did, mademoiselle."

The two of them laughed girlishly as they sat embracing one another. Angelique suddenly turned quite serious. "When I make my getaway from this miserable place you must come with me, Gabriella. My father would see that Francois LaTour would do nothing to harm you ever. He will be so grateful when I tell him what you've done for me."

Gabriella smiled warmly. "That's mighty sweet of you, Angelique. It does sound like a glorious dream but I learned long ago to forget about dreams." There was a strange look in those dark almond-shaped eyes. There was a very sultry, exotic look about Gabriella that Angelique found interesting. She wondered about her life and what had brought her to be the servant of such a man as Francois LaTour. Somehow, she knew Gabriella was not here because she wished to be.

"We'll get away from this place, Gabriella! I swear we can. I don't know how long it will take but I'll try over and over again if I have to. I'll never let that man subdue or conquer me. I swear it!"

The two of them could talk no longer for a servant came to the door to summon Gabriella and tell her that the monsieur wished to see her in his study. Gabriella left the room immediately.

Angelique was left alone to think about how she could possibly escape.

Gabriella found herself in a state of upper shock when Francois announced that he and Joseph would be leaving first thing in the morning. He explained that something had come up and he had to return to New Orleans. "A business matter I had not figured on," he remarked. He told her that she was in full charge and he was putting the entire responsibility of Angelique Dupree in her hands. "I've no other servant I trust as much as you, Gabriella. But then I don't have to tell you how I rely on you."

"I will see to Angelique, monsieur," Gabriella vowed.

Francois smiled. "I know you will. You may go now, Gabriella." She turned to leave.

Francois sat at his desk watching her. There was a certain admiration he harbored for Gabriella as she was not the usual type of servant. She was shrewd and very clever and there was a charm and grace about her that distinguished her. There was no denying that she was one of the most beautiful quadroons he'd ever seen when he brought her to Pointe a la Hache a few years ago.

It did not disturb him a few hours later that he dined alone and was informed that his little captive was having a dinner tray in her room. Tonight there was something far more important occupying his thoughts. He might have been captivated by the little beauty upstairs and gone to drastic extremes to get her where he wanted her—but nothing was more important to him than his own welfare. His old friend, Jean Lafitte, had given him much to think about this afternoon. Jean had obviously not approved of what he'd done by kidnapping Angelique Dupree.

By the time the sun rose over the muddy Mississippi the next morning, Francois and Joseph were boarding the boat to travel northward to New Orleans. He would have been very concerned had he known that there was a dockworker who noticed the name of his boat the night he captured Angelique.

The irony was that this dockworker happened to be a pal of Kirby's — and Kirby was a lifelong friend of Scott O'Roarke's.

As usual, there was that one simple thing that could spoil the best plots an individual like Francois had so cleverly planned. The dockworker's keen observation that night was enough to put Scott O'Roarke and Maurice Dupree on his trail.

When he arrived back in New Orleans by mid-afternoon, Francois went directly to his house before going to his office. He was very pleased when he heard that Desmond had carried out his orders — Bill and Mack were both dead. But what his informer did not know was that Bill had been able to talk to the authorities before he died.

So Francois had taken the time for a leisurely bath and had dressed in one of his finely-tailored suits. He looked like a dapper gentleman by the time he left his house to go to his office by early afternoon.

For the first hour Francois sat at his desk going over some papers and checking orders for imports since he'd been away for a few days. He was feeling a bit smug and would take great delight in telling Jean that there was nothing to be concerned about. In fact, he planned to taunt his old pirate friend. Jean was becoming too soft living in all that luxury on Grand Terre Island.

But the only thing disturbing Lafitte's paradise in

Barataria on Grand Terre was the constant harassing from the Governor of Louisiana, Governor Claiborne. Lafitte considered him a stupid clown. When his brother, Pierre, had been arrested by Claiborne's troops and thrown in jail, it had made a deep impression on Jean.

All their assaults and attacks on Barataria had been in vain, as Jean had always been able to win; but when Pierre was thrown in jail that had not been easy. Claiborne became Jean's enemy forever after that.

Francois could understand why his old friend was cautioning him about the authorities for taking the daughter of a very respected French Creole to his fortress at Pointe a la Hache.

But Francois's cockiness was shattered a short time later by the abrupt appearance in his office of a man announcing that he was Maurice Dupree. He was very impressive and there was an authoritative air about him as he walked up to the desk where Francois was sitting. This was a man determined to have some answers to the questions he was about to ask.

Maurice Dupree didn't care for the man he saw with his trim mustache and shifting black eyes. Francois invited him to sit down but Maurice did not accept his invitation as he stood towering over him at the desk.

Maurice wasted no time with formalities but got straight to the point when he asked if he was the owner of the *Mississippi Belle*.

"I am, Monsieur Dupree."

"Well, Monsieur LaTour, I think the authorities will want to question you about my daughter's disappearance." He added the fact that the boat had been seen leaving New Orleans before midnight and that one of the people boarding fit his description. A woman fitting Angelique's description was also seen. Francois quickly denied everything, but Dupree was not impressed. Francois found it increasingly difficult to retain a calm demeanor.

"Then Monsieur LaTour, you damned well better be able to prove it because I'm going directly to the authorities to give them all the information I have on you." He disappeared through the door, leaving Francois to ponder what he'd said.

Francois knew it was no idle threat Monsieur Dupree was making as he marched out of his office. He also recalled the venom in Angelique's voice yesterday when she had told him that her father would have his head for what he'd done to the family.

He was shaken and he had to wonder if Jean had not been right after all. Had he gotten carried away in his quest for the beautiful Angelique? He had some thinking to do and some very serious thinking at that. Oh, he could bring the divine little distraction back to New Orleans and see that she was safely back at her home and forget all his dreams about being her ardent love. But he would never be able to show his face in New Orleans again for a long, long time. So he would be losing thousands of dollars if he had to desert his very profitable warehouse filled with goods.

Angelique Dupree could identify him, which ruled that idea out. He'd done many things in his life but he had already ruled out the only sure way to keep her from pointing an accusing finger and that was to kill her. This, he could not do!

As Francois saw it there was only one thing he could do to protect himself for a while until a better option occurred to him. She must stay hidden at Pointe a la Hache. So as soon as he gave his foreman at the warehouse his orders he prepared to leave. "I've some business to attend to in Baton Rouge for a few days, Paul, so I'm going to have to leave things in your hands."

But it was in the opposite direction that Francois was heading for he well remembered Maurice Dupree's promise that he was going directly to the authorities. Francois knew he had to leave New Orleans as soon as possible.

When he arrived back home he took no time to pack any clothing. The only thing Francois gathered up was most of the gold he'd placed in the safe. As soon as he'd collected it, he announced to Joseph that he was ready to leave the city and the two of them quickly boarded the gig to go back toward the harbor.

They boarded the *Mississippi Belle* to return to Pointe a la Hache where Francois felt he would be safer than in New Orleans.

It had been a very long day for Francois for he'd left Pointe a la Hache early this morning to come to New Orleans with plans to remain a few days and scout around the city to see what rumors were floating around about Angelique's disappearance.

But he'd heard enough from the angry Maurice Dupree to know that he would be foolish to linger even overnight in New Orleans.

His haven was Pointe a la Hache!

Chapter Nineteen

Scott did not have long to wait on the pier before Justin guided the boat by for a turn around the bay as they'd agreed he would do when Scott had taken his leave from the boat earlier.

"Well, I didn't expect to catch sight of you on this turn. Got your business done faster than I anticipated, Scott." Justin was happy to hear that his young friend had been successful in finding out the owner of the *Mississippi Belle.*

"I went over to pass all this on to the Dupree family. Real nice people, Justin. I have to say they were very pleasant to me and I didn't exactly know about her father. He was very pleased to hear all I'd learned."

"I would think he would be very grateful, Scott." Justin put the fishing boat back into motion so they could fill their bins with a few more fish before the sun began to sink low in the sky.

Because their bins were full, Justin and Scott were heading back to their wharf by five. Since he'd forgotten to pick up some tobacco for his father when he left the boat that morning, Scott told Justin he'd be back in just a little while because he was rushing to the tobacco shop before they pulled out.

Justin wandered around the wharf and talked with some other fishermen who were bringing up their catch for the day. It was during this roaming that he chanced to see the two men boarding the *Mississippi Belle*. He didn't know it was that particular boat until it took a slight turn by the wharf.

One of the fellows he knew came ambling by and stopped to talk. "Pretty fancy boat, isn't it?" Justin remarked.

"Oh, yeah, that belongs to that fancy dude, Francois LaTour. He really ain't that fancy. The truth is he was one of those damned pirates out in Barataria who came to New Orleans a few years ago, becoming a so-called businessman."

"How do you know all this, Fred?" Justin asked curiously.

"Good pal of mine knows a fellow who does work for him from time to time if you know what I mean."

Justin took a long, hard look at the tall man with his slick black hair and mustache decked out in fancy clothes. He was walking along with a little hump-shouldered man dressed in faded blue garb who must have been the captain of the boat. At least, now he could tell Scott that he knew what Francois LaTour looked like. He scrutinized the man very carefully and saw what he thought was a look of tenseness on his sharp-featured face as he and his man hurriedly boarded the boat and left the docks.

But when Scott did return to the wharf and they prepared to leave, Justin had grave misgivings about telling all he'd observed. For his own selfish reasons, Justin decided to wait until they were a distance into the bayou.

He wasn't sure what wild, impulsive thing Scott might have wanted to try. Justin didn't want to go on some wild goose race after the long day he'd put in and have Mimi worrying about his late return.

When they reached a bend in the bayou that put them within a mile from Justin's pier, he told Scott he had seen the *Mississippi Belle* leave.

"You saw it leave? Damn, I wish you'd told me."

"Couldn't, Scott. You were gone and it was out of sight by the time you returned."

"Damn, I wish I'd been there."

Justin figured it was time to set the score straight. "And what would we have done, Scott? Would we have jumped in our boat in hot pursuit? I've got a wife and children I owe an obligation to. I couldn't have done that, Scott. You can but I can't."

Justin's loyalty to his family could not be taken lightly and after all, Scott couldn't expect him to feel his overwhelming torment. "I understand, Justin."

"And I understand exactly how you feel, Scott. If it were Mimi in your Angelique's shoes I'd feel the same way. I did get a good look at this Francois LaTour as he and another fellow boarded the boat. The other man was the captain, I figured, 'cause he wore the same clothing we do."

He told Scott what Fred had told him about LaTour's past and his connection with the pirates down on Grand Terre Island. This was enough to whet Scott's interest, and he wondered as Justin talked if this was where they'd taken Angelique. It would certainly be possible since it would jibe with the rumors Kirby had told him this morning.

All the crazy pieces of this insane puzzle were floating around in Scott's head as they neared Justin's pier. Justin realized this by the time they pulled up he prepared to leave the boat with two fine fish from their catch.

"If I'm not here by six in the morning, Justin, then take a nice holiday with your family, eh? I have some decisions to make tonight and right now, my head's whirling. I may just decide to go down river to search for her in the morning."

"I understand, Scott. I guess that's exactly what I'd do. I wish you all the luck in the world."

"Thanks, Justin. I'm going to need it."

"You'll find her, Scott. I've no doubt about it!" Justin leaped up on the pier with a farewell wave and went on up the path to his cottage.

Scott said nothing to his parents about his plans as he wasn't sure of them himself until after he'd had dinner with them and retired to his bedroom. It was there that he went over all the details and felt he had the puzzle put together. This Francois LaTour had hired two ruffians to abduct Angelique from the gardens. Scott figured he just happened to be an obstacle they'd not counted on and that was why he got his head slammed. Two questions were still not answered: how they knew she would be in the garden and why she was abducted.

She was apparently taken that same night aboard LaTour's boat down the Mississippi. He thought about the various places on the river that trailed all the way to the gulf.

There was one fact he knew beyond a shadow of a doubt: Francois LaTour was responsible for all of this. He would be the object of Scott's revenge.

It was not until the next morning that Scott confided in his mother. "I'm going down that river to look for her, Momma. I can't tell you how long I'll be gone or when I'll return but you'll know what I'm about."

"That's a long, winding river, Scott, and you're only one man," she pointed out.

"I know, Momma, and I've thought about that but I'm also a man determined to find the woman I love."

"Then you'll find her, son, I've no doubt of it," she declared. Knowing this, she marched over to her cupboard to pack him an ample supply of food.

"Justin knows of my plans so he'll check in on the two of you if I'm delayed. Poppa is well supplied with tobacco and we made a good catch that should cover us for a few days."

She gave him an affectionate pat on the cheek. "You know you're dealing with an evil man, Scott. He has to be to do what he did so you must be careful. If something happens to you then your Angelique will not be helped at all, will she?"

"I'll bear that in mind all the time, Momma," he assured her. "I've got to try to find her."

Scott knew he could tarry no longer. His mother watched him go with a heavy heart, afraid of what he might have to face. It was obvious that this young lady meant everything to him. For a man to love a lady that much could not be faulted. She prayed that he would find her for she was most anxious to meet this lady who'd so completely captivated her son and won his heart.

She went to the window to watch his boat pull away from the pier. The sun's first rays were just beginning to shimmer over the water. She stood there as long as she could see the boat moving down the bayou.

She knew it would be a long day and possibly a very long night. She was left with the task of telling her husband what their son had set out to do and she didn't relish the idea at all.

Scott's stops along the winding Mississippi were time consuming so he moved down the river at a very slow pace. By the time he'd been to Chalmette, Violet, and Dalcour it was mid-day. By mid-afternoon he had made his stop at Carlisle and was beginning to feel discouraged. He was almost at the halfway point before the river flowed into the gulf.

Then Scott encountered a black man loading crates on a boat soon to leave for New Orleans. "You wantin' Monsieur LaTour? You'll find him at Pointe a la Hache."

Scott thanked him and immediately left for Pointe a la Hache, which, according to his maps, lay some twenty miles down the river. By now, he was feeling his first gleam of hope, which was enough to make him push his boat as fast as possible. His eyes kept looking to see how high the sun was for he knew that once that sun set he would have to wait for another day, and he was too impatient for that!

The closer he got to Pointe a la Hache the more the blood churned in his veins and his heart pounded erratically. As his boat moved past the large pier built out over the river he saw the tall stone walls of the fortress to his left. This must be the estate of Francois LaTour, he thought, knowing that somewhere within those walls was the lady he loved.

He guided his boat past the riverfront grounds about a quarter of a mile down stream, then moved toward the bank. Scott had no scheme for rescuing Angelique—he would let gut instinct guide him and pray like hell that it worked. He had no way of knowing how many men would be behind those walls so he figured he'd play a waiting game to see who came in and out before he made any kind of move.

As he had done when he stole into the Dupree's garden, he left his boat and slowly made his way toward the back of the estate. It was quite a trek before he came to the end of the high-walled fence. Suddenly, he saw that the property lay on the cozy little cove of Black Bay.

LaTour had quite a little paradise here, thought Scott, with the river running along the front and the bay at his back door.

Sinking to the ground, he had a perfect view of the entire back of the two-story stone mansion. He did not know about the front grounds but he was surprised there were no guards moving around in the rear. Observing for almost an hour, he'd only seen one houseservant coming out to gather laundry from the clotheslines.

Scott changed spots and moved up nearer. For a moment he glanced away from the house to survey the sandy shore of the bay. His eyes caught sight of a figure far down on the beach but it was no more than a speck. The person was still too far away to detect if it was a man or a woman.

He forgot about the grounds and the house to keep his eye on the moving figure coming his way. Impatiently he waited, his eyes straining to make out the image.

His blue eyes grew wide with excitement and his heart began to beat wildly when he made out the swaying black tresses that could only belong to Angelique. He couldn't believe he could be so lucky to find her roaming freely along the shore!

He leaped up and rushed to her. Angelique saw him and feared the sun had gotten to her—it couldn't be her handsome Scott O'Roarke. She had to be dreaming.

But when they were within two hundred feet of each other, she knew she was not dreaming and the hopes she'd had that Scott would rescue her were coming true. She ran faster and so did he until she found herself gathered up in his arms, carried into the concealing shelter of a tall palm tree. Only then did he kiss her and moan her name over and over again.

"Oh, Scott—I prayed you'd come but I never expected it!" she murmured, tears flowing down her cheeks.

"Well, honey, we're not out of here yet. I'm just one man and I don't know how many men LaTour has posted around this place."

"It has amazed me that the servants are all women with the exception of his valet," she told him.

"Has—has he harmed you in any way, Angelique?" Scott's eyes searched her face and he was happy to see no signs of cruel treatment.

"He has not touched me," she declared. "But I have Gabriella to thank for that. I told him I'd die before I'd surrender to him."

He grabbed her and held her close. "Oh, Angelique! Angelique!" he cried. His happiness gave way to the realization that they couldn't linger any longer. Someone could have seen him rush down the beach a moment ago and they could be in danger.

Now that he'd found her again he didn't want to lose her! Over his dead body would anyone ever take her from him again!

Chapter Twenty

Scott helped Angelique up, urging her that they must get away as quickly as they could. They rushed back across the open stretch of beach. Once they were in the thick cover of bushes, Angelique stopped to tell him, "Oh, Scott—I promised Gabriella that if and when I made my getaway I'd take her with me. I've got to go and get her."

"Oh, honey! For Christ's sake, please hurry!"

"LaTour isn't here. Gabriella told me he left yesterday morning bright and early. That's why she allowed me to go for a stroll this afternoon."

"I happen to know that he left New Orleans yesterday afternoon and should have arrived long before I did. He had more than a twelve hour start on me."

"Well, he hasn't returned—Gabriella would surely know, Scott. But I must keep my word to her," she pleaded.

"Very well, honey, but I'm coming in that house if you aren't back here shortly."

"I'll hurry, Scott. You aren't half as anxious as I am to get away from here." Holding up her skirt so she could move faster, she ran back to the beach and up to the back entrance.

Entering the terrace door, she disappeared as Scott watched, hastily walking down the highly polished hall in search of Gabriella. But she suddenly froze as a voice called out, "What are you doing, Angelique?"

She turned to see Gabriella with her kerchief-covered head tilted to one side and a puzzled look on her face. "I saw you and your young man running down the beach a while ago and was hoping you were well away from here by now."

"I came back for you, Gabriella—remember I promised to take you with me?"

A warm, affectionate smile came to her face, which then turned serious. "God, Angelique—go and go quickly! Monsieur Francois just arrived! I'll delay him long enough for you to go out the back way. It's your only chance, ma petite. He would kill your young man without a qualm and then you'd be his prisoner again. Go—go quickly!"

The thought of Scott being killed was enough to make her turn on her heel and rush down the hallway while Gabriella went in the opposite direction to greet Francois.

By the time she reached the front door Gabriella had her usual poised air. Francois stepped inside the door and greeted her. "Everything been all right around here, Gabriella?"

"Everything is just fine, monsieur. Shall I bring you something to drink or a snack perhaps? You

164

look weary from your trip from New Orleans."

"Yes, Gabriella—I—I think I would like some tea. Bring it to my study."

"Oui, monsieur, I'll bring it." The one thought consuming her was that by the time he found out that Angelique was gone she and her friend would be a few miles up the river.

This was her prayer as she went to the kitchen to have the cook prepare his tea.

It was only when Scott saw Angelique emerge through the terrace door that he began to breathe again. What a glorious sight she was as she ran to him and he caught her in his arms and she clung to him breathlessly. "Let's go, Scott. Francois has just returned and Gabriella is going to delay him until we're gone."

They scampered along the high wall to get down to the riverbank where Scott had left his boat. It wasn't easy for Angelique to get through the thick underbrush, for she wore the dainty slippers she'd had on the night she was abducted.

But she was trying desperately to keep up with Scott's long strides. All of a sudden he felt her hand slip from his and saw her fall to the ground with an agonizing moan.

"What is it, Angelique?"

"I don't know. I must have turned my ankle," she stammered.

He quickly scooped her up and carried her the rest of the way and unceremoniously placed her on the deck. "Let me get this old girl on her way and then I'll take a look at your foot, honey."

"Just get her going, Scott," she urged. Nothing must happen to delay their getting away — Gabriella's warning was still ringing in her ears.

From the deck she could look up and see the awesome walls of her prison. It was such a marvelous feeling to be free that the excruciating pain in her foot didn't matter.

She urged Scott just to keep going down river, for her foot could wait. He smiled and nodded, agreeing that they needed more distance between them and Francois LaTour.

He could do battle with any one man but he couldn't conquer a crew sent out by LaTour.

When they were moving up the Mississippi toward Dalcour and he saw no boat on his tail, Scott felt a little more relaxed. Dusk was quickly gathering over the Louisiana countryside, for the late summer days were growing shorter.

He had only to look at her ankle to know that cold cloths should have been applied an hour ago to prevent the tremendous swelling. "Got yourself a good twist there, Angelique. Hurts like hell, doesn't it?"

"It hurts but I don't mind. I — I feel so happy to be with you that nothing else matters, Scott."

"And nothing else matters to me, my little angel." He bent down to kiss her before he went to get an old tattered blanket to place under her leg and foot.

He leaned over the side of his boat to wet an old cloth for her foot. "That feel better, Angelique?"

She smiled gratefully and assured him that it did. Scott turned his attention back to guiding his boat around the bend that would take them toward St. Bernard. By now it was dark and there were no stars or moon to guide them homeward. Scott knew he could not give way to the weariness he felt for he'd had little sleep and it had been a long, harrowing day.

Fate made the same decision he was about to make anyway when he saw lightning in the distance. His bayou home was much closer than New Orleans. He wasn't sure he could last another two hours for he'd not eaten all day.

"We're not going to make it to New Orleans, Angelique. A storm is coming up and I'm taking you to my home for tonight. It's closer."

She gave him no argument for she was also tired and hungry.

So he turned his fishing boat toward the bayou instead of northward to New Orleans.

It pleased him when she rallied from her quiet mood after they'd entered the bayou and remarked, "What an enchanting place this is, Scott!" She'd been listening to nightbirds calling and splashes in the water. The occasional flashes of lightning did not seem to disturb her.

Scott welcomed the sight of Justin's pier, for a few raindrops had begun to fall. He knew he would soon reach his father's little dock — all that concerned him was getting Angelique to the shelter of their cottage.

It did not surprise Scott that he spotted lights gleaming from his family's cottage as he pulled up to the small pier. "We're home, Angelique!"

"Oh, I'm glad, Scott. I have to admit I'm tired," she sighed as he lifted her in his strong arms.

As he carried her up the pathway toward the cottage, she gave him an uneasy smile. "I hope your folks won't mind having an unexpected guest."

"Mind? My mother will adore you and she'll be so delighted that my venture was successful. She kept telling me that God would have his protective arms around you. Obviously she was right, Angelique."

"She certainly was! You must have a very wonderful mother, Scott."

"I do, as you'll soon find out," he grinned, taking one more kiss before they entered the house.

It was a most glorious sight to Kate O'Roarke to see her handsome son coming through the door with the pretty young lady in his arms. She saw that long black hair as he cradled her in his arms so protectively. She knew now why her son was so driven to get this lady back and why she had so completely captivated his heart. She'd always known it would be a very special girl who captured her Scott's heart. This was one beautiful little miss!

"Oh, what a wonderful sight you are, Scott O'Roarke!" she declared, jumping up from her chair to greet the two of them. She'd not expected to see her son tonight for she had figured that his mission would take longer.

Scott laughed as he walked over to place Angelique on the settee. "Momma, this is Angelique Dupree. Angelique, this is my mother."

Mother hen that she was, the first question Kate asked was if she was injured. "I just gave my ankle a twist when Scott and I were running to his boat, Madame O'Roarke."

Kate O'Roarke was not accustomed to being called madame, but she suddenly remembered that Angelique Dupree was a French Creole.

"Well, let's see just what you did, child," she said, lifting Angelique's gown to examine her foot and ankle. Looking back at Scott, she asked, "Didn't you put a cold cloth on her ankle, son?"

"Not as soon as I should have, Momma. We were more concerned with getting away."

"Well, I guess you can be excused under those circumstances, son, but let's get cold cloths and some of my ointment on her ankle so we can get this swelling down. Then I'll see to feeding the two of you."

Scott went to the kitchen to get a basin of water and some cloths while his mother found the tin of ointment in a cupboard.

Angelique sat there smiling. She found herself already adoring his warm, bossy mother. Her thoughts also returned to Pointe a la Hache now that she was safely away—she was concerned that her escape might cause trouble for Gabriella.

A sudden clap of thunder broke over the little cottage and Angelique shuddered. Her nerves were raw, that was for certain.

Her private musings were put aside as Scott

and his mother came back into the parlor to administer to her bruised, swollen foot. She found it hard to absorb every word Scott's mother spoke for she talked so fast as compared to the slower drawl of her own mother.

But then, everything Kate O'Roarke did she did quickly. In a second, she had gently dabbed her foot with ointment and squeezed out the wet cloth to lay it over her foot. "Now, we'll just prop that little foot up and you can rest while I get the two of you something to eat."

As she rushed out of the room, Angelique looked up at Scott and asked, "Does she always move so fast?"

"Constantly," he laughed. "She's something, isn't she?"

"She certainly is," she agreed, smiling.

Sharp streaks of lightning flashed through the windows and Angelique was grateful they were not still on that river.

But the real gratification was being in this cozy bayou cottage instead of that awesome grey stone mansion! Warmth and love seemed to abide in this little cottage and Angelique didn't feel like an intruder at all.

It was wonderful to feel so safe and secure after what she'd just experienced!

Chapter Twenty-one

Gabriella could not see the river, for the tall grey walls denied her that privilege, but she knew that a good half-hour had gone by when she carried the tray into the study to Francois. She did not linger once she had set it in front of him but made a quick exit so he could not ask any questions.

She mounted the steps to the room that Angelique had occupied—it seemed so cold and bare without her. But Gabriella was happy that she had escaped with the handsome young man who'd come to Pointe a la Hache to rescue her. She also knew that she would probably never see Angelique again, but she'd never forget the girl as long as she lived.

Angelique would never know how temptation prodded at her to rush out of that house with her but it could have caused too great a delay. In spirit, she traced the two young people up the river, knowing about where they would be after an hour had gone by.

Slowly, she moved out of the bedroom and closed the door to go to her own room. Now, she had to put her thoughts about Angelique aside to concentrate on what she would tell Francois La-Tour. Should she rush down the steps and exclaim that she'd gone to the room to find her missing? Would it be better to play her usual calm, cool role and wait until he summoned her? This would certainly delay any action he might take to recapture Angelique.

She decided that this would be the wiser course so she remained in her room. To her delight, over two hours went by and he did not summon her. She descended the winding stairway and encountered one of the other houseservants, whom she asked about the monsieur.

Tala, the young servant girl, told her that he had gone upstairs to rest. "Monsieur did not look well, Gabriella."

"Thank you, Tala," Gabriella said as the girl went on toward the kitchen after giving Gabriella a curtsy. All of the servants paid Gabriella respect, knowing although she was a servant, she held a special place in Monsieur LaTour's house.

This was good news to Gabriella for it meant that another two hours would go by before she would have an encounter with Monsieur Francois. A sly grin crossed her face as she thought that this much time would surely see the young couple close to their destination.

She decided to give way to her frivolous mood and went back to her room to enjoy a leisurely bath. Then she dressed in a fresh frock of deep purple and tied a matching kerchief around her head.

Whenever she stood in front of the mirror and

dried off her damp body she was reminded of the man who'd sired her. He had been white and her mother had been a Negro. She had obviously inherited a fine share of white blood and each time she looked upon her tawny flesh she realized this. It showed in her fine-featured face and the exotic shape of her eyes. Never had she not known there was beauty there—men's admiring eyes had told her that.

She wondered what Angelique would think if she knew that there had been a time when she served Francois LaTour as his mistress. She had been sixteen when she was taken by him for a year—that was the reason she was now considered his special servant. He no longer desired her as his mistress but it had given her status above the other servants.

It did not bother Gabriella that she was no longer expected to share his bed, for it had provided her with a few extra luxuries. She still clung desperately to the dream that she would be free someday. Oh, she had to believe that!

There was that moment when she and Angelique had talked and Angelique had declared that when she left, Gabriella had to leave with her. Maybe this young girl would help provide her the freedom she so anxiously desired.

That daydream was shattered today, she realized, but Gabriella was very resilient so she still felt the fires of freedom burning deep within.

Miles might separate them tonight but she was sure Angelique Dupree was returning her thoughts as she sat at her dressing table putting the final knot in the turban-like kerchief.

There was nothing now to keep her from carrying out her plan and she was confident that she could do it successfully. Gabriella knew she could have been a very good actress, for many a time she'd outfoxed Francois LaTour. Tonight, she had to do it again.

It mattered not that she made Angelique look like a devious young girl for she was gone now. It was the one sure way to protect herself, so she would do it to save her skin.

She picked up the key from her dressing table and prepared herself to appear distraught as she marched down the hall toward Francois' bedroom. When she reached his bedroom door, she began to rap frantically and call out to him. When a sleepy-eyed Francois opened the door, she sobbed to him that Mademoiselle Angelique was gone. "She is not in her room and I've searched the house! The little imp tricked me this afternoon when she pretended to faint. She must have slipped the key from my sash."

Half asleep, Francois urged her to calm down and come into his room. "What—what are you saying, Gabriella? When were you last with her?"

"Just before you arrived home, monsieur. She had pretended to be faint and I had helped her into the bed as she clung to me. She must have gotten the key while I was helping her to the bed. It is the only way she could have gotten out of that room. But I must admit that it was about the time I settled her into the bed that you arrived. I must have rushed down the steps to greet you so I didn't notice that my key was missing."

"Gabriella, we all make mistakes," he soothed. How the hell could he fault her for he had made the biggest mistake of all in doing what he'd done. His delay in arriving at Pointe a la Hache had been because he'd gone to Grand Terre Island to seek Jean Lafitte's wise counsel. Jean had not been easy on him. When Francois told him what he'd learned in New Orleans, Jean was furious.

"Francois, you have managed to do something that can only bring more of Claiborne's wrath down this river to me and I'm damned unhappy with you! You have been a fool!" Francois had never seen him in such a fury and it made Francois realize the truth.

It had not been a pleasant visit he'd had with his old friend, to say the least, and when he had prepared to leave, Jean's advice had been to see that the girl was taken back to New Orleans before a patrol was sent to rescue her.

"She's not worth this, Francois. I know because I was faced with the same situation a few years ago when I became so enamored with Elise. Need I remind you of that foolish fancy?"

There was no question about Lafitte's feelings — he wanted no more problems than he already had with the governor and the authorities. Francois knew he was out of favor with his old friend, so he was not disturbed by Gabriella's announcement that Angelique was missing. The last twenty-four hours had changed not only his feelings but his plans.

Gabriella could not believe how calm he appeared and she was greatly relieved that he wasn't ranting and raving.

"I'll attend to everything, Gabriella. I'll see that the house and grounds are searched. If she's not in the house or out on the grounds, that's about all we can do tonight," he said with a shrug. Then he dismissed her.

Gabriella had to admit she was in somewhat of a daze about what had just happened. She got the impression that he really didn't care one way or the other about Angelique. She found this very strange for a man who'd gone to such extremes to get her, but she certainly knew he was a man whose moods could change very quickly.

She went to the dining room to see that things were as he'd expect them when he came to the table. She lit the candles in their silver holders and gave a finishing touch to the flowers in the cut crystal container before she went into the kitchen to see that the cook had prepared tonight.

From there she went back down the hall toward the parlor. She had permission to pour a glass of wine from the crystal decanter when she wished to in the evening. Tonight, she took advantage of that.

As she sat sipping the wine, she heard the first rumbles of thunder and rose to look at the night sky. She saw sharp streaks of lightning flashing in the blackness and all she could think about was the young couple traveling the Mississippi River. She only hoped they had reached their destination by now.

* * *

Once the rains came they stalled and lingered throughout the night, but it was a soothing sound and Angelique had not slept so peacefully in many nights. The raindrops pelting the window panes lulled her to sleep soon after Scott carried her back to his bedroom and placed her on his bed. Her protests that she could sleep on the little daybed in one corner of the kitchen fell on deaf ears where Scott and his mother were concerned.

"Scott will sleep on the daybed. You need a comfortable bed so we can get that foot propped up just right, dear," Kate O'Roarke insisted and Angelique knew there was no point in arguing so she didn't.

She saw the amused grin on Scott's face and knew exactly what he was thinking—that she might as well do as his mother wished. While he and Angelique were enjoying the snack she had prepared, Kate was busily changing the sheets so that everything would be clean and fresh for her guest.

After the two of them had left Angelique, Kate puttered around to tidy up her kitchen while Scott laid the covers on the daybed. "Don't like the looks of that foot at all, Scott. Poor little thing, she must have taken a nasty fall."

"No, I was holding her arm. She must have stepped in some kind of hole as we were running to the boat."

"Well, I hope it's better before morning and the

177

trip to New Orleans. She won't be able to put any weight on that foot. You're going to have to leave her on your boat until you can get a wagon or buggy to get her home."

"Yes, Momma—I'd sorta figured that out," he said, as he finished turning down the cover. He would not have cared if he'd had to lie on the floor tonight. All he wanted to do was sleep.

Kate sensed this and prepared to leave. Scott wasted no time in dimming the lamp and quickly sought the comfort of the daybed.

But there was no trip to New Orleans the next day for the rains continued to fall. Neither Scott nor Justin could put in the day fishing so everyone was allowed the luxury of more sleep.

Kate O'Roarke blessed the rains, for she was able to keep her guest another day and night.

She felt an instant warmth toward the beautiful little Angelique.

Chapter Twenty-two

When Angelique finally roused and looked out the window to see a steady rain still falling she knew they would not be going to New Orleans so she just snuggled deeper into the cozy bed.

It was only when she heard the sound of voices outside the door that she finally propped herself up and flung back the sheet. She looked down at the oversized gown Kate O'Roarke had provided last night. She carefully examined the smocking across the yoke of the pink-flowered gown. Kate O'Roarke had done the work, she was sure. It was so large on Angelique that she found it very comfortable especially with her injured foot. Her pastel green gown was not meant to be worn in bed.

When Kate O'Roarke came to the room to assist her and check her foot, Angelique told her how comfortably she'd rested.

"Well, it's raining cats and dogs so you'll be with us another day. Tickles me to death 'cause we can have a chance to be acquainted and that foot will have a chance to improve. I would suggest you stay in that big old gown of mine. You're just as covered as you would be in your pretty green frock," Kate pointed out.

Angelique realized she was right. She lifted the gown so Kate could take a look at her ankle. She gave it a careful examination and told her, "It's an ugly-looking mess, dear, but maybe it's not quite as swollen as it was. Best you stay in bed but we'll leave the door open so you can call out if you need something."

Kate said she would fix her breakfast and bring it on a tray. "My Timothy is anxious to meet this pretty young girl our Scott brought here last night while he was sleeping," she told Angelique with a look of mischief in her bright blue eyes that reminded Angelique of Scott.

She was curious about his father now that she'd met Kate. What would he be like and would she find him as cordial and friendly as his mother?

It was Scott who brought in her breakfast tray as he allowed his eyes to dance over her in his bed all propped up on the pillows dressed in his mother's gown. He thought Angelique looked just as beautiful as she had in her fancy, expensive dress. It was the glowing beauty of her face with her long black hair flowing so gracefully around her shoulders.

"Good morning, darling. You look like you had a good night's sleep," he said as he sat down on the bed and placed the tray on her lap. He could not resist a hasty kiss.

She smiled. "It was the best sleep I've had for nights, Scott. I don't even mind that I can't get home today."

"I must admit I'm selfish. I was glad for the downpour because that meant I didn't have to take you home," he grinned.

"Oh, Scott," she sighed as her hand went up to

caress his face. "I'll never forget that you got me out of that place."

"My soul would not rest until I did, Angelique. I was a man crazy with fear about what could be happening to you."

"And I was a lady frightened to death."

Scott kissed her again. "Don't think about that now. We'll talk later. Just eat Momma's good food or she'll give me the devil for keeping you from it while it's hot. She's a very bossy woman, as you've guessed."

Angelique nodded agreeably and began to slice a piece of ham. The eggs and flaky biscuits looked very appetizing.

"Enjoy your breakfast, angel, and I'll be back in a little while. I got some things to do for Momma. My father's ailing so she has her hands full," he added as he rose.

Angelique ate everything on the plate and was ready to get up but for her foot. All she could do was sit there feeling very irritated.

This gave her time to think about the kind-hearted quadroon she'd had to leave back at Pointe a la Hache and she hoped her escape had not caused Gabriella problems. Somehow or some way, once she got back to New Orleans, she was going to tell her father about the woman who'd helped and protected her during that horrible time. She would find a way to get Gabriella away from Pointe a la Hache.

Timothy O'Roarke could not contain his curiosity about the guest in their cottage any longer. Scott had rushed out in the downpour to get his mother some wood for her cookstove and Kate was busy in her kitchen preparing vegetables for stew.

Supporting himself on his cane he moved out of the parlor toward Scott's bedroom. He came to the open door and saw Angelique sitting on his son's bed. There was a thoughtful look on her face and Timothy wondered what was occupying her thoughts so intensely.

He could certainly see why his son was so lovestruck. If he were a young bucko she would surely have caught his eye!

"Well, Miss Angelique — I thought it was time I paid a call on you. May I introduce myself — I'm Scott's father, Timothy O'Roarke."

Angelique turned to see a stoutly-built man whose hair must have been as black as Scott's but was now streaked with grey. She saw a face that reminded her of Scott. He had the same way of smiling, but it was his mother's blue eyes Scott had inherited.

"I'm happy to know you, Monsieur O'Roarke," she declared as she greeted him.

Timothy sat down on the straightbacked oak chair. "Got to say you look mighty fine after the ordeal I was told you endured. You must be a brave little miss."

Angelique laughed softly. "I can confess I was one frightened little girl. But I'm happy to be here safe in your home, Monsieur O'Roarke."

He found her speech intriguing and like Kate he remembered that she was a French Creole. Timothy knew they had a different way of speaking. When the O'Roarkes became friends with Justin and his wife, Mimi, Timothy had found it hard to understand him sometimes.

"We're pleased to have you here, Miss Angelique. I know you must be anxious to get back to your mom and dad. But it wasn't a day to be going down that bayou this morning so Scott didn't try it."

"Oh, I understood that. All I had to do was look out the window."

"Well, miss — I'll leave you to rest but I'm happy you're getting to stay with us one more day and perhaps that son of mine can carry you into the parlor later so we can visit some more. As you can see I'm rather confined to the cottage so I don't get to visit with a nice lady like you too often," he declared lightheartedly. Angelique certainly recognized the playful look about him that reminded her of Scott.

"I would enjoy that very much, monsieur," she replied as he walked slowly from the room.

How very nice these bayou people were, she thought as she sat alone in the room. It was obvious that they were certainly not wealthy like her parents but they certainly seemed like a happy lot. There was such a warmth about them.

She could not help comparing this happy-go-lucky gentleman she'd just met to her more serious, sober father. Although he was ailing, he had a cheerful air. When Angelique thought about her doting mother, she had to compare her to Kate O'Roarke. The answer was that the luxurious home Simone Dupree lived in, the expensive gowns she wore, or the exquisite gems she owned had not made her any happier than Kate O'Roarke.

By the time the rest of the day was spent, Angelique was to learn of the lighthearted ways of this

Irish family whose son she had come to love.

They were a family who enjoyed one another as they jested and teased. But it was obvious to Angelique as she sat in the parlor that evening that there was such devotion among them. She would be sorry to leave in the morning as it was growing late and she knew they would all retire soon.

She knew she would never be the daughter her parents had known in the past. Too much had happened recently for her to return and be the same. She did not know how they would react to the Angelique they would see and live with once she got home. This could prove to be a very disturbing situation for them for Angelique was not going to be troubled by it.

She could not turn back the hands of the clock and pretend all these things had not happened. They had and she had to live the moments. It had had an overwhelming impact on her thinking.

Never again would she submit to the overprotection of her parents—she already knew they would try to be even more protective after what had happened, and she would not tolerate it!

It was late when Scott came to carry her back to his bedroom. She sensed that the O'Roarkes were reluctant to call it a night. Timothy had served all of them a nightcap of his favorite Irish whiskey before they retired.

When she was cradled in Scott's arms, she told them what a wonderful evening it had been. "Why, I forgot all about the pain in my foot," she giggled.

Timothy was feeling the effect of his bit of liquor and Kate was well aware of it, but she had dared not protest because it was good to see him in such high spirits. She, of all people, realized what it had done to him to be confined to the cottage and not be able to go out on his fishing boat.

She rose from her chair to follow Scott into the bedroom and help Angelique. She saw the special little look her son and Angelique shared as he lowered her onto the bed. There was no question about it—these two young people were lovers. She could not fault them for that, as she could recall when the handsome Timothy O'Roarke came into her life and her heart almost stopped beating. She recalled the first time they'd made love and it was long before they were wed.

She also knew that Scott was wishing she was not right there behind him so he could kiss the lady he loved before he left the room.

Ah, they would have plenty time for all that loving, she mused.

Reluctantly, Scott left her in his mother's care. "See you in the morning, Angelique," he told her as he left the room.

Once Angelique was comfortable and her foot was propped up, Kate sat down on the side of the bed. "You were a joy to have here tonight. I've not seen Timothy have such a jolly evening in a long, long time. I shall hope we will share other nights like this. You're a wonderful young lady, Angelique Dupree, and now I know why my Scott is so smitten."

Angelique smiled. "And I love Scott, Madame O'Roarke."

Kate nodded in agreement. She really admired the young girl's honesty.

"And there's no doubt in my mind that he feels the same way about you, love." She rose to leave.

There was only one thing disturbing Kate O'Roarke and that was what would happen once Angelique returned home. How would her well-to-do French Creole parents feel about their daughter loving a young Irish fisherman who was certainly not wealthy?

Could their love surmount all this?

Chapter Twenty-three

All the clouds and rain had moved out of the bayou the next morning and Scott knew there was nothing to keep him from getting Angelique back to New Orleans. He was not happy about the thought—he didn't want to part from her.

He sensed there was a bittersweet air about Angelique as she bade his mother and father goodbye and he cradled her in his arms to go down to the dock.

She was very quiet and thoughtful as they traveled the short distance to Justin's pier. Once they arrived, he left her on the boat to go up to the cottage, realizing that Justin could not know what their routine would be for the day. He found them in the kitchen having their morning coffee.

Justin had only to look at Scott's face to know he had rescued his lady love. Mimi immediately knew it, too, from his expression when he entered the kitchen.

"You were lucky, eh, Scott?" Justin asked.

"I was lucky, Justin. She's down at the boat right now. The rains delayed us yesterday. Are you ready to go?"

"I'm ready," Justin declared getting up from the chair.

"Could I come down to the pier to meet her, Scott? Justin has got me most curious about this lady." Mimi's bright green eyes sparked excitedly about the prospects of seeing this beauty Justin had tried to describe. Her husband had told her how crazily in love Scott had fallen the first time he'd seen her.

"Of course, Mimi," Scott responded.

The three of them went down the narrow pathway toward the pier. Angelique immediately recognized Justin as the man who worked with Scott and she knew that the woman accompanying them had to be Justin's wife. Angelique found her very attractive with her auburn hair piled at the top of her head.

Justin greeted her as he jumped aboard the fishing boat. "I'd like you to meet my wife, Mimi. She's most anxious to meet you, mademoiselle."

"My pleasure, madame," Angelique responded.

Mimi had the same warmth as Scott's mother as she called out as the two men went immediately into action to get the boat going on down the bayou, "Come to our bayou again, mademoiselle. It was nice to meet you."

"I will if Scott will bring me," Angelique called back as she felt the boat begin to move.

Mimi smiled warmly and waved her hand as she stood watching the boat move away. She had seen a lady who was so utterly beautiful that she could have been a queen, Mimi thought to herself. Justin had been right—Mimi had never seen a woman more beautiful than Angelique Dupree. But she was more than beautiful, she was also warm and friendly. She wholeheartedly approved of Scott's lady.

She was most anxious to talk with Kate O'Roarke to see how she felt about her. Kate was a woman who formed an instant impression about people.

When they arrived at the docks Scott left Justin and Angelique on the boat while he went to Kirby's shop to ask for the mare so he could ride out to the Dupree's to tell them the good news. Their comfortable carriage would provide the best way to get Angelique back home.

Kirby didn't have to be told that Scott was elated about something when he came dashing into the shop.

"I found her, Kirby! I found Angelique," he exclaimed.

"Well, congratulations, my friend."

"Could I borrow your horse to ride out to the Dupree's?"

"Sure, Scott. You know where she's at," Kirby told him. Before he could ask any more questions, Scott had already rushed out the door. Kirby shook his head and grinned as he turned back to his work.

Scott urged the mare to a fast pace down Old Cypress Road. As he galloped up the drive, Zachariah was in the carriage as though preparing to take someone somewhere. At the same moment, Monsieur Dupree came out of the house and walked toward the carriage preparing to board. He hesitated abruptly when he saw Scott approaching.

As Scott yanked the reins and leaped down from the horse, he called out, "I found her, Mister Dupree! I'm glad I caught you."

Scott was out of breath as Maurice Dupree stood there so stunned he was speechless. "Oh God! Dear God, you found her?"

"Yes, sir—I did. She's just fine except for an injured foot but she did that when we were running to make our getaway."

"Where is she, Scott? Where's my little daughter?"

"Left her with my partner, so I could ride out here. I couldn't bring her on a horse. She needs to ride in your carriage."

"Oh, of course she does." At first he was tempted to go back into the house to wake Simone but he thought better of it for he had no desire to wait for her to dress. Soon he would be bringing her daughter home—what a wonderful way to rouse her from sleep!

"You lead the way and we'll follow," Maurice told him as he climbed up in the carriage. There was a broad grin on Zachariah's face as he told Scott, "Knew you'd find her if anyone could, Mister Scott." Scott smiled as he threw his leg over the mare.

In a very short time they were back at the wharf. Maurice Dupree spotted Angelique sitting on the deck of the fishing boat with Scott's friend. She saw him and Zachariah as the carriage came to a halt and she threw her hand up. There was no more glorious sight that Maurice could have beheld than his lovely daughter after all the days and nights of agony he and his wife had endured.

Zachariah was thrilled to see the little miss again. "There she is, Monsieur Dupree. There she is as pretty as she can be," the old black man chuckled.

By now, Scott had dismounted and he and Maurice started down the wharf. "I owe you, young man. I owe you so much. Angelique is our life."

"You owe me nothing, sir. I care for Angelique very much," he candidly confessed.

When Maurice boarded the fishing boat and lovingly embraced his daughter, it was a tender reunion.

Scott and Justin exchanged glances and smiles. When they finally broke the embrace, Maurice smiled, "You've got a mother who'll be so happy when we get you home. She doesn't know yet because she was still asleep when Scott arrived. Shall we get started?"

"Yes, Poppa," she declared but a wave of sadness suddenly washed over her at the thought of leaving Scott. Her dark eyes looked up at him and she felt he was sharing her same thoughts and feelings.

When he moved forward to carry her to the carriage, Angelique could not have been more pleased. For one brief moment she would feel his strong arms holding her before they said goodbye.

"Goodbye, Justin. It was nice to have met you and tell Mimi I hope to see her again."

"I'll tell her mademoiselle. Come back to the bayou to see us. Our door is always open," Justin said as Scott walked away with her in his arms.

"I'll come, Justin," she replied. Maurice followed behind them, a number of thoughts beginning to race through his mind. Right now all that mattered was that Angelique was back!

Angelique gave Zachariah a big smile and wave as they approached the carriage. "A happy day this is, Mademoiselle Angelique. A real happy day!" he declared.

Scott placed her on the seat carefully so her foot would be comfortable. For her ears only, he softly whispered, "I love you, Angelique." In a louder tone of voice he told her, "I'll be seeing you soon."

She surprised him when she reached up to kiss his cheek with her father so close. "See that you do, Scott O'Roarke," she laughed gaily.

"Oh, I will," he grinned. He would have liked to

have seen Maurice Dupree's face when she had kissed him. As Scott moved out of the carriage so Maurice could get in, Angelique told him to give his mother and father a kiss for her.

Maurice took the seat across from his daughter. Once again he told Scott how much the Dupree family owed him for what he'd done. But now that he had Angelique back and they were about to depart for home, Scott was well aware that his attitude was more formal.

Right now, he had to get Kirby's horse back so he could get back down to the wharf so there was a part of the day left for fishing. His practical Irish side told him that his coffer was hurting from the time lost lately — and he knew that Justin's was, too.

He'd just have to hope that Angelique would understand. If he didn't go out daily to catch fish the O'Roarkes didn't eat and the same was true for Justin's family. He had to make up for a lot of lost time and he appreciated the fact that Justin had not complained about it.

When he returned to his boat and they pulled away from the wharf, he made a point of telling Justin that he was grateful. The easy-going Justin replied, "Ah, an extra hour for a few days and we'll catch up, Scott."

"Thanks, Justin. We will, too," Scott agreed as he got busy with the lines.

During the ride back, Maurice discovered more surprises about his daughter but he was too happy to concern himself much about anything. He didn't recall that she was such a chatterbox — she was telling him about Scott's wonderful parents and the other couple she'd met in the bayou—Justin and Mimi.

"How is it you met Scott's parents, Angelique? When he rescued you from wherever it was he found you did he not bring you directly to New Orleans?" Maurice inquired.

"We couldn't make it all the way so Scott took me to his home in the bayou. We got there just before a heavy thunderstorm."

She told her father about the two nights she'd spent at Scott's home. In that very authoritative manner of his, he asked, "And why was it necessary to spend two nights?"

"Because the rains kept up all day after we arrived. I was glad because I got to spend some time with Scott's folks—they were so nice, Poppa."

"I see, my dear," Maurice mumbled. He was already seeing that his daughter was not the same little docile miss she'd been before all this happened.

He was curious as to how this Irish fisherman had managed to locate her when the men he'd hired had not been able to do so. "And where was it Scott found you?" he questioned.

A strange look came over her face as her dark eyes looked directly at him. "I wish to tell this tale only once so I shall tell you everything when I can also tell it to Momma."

"I—I understand, Angelique," Maurice replied. He said nothing else for he saw the determined look on her face and knew it had to be her way.

Her next words made a very definite impression on him and he would recall them often in the days to come. "I've got Scott O'Roarke to thank for rescuing me and I think you'd better remember that, Poppa!"

Chapter Twenty-four

For the rest of her life Simone Dupree would never forget the sight of her daughter sitting on the side of her bed waking her up. As Angelique bent down to kiss her cheek, for a moment Simone thought she surely had to be dreaming. If this wasn't true then she didn't wish to wake up.

But it wasn't a dream—she reached out and touched the soft flesh of her daughter's arm. She was real.

Their reunion was much more emotional than the one she'd shared with her father on Scott's fishing boat. The two of them allowed the tears of joy to flow.

After they had spent a half hour together, Simone decided to get up and dress. "We'll have lunch out on the terrace and talk for the entire afternoon. I know you have so much to tell me." Suddenly Simone remembered her daughter's injured foot. "Forgive your foggy-headed mother. You can't be on that foot. I think we should summon our doctor to have a look at that, don't you, Maurice?"

Maurice had been sitting quietly over in the overstuffed chair by the window as the two of them had been having their precious moments of being reunited again.

"That was my thinking, Simone. Angelique needs to get in bed and rest after the trip." Rising from the chair, he went to summon Big Jake, the black man who'd brought Angelique from the carriage up to her mother's room. "I'll have him take her to her room and then I'm sending for Doctor Delovier. I'd advise that you visit with Angelique in her room this afternoon, Simone."

His manner was so curt and abrupt that Simone wondered what had Maurice so disturbed. But she was not going to allow him to dampen this wonderful morning for her. "It matters not to me where I spend my time with her, Maurice. Call Big Jake so we can get Angelique comfortable."

Angelique wondered what this sudden explosion of tension was all about. She knew that her father's brusque manner had upset her mother. When the two of them were alone, she tried to soothe her mother. "I think Poppa has had too much to deal with this morning. My sudden appearance must have been very traumatic. He may still be in a state of shock."

"I think you could be right, Angelique," Simone agreed. Nothing else made any sense. She got out of bed and slipped on a wrapper as Maurice returned with the black man. Angelique was picked up and taken to her own room across the hall.

Simone went to the armoire to get a gown. She did not wish to summon her maid for she wanted to be alone. She wondered if all of this had had a more drastic effect on Maurice than she'd realized. Of all people, she knew how devoted he was to

195

their only daughter. In her own misery had she not been aware of how it had affected him? She would have expected him to be a happy man this morning.

She did take the time to summon Celeste to assist Angelique with whatever she might need.

Once she was dressed and her hair was neatly styled, she went across the hall to see that Celeste had removed Angelique's green gown that she'd been wearing since the night she was abducted. "Take it and burn it, Celeste. I never want to see it again." The dress was in tatters and had soil spots on it.

Angelique shared her sentiments—she never wanted to wear it again. As Celeste helped her out of the green gown and into her blue nightgown, Angelique was reminded of Kate O'Roarke's pink flowered nightdress.

Celeste left the room and Angelique sat propped up on her pillows waiting for her father to return with the doctor. She urged her mother to stay so they could talk.

As she had told her father, she told her mother about the kindhearted bayou people. "Scott's parents are so nice. Maybe someday you and Poppa can get to meet them."

"Well, from all you've told me they sound very nice and it would be a pleasure to meet them since we owe their son so much. I shall never forget what he's done for you and us."

They talked only a few more minutes before Simone reached to the foot of the bed for Angelique's wrapper because she heard the two men talking just outside the door. "Here, dear, slip into this. Doctor Delovier and your father are here."

Angelique had known the doctor all her life. He had come to the house many times over the years to attend to their needs so it was like greeting an old friend when he entered.

"Well, young lady what is this I hear about you injuring your ankle?" he said with a fatherly smile as he took a seat near her bedside.

Maurice and Simone quietly left the room. "We'll be in my study, doctor, when you have finished your examination," Maurice told him.

But once they went downstairs, Simone turned to go in the opposite direction from the study. "I've some things to talk over with the cook, Maurice. I'll join you later."

When Simone had given the cook the changes for their dinner she went toward the study. She wanted the meal to be one of Angelique's favorites. There had to be an egg custard pie for her daughter's first meal since she had returned.

It did not surprise her to find Doctor Delovier already in the study. She didn't think it was too serious and she was certain that Scott's mother had properly attended to her daughter.

"Just a little sprain, Simone. She'll be breezing around the house in another day or two as good as new," he told her.

"I rather expected that was what you would tell us, doctor. May I offer you something — some tea or coffee?"

"Not this afternoon, Simone. I've a baby that's going to arrive sometime this afternoon or evening. I have to get over to the Montroses. I told Angelique she will have to be the judge of when she tries to walk on her foot. However, I did tell her to stay off it for the next twenty-four hours."

He told them goodbye and prepared to make his usual hasty departure.

When they were alone, Simone sighed deeply. "Well, Maurice we have our daughter back. What a difference twenty-four hours can make!"

"Yes, Simone we have her back but you might as well face something I've faced already. Angelique is not the same girl as she was when she was taken from this garden."

Simone turned her head slightly with a skeptical look. "Why, Maurice—I think she's come out of all this in remarkable form. She doesn't seem troubled or frightened as I might have expected."

"Damn, Simone—that's not what I'm talking about," he said in an irritated manner.

"Well, then tell me what you *are* talking about, Maurice. I don't understand your sullen mood and manner when it should be the happiest day of your life."

"You have not noticed this very independent air she has after this odyssey away from home and around strange people?"

"I consider that this odyssey, as you call it, was enough to force her to be independent for she was on her own with no one to look to but herself. If she's feeling very self-assured then I say good for her, Maurice," Simone retorted as she marched out of the room.

As she mounted the steps she knew what was bothering Maurice since he'd arrived home with Angelique. She hated to confess it, even to herself, but he would have been happier if Angelique had fallen into his arms trembling and scared as she had at times when she was a child. Perhaps he would even have hoped that she would be reluctant to leave the house again for fear that something like this would happen.

Simone knew that Angelique would not feel that way. In fact, she would wager that she would be taking more liberties and demanding far more freedom than Maurice would allow. That was where the problem would arise, for Angelique would not always abide by her father's wishes as she once had.

By the time the evening was over and Big Jake carried Angelique back to her bedroom, many things had been explained to Simone. As a woman, she had a clearer understanding than Maurice could ever have.

In her gown and wrapper, Angelique had been carried down so she could sit at the dining table and enjoy the fine feast — she especially enjoyed the custard pie.

After dinner the family moved into the parlor and Angelique was placed in one of the overstuffed chairs, her foot propped on a footstool.

Impatient to hear exactly what had happened that horrible night, Maurice asked if she felt up to telling them about it. He walked over to pour himself a glass of wine from the decanter.

"Would you pour a glass for me, Poppa? Can you and Momma tell me where Cuddles is? I've wondered about her all afternoon."

Maurice poured her the glass of wine as Simone explained about Cuddles. "Zachariah has been keeping her since all this happened, Angelique. We were so beside ourselves those first few days that he took charge of her."

"Well, I'm home and I'm fine now so could Big Jake go get her?"

"Of course he could. I know how happy she'll be to see you." She rose from her chair to ask Big Jake, who was sitting in the kitchen, to go to Zachariah's quarters and get the little pup.

Angelique took the wine her father gave her and without any further hesitation told them how she'd gone into the gardens with Cuddles to meet Scott O'Roarke as they had planned earlier that day.

"A man was sitting on the bench where I would have expected Scott to be waiting for me. By the time I saw that it wasn't Scott it was too late and another man grabbed me from behind." She told them how a gag was pushed into her mouth and she was carried over the fence and loaded into a wagon.

"I was taken to a house somewhere here in New Orleans but I could see nothing for I was blindfolded." She told them how she had no inkling of how much time passed before she was herded down the steps again to board a boat.

"I lived in darkness until we reached a place down the river, Pointe a la Hache. Only then, when I was behind the high walls of a place that looked like a fortress, did I get rid of the blindfold. I also learned who had abducted me because he had seen me and become obsessed with possessing me."

Being a woman, Simone was living this shocking story her sweet, innocent daughter was telling her as if it were happening to her. Mon Dieu, no wonder Angelique had changed!

"The man who did this is Francois LaTour. Momma, you recall the day we had lunch at the little tearoom when we'd shopped before Poppa's birthday? I'd noticed him ogling me every time I looked up. There had been a couple of other times our paths had crossed."

"I remember the day, Angelique, and I'd wager that he was also the one sending the baskets of flowers?"

"He was. He admitted that to me." At this point there was an interruption as Big Jake came into the room with a big grin on his face. He held a wiggling, excited little pup and placed her on Angelique's lap. For the next few moments, Cuddles and Angelique enjoyed a grand reunion. When the dog contentedly curled up on her lap as Angelique's hand gently stroked him, she told them about the wonderful Gabriella and how she had connived with her to pretend to be desperately ill. "I played a very convincing role and pretended I couldn't keep my food down," she said impishly. Otherwise, LaTour would have taken his pleasures with her.

She told her parents that she was indebted to Gabriella, for it was she who helped her and Scott get away. "Gabriella is a quadroon. I won't forget her, Poppa. You have power and influence here. I'll do anything I can to get her away from that place."

The expression on her father's face gave her no inkling of what he was thinking but she saw a

201

change of expression when she added, "Scott and I are both indebted to her. Scott has assured me that he will help me figure out a way to get her away from LaTour."

"Well, this is something that can't be acted upon impulsively, dear," Maurice told her.

But this was not the answer Angelique wanted from him. "Nor is it a matter that will be put aside and forgotten, Poppa. At least, I won't forget her—ever! Gabriella saved me more than once."

Maurice glanced over at his wife and Simone knew what he was thinking, but she also saw the determination in her daughter's face as she was talking. She never admired her daughter more than she did tonight. Never was she prouder!

Maurice should take her seriously and not look on her as a little girl any more! She was a young woman with strong convictions and a firm idea of what she felt was just and right.

If Maurice tried to shrug this away, he would regret it, Simone decided as she carefully observed the two of them.

Angelique would never allow that to happen! From now on she was going to be in full charge of her life, Simone suddenly realized listening to her talk to them tonight. No longer would Maurice tell her what she could or should not do for she'd lived through too much for a young lady her age for it to be otherwise.

She had survived this ordeal, and it had not been because of Maurice's influence and wealth. It had been Angelique's wit and cleverness, along with the help of this quadroon.

Scott O'Roarke was also to be credited for his dogged devotion and determination to find her — and he had!

Chapter Twenty-five

As Doctor Delovier had predicted, Angelique was walking within a couple of days with the aid of a cane. The news of her return had reached the Benoits so Nicole sent word she would like to come for a visit. Angelique eagerly agreed to accompany her to town for lunch the next day. It did not matter that her parents did not seem to approve that she had planned a jaunt around New Orleans with Nicole so soon after she'd come home.

But Angelique eagerly anticipated it. She was ready to leave the house after being home a couple of days and already finding herself bored.

She had Celeste lay out one of her most attractive gowns and matching parasol in a robin's egg blue, the shade she considered her most flattering color.

Simone was happy to be settled back into her peaceful routine; the last two days had been divine. Maurice was starting to return to his routine, too, but the first thing he'd done the morning after Angelique had arrived was bring charges against Francois LaTour. He told the authorities about the place at Pointe a la Hache but Maurice was told that they would have to await LaTour's return to New Orleans to arrest him.

This did not please Maurice, as he feared that La-Tour could slip into New Orleans and the authorities would never know it. So he posted notices of a reward for anyone spotting LaTour and placed them all along the wharves.

The last two days, Scott and Justin had been making up for lost time. But as Scott put in long days from sunup to sunset, he thought about her and wondered how she was now that she was home. He also knew there was a score to settle with Francois LaTour. And there was also the debt he felt he owed to a woman he'd never seen—Gabriella, who had been so kind to his beloved Angelique. There had to be one more trip to Pointe a la Hache.

Another two or three days would make up their losses if he and Justin were as lucky as they had been yesterday and today. Then he was going to enjoy an evening off so he could see Angelique.

But this time he was not going over the garden fence! This time he was going to the front door!

The Benoit carriage arrived promptly at two and Angelique eagerly went out to join Nicole. Seeing her friend use a walking cane whetted her curiosity as her driver went to assist Angelique down the steps and into the carriage.

"Oh, Angelique! God, I'm so glad to see you back here. But I was surprised by the cane," Nicole told her as they embraced warmly.

"I injured my foot while Scott and I were running to his boat. It's practically back to normal now," Angelique replied.

"Dear lord, what an adventure you've had since we

last said goodbye! I must say that none of it seemed to leave a mark on you, though. You look absolutely magnificent!" Nicole's dark eyes surveyed her carefully.

"Yes, I guess it could be called an adventure and one I don't want to have again, I can tell you!"

"God forbid!" Nicole echoed.

Soon the carriage was leaving the outskirts of the city and heading for Chez Lilly's where they planned to have lunch. While they enjoyed the meal and talked about all the madness that had been thrust into Angelique's life, neither of them noticed the stares and whispers of the other women dining there.

But suddenly Angelique did notice and she knew that she was the focus of their attention. She had not thought about that possibility.

"Guess the subject of what happened to me has been a topic of gossip in New Orleans?" She knew Nicole would certainly know if it was true.

Nicole had been busy eating so she had not paid much attention to those at the adjoining tables. "Everybody was talking about it," she mumbled, still nibbling.

Nicole then began to notice how some of the women were staring at them when she happened to glance around the room. There was no denying that their faces were filled with scorn and disapproval.

"They're just a bunch of curious cats, Angelique. Ignore them," Nicole said, trying to console her friend.

"Oh, they don't bother me, Nicole," she told her. She threw back her head with a little laugh. "I just never thought of myself as notorious. I'll find that no problem but I'm not sure how this will affect my father or mother."

"A day or two and they'll turn their gossip in another direction. You know how a bunch of old busybodies are," Nicole giggled.

The frivolous Nicole was hardly ready to call it an afternoon, for there was still more she wanted to hear from Angelique. "Shall we leave here and go to The Gardens for a light dessert and a glass of wine? Would you want to? I've got to hear about Scott."

Angelique gave her a sly, little smile. "Scott was wonderful!"

"Well, surely your parents will have to consider all this. He should not have to meet you in secret any more," Nicole declared as they prepared to leave.

"There will be no more secret rendezvous. I'll insist on that. Scott will use the front door and be welcomed as graciously as I was welcomed by his family, I pray," Angelique responded. Nicole could see how her friend had changed since the last time they were together. Angelique would not have made such a bold statement a few weeks ago. Now that she thought about it there were several little things that were different about Angelique. She'd always considered Angelique shy and reserved, but she hadn't been today. She'd talked openly about everything that had happened.

They went to The Gardens and enjoyed their famous desserts and a glass of wine. Nicole watched Angelique's face as she spoke with such warmth about Scott and his family. Knowing her family and Angelique's as she did, Nicole wondered how everyone would feel about the great admiration she felt for this Irish family who lived in the bayou and earned their living as fishermen.

Nicole knew that the French Creoles could be a snobbish lot at times. She'd seen it in her own parents and that was why she had slipped around to see Mark.

Both young ladies were so busy chattering and indulging themselves with the divine dessert that they did not know they had caught the eye of young reporter. He'd made a point of quizzing their waitress about the beauty with the long black hair, a fetching figure in the blue gown and matching bonnet.

"That is Mademoiselle Angelique Dupree. She was the young lady who was kidnapped from her parents estate a short time ago," the waitress told him.

That was all Mason Ames needed to hear to fire his interest to a full-blown flame. No one had to tell him that the two young women were daughters of very wealthy New Orleans families. All he had to do was look at their expensive silk gowns. A fancy carriage awaited them to take them back to their luxurious homes.

Mason didn't have much admiration for most of New Orleans' society. He found them to be an overbearing lot who thought they were better than the ordinary man. Too often when it had been his job to speak with them, he detested their attitude and the way they looked down their noses at him.

Fortified with a generous shot of liquor, he sauntered over to the table where Angelique and Nicole were sitting. He heard their lighthearted laughter as he approached.

"Mademoiselle Dupree, isn't it?" he inquired as he came up to the table.

Angelique turned to see the dapper young man who had a rather cocky look on his face. "Oui," she responded.

He introduced himself and told her he was a reporter with the local paper. "My paper would be very interested in having an account of what happened to you. It would be a sensational story."

He'd never seen such beautiful eyes even though they were looking at him with sparks flying. Her voice was soft, almost gracious, but very firm as she told him, "No, Monsieur Ames—I shall not give you or your paper some lurid story. You'll have to look elsewhere. Now if you would be so kind as to leave so we can continue our conversation. We would appreciate it."

Nicole Benoit sat there marveling at the sophisticated way Angelique handled the man. Exploding with laughter, she said, "Dear God, Angelique, you HAVE changed!"

Angelique smiled. "Yes, I've changed a lot, Nicole."

By the time they left the Gardens both of them were completely sated and swore that neither would be eating much at dinner. It had been a wonderful afternoon.

As they approached Angelique's home, Nicole suggested she come over in a couple of days to go for a ride. "I've promised Mother I'd go with her to a tea tomorrow. Such a boring little ritual but once in a while I suffer through one for her sake."

"I'll see you the day after tomorrow," Angelique promised.

Angelique realized that most of their time had been spent discussing her. Just as the carriage was approaching the long drive to her house, she asked Nicole, "How about Mark? Are you still seeing him?"

"As much as I can. I'm hopelessly in love with him, Angelique. I can admit this to you, knowing how you feel about Scott, but I don't know how I'll ever get him accepted by my family," she said dejectedly.

"Why, Nicole—I can't imagine that this would stop you! I know it won't stop me where Scott is concerned. I would hope they would accept him, but I will marry no man I don't love with all my heart and soul just to please my parents."

"Damn, Angelique—you've amazed me today! You've been good for me and I must tell you I think things have reversed themselves in the last few weeks. Remember that weekend you spent with me and I told you I'd teach you a few tricks before you returned home?"

Angelique remembered that weekend vividly, for that was when Scott had first made love to her. With all the other things that had happened that seemed like a lifetime ago. "I remember, Nicole."

"Well, I know that I'm not going to to teach you any tricks from now on," Nicole said, grinning impishly.

Angelique was about to leave the carriage at the front entrance of her house. She had no answer for Nicole, for she rather doubted that her friend was as experienced as she was now. It had taken only a few days and nights to change all that.

"I'll see you day after tomorrow, Nicole. It was a wonderful afternoon," she said as she allowed the driver to assist her out of the carriage.

As she walked into the house, she recalled the stares she'd received this afternoon and then her encounter with the reporter.

There was a hint of scandal and malicious gossip about her floating around New Orleans!

Chapter Twenty-six

Usually Simone Dupree always enjoyed the annual tea Virginia Pecherie gave every summer in her magnificent garden setting. On the warmest day it had always been pleasant, with all the trees shading the area where small individual tables and chairs were placed on the thick carpet of grass.

There were usually fourteen women and their daughters invited. The most divine pastries were served at the mid afternoon gathering and two or three different teas were brewed to please the taste of the various guests.

Virginia's teas signaled the last women's social before autumn arrived. The ladies made a very colorful picture in their colorful gowns and hats, usually in shades of lavender, pink, blue, and yellow. The same colors were repeated in the garden where myriad flowers were at their peak.

But as Simone returned home this late afternoon she was angry and glad that she had not asked Angelique to accompany her. She had assumed that her daughter was probably not ready to attend such a gathering with so many people around after what she'd been through. To go with Nicole on the little jaunt yesterday was different. In fact, Angelique seemed in very high spirits when she returned home.

Had Angelique chanced upon two of the women having a very lively conversation about her, she would have been shattered. This had happened to Simone and she had not turned her back. Instead, she marched up and addressed the one who was talking. "No, Denise—I think you've got that wrong. Maurice and I are not the least bit ashamed of Angelique. The shame is that it happened to such a sweet girl and that women who have known her all her life would talk about her as I just heard you doing."

"Oh, Simone, you just—you're wrong. Jean and I meant no harm," Denise stammered feebly, darting a glance at her friend. Jean's face had suddenly paled and she saw no way to wiggle out of it.

"If those weren't catty remarks I just overheard then I'm crazy." With fire in her eyes, she pointed a finger at them as she warned, "Watch your mouths, ladies. They could get you in trouble."

When she turned to walk away, Denise took a deep breath and moaned, "God! I had no idea she was anywhere nearby. Just a moment ago I saw her across the garden strolling and talking with Virginia. Suddenly there she was right behind us."

"Oh, mercy—she'll never speak to us the rest of her life, Denise. Oh, she was so angry! Rest assured, our family will never be invited to the Duprees nor will yours," Jean said, her voice cracking because the whole episode had upset her so.

"Just wait until she goes home and blabs to Maurice. He worships Angelique so he might just be paying a call on our husbands," Denise added with concern.

"Oh, no! Don't say that! George will feel like killing me," Jean shuddered.

The two of them were so nervous that they were the first guests to leave. The gay time they'd been having had come to an abrupt halt.

Virginia Pecherie had no idea of the little episode that had happened involving three of her guests. She had thoroughly enjoyed herself and managed to have a chat with each of them before the tea was over. It had pleased her that Nicole Benoit had come with her mother and she certainly understood why Angelique Dupree had not attended but when she and Simone had managed to have a private little chat Simone had explained why.

"You and Angelique will have to come over soon and we'll have our own private tea party here in the garden," she'd consoled Simone. Virginia had been very sweet and understanding.

When she arrived home, Simone went directly to her bedroom and took off her hat, flinging it on the bed. She didn't know if she could ever forgive Jean and Denise after this afternoon!

It was terribly disillusioning to see this side of two women she'd considered her friends for years. She was glad that she'd not encountered Angelique when she'd arrived home for she needed time by herself to gain control of her nerves.

By the time an hour had gone by, Simone did find that she was calmer and she also noticed that Maurice was running late. She wondered what was delaying him.

But at least she was now in control of her emotions and ready to face her daughter as she made her way toward the parlor.

Maurice had taken the gig into the city, leaving Simone the use of the carriage and Zachariah's services to go to her tea. He knew how she always looked forward to this annual event of Virginia Pecherie's. She would be in very gay spirits tonight and he wished he could feel the same way.

When he left his office after going over the books with his bookkeeper, he'd taken a ride along the lake road just to think about the things that had happened to him today when he'd gone to lunch. He couldn't believe the audacity of people.

Gents in the dining room of the hotel had come up to his table as he'd been dining with an old friend to question him about what had happened to Angelique and if the rumors were true. He'd wanted to say that it was none of their damned business.

But he acted with more finesse but at the same time he did not satisfy their curiosity. His friend knew he was seething inside and noticed that Maurice's usual hearty appetite was gone.

He felt deep compassion for Maurice, for he knew how much he doted on his only daughter. For the slightest hint of scandal to touch Angelique was very disturbing to him.

As they left the hotel, he'd patted Maurice's shoulder and remarked, "Some people can be so thoughtless and rude."

"But I would not have expected it from any of them, Anton. Two of them have daughters about Angelique's age. Dear God!"

"I know, Maurice. I would feel just as you do right now," Anton assured him as they walked toward the gig and mounted the seat.

"Well, thank God for a friend like you, Anton. It makes up for others just now." But Maurice Dupree had never been a very forgiving man so he would not forget the behavior of these gentlemen for a long time to come.

He stayed in a riled state the rest of the afternoon so that was why he'd wanted to try to simmer down before he arrived home to meet his wife and daughter.

The ride around the lake road did have a soothing effect as he looked out at the water with the sun sinking lower and lower in the sky.

He was still indignant but some of the anger had mellowed by the time he finally turned the gig toward home.

It suddenly dawned on him that he was arriving almost an hour later than usual. He thought Simone would be vexed but when he entered the house and she greeted him he was grateful for the smile on her face.

"You better get on upstairs, dear, to prepare for dinner. It's almost ready," Simone told him.

"Yes, Simone, I will. I realize how late it is," he quickly replied.

He met his daughter coming down the steps as he was going up. "Papa, you just getting home?"

"Yes, Angelique. Had a busy day," he said as he leaned over to kiss her cheek. Looking at her angel face, he was reminded of the blunt questions thrown at him and it was enough to put him in a foul mood again.

By the time the three of them were at the table, Angelique asked her mother about the tea. "I didn't have a chance to ask you after you got home. Was Nicole there with her mother? She told me yesterday that she was planning to go."

"Yes, she was and looking pretty as a daffodil in her yellow gown and straw bonnet. She told me to tell you she would see you tomorrow. Now what are you two planning?" Simone smiled at Angelique, sitting across the table looking lovely in her pink frock.

"We're going for a ride."

Maurice started to make a remark but he bit his tongue for he knew he was not in his best form tonight. This was a change in Angelique—she no longer asked their permission but seemed to do as she wished. This was something he planned to discuss with Simone when they were alone, he promised himself as he cut into the potato on his plate.

He noticed something else as the meal went on—his chatterbox wife was unusually quiet. "The usual group of ladies attend this afternoon?" he asked.

"Yes, dear, the same ladies."

"Well, usually you're bubbling over when you've gone to one of Virginia's little get-togethers."

"It was nice as usual, Maurice," Simone replied, praying that he would let the subject drop for now at least. Later when they were in their bedroom she would tell him what had happened but she didn't want to do so in Angelique's presence.

After dinner, Angelique picked up her little pup as she scampered down the highly polished hallway and announced that she was going to take her for a walk in the garden. She immediately saw the stricken look on her parents' faces and a protest about to come from her father. But she stopped him by declaring, "I know what you're thinking, Poppa, but I won't become a prisoner of this house. I'd rather be dead than live that way."

She left them with Cuddles still cradled in her arms as her parents went on to the parlor exchanging glances. "Can't get over how independent that girl's become lately!" Maurice remarked as they sought the comfort of the matching overstuffed chairs.

"Yes, she is certainly that, I'll have to admit," Simone agreed. Like Maurice, she saw it more and more as each day went by. There had been a time that Angelique would have asked her about going riding with Nicole Benoit before she accepted the invitation but now she didn't.

She waited to mention what was gnawing at her until he had poured himself a brandy and a glass of sherry for her. Once he was settled in his chair and began puffing on his pipe she revealed to him what had happened at tea.

"I trust that you didn't fail to tell them off," Maurice bristled angrily.

"I told Jean and Denise in no uncertain terms what I thought of them and that I'd advise them to watch their foul mouths," Simone declared.

"Well, good for you, Simone. Now, I've something to tell you that happened to me today," Maurice said, feeling very angry that his dear wife had been so hurt. In the future the Dupree family would omit two couples from their guest list, Maurice decided.

But what Maurice and Simone did not know was that about the time he was beginning to tell his wife about the melodrama in the hotel dining room, Angelique had entered the front door. They didn't hear her soft footsteps coming into the parlor.

When he had finished his tale and before Simone could respond, Angelique made her presence known. "Yes, Poppa and Momma—it is so! Angelique Dupree is tainted with scandal even though it was not of her doing. Shall I tell you what happened to me yesterday? I had not intended to, but it's obvious that we can't escape it."

"Sit down, Angelique, and tell us what happened," her father requested.

She let the little dog down and took a seat. "Ah, yes Poppa — it seems I've become notorious! But it won't bother me, I assure you, and I hope it won't disturb the two of you. I simply could not care less."

Her parents saw a hardness about her. That lovely, delicate face had the expression of someone with a headstrong, willful air.

Chapter Twenty-seven

As soon as Angelique was seated, Simone immediately wanted to know what had happened when she and Nicole were out that afternoon. "You seemed in such high spirits when you returned home."

"It was because Nicole and I had had such a delightful afternoon. What happened when we were in the Gardens did not bother me so much as it disgusted me. Someone had obviously alerted the reporter that I was Angelique Dupree or he would not have approached me while Nicole and I were at the table enjoying ourselves."

"You're telling me that a reporter from the paper had the gall to speak to you—and about what?" Maurice snapped as he reared out of his chair.

"He said he wanted to interview me for a story about what had happened to me."

"Who was this man? What was his name?" Maurice demanded to know.

"I don't recall his name," she lied. "It doesn't matter because I told him there would be no story for his curious readers. He walked away because he knew he had been dismissed. You see, Poppa—I'm not a helpless child anymore. That time is over," she said pointedly.

"No, Angelique, you're not a child any more. Your mother and I are very aware of that," Maurice told her.

"We're very proud of you, dear," her mother said. "We hold our heads high with pride about your courage. Few young ladies have faced what you had to endure. You're a very strong young lady." Ever since Angelique had been back home Simone had thought about how she reminded her of her own very adventuresome grandmother, Delphine. There was a lot of her in Angelique, Simone thought, and even more as her daughter grew older.

Simone was like her mother, Delpine's daughter, but now some two generations later it seemed that her own daughter had inherited that fiery spirit of her great grandmother.

"Thank you, Momma. I'm glad you feel this way for I have great pride in the name Dupree and would never want to do anything to shame it."

"You'd never do that, Angelique," Simone declared, as Angelique prepared to take Cuddles and go upstairs to her room.

Angelique kissed both parents and departed with the little pup snuggled in her arms.

It was bright and sunny when Angelique awoke the next morning to get dressed and meet Nicole for their morning ride. She dressed with eagerness to get to the Benoit's and was also finding herself eager to have Scott pay a visit, but she knew he had to be making up for the lost time he'd spent searching for her.

Being around the O'Roarke family for that brief time and from what Scott had told her, she knew

220

that they survived on the fish he caught daily.

So many things had happened to her in the last few weeks. It had broadened her horizons about life, which she found startling. She thought about the little cloistered world she'd lived in all the sixteen years of her life. Then suddenly this handsome young fisherman had come into her life and she had so completely surrendered herself to him. This was enough to amaze her.

For her to be so daring as to slip out of the house to keep a rendezvous with him in the garden was something she'd never been tempted to do before Scott O'Roarke had come into her life.

Because she was so eager to meet him in the gardens one night a few weeks ago, she had made herself vulnerable to the evil plans of Francois LaTour. That had been an experience she would forever remember. But it had also made Angelique realize that it was wrong for a young lady to be as overly protected as she had always been. Somehow, she knew it had to be her father who'd laid down such harsh guidelines the last few years—her mother would not have been so strict and rigid.

Never again would she allow herself to be so restricted which was why she had made a point of telling her father that she was no longer a child. He had to accept that!

When she emerged from the house and started for the stables she encountered old Zachariah, who greeted her with a warm, friendly smile. "You sure look mighty pretty, Mademoiselle Angelique. That Cuddles behaving herself? She's a handful, I found out."

"A delightful handful, though. Yes, Zachariah, she's fine! Bet you spoiled her, eh?"

He chuckled, "Guess I did."

He watched her go on toward the stables and it was good to have her back here for there was a gloomy shroud hanging over this place during the time she was gone.

Angelique rode into the drive of the Benoit estate at the appointed hour to meet Nicole but she had no knowledge that she was also going to be greeted by Nicole's cousin from Baton Rouge. Nicole did not know he had arrived in New Orleans the previous night.

So it was the three of them who rode out of the estate to go on a jaunt around the countryside. Nicole was not pleased to be saddled with her cousin for she had hoped to be able to meet Mark in the woods. She knew Angelique would understand but now Louis was along and it was not going to work out as she'd hoped.

When she had the chance to whisper to Angelique about her dilemma, Angelique suggested that she try to keep Louis occupied while Nicole left them under the pretense of searching for something in the woods like wild herbs to take back to her mother.

"God, Angelique—you never cease to amaze me! How clever you are! How could I have believed you were so naive and innocent? That's perfect and I thank you for helping me out!" Nicole exclaimed as they urged their horses up to join Louis.

Angelique laughed, "You weren't fooled but I find that certain things make you a little smarter. So I guess that's what happened to me."

"Well, all I can say is I never saw it happen to anyone as fast as it did to you. I do appreciate your taking Louis off my hands for a while if Mark does happen to show up."

"Well, he seems very nice, Nicole."

"Louis is sort of the scholarly type, if you know what I mean. He's so smart that I never know what to talk about when our families do get together."

Louis Benoit had not kept pace with the two girls. He had taken time to absorb the countryside they were riding through. Nicole had had her chance to have this little private talk with Angelique, and now that it was done, she and Angelique waited for Louis to catch up with them.

"This is beautiful country around here, Nicole. My uncle certainly has a beautiful place," Louis exclaimed. It was obviously delighted that he'd spotted so many varieties of birds since they'd left the house.

"Cousin Louis is an avid birdwatcher, Angelique," Nicole explained.

"Well, so am I, Louis," Angelique said with a friendly smile. "I love watching them gather in my mother's garden. They always have plenty of water to cool themselves there. Old Zachariah carries a pocketful of breadcrumbs to toss around on the grounds."

A smug grin came on Louis' face as he playfully teased his young cousin. "You see, Nicole—I'm not the only one who watches birds."

Tossing her head and shrugging her shoulders, Nicole retorted, "Well, she never mentioned it to me." But then there were many things she was learning about Angelique lately. The three of them were in a very gay mood as they rode on a few more minutes. They heard the call of a certain bird, which was the signal that Mark was close by, and it immediately caught Nicole's attention. It was the call of the whippoorwill that Mark used to signal Nicole.

She halted her horse and began to dismount as she told Louis that she was going into the woods to get some wildflowers and herbs. "I always try to bring them to Momma when I ride this way. I'll catch up with you and Angelique in just a few minutes."

"We'll ride slowly, Nicole," Angelique told her with a wink.

"Yes, Nicole — we'll ride slowly. I'd like to spot that whippoorwill I heard just now," Louis told his cousin.

Nicole had to turn swiftly to keep him from seeing her amused smile because she certainly didn't want him to spot this "whippoorwill."

After Angelique and Louis had gone another two hundred yards, she suggested that they dismount and sit by a fallen tree. "Maybe we'll spot him and Nicole will also spot us as soon as she rides down the lane," she pointed out.

"That's a good idea, Angelique," Louis agreed. He found himself liking this friend of Nicole's. Some of them he'd met on previous visits he'd not cared for at all. They had been prissy little bores but the beautiful girl joining them today was not only pretty she had some brains, too. His aunt usually gave a dinner party while he was visiting and he hoped that Angelique Dupree would be on her guest list.

As they dismounted and sank down on the ground, Angelique smiled, "This is a perfect spot to scan the trees, isn't it?"

"Yes, it is but I hope you don't spoil your riding skirt, Angelique." He gallantly offered to lay his vest on the ground for her to sit on.

"Oh, thank you, Louis, but this skirt will wash up if I do get a grass stain on it so don't be concerned."

"Well, if you're sure."

"I'm sure, Louis. I wear it often when I go riding so I often sit on the ground and take a rest."

Louis surprised himself when he realized that he was staring at the girl beside him more than he was looking up at the trees.

He also surprised himself when he found himself boldly asking about her silky black hair for he could never remember seeing such hair on a young lady. "Tell me, Angelique, how many years has it taken for your hair to grow that long? I've never seen a lovelier head of hair."

"I guess my entire life. It has never been cut, only trimmed from time to time. Thank you for your compliment. At least, I can never remember it being cut, Louis."

He smiled, "I bet you're the envy of all the girls around here."

Angelique found Louis a very easy person to talk to and more than a half-hour had gone by as the two of them sat leaning back on the huge trunk awaiting Nicole. Louis had been so absorbed in his conversation with Angelique that he'd no inkling of how long his cousin had been gone when she came riding up the lane holding three or four bunches of wildflowers.

Angelique knew she had seen Mark from the glowing look on her face. But she brought back no herbs.

Her sly friend had already conjured up an answer to that. "Couldn't find any herbs anywhere. I looked all over the place. That's what took me so long," she said very convincingly.

Angelique could hardly suppress a giggle. It was only when she and Louis got up to mount up their horses that she realized that they had been sitting in the spot where Scott had first made love to her. That was enough to make her yearn desperately to feel his arms holding her and his sensuous mouth kissing her.

She wondered how much longer she would have to wait before he would come to her as Mark had come to see Nicole today.

Chapter Twenty-eight

It was almost five in the afternoon by the time Angelique was headed toward home. After the three of them had arrived back at the Benoit's, they'd sat out on the side veranda and enjoyed refreshments. Nicole could tell that her cousin Louis was very attracted to Angelique for she'd never seen him so attentive and entertained by any of her other friends.

"Mother is going to have a dinner party for Louis at the end of the week before he returns to Baton Rouge. I don't have to tell you that you're invited," Nicole said. She saw by his pleased expression that he was happy to hear her say that.

Angelique knew that it was time she was leaving so she told them what a wonderful afternoon it had been and what a pleasure it was to meet Nicole's cousin.

"I'll look forward to coming to the party and seeing you again, Louis, before you return to Baton Rouge. Now I must go," she told them as she prepared to leave the veranda.

Nicole quickly got up from the table, asking her cousin to excuse her for a moment while she walked Angelique to her horse. When they were far enough away so Louis would not overhear them, Nicole sighed, "Oh, God, thanks—thanks a million, Angelique."

"I enjoyed talking with your cousin. I think he's very nice—a real gentleman." Angelique prepared to mount her horse.

"Well, I can tell you I think you've won another admirer. Never seen Louis so talkative and outgoing as he was around you. I think he's smitten. I'll bet you this is all he'll talk about tonight and tomorrow," she giggled with an impish twinkle in her eyes.

Angelique just smiled and shook her head as she prepared to ride home. She had no doubt that her mother was already pacing the floor and looking out the window for her.

It was true that the last hour Simone had paced the floor and watched the clock. She questioned just how long those two young ladies could ride around the countryside. She knew they were not riding this long. Angelique had left here before noon.

Finally, she saw her coming up the drive—it was a sweet relief to Simone to see her daughter returning home safely.

Angelique rushed into the house to greet her but she didn't seem to want to linger. "Oh, I feel the need to have a bath and change of clothes, Momma. I'll tell you about my afternoon later."

Before Simone had a chance to protest, Angelique dashed on toward the stairs. Simone stood watching her go and shook her head with a smile. She had changed! Simone went back to the parlor and picked up her needlepoint.

That night as the three of them dined, Angelique told her parents about the delightful afternoon she'd had riding with Nicole and meeting her cousin, Louis Benoit. Maurice and Simone knew about Louis and were secretly sharing the thought that he would be an ideal suitor for Angelique. He came from a fine French Creole family in Baton Rouge and his background and upbringing had been like Angelique's. As Maurice recalled he was about twenty-four or twenty-five, which was about the right age for his daughter's suitor and future husband.

The Duprees had no dearer or closer friends than the Benoits, so they found his nephew perfectly acceptable. The next morning when the invitation arrived to a dinner party at the Benoits, they were delighted.

The excitement washed away the hurt Simone had felt from the encounter with her two friends, Jean and Denise. She was so thrilled that she immediately planned a trip into the city to purchase a new frock or pair of slippers for herself and Angelique.

It had been almost a week since Scott had stopped by the smitty shop to have a chat with his old buddy, Kirby, or to have a few drinks. This late afternoon he felt he could afford an extra hour or two since he felt that Justin had been fully compensated. His share of the daily catches had made up for the time Scott had caused him to lose.

Kirby was happy to see him saunter through the door about the time he was ready to call it a day and go home to fix some supper for his ailing father.

"Well, if you aren't a sight for sore eyes, pal! Thought maybe one of those 'gators finally got you," Kirby jested.

"I'm too ornery. Don't you know that by now, Kirby?" Scott laughed huskily. On a more serious note, he confessed the truth about working longer days to make up for lost time. "But now I've got Justin squared away so I thought I'd come by to see how you've been getting along."

"Glad you did. Give me another minute and I'll be ready to get out of here. We'll go up to the house, have a little supper, and then you and I'll go have some drinks and do a little talking, eh?"

"Sounds good to me, Kirby."

A short time later they were walking up to the little cottage. Scott had never known anyone who could move as fast and put a damned tasty meal on the table as fast as big, burly Kirby could. It was simple fare, nothing fancy, but it was always good eating at Kirby's cottage.

Scott tried to help with the dishes but Kirby had insisted they wait as he excused himself to take a bath and shave.

For a big guy Kirby could move fast. Scott had only had time to pour a cup of coffee and drink it when Kirby reappeared in clean pants and shirt. He'd seen that his father was back in bed and comfortable. "Pa's down for the night so we can go."

The two of them left the cottage for the nearby tavern. It was a busy night but they found a vacant table and ordered a round of drinks. It was always good to be with Kirby and have a few laughs.

Finally Kirby asked him, "And how's the pretty lady, Angelique?"

"Haven't seen her since I got her back home."

"You haven't seen her? I think it's time you did if you're as crazy about her as you led me to believe."

"I'm crazy about her, I can tell you that. But I had to make up to Justin and I got that done today."

Kirby took a generous sip from his drink. "You never have told me about that wild, crazy trip you made to Pointe a la Hache. Want to tell me now?"

Scott told him everything that happened from the moment he arrived at Pointe a la Hache until they got back to New Orleans.

Kirby listened intensely and had to admit that Scott and Angelique certainly owed this Gabriella a favor or two. "Damn, you say the word and I'll go with you to get that lady out of there!"

"I might just be taking you up on that, Kirby, if you're serious," Scott challenged.

"Never say anything I don't mean, Scott. She sounds like a lady worth her salt and there ain't many of those around."

"You mean you'd be willing to go to Pointe a la Hache and help me get Gabriella?" Scott asked.

"Damned right I would. You say the word and we'll go. You and your little Angelique might not have got out of there but for her. You sure as hell owe her, Scott!"

"You don't have to tell me that, Kirby, but I do appreciate your offer. I may be calling you sooner than you think," Scott added as they finished their drinks. He knew it was time he left the tavern and

Kirby's good company to get traveling toward home.

As they walked to the wharf, he found himself wondering why a goodhearted, happy-go-lucky fellow like Kirby had never married. He was a robust man, even good-looking in a rugged sort of way and in the prime of life. But as far as Scott could remember he'd never had a girl. Oh, he'd jested and teased some of the girls he encountered at the taverns when he and Scott had gone there, but Scott knew he was just playing around.

He'd never asked Kirby why he'd never married but tonight he decided to.

Kirby did not hesitate. "I only loved one girl, Scott, and she died before I could marry her. Never met anyone to come up to her so I couldn't bring myself to settle for less. Guess it was just as well for the way things came down with Pa. A young bride would not want an elderly one to tend to and someone's got to do it. So I guess things turn out for a reason, eh?"

"I suppose you're right, Kirby."

As Scott was preparing to step into the canoe, Kirby called out to him, "You going to marry Angelique Dupree?"

Scott laughed, "If she'll have me but I'm not too sure about that."

"You ask her?" Kirby yelled, for the canoe was already plowing through the waters.

"Not yet!"

"Better get to asking, O'Roarke," Kirby chuckled as he turned around to leave the wharf.

Since the day Francois LaTour had returned to Pointe a la Hache Gabriella had found him acting very strangely but she was absolutely convinced that he suspected her of nothing. She was even more convinced when he suddenly announced he was sending her and Joseph back to New Orleans.

"I need to have you there to see after things for me, Gabriella. I'll remain here a while longer."

"If this is what you wish, monsieur. What am I to say if someone asks for you or where you are?"

"Tell them I've gone on a trip—a very long trip, Gabriella. You know what I mean. Tell them or anyone who inquires that I've gone back to France to visit my brother."

Gabriella nodded, letting him know she understood that he wanted no one to know he was down at Pointe a la Hache.

Now she knew why he was sending her back. She was shrewd and Francois had obviously decided that it would be to his advantage to have her back at the house in the city. If she was there and anyone came to inquire about him she could steer them wrong and that was exactly what he wanted.

He was grateful that a patrol had not come to Pointe a la Hache to arrest him and cart him back to New Orleans to rot in a jail cell.

"You and Joseph will leave the first thing in the morning, Gabriella," he said as he prepared to leave the room.

"Oui, Monsieur LaTour." The minute he left, an amused smile crossed her tawny face. No one had to rescue her as Angelique had promised. She was going to New Orleans and once there she would be free of this yoke. She knew Angelique was sincere in her promise to help.

Gabriella knew this was her moment to make the break or she'd never be able to do it. She wasn't too old but the years went by so quickly. Living as she had, she saw herself as much older than Angelique, although she wasn't.

She would be willing to do anything just to be a free woman!

Chapter Twenty-nine

Simone spent a delightful day with her daughter shopping and having lunch in the city. They couldn't believe that both of them had found new gowns in Madame Eugenia's Shop. They knew there was no time to pick out material and have anything made, so luckily they'd found them.

After lunch they made one more stop — at a small boutique on a side street — in search of slippers to match their gowns. They were also successful there and found exactly what they were looking for. As they were leaving to board their carriage, Simone told her daughter to go ahead. "I forgot something but it won't take me a minute." She rushed back into the shop as Angelique stepped into the carriage and Zachariah climbed into the driver's seat.

Two finely-attired men in their twenties were sauntering down the street. Neither Angelique nor Zachariah had noticed that they were ogling her with lecherous looks. One of them smirked, "That's her! She's the one."

The other man smiled as he commented, "I can see why someone would want to take that pretty thing. She's one fine-looking female."

Angelique chose to ignore them by pretending she didn't hear them. She looked straight ahead and held her head high but she saw that Zachariah was not prepared to ignore it. Her gloved hand took hold of his arm. "No, Zachariah! Get back in the seat! I can ignore scum and so can you!"

The elderly black man obeyed her and about that time Simone came out of the shop. Angelique quickly admonished him to say nothing as she moved over in the carriage to allow her mother to take a seat.

But the first chance Zachariah got to be alone with Angelique, he let her know he could not stand by and see her insulted.

"And I cannot stand by, Zachariah, and see you harmed or injured. I care not what the likes of those men were saying about me but I care very much about you. This thing will pass just as soon as the city has something new to gossip about, Zachariah."

"Always knew you were sweet and pretty, Mademoiselle Angelique, but just never knew you were so wise. We'll just hope then that something happens fast," he declared.

As he was going to his quarters, Zachariah knew he could not have done battle with the two young bucks but a rage shot through him when he heard them talking like that about Mademoiselle Angelique.

Later that evening as he was taking an evening stroll around the stable, he was delighted to see that nice young fisherman come riding up the drive with a big bouquet of flowers in one hand. Zachariah had been wondering when he was going to come around. He had to figure it was because he was working from sunup to sundown on that fishing boat. A working man didn't have a lot of time to go courting.

Perhaps that was why Zachariah felt free to walk up to him before he went to the front entrance. Scott greeted the old black man with a friendly hello and Zachariah told him how glad he was to see him again.

"Hope I'll find Angelique home. Had no way of letting her know I was coming by," he told Zachariah.

"Oh, she's home. I'll just get on my way but it was good to see you again."

The truth was that Scott would have felt far more comfortable climbing over the garden fence than he felt knocking on the front door. He'd worn his best shirt and pants and taken special care to brush his thick, unruly hair. He knew when a man came to visit a girl like Angelique he should bring her flowers, so he'd purchased these late in the afternoon from a vendor down on othe wharf.

When the servant opened the door, he said he was calling on Miss Angelique. The young black servant girl invited him to enter and have a seat on the deep green brocade settee in the long hallway while she went to summon the mademoiselle.

But as the servant was climbing the steps, a bouncing ball of fur came scurrying down. Scott recognized the pup instantly and she obviously recognized him, too, running directly to him with her short tail wagging furiously.

"Well, Cuddles—you remember me!" He scooped her up with one hand as she eagerly licked the side of his face. Scott laughed and placed the flowers on the other side of him for it was going to take both hands to control this feisty little pup.

All the commotion out in the hallway drew the attention of Simone and Maurice who were sitting in the parlor waiting for Angelique to join them for dinner. Scott would have been very upset to know he had arrived before the Duprees had dined.

They emerged from the parlor just about the time Angelique was bouncing down the steps to see if it was Scott who was calling on her. When she reached the top of the stairs and saw that it was, she was thrilled. She observed the warm reception Cuddles was already giving him.

But she was also privy to the displeased looks on her parents' faces before she announced her presence at the base of the stairs.

Before they had a chance to address him, she rushed up to greet him. "Scott, it's so good to see you. I see Cuddles has already welcomed you," she said laughing softly. She turned toward her parents. "Isn't this nice, Momma and Poppa? Scott can join us for dinner."

Scott was ill at ease and feeling very awkward now. "Oh, no, Angelique! I've already eaten."

Angelique was determined to make him feel welcome in her home as she'd felt in his. "Well, you'll keep me company at least and share a cup of coffee or a glass of wine?"

"Of course, Angelique. I will if Cuddles will allow it," he told her, his Irish wit taking over. He had eyes for no one but her. He did not notice the glances exchanged between her parents. It had been almost a week since he'd seen her and it had seemed like forever. Dear God, she looked absolutely gorgeous!

He offered her the bouquet and she took it, graciously thanking him. "They're beautiful, Scott, and it was sweet of you to be so thoughtful." She called to the young servant girl who'd answered the door to take them and put them in a vase. "Take them to my room, Tessie."

Maurice and Simone found themselves onlookers, for there was no doubt that their daughter was in charge. They realized that they'd best try to be cordial for her sake if nothing else.

The four of them went into the parlor and Maurice poured Scott a glass of his cherished Madeira.

A few minutes later Scott accompanied the family into the spacious, lavishly furnished dining room aglow with candlelight. He could not help comparing this to his mother's little kitchen where they also dined in the evening. At Angelique's urging he did have dessert. It was very tasty and served on fine china but it was not as good as the flaky crusts of his mother's pastries.

After the meal, they all returned to the parlor and Maurice took up his pipe. "You smoke, Scott?"

"Yes, sir, but not a pipe. My father smokes a pipe. I like a cheroot," he told Maurice.

"Well, I shall offer you one I keep here for my friends. Try this," he said, as he lifted the lid of a fine teakwood box on the table.

A few minutes later, Scott confessed, "A much better cheroot than I can afford, sir."

Angelique allowed this casual conversation to go

on for several minutes before she suddenly decided to make her bold move. She'd not seen Scott for days and she had no desire to spend more time in the parlor with her parents. She looked at the clock on the mantel and knew that tomorrow was another working day for him.

Cuddles was at her feet fidgeting back and forth which gave her the perfect excuse to ask Scott to take a stroll with her in the garden while she allowed her pup to run.

Scott was more than eager to accept the invitation and took the opportunity to express his thanks to her parents. "I'll have to be leaving shortly. A fisherman's day starts very early," he added.

Maurice and Simone watched the young couple leave with the pup scampering after them. It only took the cover of darkness for the two of them to fall into one another's arms.

Angelique knew he was as eager as she'd been to be alone. It was a long, lingering kiss as they clung together, his arms encircling her tiny waist. There had been no need for words as their eyes had spoken of their yearnings all evening. But now they could enjoy that moment they'd been denied until now.

When he finally released her, he sighed, "God, I've missed you! You must know I would have come sooner if I could have."

Breathless from his kiss, she told him that she understood. "But I have to admit I was becoming impatient."

"Good, I always want you impatient to see me."

His hand held hers as they walked over to the bench. "Has everything been all right with you since I brought you home, Angelique?"

"Everything is all right, Scott. I guess I've become a little notorious. This doesn't bother me as much as it does my parents." She told him about the gossip.

"Don't let it! I've got something to tell you while we're together for I don't know when I'll be able to get back. Kirby, my friend, is going to help me get Gabriella away from Pointe a la Hache. We'll keep our word to her, Angelique. I promise you that."

"Oh, Scott—how wonderful! I'll have to meet Kirby. Will you take me to meet him sometime?"

"Oh, honey, it would be a pleasure and Kirby would be delighted to meet you since he's heard so much about you."

Scott knew he could not make love to her as he ached to do but it was wonderful just to be with her and feel her warmth so close to him.

He did not want to leave her but he knew he must for both their sakes. After he took another kiss, he told her, "My folks and Justin and Mimi want to see you again. Can I ever take you back to my bayou for a visit?"

"I'll go any time you say. I'm eager to see them, too," she confessed.

"Well, I'll come for you very soon, my darling. I just wanted to be sure you were willing."

"I'm willing, Scott. I loved your bayou."

Scott looked at her sitting beside him with the moonlight shining down on them and he had to confess that Mimi was right. She did look like a princess. He'd never seen such charm and beauty!

Scott O'Roarke was filled with mixed emotions when he took a last kiss and saw her to the front door before he went to mount up on Kirby's horse. Maybe she was not aware of it, but after tonight he knew the Duprees would never approve of him. They did not consider him good enough for their daughter.

He had to admit that he had nothing to offer but his love. But it was a love that was endless and eternal!

He only hoped that would be enough for Angelique!

Chapter Thirty

Monsieur Benoit and his wife always gave very grand parties with just the right number of people so they could spend time with each of them. It was her vivacious mother whom the feisty Nicole resembled in looks and temperament. Her father possessed a quiet dignity and Angelique had always imagined he must have been very handsome when he was younger. Unlike her own father, he'd remained trim after he'd reached middle age.

While she had not noticed it the other day, she saw a striking resemblance between Monsieur Benoit and his nephew. They even had the same mannerisms in the way they walked and held their heads.

Many things were obvious to Angelique during the dinner party at the Benoits. Her parents heartily approved of Louis Benoit. They displayed a friendlier attitude toward him than they had toward Scott when he was at the house.

She noticed their pleased smiles when Louis took her arm to escort her into the dining room. They heard him tell her how beautiful she looked.

When Simone got the opportunity to whisper in

her husband's ear, she murmured, "He seems very taken by our daughter, wouldn't you say?" Maurice gave her a nod with a pleased smile.

Nicole's mother came up to them as she rushed to catch up with her husband but she paused a moment to ask, "Well, what do you think of our nephew?"

"Charming young man, dear," Maurice told her. Simone echoed his sentiments.

"Well, Louis will want to come back very soon, I think. Speaking of charm, I think he's quite taken by your little Angelique." She would have chatted longer but for the sight of her husband motioning to her.

There were fifteen guests gathering around the dining table bedecked with a fine white linen tablecloth. Tapers glowed in the matching silver candelabras and a silver urn was filled with greenery and white flowers from Celeste's garden.

A special crawfish soup was always served at the Benoit dinners—it was a tradition. But Angelique enjoyed even more the little pastry shells filled with creamy sauce and generous chunks of shrimp.

By the time dessert was served she gave Louis a helpless smile, confessing that she did not know whether she could eat another bite. He grinned, amused by her honesty, for he had noticed how she'd been eating with relish.

"Then don't force yourself," he urged.

"I won't, Louis. My gown might just split at the seams."

He could not suppress a laugh. Monsieur Benoit glanced down the table to see that his nephew was having a very merry time. Usually, he was not too outgoing at these gatherings his aunt planned when he came from Baton Rouge. He could not say that his daughter, Nicole, was enjoying herself too much as she was seated by the rather dull daughter of one of their friends. The only other person Nicole's age was the son of a couple who'd been friends of theirs for years. But he was far too meek and quiet for his gregarious Nicole, so it was a boring evening for her.

Maybe the evening would become more interesting for her when she joined Louis and Angelique again, he hoped. He worried about her often for there was a reckless streak in her that surpassed even the vivacious ways of his wife.

As soon as dinner was over and the guests headed back toward the parlor, Nicole did make a quick exit to join her cousin and Angelique. She urged them to join her in the garden for a little while. "I need to be delivered from that babbling Roxanna. God, she gets on one's nerves."

Reluctantly, Louis was persuaded to take her and Angelique for a stroll but he told her it would have to be brief. He didn't want to offend his aunt and uncle because he knew the party was in his honor. His aunt was right—he wanted to return to New Orleans before another year went by, though he usually only visited once a year.

He knew he could become very serious about Angelique Dupree and if he did, what he really wanted was to remain with her alone the rest of the evening as he was leaving in the morning.

With Nicole on one side and Angelique on the other, he led them out through the doors leading to the veranda. The minute they were outside, Nicole

sighed, "Thanks, Loius. I'll do you a favor sometime."

"I might just call on you," he teased.

"Any time," she replied as they ambled along the
pathway.

They moved only a short way when Nicole's impish mind exploded with an idea of how she could
repay his favor to her on his last night here. As
they were nearing one of the little wrought iron
benches, she moaned in discomfort, "These darned
slippers are killing my feet. You two go ahead and
enjoy yourselves. I'll sit here and wait for you and
get off my feet for a few minutes." She moved to
the bench and sank down, wasting no time taking
off her shoes.

It never dawned on Louis that it was just a little
ploy she had conjured up but he had to admit he
was grateful for the precious few moments to be
alone with Angelique.

He was not known to be talkative but for whatever reason, he had found Angelique easy to be
with the other day when they'd met. Young ladies
he'd known all his life had not made him feel that
comfortable back in Baton Rouge.

"It's been a very pleasant experience meeting
you, Angelique, and I hope I can call on you when
I return."

"Why, of course, Louis. I'm sorry you won't be
staying longer."

"You mean that, Angelique?"

"Of course, I mean it. It was fun the other day
when the three of us went out riding."

Her straightforward manner was probably what
made Angelique so different from most of the girls

he'd always known. He liked that. Being on the serious side, he sensed there was a serious side to her, too.

She was not a wild little madcap like his cute cousin, Nicole, and yet, she could be gay and light-hearted with the most infectious laugh.

"Well, I'll be coming back sooner than I usually do just so I can see you, Angelique," he said smiling, but he was serious.

"That would be very nice, Louis."

"I shall certainly look forward to it. You—you're not engaged or spoken for, are you, Angelique?"

Suddenly, her thoughts turned to Scott O'Roarke. She found herself stammering when she answered, "No, Louis—I'm not engaged or spoken for." Once again, she was being truthful. Scott had not mentioned that he wanted her to marry him, but he'd said he loved her.

Her answer was enough to give Louis hope that he had a chance to win her. He was happy as he suggested they better be getting back to Nicole and to the party. "After all, I don't want to insult my aunt and uncle. Then I'd find myself an unwelcome guest when I want to come here again."

"No, we wouldn't want that, Louis," she answered, for she wanted to get back. It dawned on her that Louis was thinking in far more serious terms about her than she'd realized. She did like him very much but it was not in a romantic way. She could not imagine his lips stimulating the magic that Scott's did when he kissed her. As good looking as he was, she could not believe she'd burn with desire if he took her in his arms and pressed his body against her.

She welcomed his suggestion that they go back to the house for never would she want to hurt his feelings. He was too nice.

Nicole could see from the look on Louis's face as he and Angelique came back up the pathway that she had certainly done him a favor. Reluctantly, she began to slip her feet back into the slippers. It wasn't that they hurt, for they hadn't, but she was enjoying the quiet of the garden and thinking about her handsome Mark.

The trio went back toward the veranda and entered the house. The guests were beginning to say their goodbyes to the Benoits and Louis had arrived just in time to join his aunt and uncle to say farewell.

Angelique joined her parents as Nicole slowly ambled over to stand with Louis and the Benoits. Maurice and Simone were feeling very smug that their daughter had spent the entire evening with the guest of honor. Simone was thinking to herself that this would provide a different kind of gossip around New Orleans for her friends, Jean and Denise, to ponder next week. She was in very high spirits.

Maurice had his own private musings. He could not help being a little irritated when Angelique leaned over to her mother to suggest that perhaps they, too, should leave. What a bossy little belle she had become!

But Simone had not taken it that way and agreed with her daughter. "Are you ready, Maurice?" she asked, turning toward her husband.

He mumbled an answer and took the lead to guide them toward the archway where all the

Benoits were standing. It seemed that the rest of the guests were taking their cue and following behind them.

"It was a wonderful evening, dear," Simone told Celeste as the two of them embraced warmly. Maurice was saying farewell to Louis and Nicole was telling Angelique that the two of them would have to get together again very soon. With a curious look on her face and her dark eyes flashing, she whispered in Angelique's ear, "Has Scott been around yet?"

Angelique gave her a nod and a radiant glow came to her face. "I'll tell you all about it when we get together."

Nicole's dark eyes sparkled brighter for her curiosity was whetted. "We'll go to lunch Monday?"

"Monday is fine," Angelique agreed as she moved down the line to say farewell to Louis.

He took her hand and held it. "I shall see you, Angelique. Remember what we talked about."

She knew his words had been heard by her parents and had suddenly caught their attention. As they slowly drifted on out the entranceway to their carriage, her mother remarked about what an absolutely grand evening it had been.

An amused smile was on Angelique's face but she said nothing. Let them think what they wanted to about her and Louis, but it was not Louis Benoit she loved. It was the bayou fisherman.

She would have to love the man she married deeply and completely!

Chapter Thirty-one

The day after the Benoit party was not pleasant for Angelique because all her parents could talk about was Louis Benoit and how very nice he was. It was all too obvious what was going on.

Her father rambled on and on about what an ideal young man he was and how intelligent. "A lucky young lady she will be whom he takes for his wife. Fine family and heritage—that's very important, Angelique, and you must be mindful of this now that you're grown up."

She playfully teased him, "You heard him, Momma. He admits I'm no longer a child."

Simone smiled but said nothing. As the day went on, Angelique was to hear similar praise from her mother about how very nice and mannerly Louis was. By the end of the day she figured that she had responded a dozen times or more to how nice Louis was. She was sick of the subject and that was not poor Louis' fault or failing.

By the time she was ready to excuse herself to go up to her room she knew there was only one way to settle this matter once and for all. When Simone remarked that it was probably time they all retired after such a festive evening last night, she could not resist one last remark to her daughter. "Tell me, dear—tell me what you think about Louis? You haven't really said."

Angelique's patience was at an end and her voice had a hint of sharpness as she turned around to look at her mother. "Louis is very nice and sweet and I like him. But liking a man is hardly loving him, Momma, and I don't love him."

She swished her skirt around and quickly rushed out of the room. Simone glanced over at Maurice who was frowning. "That girl is just not the same. She hasn't been since she got back home. God, I wish she'd never gone through all that. The experience has changed her forever, Simone."

"It was out of our hands, Maurice. We can't change that, I'm afraid." Simone slowly moved toward the door.

"It's that fisherman, O'Roarke, whom Angelique fancies instead of Louis Benoit. I'm telling you here and now that I'll not be able to accept that," he declared gruffly to his wife as he lay aside his pipe and prepared to go upstairs.

"You might have to accept it, Maurice. Angelique will choose her own husband. She will never allow us to pick him out. This I can assure you! There might have been a time a few weeks ago that we could have influenced her but that was the past."

He snapped, "I won't! Never! I appreciate what Scott O'Roarke did but that does not give him the right to marry my daughter."

"But Angelique could give him that right," Simone pointed out. It was not to Maurice's liking to hear what his wife was saying. He was in one of his sullen moods by the time they reached the second landing and went into their room.

Simone sensed it and went about preparing to undress and take down her hair.

"Maurice, you must bear in mind that we could drive Angelique away from us if we take a negative attitude toward Scott. He may only be a fisherman in your eyes but he's a very handsome young man. As a woman I can understand Angelique's feelings better than you. He would turn many a young girl's head."

"For God's sakes, Simone—you talk like you're moonstruck over that—that Irishman," he said as though it left a foul taste in his mouth.

Simone saw it was imposible to make Maurice see the truth. So she said nothing more, allowing him to think whatever he wished.

Getting up from the dressing table, she dimmed the lamp and said goodnight. Maurice should be very grateful that she had not taken after her grandmother, Delphine, for their marriage would never have lasted. But Maurice was not going to be spared, for his daughter had a lot of Delphine in her.

Joseph had never seen LaTour's quadroon as angry as she was the evening they arrived at Francois' home in New Orleans. She had a right to be, old Joseph figured. The house had not been properly cared for during her and Francois' absence. When Gabriella marched around the house after they arrived he saw the house servants shiver with fear as she admonished each and every one. Joseph followed behind her like a dutiful pup. He knew the one who was going to receive the brunt of her fury—the lazy housekeeper Francois had left in charge of things when they'd made their hasty departure.

For a long time, Joseph had known why Francois had prized this lovely lady so much. She was as smart as they come and in terms of beauty, she surpassed most women Joseph had seen in his lifetime. She might be considered black in some circles but to Joseph she was a lot more white than black.

She made her final stop in the kitchen to find Josie at the table enjoying some of Francois' fine wine. The imposing sight of the quadroon glaring down on her with almond-shaped eyes flashing was enough to make Josie jump up and make awkward gestures of straightening her apron and skirt. She and all the other servants knew the power and authority Francois LaTour gave to Gabriella.

She attempted to greet her but Gabriella snarled, "You're drunk, Josie! Get your belongings packed. I want you out of here in a half hour!"

A shocked look came to Josie's face as she gasped in protest but Gabriella quickly assured her that she meant exactly what she'd said. Then she turned to check the pantry. It was a pathetic sight, almost bare despite the well-stocked shelves they'd left.

It was not until two hours later after she'd gone to her room that Gabriella asked herself why she should be concerned about this house. It didn't belong to her and she didn't plan on remaining here that long now that she was free to do what she wished.

She realized it was a habit that she was leaving behind, but she couldn't make any plans because of Joseph. After she had bathed and dressed, she went downstairs to find him in the kitchen. He'd managed to brew a pot of coffee and told her, "Josie just left. She was one scared gal."

Gabriella managed to find enough in the pantry to prepare a meager meal for the two of them. "Hate to have to leave you here in this mess, Gabriella, but monsieur wanted me to get you here and come back to Pointe a la Hache tomorrow. I was planning on leaving first thing in the morning."

"You do what Francois told you to do and don't worry about me, Joseph. I'll be fine," she assured him. In fact, she was delighted to hear he would be leaving in the morning for she could then go about making her own plans to leave leaving forever the "prison" she'd been in since Francois had possessed her.

Perhaps that was the thing that had made her heart mellow so much when she saw another pretty girl, so young and innocent, taken by the lecherous Francois.

Once Joseph was gone, she could seek out Angelique for she had to know if she was sincere and would help her as she'd said. Oh, she had to believe that she'd meant what she said! It was very important to Gabriella.

The next morning, she went down to give very specific orders to the servants and handed Joseph a farewell message to carry back to Francois. "I'll tell him, Gabriella," Joseph assured her as he prepared to leave.

254

When he had left and she had the servants working as they should be, she went up to her room. She figured she'd more than earned all the clothes Francois had bought her as well as the few pieces of jewelry in the little teakwood box. When she had done all this, she asked herself what was the price of bondage for all the years she had served Francois and been his mistress before he tired of her?

Without a qualm of conscience, she went down to his study and emptied the little pewter box of all the gold coins Francois kept there. Then she went over to the desk where there was a little secret money drawer he had told her about so she could run the house when he wasn't there.

She took this, too, and left the room. She felt no guilt for she knew that Francois had certainly not worked by the sweat of his brow to earn his money. He was still a pirate at heart and his wealth was still being gained by robbing people in a different way.

She knew much about this man after five years of being privy to his comings and goings. His undoing was that he dared to trust her as a dutiful servant, loyal and true. No white man would ever bend her to his will. Not even Francois had managed to do that even though he thought he had.

By afternoon she was ready to make her move to the road to freedom. She dressed with special care and had the young black boy, Nat, prepare the buggy so he could drive her.

Finally, she was ready to go on her search for Mademoiselle Angelique Dupree. With Nat guiding the buggy, she left the house and it took only a few inquiries to be directed to the country estate out on Old Cypress Road.

Nat pulled the buggy up to the front entrance and leaped out to help Gabriella down from the buggy. It did not surprise Gabriella that Angelique lived in such lavish surroundings.

With her kerchiefed head held high, she gracefully walked up to the door and knocked. As it would happen, Simone was nearby so she was the one to open the door.

"I wish to see Mademoiselle Angelique. I am Gabriella."

Simone did not invite her into the house for she was not sure how Maurice would react. She was a very attractive young woman, Simone thought, as she gazed at her.

"Would you tell her I came to call? I trust she's fine, madame?"

"She's just fine and I shall tell her you came to see her. I'm sure she'll be sorry she missed you," Simone said as she dismissed the quadroon.

Gabriella knew when she had been graciously dismissed so she bowed politely and turned to leave. "Good day, madame," she said. It was obvious she'd made Simone ill at ease.

"Good day to you," Simone replied as she watched the woman leave. She found herself intrigued by her exotic beauty with those almond-shaped eyes and tawny, satin complexion. She was striking!

So this was the Gabriella whom Angelique had spoken about—the woman who had helped her escape from Pointe a la Hache. Simone could believe it for she had seen the strength and force in this woman as she'd talked to her for a few brief moments. For what she'd done for her daughter, Simone was beholden to her.

Maurice would probably not feel as she did but that didn't matter to her. This woman, Gabriella, would forever have her respect and gratitude.

As soon as Angelique returned from her trip into the city with Nicole, she would tell her of Gabriella's visit.

It mattered not if Maurice approved or not! Simone had to tell her daughter about Gabriella.

Chapter Thirty-two

She was disappointed that she had not seen Angelique, but Gabriella would go back tomorrow. Sooner or later, she would see her. On the way back to the house she made a stop by the marketplace for it was Monday and the freshest vegetables and fruits would be there today.

She visited some of the stands to pick up a few things to carry her through another day or two. Why should she spend extra money to furnish Francois' empty pantry if she would be leaving as she expected to do? But tonight she had to eat and knew what she found the previous night when she tried to put a meal together after she'd kicked Josie out of the house.

She bought all the makings for a tasty fish chowder—a small sack of crawfish, onions, a few carrots and potatoes.

As soon as she returned to Francois' house she instructed one of the young servants to make a fire in the cookstove and start heating some water in the cast iron kettle. She went upstairs to change into one of her more simple muslins, then returned to the kitchen to enjoy a feast of her favorite fish chowder and one of Francois' best white wines. In the morning she would go back out on Old Cypress Road to seek Angelique. This time she would arrive in the morning before Angelique could possibly leave for an appointment.

She found herself wondering about her and that young man who'd rescued her from Pointe a la Hache. Had the whole episode heightened their affections for one another?

She imagined that it had. Seeing the two of them scampering across the beach that day, she had to say that Mademoiselle Angelique had one very handsome man as she'd watched his trim body move and his long legs stride along the sandy beach. Even from a distance, she saw that he was good-looking enough to turn any young girl's head.

As she indulged herself with these musings, she cleaned and prepared all the vegetables and crawfish. There was an ample supply of herbs in the pantry and that was the secret of her chowder. Once everything was tossed into the pot the rest was waiting for it all to simmer.

She left the kitchen for the parlor and as she went by the large mirror over the library table she stopped to stare at her reflection. She could have been the mistress of such a fine house and the wife of a wealthy gentleman. She looked almost as white as Angelique Dupree and was certainly attractive with a very fine figure.

She had to wonder though if her life would have been worse had her mother lived instead of dying when the fever spread up and down the river country some eight years ago. Gabriella was old enough to remember the shack they lived in and how her mother did washing for the boatmen. They would drop it by and pick up the clean, pressed clothes the next week.

She also wondered which of these white men might have been her father—or was he one of the wealthy sugar cane planters living near their shack.

Her mother, Cornelia, had been a beautiful woman, Gabriella thought. She wasn't as black as most of the Negro women in the shacks along the river. Crazy as it might seem, Gabriella did not know her mother's age but she'd have judged her to be about her own age when she suddenly took ill and died.

Her mother always wore a turban-like kerchief around her head and, perhaps, that was why Gabriella had adopted the habit. She never remembered seeing her mother in anything but a straight-lined cotton shift, which she had sewn herself. But even in the shift, the full bosom, wasp-like waist, and rounded hips were evident.

Never could she get her mother to reveal who the white man was who'd fathered her. All she would say was it was no boatman coming and going up the river. Her father was a man of fine breeding and good stock.

Gabriella was doomed never to know who her father was, for that knowledge had gone to the grave with her mother.

For the rest of the afternoon and evening she gave way to the whimsy that she was a lady of class as she lingered in Francois' elegant parlor and later dined in his dining room by herself, enjoying the delicious chowder and sipping the white wine.

When she went upstairs, she picked one of her nicer gowns in a rich purple to wear tomorrow when she traveled out to the Duprees.

When she had done that, she was ready to get undressed and go to bed.

Angelique was devastated that she had not been home when Gabriella had come to the house. "Did she mention where she was staying, Momma?"

"No, dear, she didn't. I didn't ask her," Simone admitted. She saw the distraught look on her daughter's face and tried to soothe her. "She'll come again, I'm sure."

Angelique nodded her head, but what her mother did not know was that Gabriella might have been desperate for her help if she'd managed to escape from Pointe a la Hache and Francois La-Tour.

"I—I guess there's nothing I can do but pray that she comes again tomorrow," Angelique muttered dejectedly. She recalled that Gabriella had told her about a house Francois had here in the city but she had no idea where it was. According to Gabriella, it was to this house she was first taken the night she was abducted from the garden but being blindfolded she had no inkling where it was.

Tomorrow she was staying at home all day hoping that Gabriella would appear again for if she left to go out searching, she could miss her.

The rest of the late afternoon and evening all Angelique could think about was Gabriella. What had happened since the two of them had said goodbye? She prayed that she had paid no price for allowing her to escape with Scott.

She did not linger in the parlor with her parents

after dinner. Instead, she took Cuddles and retreated to her bedroom.

Maurice frowned, asking his wife, "And what's the matter with her tonight? She seemed so preoccupied all during the meal. With everything else is Angelique becoming temperamental?"

"It's not that, Maurice! Her friend, Gabriella, came here today while Angelique was with Nicole. You recall her telling us about the woman at Pointe a la Hache who helped her escape? She told us about the woman and how she felt the need to help her?"

Impatiently, Maurice shrugged his shoulders. "Oh, yes, I seem to recall Angelique mentioning her now," he remarked. He had seen the young woman leaving but he did not wish to mention it to Simone. He was glad his daughter was not home to greet this young quadroon.

"As I recall, Angelique said she was black?"

"She said she was a quadroon, Maurice." More and more Simone was finding herself short-tempered with her overbearing husband who seemed to think he had the God-given right to pass judgment.

"That's a Negro woman as far as I'm concerned."

"To me that's a woman who was fathered by some lecherous white man, Maurice, so we have a difference of opinion. But the truth is that you better be prepared for the fact that Angelique considers this Gabriella her dear friend," Simone declared, turning her attention back to her needlepoint.

Maurice did not like the attitude of his wife or his daughter lately. He had always been the one in charge—his word had always been law. But now his daughter had become defiant, boldly declaring her independence. His wife had always been a sweet, passive lady who'd seemed happy to let him have his own way. Lately, he'd observed that she dared to argue with him and have her own feelings be known. This had never happened before and it was becoming very unsettling to Maurice.

He bluntly announced to Simone that he was going out into the gardens for a breath of fresh air before he retired. He needed a moment of solitude.

Never looking up from her needlepoint, she told him she was going upstairs shortly. "I'll probably be upstairs. I'll leave the lamps for you to attend to, Maurice."

Maurice walked in the gardens for almost an hour but he found no answers to what was troubling him. It seemed that nothing had been right in this household since the night Angelique had been taken. The authorities were doing nothing to apprehend this Francois LaTour so he was in a disgruntled mood about a lot of things.

As he walked in the dark he got to thinking that the real problems in his family had started when Angelique had chanced to meet that Irish fisherman, Scott O'Roarke. But for the fact that she'd dashed out in the garden for their secret rendezvous, LaTour's hired ruffians could not have grabbed her and all the other horrible things would not have happened.

Yes, he had to lay the blame for everything that had suddenly gone wrong in this family at the feet of Scott O'Roarke! He didn't particularly like the familiar way this O'Roarke had about him the day

Angelique had arrived back home and he'd taken charge by carrying her up to the carriage. The man was too damned bold to please Maurice, now that he thought about it.

Who did he think he was to be so presumptuous as to come to their home the other night and be their uninvited guest at the dinner table?

By the time he finally left the garden, Maurice had conjured up many reasons why he didn't like Scott O'Roarke. But the most imposing threat was that his daughter might be in love with this lowly fisherman.

Maurice could never tolerate that! Angelique must marry a young man like Louis Benoit. The daughter of a wealthy French Creole gentleman just didn't marry the captain of a fishing boat. Angelique surely had to realize this—for her to think otherwise meant that she had taken leave of her senses.

He was beginning to wonder if his beautiful daughter had inherited the unfortunate traits of Simone's family instead of his. He recalled all the tales he'd heard Simone tell about her adventuresome grandmother, Delphine.

Dear God, maybe Angelique was like her!

Chapter Thirty-three

Angelique woke up much earlier than usual and wasted no time getting dressed to go downstairs. Oh, Gabriella would surely come back again this morning! Angelique knew she was hopelessly lost as to how to seek her out if she didn't appear again. If only she could rush to Scott and seek his advice. The vast area he covered in that fishing boat made it impossible for her to get word to him. She wished it was Friday so he would be by the docks but it wasn't. All she could do was wait and hope, which is what she did for the next three hours.

It would have pleased Gabriella to know that her little friend awaited her arrival with such eagerness as she dressed and prepared to leave the house. A short time later she and young Nat were boarding the buggy to go out on Old Cypress Road.

They traveled down Dumaine Street where people were already milling around. The wharves were a beehive of activity, for New Orleans was a constantly busy port city. Gabriella noticed that Nat was slowing the pace of the bay and she inquired why he was stopping.

"Something wrong with that bay, Mademoiselle

Gabriella. He limpin'," he said as he prepared to jump down. It didn't take him long to discover what was making the horse limp and slow his pace. "He's thrown a shoe."

He took the reins to lead the bay as easy as he could to a smitty shop a short distance away. "Kirby will take care of it for us, mademoiselle. I know him. He's a good man," young Nat assured her.

"All right, Nat," she replied as he started guiding the bay toward the shop.

It was obvious to Gabriella that the poor bay was moving laboriously and she knew he must be in pain. So it was a welcome sight to see the sign saying Kirby's Smitty Shop right ahead.

The familiar camaraderie young Nat seemed to share with the huge man who must have been the blacksmith was interesting to her. He greeted the black boy as he sauntered up, "Hey, Nat—got a problem?"

"Horse threw a shoe," Nat told him. Gabriella could see Kirby's firm-muscled legs making long strides just inside the shop. When he came out Gabriella saw the whole of him and was immediately impressed by the way his cotton pants molded to his body and his broad chest glistened with sweat.

Kirby was stunned by the sight of the tawny beauty sitting in the buggy. She made a striking sight in the purple gown and the matching turban. His husky voice stammered, "Good morning, ma'am. Nat tells me y'all got a problem."

"Yes, monsieur. He says the horse threw a shoe," she said. Kirby looked at the horse's hoof and nodded his bushy red head.

He immediately led the buggy through the wide double doors as he explained to Gabriella that she would be more comfortable inside while he unharnessed the horse.

When Kirby got the chance he whispered to little Nat, "Who's that pretty lady you're carting around this morning? Never saw her in that buggy before."

"That's Mademoiselle Gabriella. She *is* pretty, isn't she?"

"Very." For a moment or two he did not realize that this could be the woman Scott had spoken about. Actually he had only found out recently that this little black boy, Nat, worked in the La-Tour household and stables. Knowing that and that this woman's name just happened to be Gabriella, he was sure she had to be the one Scott knew. If so, then Scott did not have to go to Pointe a la Hache to get her for she was already in New Orleans.

But how could he approach her without offending her? What if his assumption was wrong? He would look like a fool. All the time he went about the task of shoeing the horse he kept stealing glances at her. Once Gabriella caught him looking and a slow smile came to her face. Kirby felt himself blushing with embarrassment.

When the task was almost finished, Kirby still could not decide how to find out if she was the Gabriella who had befriended his pal and Angelique Dupree.

He'd never had as glib a tongue as his pal, Scott O'Roarke. Some would have actually called him shy. But he couldn't let them go on their way without finding out who she was. He owed it to Scott to keep him from making that long trip to Pointe a la Hache.

Kirby knew no other way to do it than just come right out and ask him.

But he never got the chance because Nat came rushing from the door, his big black eyes wide as he ran to the buggy. "Lord Almighty, Mademoiselle Gabriella—I just saw Monsieur LaTour and his man, Paulo, going down the street toward the house!"

Gabriella's face was panicky. "Are you sure, little Nat?"

"Yes, ma'am! I'm sure! It was him and I know that mean-looking Paulo when I see him."

Gabriella forgot that Kirby was near as she moaned in despair, "Oh, God, little Nat!"

Kirby was convinced by the way the two of them were acting that this had to be the lady Scott had talked about. He started moving toward the wide doors of his shop. When he had one door closed, he pulled the other one in and moved the bar to secure them. By this time Gabriella was aware of what he was doing and that she and little Nat were imprisoned inside the shop.

"What is this, monsieur? Why have you done this?" She reared up in the seat indignantly, but it was actually fright consuming Gabriella.

"To help you, miss, if you're who I think you are. I've only one question to ask you and that is if you are the one who helped Miss Angelique escape?"

This startled Gabriella and she asked in a faltering voice, "How—how do you know this?"

"My friend, Scott O'Roarke, told me about you

and how he is beholden for what you did for him and his lady. Fact is, the other day he was in here and we were talking about going to Pointe a la Hache to get you. I don't need you to answer me — I know you're the lady," Kirby told her.

"I am, monsieur."

"Then you have to allow me to help you and that's why I locked the front of my shop. I owe Scott a favor as he feels he owes you. We'll send little Nat back to the house with the buggy while I get you to your friends and safety."

He lectured little Nat carefully, telling him to say he had gone from the house on errands and the horse threw a shoe so he had to get it fixed.

"But he's going to ask me about Mademoiselle Gabriella 'cause them other servants know that she let the cook go so what am I to tell him about her, Kirby?" Nat asked anxiously.

"You're going to tell him you left her at the marketplace to shop while you attended to the horse. You understand, son? He can't fault you because she wasn't there when you returned to get her."

Nat nodded. Kirby was trying to help Mademoiselle Gabriella and he wanted to do that, too. He didn't want to get his hide skinned by monsieur, but if he did exactly as Kirby told him Nat knew it would be all right.

"While you're on your way back to the house, I'll get Miss Gabriella to her friends where she'll be safe. Now, I'll open the back doors and you get hopping out of here, little Nat."

Kirby lifted Gabriella out of the buggy and went to the back to swing open the two wide doors. Nat did exactly as Kirby had instructed him to do, turning back to wave at them. Kirby wasted no time closing the doors after him.

"Now, Miss Gabriella—we've got some talking to do. I'm taking you to my house because it's closer and LaTour knows nothing about me. My pa is there—he's sick in bed most of the time but I know you'll be safe there."

"Whatever you say, monsieur," Gabriella said, grateful that he was being so kind.

"Now, please ma'am, I don't want to offend you but we got to do something to disguise you. Would you consider it an insult if I ask you to throw one of my old horse blankets around that head of yours to cover that pretty kerchief and your dress just a little?"

Gabriella could not resist a soft giggle. "Ah, Monsieur Kirby—I'm not so proud that I would not do anything if it was necessary."

"Well, it's broad daylight and I don't want to call attention to us. A lady dressed as fancy as you would certainly draw stares, if you know what I mean," Kirby said with a warm smile.

Gabriella found herself liking this smitty more and more. He did not know what it had meant to her for him to call her a lady. "You get me the blanket and I'll drape it around my head and shoulders."

A few seconds later the two of them slipped out the back doors and walked hastily up the incline to Kirby's cottage.

As they made their way to the house, Gabriella explained that it was to the Dupree home little Nat was taking her when he discovered the problem with the bay. She told him that she had also gone there yesterday only to be told by Angelique's mother that she was not there.

"Well, that's why I'm taking you to my house instead. I don't know what our reception there could be, if you get my meaning. It's most important that you're not spotted here in New Orleans if this Francois is back in the city."

Gabriella knew he was exactly right for Francois would deal very harshly with her if they ever met now. She had thought it her good fortune when she chanced to meet Angelique Dupree and now she knew it was her lucky day when the bay threw his shoe causing her to meet Kirby.

The trek from the shop to the cottage was without any incident; Kirby was glad he'd met no one he knew along the way.

He was greatly relieved when they got to his front porch and he ushered Gabriella inside. She was eager to get the blanket off of her shoulders for it had been heavy and warm.

Kirby excused himself, leaving her alone in the small parlor while he went to the bedroom his father occupied. He found him asleep and gently woke the old man so he could explain about their unexpected guest.

He made the explanation very simple: she was a friend of Scott's and would be at their cottage until he could get word to Scott.

"Now, Pa, you just go back to sleep and I'll tell Gabriella to make herself at home 'cause I got to get back to the shop."

In a sleepy voice, his father mumbled, "Tell the lady to make herself comfortable, Kirby. Think I will get a little more sleep."

"You just do that, Pa," Kirby urged as he rose from the side of the bed.

The house was very small so Gabriella had heard the sounds of the two men's voices at the back of the house. She'd also had time to observe the parlor—it was obvious it had lacked a woman's touch for a long time. She had to assume that Kirby's mother was no longer living and it was just him and his father occupying the cottage. She found it hard to believe that a fine looking, hard working man like Kirby had never taken a wife.

When Kirby returned to the parlor, he saw the thoughtful look on her lovely face. He hesitated for just a minute to savor the sight of her. Gabriella was not aware that he'd been admiring her before he let his presence be known. She was dwelling in a moment of foolish fancy—it would be wonderful to live in a simple little cottage like this and make it cozy and attractive. It would be so nice to have a good man like Kirby for a husband who would love and protect her from men like Francois. At least, she could daydream as all young women do!

Reluctantly, he said, "Pa knows you're here and he said to tell you to make yourself at home. He's still napping."

"I'll try to be very quiet so I won't disturb him, Kirby."

"Oh, you won't disturb him, Gabriella."

Neither of them had realized that they were addressing one another with less formality. It had just happened.

Kirby took her to the kitchen to show her where

272

certain things were in case she wished to fix something to eat before he returned.

"Guess I don't have to tell you that men aren't as good housekeepers as ladies. You can see that for yourself," he laughed goodnaturedly.

"Kirby, you just get back to work. I've already created enough trouble. I'll be fine," she assured him.

"I know you will be and that's why I wanted you here. So I'll leave you, Gabriella. See you this evening about sunset," he said as he started backing out of the kitchen. He felt awkward and bashful like he might have back when he was a lanky youth of sixteen or seventeen.

"I'll see you around sunset then, Kirby," she said as she watched him backing out.

When he disappeared, Gabriella thought to herself that he had such a rugged look about him with that powerful body but he had such a gentle way.

It was nice to say that she'd see him at sunset. It dawned on her that she'd never known anyone like Kirby Murphy before. Due to the sordid life she'd been forced to live she had always felt as old as the ages — but suddenly she felt as young as springtime.

It was a wonderful feeling!

Chapter Thirty-four

Gabriella did exactly what Kirby had told her to do and made herself at home in his cottage. For an hour she puttered around in the kitchen with an old flour sack tied around her middle for she found no aprons there. When her biscuits were baked and a pot of tea brewed, she sat down at the table to enjoy a couple of biscuits, lavishly spread with a jam she'd found in the cupboard, and sip two cups of tea.

Wondering if Kirby's father might be awake and hungry, she slipped back to check him. She could tell from the way his head was lying on the pillow that he was sleeping soundly so she quietly moved back down the hall.

She had time to explore every corner of the tiny cottage in the next few hours. She felt so grateful to Kirby for what he had done that she dusted everything that needed it. She opened the windows to allow fresh air to blow in. There were very few flowers growing in the small front and back yards. It was obvious that Kirby had no time for gardening with an ailing father to tend to when he came in from working hard.

But tonight he would come home to a good meal, she thought, after surveying the cupboard and pantry. There was a jar of peaches so she baked a peach pie. She found a ham hanging in the pantry so she sliced some of it and discovered two nice heads of cabbage. A neighbor had apparently brought them because there was no garden in their back yard.

She prepared the cast iron pot with water and seasonings before she dropped the chunks of cabbage into the steaming water. All the time she busily moved around the kitchen, she could not help thinking that she had not had the chance to take all the belongings she'd gathered up yesterday. All she had was the clothing on her back, but there was the gold and money she'd put in her reticule. Thank God for that!

The boiling cabbage had simmered about an hour when its special aroma began to permeate the kitchen as well as the rest of the cottage. Gabriella sat at the table thinking about all the things that had happened which were certainly not according to her plans.

But her solitude was interrupted when she noticed the feeble old man on a walking cane coming into the kitchen. His thick mane of white hair was tousled and reached down over his collar.

"Smelled cabbage, I did. Haven't smelled that in this house since my Mary died." His watery eyes had the hint of a sparkle. "Tell me I'm right, missy. Tell me you're boiling up some cabbage and I ain't just dreaming it."

Gabriella got up from the chair and went over to help him the rest of the way to one of the kitchen chairs. He looked like he could tumble to the floor at any moment.

She gave him a warm smile. "It *is* cabbage cooking. I hope you'll like it."

"I'll love it, never you fear. Kirby does his best but it just ain't like his ma's."

When she had him safely seated, she asked if she could get him a cup of tea. "I'm having one," she added.

"Sounds mighty fine. Got to say it's a sorta nice sight to see a lady puttering in the kitchen again."

Gabriella brought the cup over to the table. "Be careful—it's very hot," she warned him, seeing how his hands trembled.

"Sit down now and quit your fussing over me, miss. Kirby told me you were our guest. Appears to me you're hardly being treated like a guest, working and stewing around here in the kitchen."

"Well, I was hardly an expected guest and for that I must apologize," she said as she took a seat.

"No call for that. Your company is certainly welcome for it's a long day with Kirby working. Can't get out and take walks to visit with my neighbors like I used to."

They talked for a while longer until he had finished the tea. When she saw he was attempting to rise out of the chair, she insisted that he allow her to help him. "Do you want to get back to your room?"

He nodded and allowed her to take him back. "Got to get me some rest now so I can enjoy some of that cabbage after Kirby gets home," he said with a weak smile.

"Well, if you don't feel like coming to the table I'll bring you some on a tray. Now you rest," she urged.

She left and returned to the kitchen to check the pot. She wondered what his illness was and how long he'd been this way.

She was also wondering how long it would be before Kirby would be home. To make the time pass faster she set up the table and got the skillet out so she could fry some slabs of the ham once he did arrive.

As dusk gathered, Kirby came bouncing through the front door and everything seemed different to him from the minute he entered. The delicious aroma coming from the kitchen was the first pleasant surprise and then he was greeted by the lovely Gabriella who wore a warm smile.

Knowing what a sight he must be, he asked her to excuse him until he got cleaned up. He hesitated only long enough to inquire about his dad.

"Just fine. He's resting again but he did sit in the kitchen with me to enjoy a cup of tea."

A surprised look came to Kirby's dirty face. "Well, he loves hot tea."

"He also likes cabbage, I found out," she laughed.

"Oh, that he certainly does. That pot of cabbage will put you in his good graces forever." He rushed out of the room to make himself more presentable.

Once he had bathed and put on a clean pair of pants and shirt, he slipped into his father's room to see that he was peacefully resting. Then he went back toward the parlor where he'd left Gabriella but she wasn't there. She'd gone into the kitchen to start frying the ham, so he joined her and ambled around for he was usually the one standing at the stove this time of the evening.

"Don't know how to act at being so idle," he laughed.

"Well, just sit over there and talk to me, Kirby. I trust you had no one coming to the shop to cause any trouble?"

"Nope, Nat must have done as I told him." He also told her that he'd not had any way to get word to Scott all afternoon.

Kirby poured two glasses of milk, as Gabriella had told him she would be having another cup of tea. About the time she was placing the slabs of fried ham on the platter, Tom Murphy came wobbling through the door once again. This time Gabriella noticed he'd made a feeble attempt to run a brush through his unruly hair.

Kirby was pleasantly stunned and went to help him get seated. "Wasn't about to let you young scamps have all that good food," he jested.

It was a very pleasant meal the three enjoyed together, thanks to Gabriella. The two men had not had such grand food in a long time. It was sheer paradise to have the juicy peach pie after they'd had their fill of the cabbage and ham. They savored each bite of the pie.

"I think we should keep Gabriella with us so we could have a fine meal like this every night, don't you, Pa?" Kirby smiled.

"Heck, I might just get well if this fine little lady stayed around."

It was very gratifying to Gabriella that she had been able to do something for Kirby and his father to repay them for all that had been done for her. She didn't know what she might have faced if she hadn't been in his shop this morning.

She only prayed that little Nat had fared all right as Kirby seemed to think, for she knew the outrageous temper tantrums Francois could have.

When the meal was over and Kirby had his father comfortably settled in for the night, he went back to the kitchen to help her with the dishes. After the kitchen was in order, he invited her to sit on the front steps. "A breath of fresh air will do you good after being in the house all day."

A gentle breeze did seem refreshing and Gabriella suddenly realized she had put in a busy afternoon. For a few moments it was nice to sit there quietly with neither of them talking. But finally Gabriella spoke for she did not wish to impose on this nice man and his father. Kirby Murphy had all the responsibility he needed without her hanging on to him, too. She told him this, adding that maybe there was some way she could manage to get word to Angelique tomorrow.

Kirby's rough hand reached out to take hers. "Look, you wouldn't be imposing on us if you stayed here a week or a month. We can't afford to take any chances now that we've got you away from that idiot, Francois. Look what he did to Angelique Dupree just because he took the notion. I got to be the last person in the world to tell you he has no scruples."

A sad look crossed Gabriella's face as she solemnly declared, "Scruples Francois LaTour does not have!"

After they had talked for another half hour, Kirby knew he had to get to bed to be able to get up early. As they went back into the parlor, he told her to let him get a few things from his room. "I'll sleep with Pa and you can have my room, Gabriella." He would not allow her to protest. With his usual warm smile he shook his head and marched out of the parlor.

A few minutes later, he came back. "I lit the lamp by my bed and I hope you get a good night's rest, Gabriella. You need it and I'll see you tomorrow but probably not before I leave to go to the shop. It's too early!"

"Thank you, Kirby—thank you for everything. I shall rest well and you do the same," she said. Leaving the parlor to go to his room, her hand went up to wipe her eyes and she was glad he couldn't see her. Tears did not come easy for Gabriella and she could not recall the last time she'd cried but tonight she felt the need to.

Such overwhelming emotions flooded through her. Never had she known such kindness. Kirby Murphy had to be the nicest man in the whole world. She did not know that such goodhearted, gentle men existed on the face of the earth. Today, she'd met one!

She was a stranger and he had taken her in and offered her refuge. He'd as good as told her tonight that his home was hers for as long as she needed it.

As she undressed and slipped into his bed, she thought to herself that it would be a very lucky woman whom Kirby asked to be his wife. She could not deny that she envied that woman with all her heart and soul.

If only she could be that woman, she would have been so happy. But Gabriella was never one to fool herself about certain things in life and she knew this could never be.

But for tonight as she lay in his bed, she would pretend it could be so!

Part Three

The End of a Bittersweet Summer

Chapter Thirty-five

A late summer shower moved in over the coast of Louisiana. Scott and Justin were glad that the rain didn't start until after four so they had put in most of the day before they headed for the bayou.

"Sort of messed up my plans, I got to admit," Scott told Justin as they moved around the bends of the bayou with the light rains pelting them. "Had it on my mind to go by Kirby's, but guess it will have to be tomorrow."

"Well, I got something to talk to you about. It's Mimi's birthday. She wants us to have a little celebration. Suppose you could get that little lady of yours to come? Mimi would be thrilled to pieces."

"I can try, Justin, and I will. Got the feeling that the Duprees weren't too happy to see me the last time I saw Angelique. Of course that isn't going to stop me from trying to see her as long as she doesn't start acting cold like they did. It's not easy, Justin, when you're in love with a girl like Angelique whose family is wealthy and I happen to be a poor fellow according to their standards."

Justin laughed. "Well, Mimi and I had no problems — both of us were poor."

They were glad to see Justin's pier for the rains

were becoming heavier. Scott was not so lucky because he was drenched by the time he got to his own pier and managed to run up the path.

The day was drawing to an end for Kirby, who was like a young man courting as he had been a few years ago. Oh, he knew there was a part of Gabriella that was Negro but he couldn't lie to himself—he had been attracted to her since the moment he'd seen her in the buggy. She was not much darker than the French Creole beauties around New Orleans, and they were the most beautiful ladies he'd ever seen.

He was also wondering what magic she'd create next on that old cookstove of his mother's. It had been good to see his father eat with such relish again.

He noticed that a light shower had begun to fall. At the same moment, little Nat guided his buggy right through the open double doors of the smitty shop. Excitedly, he leaped from the buggy to tell Kirby, "Got something for you to give to Mademoiselle Gabriella. She was always my good friend so I wanted to help her." He motioned to Kirby to help him get the baggage from the buggy. "These are hers and I thought I'd get them to you so you could take them to her."

As soon as he and Kirby had unloaded the last one, little Nat wasted no time getting back up in the seat. "I got to get back before monsieur returns or my tail will be in a crack, Kirby."

"You be careful, Nat!" Kirby warned the young boy who'd dared to load all this stuff in the buggy for Gabriella. Such bravery could cost him if LaTour found out.

A sly grin broke over his face. "I'm going to market to get some things for the woman in charge of the kitchen now that Mademoiselle Gabriella kicked Josie out."

"Better get on your way," Kirby called out.

Little Nat called back as he was rolling out of the smitty shop, "Tell Mademoiselle Gabriella I'll be missing her!"

Kirby nodded. He found himself wishing he could take young Nat under his wing. He was such a cute little tadpole with that happy look and eager smile.

Looking at the pile of baggage, Kirby knew it was impossible to carry all this to the cottage tonight. He had no wagon or buggy, so he took it to the back stall and piled it there. Little by little, he would get it home.

By the time he was ready to leave, rain was falling steadily. He carried two of the smaller valises under his arms as his hands gripped two of the larger ones.

Gabriella was elated when he told her how little Nat had gathered up all her belongings and brought them to him this afternoon. Nat had obviously fared all right yesterday.

"Oh, that little monkey! I adore that child! I—I wish I could free him as I am free now," she sighed.

Kirby found it interesting that the two of them were feeling the same way about Nat. She was a woman with a kind and generous heart which endeared her to him.

When he went in to see about his father after he'd carried all the baggage to his room for Gabriella, the old man was sitting up in bed ready to praise their young guest.

Kirby sat on the bed as his father told him about the tasty broth she'd made. Kirby could see for him-

285

self that his father seemed in the best spirits. "Damn, Kirby, it's a woman we've needed around this place!"

A laugh exploded from Kirby and he found himself even more amused when his father told him that Gabriella was going to cut his hair tomorrow. Old Tom was wallowing in all the attention.

But he was in for more surprises when he learned later that Gabriella had ventured out to the street when a vendor moved down the street selling vegetables and fine young fryers from a coop in the back of his flat bed wagon. She had purchased the three remaining hens and bargained for the coop, asking the vendor to put it in the back yard.

They dined on delicious stewed chicken and dumplings. Kirby was delighted. "You're a most amazing lady, Gabriella! I don't think I want to take you to Angelique Dupree after all."

She burst into a lilting gale of laughter and Kirby thought she looked exotically beautiful. She'd obviously found some clothing in the valises he'd brought home. She wore huge gold hoop earrings and her dress was a delicate coral.

Gabriella was in very high spirits for she had all the beautiful clothes she'd thought she'd lost forever and some jewelry she'd felt very sad about losing. How she had worked to earn these few luxuries for the last five years!

She'd purchased the chickens and coop from the vendor with a coin from her reticule. That one gold coin had bought the chickens, coop, and a nice supply of vegetables.

After the meal was over and Kirby had seen that his father was in bed for the night, the two of them cleaned up the kitchen and went out on the front step to sit in the darkness and talk.

Kirby's husky voice was filled with sincerity and emotion. "I can never tell you what joy you've brought to this house in the last two days, Gabriella. My father looks better than he has in years."

"Oh, thank you, Kirby. I would like to think that was true."

"Well, it is. I'm not a guy for sweet talk unless I mean it. The truth is, Gabriella—damn it, I don't want you to leave!"

Gabriella was shaken. But she knew that as much as she wanted exactly what he wanted, it was impossible.

She took his huge hand in hers. "Oh, Kirby, I could so easily say that I would be the happiest woman in the world to stay right here with you but you must know that it can't be. I'm—I'm a quadroon!"

"I know that, Gabriella, but you've made me happy—happier than I've been in a long time, so why should that matter?" The look on his face told her he meant it.

She leaned over to rest her head on his broad shoulder as she sighed, "It doesn't matter to me either but would you be able to tolerate the gossip and ridicule? I couldn't do that to you, Kirby."

"Test me, Gabriella. Don't leave me yet. I'll get word to Angelique if this is what you wish but stay here with me a while longer."

"This I'll promise, Kirby. I'll stay with you for a while if it would make you happy," she said as she tilted her head to look up at him.

"It would make me very happy, Gabriella," he murmured as he took her hand and gently kissed it. Gabriella loved the gentleness of this man who was in no hurry to persuade her to share his bed. Kirby

Murphy was a most unusual man.

"I could not be happier than I am right here with you, Kirby Murphy, and here I shall stay."

Gabriella was convinced that fate was finally going to be kind!

It was to little Nat's advantage that Francois and Paulo had a difficult time locating the fierce giant, Desmond, whom Francois always hired to do distasteful jobs so his own hands would not be sullied.

They had to go to several places before he was finally spotted. Because of his massive size it didn't take long to spy him.

Long before Francois and Paulo returned to the house, Nat had attended to the buggy and bay and delivered the food to the newly appointed cook. In fact, he had curled up in one of the empty stalls to take a short nap when he heard the two men returning.

The last time Desmond's services were called upon was when he took care of the two men hired to abduct Angelique Dupree. They had not obeyed his very specific orders to put no marks on her beautiful flesh. Now, he'd like to be the one putting some marks on that satiny flesh. Never had he allowed a woman to get under his skin as she had and it could have cost him his life.

But the need for Desmond's services was not for Angelique Dupree but for Gabriella. Desmond would recognize her immediately if he saw her and Francois knew she had to be somewhere in New Orleans.

Never would he have suspected her to play him for a fool by running away. That was going to cost her dearly. He'd given Desmond orders to find her and kill her. He'd say one thing about that big ugly giant; he always carried out an order and earned his fee.

As they prepared to leave the stable, Nat heard Francois saying to Paulo, "That bitch should have known better. Desmond will find her and when he does she won't look too pretty. I was too nice to her and got her to thinking that she wasn't a servant any more."

"Gabriella never acted like a servant. Always walked around with that head of hers held so high and mighty," Paulo remarked. He, too, had considered her one beautiful woman as all of the men did who were associated with LaTour.

What little Nat heard was enough to make him tremble with fear. He had to let Gabriella know that Desmond had been hired to kill her but he could do nothing until tomorrow. As soon as it was daylight he had to get to Kirby and warn him about Francois' plans for the beautiful Gabriella.

Little Nat shuddered to think about what Desmond could do to her lovely face and body if he found her. He was a vile monster who enjoyed inflicting pain. Gabriella could not fall prey to him!

Nat didn't sleep all night just thinking about this evil plot of Francois LaTour's.

More than ever Gabriella was in danger and Nat had to do what he could to keep her from being harmed.

Chapter Thirty-six

Scott swaggering through the shop doors was about the best sight Kirby could have seen. "Was beginning to wonder if I had to get in my canoe and come to the bayou to tell you my good news."

"So wait no longer 'cause here I am," Scott declared as he walked over to where Kirby was working on one of the horses.

"Gabriella—you won't have to go to Pointe a la Hache. She's right here in New Orleans," Kirby declared with a smile.

"How do you know?"

" 'Cause she's been at the house with Pa and me for the last three days." He went on to explain to Scott how it had all come about. His pal was slightly stunned, but pleasantly so when he finished telling him everything.

"God, I got to ride out to the Duprees right now to tell Angelique. She'll be so happy to hear this." It mattered not to Scott that he'd taken the brief leave of the fishing boat just long enough to come up to the tobacco shop for his father and had just intended to say a quick hello to Kirby.

Before Scott could ask for the loan of a horse,

Kirby offered one and Scott wasted no more time in conversation.

He spurred the horse into a fast gallop toward Old Cypress Road and as he was riding toward the Dupree estate he realized this would give him the perfect opportunity to invite Angelique to Mimi's celebration.

The sight of the handsome O'Roarke galloping up on the horse as she was out in the garden was enough to make Angelique lift her skirt so she could run to meet him. He saw her running across the grounds as he was leaping off the horse. He, too, darted hastily toward her and neither of them cared who saw them when they met. Scott lifted her in his arms to plant a kiss on her lips and swung her around. "Oh, Angelique! Gabriella—she's back! She's away from LaTour," he exclaimed, explaining that she was safe with his friend, Kirby, and how it had happened.

"So that's why she came here the other day wanting to see me! I was gone so I've been praying she would return but she didn't. From what you've told me she was on her way here when they were forced to stop by your friend's smitty shop. Lucky for her they did."

Oh, how glad she was to know that Gabriella was away from Francois and in safe surroundings.

"I can't wait to see her, Scott," she exclaimed, her eyes shining.

"And you will very soon. As a matter of fact, you're invited to a celebration in the bayou. It's Mimi's birthday celebration. Will you come with me?"

"Nothing could stop me. I'll be delighted," she promised.

A broad smile came to his face, "Oh, Angelique— nothing's going to keep me from you as long as that's what you want."

"I'll always want that, Scott. You surely must know that!"

"That's all I need to hear. I wish I could linger longer but old Justin is thinking that I left the boat just to go to the tobacco shop. I happened to stop to say hello to Kirby and that's when he told me about what had happened with Gabriella. I was really stunned by his news. I couldn't go back to the boat until I rode out here to give you the good news."

"Oh, I'm glad you did!"

"I figure that Justin will invite Kirby to their shindig so Gabriella might just be coming with him. That will be a happy reunion. I'll be here at five to get you, Angelique, but waiting for Saturday is going to seem like forever."

She smiled up at him, "Tomorrow is Friday, Scott."

"I know but it's still going to seem like forever," he declared. "A kiss to keep me until I see you at five, eh?"

She reached up on tiptoe to meet his lips and her arms encircled his neck. He felt the warm softness of her body pressed against him. His whole being ached to linger longer and love her as he so desperately wanted to do.

"Oh, God, Angelique!" he moaned huskily for it was agony to force himself to release her. He reluctantly turned to go back to the horse but he called back, "Saturday evening at five!"

She smiled and gave him a reassuring nod. Excitedly, she went back through the gardens and up the veranda to the house. Going to Mimi's party Saturday night was far more exciting than the Benoit's party and she wanted to look through her wardrobe for just the right dress. She wanted to look pretty for Scott but it could not be too fancy or frilly.

When she had gone over all the things hanging in her closet none seemed right for the occasion, so she immediately made plans to go shopping for a simple frock for herself and a gift for Mimi. She sent word to Zachariah that she wished him to take her to town.

An hour later, she bounced down the steps looking as beautiful as the pink roses in her mother's garden. In her hand was a pink parasol that matched her dress — she chose not to wear a bonnet.

Zachariah gave her a warm greeting as he helped her into the carriage. "Nice afternoon to go shopping. Now where will we be going, mademoisell?" he asked as she settled on the seat.

"I'll just have to direct you, Zachariah, because I don't know the name of the little boutique," she told him.

When they arrived in the city she began to direct him toward the side street where she'd seen the dress she was looking for in a shop window. Oh, if only it was still there!

"That's the street, Zachariah. Turn right here!" she called out and he did as she'd requested.

"Right here. Stop right here, Zachariah!" she told him anxiously for the little floral cotton dress was still on display. The bodice was a soft white voile with two tiers of ruffles lining the scooped neckline. It was sleeveless but the ruffles covered part of the arm.

She dashed into the shop and asked the young clerk if she might see the dress in the window. Elsa, the young clerk, quickly told her, "Oh, we've some new things you might wish to see, mademoiselle."

"No, it's this dress I'm interested in," Angelique replied firmly.

Elsa would have suspected this young lady to want something fancier like the dress she was wearing. But she took the frock from the form and handed it to Angelique. To her delight, it was her size.

"Yes, I'll take it and I have to buy a gift for a friend before I leave," she told the young lady. Elsa began making suggestions. "Oh, I have some beautiful lace shawls that just arrived today. There are three different colors. I have only one black one left but there are some in white and ecru."

Angelique asked to see the ecru shawl. She thought it would be perfect for Mimi with her coloring. By the time she left the boutique, she'd purchased the dress and an ecru lace shawl and tortoiseshell comb for Mimi. She was very pleased as she came out of the shop ready for Zachariah to take her home.

"Mademoiselle Angelique, you seem to be glowing with happiness today and that makes old Zachariah happy too," he told her as he helped her into the carriage.

"I am, Zachariah," she confessed. As they drove back home she told him about Scott's visit and his good news. She even told him about the celebration she was attending with Scott.

"Saturday night in the bayou, eh?" The old black man raised a skeptical eyebrow for she could only see his back. He had grave doubts that Maurice Dupree would give his approval.

"Yes, and I'm so excited."

Zachariah had the urge to tell her that she better

294

not get too excited for she might end up disappointed, but he remained silent.

He feared that as soon as she mentioned all this to her father that radiant look on her face would suddenly be gone.

Simone had returned from an appointment to find Angelique gone and the only information she could get from the house servants was that her daughter had ordered Zachariah to drive her somewhere.

She could not argue with Maurice about the fact that Angelique had surely changed. There would have been a time when she would have left a note telling her where she was going. Now she did as she pleased, it seemed.

But Angelique's jaunt into New Orleans had not taken more than an hour so Simone did not have to wait too long before she saw the carriage rolling up the drive. The sight of it made her heave a deep sigh of relief and she wondered if she would ever get over the fear that some awful thing was going to happen to her daughter again.

When Angelique entered the house she was prepared to go directly upstairs but her mother summoned her from the parlor. As she entered with the packages in her arms, Simone commented that she did not know that she was going shopping.

"Nor did I until this afternoon. Scott came by this morning to bring me the wonderful news that Gabriella is safe. Isn't that wonderful, mother?"

"Oh yes, dear," Simone responded casually. "But how would that have caused you to go shopping?"

Angelique enthusiastically told her about the celebration Scott had invited her to attend. "I wanted a simple frock to wear. They don't dress that fancy back in the bayou. And I wanted to get Mimi a little gift."

Simone wondered if her daughter had taken leave of her senses. Maurice Dupree would never agree to such a thing. "Darling, a trip into the bayou with a young man just isn't proper."

"Oh, it wasn't proper that Scott and I were all alone when he came to Pointe a la Hache and we traveled up that river. We were unescorted when he brought me back. Don't you realize that my being kidnapped sets me apart from other girls my age and our little circle of society? Nothing can change that back to where it was before."

Before Simone could say anything Angelique had gathered up her packages and marched out of the room. Every word she'd said was true and Simone knew it but she'd never get Maurice to agree.

The evening was not going to be a pleasant one, she suspected.

Upstairs Angelique was thinking the same thing but she was not going to allow either of them to spoil the joy consuming her this evening. Her dear friend Gabriella was here, free at last from Francois LaTour, and soon she would be seeing her. Saturday night she was going to be with the man she loved, enjoying a festive occasion with her bayou friends. Her parents could not deny her this and if they tried she would have to defy them. Nothing could stop her from going with Scott.

When she joined her parents later for the evening meal she knew her mother had not mentioned their conversation for her father's mood was too pleasant. She knew it would not remain that way for the entire evening. Amazingly, it did for Angelique did not mention anything about her plans and obviously her mother had decided not to say anything yet.

Simone had her reasons for not telling Maurice. Something told her that nothing would stop Angelique from doing exactly as she wished despite any ultimatum Maurice laid down. She wanted to delay the terrible explosion for as long as possible.

She knew it was going to happen the minute she or Angelique told him. Maurice could be such an unbending man that he might do something he'd later regret.

For Angelique, Friday was an endless day for she was counting the hours until Saturday at five when Scott would be coming to get her.

Justin and Scott had been so busy that the day went by swiftly. They'd sold all of their fish and their pockets were filled with money. They were in the best of spirits as they secured the fishing boat to go up the street to buy Mimi a birthday gift.

Justin found a pair of creme leather slippers that he knew would delight her. Scott couldn't find anything in that shop so he suggested that they go a little farther up the street. In the jeweler's window, Scott spotted a delicate gold cross and he remembered how Mimi was always admiring the one his mother wore. "What about me getting that cross for Mimi's birthday, Justin?"

"Needless to say, she'd love it, Scott, but you don't have to do that. Something simple will please Mimi, knowing that you thought of her."

"My expenses are covered after today and I want to do it. She's deserving of a fine reward on her birthday," Scott smiled, urging Justin to go in with him.

When he left the jewelry shop, he'd also made another purchase. He bought the gold cross for Mimi and a gold locket for Angelique.

Justin laughed lightheartedly and told him that they'd better get back to the boat and head for the bayou before he spent all his money.

"I'm ready now," Scott laughed as he broke into a fast gait.

Gabriella spent the entire day in a state of bliss due to Kirby telling her last night that they were invited to a party down in the bayou and that she would be reunited with Angelique.

She'd had a girlish enthusiasm all day about the thought of seeing Angelique again and what she would wear to accompany Kirby to his friend's home. The only thing she wished was that she had a gift to take to this Mimi whose birthday they were going to celebrate.

She started going through the valises that Kirby had finally managed to get to the house, and she found what she had been looking for. The three dainty handkerchiefs edged with delicate French lace would be a perfect gift.

Tom Murphy watched her as she busied herself in the house all day. He was glad to see her cheerfully humming a tune as she went about what had become her daily routine.

The cottage had not been so clean since Mary Murphy had died and all the good meals Gabriella had prepared had to be the reason for Tom's renewed strength.

It was time the young lady got away from the cottage to enjoy some free time after all the cleaning, cooking, and washing she'd done.

Kirby's spirits were as high as hers until little Nat showed up at the shop to tell him the latest news about what he'd overheard Francois discussing with Paulo.

"Tell Mademoiselle Gabriella to watch out. She knows that Desmond and he would recognize her on sight, Kirby. She knows what a mean son-of-a-gun he is. You tell her what I said." Like a phantom, he was gone and Kirby knew that Nat had placed himself in jeopardy again by coming.

He thought about many things as he worked the rest of the afternoon. Should he say anything to Gabriella tonight? He decided he'd do nothing to destroy the gay mood she was in about going to the party with him.

Should he talk to Scott about her staying in the bayou for a while until some time passed?

By the time he left the shop to go home, he knew he wasn't going to leave her in the bayou. He wanted her with him!

Chapter Thirty-seven

Kirby knew he'd made the right decision to keep Nat's news to himself after he'd been home for a few hours. Gabriella's face was radiantly beautiful tonight and he wanted her to have this happiness.

It wasn't purely selfish on his part that he wanted her with him. As he saw it, Francois LaTour knew about Scott O'Roarke so Desmond could be stalking him and it could lead him to the bayou.

Desmond knew nothing about him nor did Francois LaTour. As Kirby saw it, she was much safer at his cottage. He was going to tell her about what little Nat had said so she would be aware of the threat but it was not going to be until they were coming back from the party. He only prayed that little Nat hadn't been followed.

Rarely did he give himself a holiday from the shop but tomorrow, he was. He wanted to buy a gift for Justin's wife and there was something he wished to purchase for Gabriella.

He told Gabriella that he was not going to work the next morning but he would be doing errands. Gabriella knew the day would go slowly until she and Kirby were in his canoe paddling down the bayou.

By noon, Kirby had returned to the cottage with gifts for Mimi and Gabriella. He was proud of the little teakwood trinket box he'd selected for Justin's wife. "I figure she isn't a lady who gets too much luxury or little pretties, as my mom used to call things like this."

"It's exquisite, Kirby. You made a fine choice. She'll be thrilled," Gabriella exclaimed as she examined the box.

"Well, this is for you and I hope you like it," he said as he handed her a small package containing a frosty white lace head scarf.

Gabriella caressed the delicate lace and thanked him. But he had to know that she always wore a kerchief like a turban. She never wore a scarf.

"You can wear it around your neck, Gabriella, but tonight until we get into the bayou wear it — wear it for me. Take your kerchief with you to wear later but down on that dock please wear this. You're so distinctively stunning and I don't want to attract attention as we depart. It's for your sake I'm asking you to do this."

She ached to reach over and kiss him but she didn't. Never had she had a man concern himself so about her welfare and in that moment she knew that she'd love Kirby Murphy until the day she died.

"Oh, Kirby, I'll be happy to wear your beautiful scarf but I'll take my kerchief so you'll know it's me you're with tonight."

Kirby laughed, "I would know I was with you with or without the kerchief or scarf, don't you know that, Gabriella?"

"I would wish it to be that way, Kirby," she said smiling up at him.

"Well, that's the way it is."

If Tom Murphy had not come wobbling into the parlor where the two of them were sitting, Gabriella could have sworn that Kirby was about to bend down to kiss her. She yearned desperately for his lips to meet hers.

Gabriella left them in the parlor to go back to the bedroom to put her new lace scarf with the gown she planned to wear. With a large comb, the white scarf would have the effect of a mantilla. How perfect it would be with the bright yellow frock trimmed with white lace she was wearing to the party.

But she still left the bright yellow kerchief there on the bed with her reticule. Always, she wore the massive gold hoop earrings and six gold bangle bracelets on her right arm. They were the first jewelry she'd ever owned and, even though it had been Francois who'd given them to her, she loved them.

Before she began to bathe and dress for the evening, she served old Tom his dinner and Kirby got him into bed. What neither of them realized was that Tom did not usually lie in his bed after he was tucked in after dinner. He sat up and read as he puffed on his pipe; he didn't find the need to sleep as much as he used to and he thanked Gabriella for that.

He was also walking around the cottage more during the day — lively conversations with the nice young lady not only entertained him but filled many empty hours. He had a lot to thank Gabriella for!

Gabriella took extra time to primp before the mirror for she wanted Kirby to be proud of her as she stood by his side to meet his friends.

After she slipped into her yellow gown, she sat before the mirror and instinctively reached for the kerchief to flip it around her head. She laughed at herself as she tossed it back on the bed. It took a couple of attempts before she got the high comb holding the lace scarf exactly as she wanted it. Finally, she was pleased with the reflection in the mirror. She gathered up her reticule and the kerchief and as she started out the door, picked up her gift for Mimi.

Twilight was gathering and Kirby had planned it that way even though Scott had told him he was picking Angelique up at five. Kirby didn't want to get down to the river that early.

Angelique had been ready and waiting long before Scott was to arrive. Her simple gown with its white voile top and brilliantly flowered skirt looked very attractive. She'd rushed down to the gardens to find a scarlet hibiscus and pinned it in her hair.

On the bed beside her scarlet silk reticule was Mimi's gift. She went back to her dressing table to dab some toilet water behind her ears and at her throat; now there was nothing to do but sit impatiently by the window so she could see Scott when he came.

She looked at the clock—it was four-thirty and she thought if she was lucky she might be gone when her father arrived home. She prayed that she would be.

Then she remembered it was Saturday and she'd not be gone for he always got home earlier. She'd already faced the worst possibility—that he might forbid her to leave the house with Scott. But she knew she would go anyway despite what he might threaten. This night meant too much to her.

Every five minutes seemed like five hours as she stared out the window. Nervously she kept getting up and looking in the mirror to see that she looked as pretty as she wanted to look.

At the moment she was pacing back and forth, Scott was at the livery where he knew the owner, Enos Harley. He'd struck a deal for the loan of one of his buggies in exchange for a nice package of fish. It was one time he did not ask to borrow Kirby's mare for he could hardly expect Angelique to ride with him that way.

Enos was more than willing to oblige him for Scott had brought enough fish to feed his family for a couple of nights. He had always admired the young man who'd taken over for his dad and worked so energetically to keep the O'Roarke family out of debt.

Now that Scott had the buggy, he was ready to travel down Old Cypress Road to get Angelique. He still had to face the fact that Angelique might not be coming with him. She had told him nothing would stop her but Scott was convinced Maurice Dupree would try.

He was prepared to face Maurice but would Angelique be able to stand up to her father if he flatly refused to allow her to leave the house? Scott hoped she would because if she couldn't, then any future for them would be utterly hopeless.

As his buggy traveled down the road, he did not know that another buggy was trailing behind him about a quarter of a mile—carrying Maurice Dupree.

Angelique recognized Scott as he pulled into the long drive. His black hair was blown over his forehead as the buggy moved swiftly to the front entrance. She laughed gaily as she jumped up to rush downstairs. He had arrived before her father and nothing could have pleased her more.

As she rushed down the hall toward the front door, Simone was sitting in the parlor awaiting her husband's arrival. She called out but Angelique did not stop as she wanted to be the one to greet him.

When she flung open the door before he'd had a chance to knock and she looked so breathtakingly beautiful, he began to breathe easier.

"Well, are you ready, angel?"

"I'm ready!" she declared, her reticule and gift in her hand.

Simone had moved into the hall to see the two young people at the door. She came up behind her daughter. "Angelique, you know your father has not been told of this. I didn't tell him for your sake but he'll be home any time and he's going to be furious."

Angelique patted her mother's shoulder. "I thank you for that, Momma. I'm doing nothing wrong, just going to see and enjoy my friends. If this makes Poppa furious then so be it!"

She bent over to kiss her mother and assure her it would be all right. Simone watched as Scott helped Angelique up to the buggy seat, but she also saw her husband's gig enter the drive. As he pulled up by the side of Scott's buggy, Simone saw the look on Maurice's face. She couldn't hear their conversation but she could see the fury on Maurice's face, flushed with anger.

As Scott's buggy began to pull away she heard Maurice roaring like a lion to his daughter, "Then why don't you just stay there with your bayou friends!"

Simone felt sick. For a moment she felt so faint that her hand clutched the casing of the doorway. After she had steadied herself, she moved back to the parlor.

By the time she had taken her seat, she was prepared for Maurice as he came through the door. He reacted exactly as she'd suspected he would. Like a raging bull, he entered the parlor.

"Did you know of this, Simone?" he demanded.

"I did," she declared with an air of boldness. "But all your ranting and raving would not have stopped her, Maurice, so I sought to spare you both."

"I—I find it hard to understand you lately, Simone!" he snapped.

"And we both know why, don't we, Maurice? I'm facing the truth which you find hard to accept. If it was Louis Benoit she was with, you wouldn't be this riled."

He could not reply for he knew she was right. He went to the liquor chest to pour himself a drink, but Simone had more to say and she did not hesitate. "I hope you don't live to regret what you said to your daughter, Maurice. She might just take you up on staying in the bayou with the people she considers her friends."

She rose from her chair to walk out of the room.

His wife's words had a tremendous impact on Maurice as he sank down in the chair with the brandy.

Why had he not bridled that caustic tongue of his? He knew the answer. It was because he could not tolerate his daughter defying him as she'd done constantly since she returned from that place, Pointe a la Hache.

Oh, how he wished he could take those words back! How much wiser Simone was. He saw her look of disfavor as she left the parlor. His whole world seemed to be crumbling and he knew not what to do or how to stop it.

Never had Maurice Dupree felt so helpless! No longer did he control his household as he always had in the past.

Chapter Thirty-eight

By the time Scott and Angelique got to the dock and boarded the *Bayou Queen* the sun was low in the sky. Although it was late summer, there was a cool breeze once they started moving. As New Orleans receded in the distance she noticed several pirogues trailing behind them.

"Are those people from the bayou, Scott, on their way home?" she asked.

"Well, at least some are. I recognize a few familiar faces back there," he said as he glanced at the dugout canoes that served people in the bayou as a means to get to New Orleans.

"Will there be a big crowd at Mimi's party?"

He turned and grinned, "There'll be a fair gathering of friends and neighbors. My mom and pa will be there. You know Justin and Mimi. Kirby will be there with Gabriella and he'll finally get to meet you. He's been most curious about Mademoiselle Angelique Dupree," he teased playfully.

"And I'm anxious to meet him. I like him already for what he's done for Gabriella."

He was glad to see that her mood seemed gay and lighthearted—he had feared the encounter with her father might have dampened her spirits. If it did, she seemed to have swept it all behind her.

He was sorry it had to happen that way but it did not surprise him. It was obvious since the day he took Angelique home that Maurice Dupree's seemingly cordial manner would quickly vanish. Once his daughter was safely at home, Dupree seemed ready to dismiss Scott.

Madame Dupree had remained friendly but she acted a little restrained around her husband.

"Happy you got to come with me, honey. It's going to be a wonderful evening. Justin is roasting a whole pig for the occasion and that sauce Mimi makes is like nothing you've ever tasted. Be prepared — it's hot!" he said laughing.

Twilight was on them but Angelique could still see and remember some of the bends and turns of the stream, for it had been daylight when she and Scott had left to bring her back to New Orleans. She knew that they were not too far from Justin's pier.

It was about this time that Kirby and Gabriella were getting into his canoe to take the same route Scott and Angelique had just traveled. He tried not to be too obvious as he constantly glanced around and over his shoulder as they walked from his cottage to the dock. He began to relax some time later as they left the city in the distance.

"It's a beautiful evening, Kirby."

"Not half as beautiful as you tonight, Gabriella. Don't know whether you look prettier with that lace scarf or a bright kerchief," he said. He vowed that this Desmond would have to kill him first before he harmed her.

He spotted some of the pirogues a distance ahead of him but none was behind, which suited Kirby just fine.

They would arrive at Justin's just about the time it got dark. He knew there would be flambeaus by the pier and along the pathway to guide his guests through the darkness — he'd been to Justin's festive get-togethers before.

By the time Kirby had guided his canoe into the deep of the bayou, Scott was helping Angelique off the boat. He thought how beautiful she looked this evening with the huge red blossom tucked at the side of her head. She seemed like a different woman tonight. This was nothing like the fancy gowns or finely-tailored riding ensembles he'd always seen her wearing. If it was possible, she was more beautiful than ever in her simple cotton frock.

They walked up the pathway lit by torches, hearing the sounds of laughter and talking as they approached Justin's cottage. Acadians were a happy lot — like the Irish, Scott thought.

Three or four couples were already there and the first to rush up to greet them were Justin and Mimi. "Oh, I was hoping you'd come, Angelique," Mimi declared excitedly as she gave her a warm embrace.

"I wouldn't have missed it for anything, Mimi. Happy birthday," Angelique said smiling as she handed her the gift. Scott gave Mimi a hug and a kiss as he gave her his gift. In his pocket he had the gift he'd bought for Angelique.

They walked over to where Scott's father was sitting in a chair. He certainly didn't look like he was ailing, dressed up in his bright shirt and best twill pants. Kate O'Roarke was across the grounds visiting with one of her neighbors but when she saw that her son had arrived she dashed over to greet Angelique. Without any hesitation, she threw her arms around her. "Mercy, if you aren't a beautiful sight. Prettier

310

than that flower in your hair, child," she declared.

"Good to see you again too, Madame O'Roarke," Angelique greeted her warmly. Kate supposed that in time she'd get used to being called 'madame.'

By the time Gabriella and Kirby approached the pier, Angelique had met everyone. She swore that there couldn't be nicer, friendlier people anywhere than the ones she'd met in this bayou.

She drank the wine that Mimi and Justin had made and she could tell the pig roasting in the pit was going to be delicious from the aroma. Long planks were laid over sawhorses as tables and Mimi had draped them with tablecloths. This provided enough room to seat all the guests for the feast she and Justin had been preparing for days. Cakes and pies had been baked ahead of time; fresh corn simmered in a big cast iron pot; jars of relish Mimi had canned were on the table for her guests to sample as they wished.

Varieties of freshly baked loaves of bread were on the table and Kate O'Roarke busily helped Mimi put the finishing touches to the meal as most of the guests were there. Mimi's children were romping and playing with some of the neighbors' children who'd come with their parents.

Angelique was amused as she watched the easygoing Justin reprimand the rambunctious children who had almost knocked over the pitcher of cider. All the time she watched the kids scamper around the table and chairs where couples were sitting, her eyes kept scanning back toward the pathway for Gabriella. She leaned over to Scott to whisper, "You suppose that they aren't coming?"

"They'll be here. Kirby figured it would be safer if they didn't go to the dock until dark. Kirby is a pretty sly fox so he would be smart enough to know it wouldn't do for her to be seen by someone who would recognize her and run to LaTour."

"I hadn't thought about that," she confessed. Gabriella was free but yet she wasn't.

As Scott had told her, a short time later Angelique saw the stately figure of Gabriella moving up the pathway with a tall, husky man who had to be Kirby.

She was stunning in her bright yellow dress and her usual matching kerchief. Angelique lifted her skirt so she could rush across the grounds to greet her, leaving Scott back where they'd been standing. As he watched her go, he realized the bond that existed between these two even though their time together had been brief. A friendship like theirs was rare!

The two embraced as Kirby stood feeling very much like his pal, Scott. When they finally released one another, Angelique turned to Kirby. "You must be Kirby and I thank you from the bottom of my heart for what you've done for my friend, Gabriella."

"Been my pleasure, Miss Angelique. I know that's who you've got to be," Kirby said with a broad smile. Now he could see why Scott lost his heart to this little miss with the glorious black hair. She was so pretty that any man would find himself staring at her.

Scott ambled over to join them and laughed when he saw that Angelique and Gabriella were already engrossed in private conversation. He suggested that he and Kirby leave them for a few moments before they made the rounds to introduce Gabriella and Kirby to the other guests.

Angelique and Gabriella were pleased to have a

little time together. The two men ambled a short distance away to have their own private discussion and Kirby told him about the latest development. "LaTour's back in New Orleans and little Nat brought me the news today that he's hired that mean sonofabitch, Desmond, to kill Gabriella. He knows her, having been at LaTour's house various times, or so little Nat told me." Kirby added that was why he'd left the city late.

"Maybe Gabriella should just stay here in the bayou, Kirby?"

"Thought about that but then I got to thinking that he knows of you but he doesn't know me. Think she'd best stay with me."

"What does she think?" Scott asked.

"Haven't told her yet. I didn't want to spoil tonight for her. I'll tell her when we're back home but I wanted her to have this night without that hanging over her head, Scott."

"I understand, Kirby. I'd have done the same thing."

They began to walk back over to the two ladies, who were still talking.

Together the four of them walked over to introduce Gabriella to Justin and Mimi, as well as Scott's parents. Now that all their guests were there, Justin invited everyone to come to the table to eat.

It was a real feast on the grounds of Justin and Mimi's cottage in the splendor of the torchlights. It was nothing like anything Angelique had ever experienced before and she knew whatever price she had to pay because her parents had opposed her coming here was worth it.

Everyone around the table enjoyed the good food Justin and Mimi had so lovingly prepared. To Angelique, preparation for parties was done by servants in the kitchen when her mother or Madame Benoit had social affairs. But there were no servants in Justin's house.

When everyone had their fill, Justin stood up to give his wife a toast and wish her a very happy birthday. Then everyone cheered, insisting that Mimi open her gifts. Mimi eagerly obliged and it was Justin's gift she opened first. The pretty slippers delighted her so much that she put them on immediately. Kate O'Roarke had made four new aprons for her. When she opened Angelique's gift, she sighed with delight, draping the lace shawl around her shoulders and tucking the comb in her hair. Justin had not seen her so happy for a long time.

Kirby knew he'd gotten her the right gift when he watched her gently caress the little trinket box. Mimi was overcome by the fact that a young lady who'd never met her was so thoughtful: she passed around the lovely lace-edged handkerchiefs for everyone to see and thanked Gabriella for being so nice.

One of her neighbors had brought a whole smoked ham and another had crocheted an afghan in lovely pastel colors. Her close friend, Yvonne, had made a pretty pillow with needlepoint on the cover.

Scott's gift brought tears to her eyes for she had wanted a gold cross like the one Kate always wore around her neck. "Oh, Scott," she sighed, her voice cracking.

She knew that this would be a night she would never forget. As her guests headed for the pathway to board their canoes, she bade them all a heartfelt farewell.

Kirby announced to Scott that he was going to

leave. "Pa's been on his own for awhile so I need to get home. Stop by when you get a chance."

"We'll see each other soon, Gabriella," Angelique promised. The two of them gave each other a warm embrace.

Justin urged Scott to let him escort his folks home since Scott had the long trek back into the city and Scott accepted. He and Angelique were the last to take their leave but Mimi made a point of telling Angelique she must come more often. Angelique laughed, "If I could ride a horse to get here instead of taking a canoe I could come more often."

Mimi told her, "Catch the fishing boat and stay for a whole weekend with me on Friday, Angelique."

Angelique could only nod, for Scott was rushing her down the pathway. The hour was not late but by the time they went up the bayou and got to the city there was still the few miles to go down Old Cypress Road in the buggy. Not that this mattered to him, but he didn't know what to expect from Maurice Dupree.

Reluctantly, Angelique said her farewells. She had enjoyed herself too much and it was only when she and Scott were aboard the *Bayou Queen* that she began to think of what she might have to face at home.

Scott sensed the sudden quiet mood consuming her and reached into his pocket to take out the locket. "I've something to give you so you can always remember tonight."

Her dark eyes looked up at him. "You know I'm sorry to see it end, don't you?"

"I know and soon there won't have to be an end, Angelique." All the time he was talking he was preparing to place the gold locket around her neck. The moonlight seemed to gleam down on the heart-

315

shaped locket as Angelique saw what was in his hand.

He gave her a boyish grin. "I'm giving you my heart forever and ever, Angelique Dupree."

"Oh, Scott—don't say that if you don't truly mean it!" she sighed.

"There's only one thing that makes me hesitate to ask you to be my wife and that is that I'm not a wealthy man. But I love you as no other man would ever love you."

"And I love you, Scott. It doesn't matter to me that you aren't wealthy," she declared convincingly.

"To be my little bayou queen would be enough to satisfy you, Angelique?" His blue eyes searched her lovely face.

"Just to be with you and have your love is all I ask. I could love no man as I love you, Scott O'Roarke," she murmured softly as his strong arms encircled her.

Holding her in his arms after what she had just said, Scott didn't care whether he took her home tonight or ever!

He was damned well tempted not to return to New Orleans but he wanted neither of them to have any regrets later.

Part four

The Splendor of Autumn

Chapter Thirty-nine

It wasn't a pleasant evening at the Dupree home as Simone and Maurice sat at the dining table nibbling at their food. They made no conversation so the room was shrouded in deadly silence.

The longer Simone looked in her husband's direction and saw his sullen face the more her sympathy went to Angelique. She hoped she was having a wonderful evening and that her father had not dampened her merry mood.

After dinner, they retired to the parlor; Simone had decided if he didn't wish to talk to her, she had no need to talk to him either. She took a piece of needlepoint out of her sewing basket and started to work. Maurice sauntered out of the room without saying that he was going for a stroll in the gardens.

The more Maurice thought about it, the more he was vexed with Simone. He found her calm, casual air hard to understand. He would have appreciated it more if she had been as disturbed and angry as he was. Damned if he could understand the woman!

This was their daughter who'd gone unescorted to a place in the bayou where they knew nothing about the people she was going to see. He would have expected Simone to be distraught about Angelique going to the bayou after dark through waters infested with snakes and alligators.

As his daughter had changed, so had his wife. He faulted Simone for Angélique's reckless behavior.

Simone would have been the first to admit this but she could not have told him what had sparked it. She did know it had happened when Angelique was abducted. She also knew it had made her realize that she and Maurice had allowed their lives to revolve around their daughter instead of the two of them. Now they were strangers!

Perhaps she had never thought about the time when Angelique would no longer be living under their roof; like all young ladies, there would come a day when she would marry and leave home.

When she was abducted and the house was without her, Simone felt a depth of loneliness she'd never known.

Putting aside her needlepoint long enough to pour a glass of sherry, she sighed as she thought about her husband.

Maurice had been outside for almost an hour before he returned. He went over to the liquor chest to pour himself a nightcap before he went on upstairs. In a gruff voice, he declared, "The hour's getting late."

"Is it? I hadn't noticed, Maurice. What time is it?"

"It's after nine," he muttered as he came over to sit down in his favorite chair.

She gave him a slow smile, "Well, that's not so late, Maurice.

"What is it with you, Simone? You don't seem the least bit concerned about Angelique. You're not like the mother you used to be, I can tell you."

"No, I'm not and for a very good reason, Maurice.

I see nothing to be worried about because she's with the young man who risked his life to rescue her. You seem to forget that. She has gone to a birthday party with friends she met some weeks ago. So tell me, Maurice what's wrong with that? What was wrong was what you said to your daughter about staying in the bayou with those friends. She might just do that and you can thank yourself for that if she does."

"So am I to assume you'd have no objections if she married this—this Irish fisherman?" Maurice bristled.

She looked at him coldly. "I pray that Angelique marries the man she loves, Maurice, and I don't care if he's a fisherman or wealthy like Louis Benoit. Look at my own grandmother, Delphine. She married a man she didn't know. He received all the money she'd brought from France and was cruel and mean. Who could blame her for taking lovers? I didn't. Perhaps you'd have found fault with that."

"What has she got to do with what I'm talking about, Simone? I don't see the connection." Maurice said impatiently.

"She's a part of me—a part of my past. Now, look at your past and your family. All French Creole families are not pure or free of sin. Look at your older brother, Jean Gabriel. Even the esteemed Dupree family had their little scandals. Remember?"

"I know that!" he snapped. "Jean Gabriel was always the black sheep. But none of that scandal would have been known had his wife not committed suicide."

"Poor Cassie would never have been driven to that if he hadn't fathered a child by a black woman. My heart went out to her—I saw the agony she was feeling, Maurice. Our daughter may not live up to your so-called conventional ways. But who knows, Maurice—she may end up happier!"

Maurice did not want to hear any more of this kind of talk so he made a hasty exit telling Simone he was going to bed. His face was twisted in agony.

Simone had a sly smile on her face—he could never face certain truths, so he always chose to walk away. Often during the last fifteen years she had thought about poor Cassie. Jean Gabriel had not lingered long in sorrow for he took a new wife six months later. But Simone had wondered about the poor black girl and the baby who had Dupree blood flowing in her veins.

Her curious nature had always wondered what that child would look like for Jean was dashingly handsome. She would be a few years older than her darling Angelique. She and Maurice had just gotten married about the time all this happened. Poor Cassie didn't find out about this until five years later so the child was a toddler by then.

But if Simone were to guess it would be that the child had had as despairing a life as her black mother. Often when their carriage was driving up Bourbon or Dumaine Street and she noticed one of the lovely quadroons, she'd wondered if one of the young women might be the daughter of her brother-in-law.

She'd also wondered if God had punished Jean Gabriel for his sins for he and his new wife had never had children their marriage had not been happy. There had been rumors that his second wife had a roving eye as she was some twenty years younger than Jean Gabriel.

By now, Simone's sherry glass was empty and she was ready to put her needlepoint aside. She went around the parlor dimming lamps. Would Angelique come home tonight, she wondered. The clock was chiming eleven. Whether she did or didn't, Simone knew it was out of her hands.

It was not easy for two young lovers like Angelique and Scott to part when he brought her to the front door. Scott was just grateful for her sake that Maurice Dupree was not standing there in a rage.

After he'd kissed her for the last time, he vowed that he would not wait so long to come to her ever again. "Now that I know you feel as I do, nothing will stop me."

He lingered until she had gone through the front door before he turned toward the buggy. By the time he got it back to the livery and then continued to the dock it was the midnight hour. He was glad tomorrow was Sunday and he didn't have to get up early. How sweet his sleep was going to be tonight—Angelique loved him as much as he loved her!

He could not have been happier as he moved through the bayou listening to the night birds calling and the splashes of alligators and fish.

It didn't matter to her that he wasn't rich. She had told him so, and what he couldn't give her materially Scott knew he could more than make up for with love.

As he made his way homeward at the midnight hour, he was also thinking about Kirby. He noticed the way Kirby's eyes were constantly on Gabriella all evening and he wondered if it was just his imagination because he was in such a romantic mood. He was sure he saw something in Kirby's eyes that made him think old Kirby was smitten. There was no denying that Gabriella was a very sultry lady. He knew one thing—he'd never known Kirby to act around a woman as he had tonight.

If he was a betting man, he'd bet he was right!

A quadroon she might be but the people of the bayou had warmly accepted her. Anyway, it wouldn't matter to Kirby, Scott mused.

It didn't surprise him to see a light still shining from the cottage window as he pulled up to the pier. He had no doubt that his mother was sitting in the parlor awaiting his return.

As he went in and saw her napping in the chair he gently admonished her. "How old am I going to have to be, Ma, before you quit sitting up until I get home?"

With a half-smile she said, "Only after you have a good wife who'll do the same, Scott O'Roarke!"

The two of them left the parlor together to go to their bedrooms. "It was a grand night, wasn't it son?" She looked up at Scott, who towered over her.

"It was a wonderful evening!" He bent down to give her a kiss on the cheek as he went on into his room.

Angelique was relieved to find the downstairs deserted and dark when she entered the front door. Quietly, she tiptoed up the steps toward her room. When she was inside she brightened the lamp so she could look in the mirror to see the gold locket Scott had placed around her neck. Her finger caressed it. He'd told her that it represented his heart which he was giving to her. She wanted to believe him and she found it hard not to because he spoke with such sincerity.

As she undressed and slipped into bed, she cared little for what tomorrow would bring for tonight had been so wonderful. She would never forget this late summer night!

So deep was her sleep that it was almost noon when she finally woke up. She was reluctant to leave the soft comfort of her bed as she flung her legs over the side.

She was certainly not eager to go downstairs for her father would be home today. But since she had to face him sooner or later, she began to dress. When she was dressed and had brushed her long hair free of tangles, she left her room.

Since she had missed breakfast, she went to the kitchen to see if the cook could serve her a light lunch. She sat in the sunny kitchen alcove instead of the dining room to eat. It had been a surprise that she could come downstairs and to the kitchen without meeting her mother or father. But as she was finishing the last bite of food, Simone did come in to find her daughter sitting alone at the table.

"I—I didn't know you were up, dear. Why didn't you let me know? We just had lunch out on the veranda." She was coming into the kitchen to tell the cook how delicious it was.

"It is delicious!" Angelique agreed, which was obvious since she'd left nothing on her plate. Simone came over to sit down at the table with her.

"Did you have a nice time, Angelique?"

"It was a wonderful evening, Momma, and it was so wonderful to see Gabriella and know she's safe. I've never known so many nice people as I know out there."

"I'm glad you enjoyed yourself so much, dear." Simone noticed the gold locket so perfectly displayed with her scooped-neck gown. "Scott give you that last night, *ma petite?*"

"Yes, Momma—isn't it pretty?"

"Very pretty, Angelique, and that was very nice of him," Simone replied.

Simone was grateful for this private moment with her daughter for it was an opportunity to let her know she did not condone her husband's harsh reprimand.

"I care for him very much, Momma. You might as well know it. I don't care that he's only a fisherman and not the type of husband Poppa had in mind for me. My husband will be my choice, not his. I don't wish to hurt him but I might have to."

"If you do, Angelique then so be it. Better Maurice be disappointed and hurt for a few weeks than for you to suffer for a lifetime because you married a man you didn't love."

Angelique embraced her mother. "Thank you, Momma. What you just said means a lot to me."

The two of them spent the next hour together and Simone listened intensely as Angelique told her about the gay evening she'd shared with Scott and his friends. There was a glow of happiness on her face and a genuine feeling for these people out on the bayou; nothing would make it any different. Maurice would have to try to understand if he didn't want to lose his daughter.

"I'd like to meet these people sometime, Angelique," Simone said, which pleased her daughter very much.

"I'd love to have you meet them—you couldn't help but like them."

The two of them would probably have talked longer except that Nicole Benoit arrived to visit

Angelique. After a few minutes of conversation, Simone excused herself so the two young girls could have privacy.

"Could we go to the gardens, Angelique? I know what big ears servants have and I really need to talk to you."

"Of course we can." She had never seen Nicole look so serious and wondered what was disturbing her.

They went out to the veranda and down the steps with Cuddles rushing out the door to join them.

When they got to the area where the fountain stood they sat on the benches. "I don't think we have to worry about anyone hearing us out here. No gardeners are working today. Now tell me, Nicole—tell me what is so serious."

"Well, I just had to talk to you before I go to meet Mark. Mother thinks I plan to visit with you this afternoon—that's why I came by here first."

"Well, you know I wouldn't give you away, Nicole."

"I know you wouldn't, Angelique. It's good to have such a friend as you. God knows, I need you right now. I'm scared for the first time in my life. I'm almost sure I'm pregnant, Angelique."

"Then you must not delay telling Mark, Nicole. I know it's his baby if you're pregnant. But are you sure?"

"I'm very sure! I've heard about all the signs and I've got all of them."

"How long have you suspected, Nicole?" Angelique asked.

Nicole confessed that she had suspected it for almost two months and had given Mark little hints. Angelique saw no signs of frivolous, flippant Nicole as she confessed, "I guess what has me so scared, Angelique, is his attitude. He didn't seem the least bit concerned and shrugged it aside. Damn, Angelique—I'm—I'm so scared."

Angelique gave her hand an assuring pat. "Go to Mark and tell him that he has a responsibility to assume, Nicole. It isn't your burden to bear alone. I would go to Scott immediately if I were in your shoes."

"I'm going to and thanks, Angelique. I needed to talk to you. Come over tomorrow and I'll tell you what happened when I talked to Mark."

"I'll see you tomorrow. It will be all right, Nicole," she said soothingly. But she wasn't so sure it would be all right. It suddenly made her realize that she, too, could be pregnant with Scott's child but she could not believe that he would react as Mark had with Nicole.

The rest of the afternoon Nicole was very much in her thoughts!

Chapter Forty

It did not matter to Angelique that her father was quiet and withdrawn during dinner just as long as he kept his caustic tongue to himself. At least she knew that her mother seemed to understand.

She knew what a prideful man he was and never more than tonight. When the meal was finally over, he said almost begrudgingly, "Well, it's nice to have you home with us tonight, Angelique."

"Thank you, Poppa." It was difficult to suppress an amused smile for she could not resist glancing over at her mother. She got the impression that she was sharing her feelings.

As the evening went on and the three of them were in the parlor, he asked more questions about the party.

"Best barbecued pork I ever ate in my life, Poppa. Justin cooked it all day long and it was delicious." She made it a point to tell him that all the cooking and labor for the celebration was done by Justin and Mimi. "They have no servants. Their ways are simple but they're happy. Their little cottages don't have luxuries like our home or the Benoits but they don't seem to need them, Poppa."

There was no comment Maurice sought to make

and Simone sat silently. Strange that he should think of something Simone had said to him almost two years ago about Angelique. She had surely seen the handwriting on the wall when their daughter had been about fourteen. She had told him that Angelique would have a streak of independence and daring about her that neither of them possessed.

He remembered that he asked her why she had said that and she'd told him that she saw traits in their daughter that reminded her of her vivacious grandmother. Simone's mother was a completely different personality and Simone was very much like her own mother, so neither of them had inherited the ways of Delphine.

Angelique had and Simone had seen it even then!

Francois LaTour would have been the first to admit that wealth could not buy happiness. He was finding that his wealth could not buy him revenge against the lovely Gabriella. Desmond had come to his house to admit that for once he had not been able to carry out Francois' orders.

"I've checked everywhere around the city and it's as if she's been swallowed up, monsieur. I'm at the point of believing that she is gone from New Orleans. It's been over a week since she left the house," he added.

Francois knew that Desmond never lied. He'd done too many jobs for him in the past for Francois to question him. He didn't have to come here tonight to say this.

"Just keep looking, Desmond. I still want her dead. More than ever, I want her dead now—the bitch took gold from my safe. I—I don't care if it takes months," Francois muttered darkly.

Desmond nodded and made an exit from Francois' study. Francois moved from his desk to the liquor chest to pour another drink.

His damnation was the day he ever set eyes on the enchanting Angelique Dupree and she cast her spell on him. Everything had gone wrong since then. More and more, Francois realized how he was suffering from the loss of Gabriella. He had not known how insidiously she'd taken charge of his life. Only after he'd returned to New Orleans to find his house in a shambles and Gabriella not there did he begin to realize just how much she did for him.

She had been a rare jewel and he had just not realized it sufficiently. As young as she was there was an air about her that made the servants of his houses respect and obey her. But she was so much more than that. Gabriella drew the admiration of his business cohorts when he'd entertained them. The woman possessed a charm and grace that made her outstanding and he was finally realizing it fully.

There were so many other things she did for him over the years and that was causing his frenzy for he knew he would never have that sort of devotion again. She was gone!

It was not only her exotic loveliness that placed her far above the ordinary servant, it was her clever, sharp mind that Francois had admired from the moment they'd met. He knew that if Angelique

331

Dupree was not his damnation then Gabriella would surely be! She knew too much about him and his business. She had to be eliminated!

It was with a heavy heart and much reluctance that Kirby made himself tell Gabriella about what little Nat had told him. After they'd got back from the bayou he'd urged her to sit on the steps with him before retiring. "I've something I've got to tell you and if I could spare you I would but I can't—damn it!"

Gabriella sat down with him and thought of a number of things that he might be going to say. "Then tell me, Kirby. I'm a big girl and I can take it," she assured him.

"Little Nat came to the shop. He'd overheard Francois and Paulo talking in the stable—they didn't know he was back there napping. Francois has hired Desmond to kill you. Little Nat says that Desmond can recognize you."

She seemed unusually calm. "Oh, yes—Desmond knows me quite well. He should for I've been there on several occasions when Francois assigned similar jobs to Desmond." The news did not shock Gabriella.

"This is why I wanted you to wear the lace scarf tonight, Gabriella. I don't want anyone recognizing you."

"I know, Kirby."

Kirby told her about Scott's offer of refuge with his folks but that he'd turned him down because Francois knew about Scott. "He doesn't know about me so I felt you'd be safer here, Gabriella. Tell me I made the right decision."

"You did, Kirby. Here is where I wish to be. My only fear is that I might put you or your father in danger. Francois can be vicious!"

Kirby admired her courage. She was the one threatened but her concern was for him and his father. Now he knew why he'd been so attracted to her and found himself falling more and more in love—she was so giving. He had only to think about the first day he'd brought her home and how she'd worked the whole afternoon to cook for him and his father. There was the attention and gentle care she'd given his father and he could swear that the old fellow had responded to it. He was better than he'd been for a long, long time.

Kirby didn't care that she was a quadroon. He had felt proud to have her standing by his side at Justin and Mimi's party. As far as Kirby was concerned, she was the most beautiful lady there.

It was not her fault that some white man had taken liberties with her mother. The sin was on that man and not Gabriella.

"You don't worry about me and Pa, Gabriella. Me or Pa would willingly lay down our lives for you. You must know by now how we both love you." His strong arm snaked around her waist.

Her almond-shaped eyes stared up at him. "Love is a very strong word, Kirby. I know that you both like me and for that I've been very grateful. I've never known such happiness as I've known here in this little cottage."

"Think you'd always feel that way, Gabriella?"

"There's nothing certain about life, Kirby. I learned that at a very early age. I live one day at a time."

"Want to live one day at a time here with me, Gabriella?"

"Are you asking me to stay here with you, Kirby?" she asked with a provocative gleam in her eye. There was a shyness about Kirby beneath his robust, husky image.

"Yes, I guess that's what I'm asking, Gabriella,' he told her in a deep bass murmur that was touched with all the emotion he felt.

Her hands went up to touch the sides of his face and her soft fingertips on his cheeks filled Kirby with a flaming desire to make love to her.

"I'll stay with you as long as you want me, Kirby."

He could no longer fight the urge to kiss her for he'd wanted to do it for so long. He drew her into his arms and his lips captured hers in a long, lingering kiss which gave Gabriella the answer: he wanted her to stay. She felt a consuming passion when he kissed her.

He immediately sensed her passion by the way she responded to his kiss. His body was consumed with a raging desire to make love to her and the way her sensuous body was pressing against him he knew she was as eager as he was.

Scooping her up in his arms, he moved through the front door and went directly to his room. Tonight, he was going to share his bed with the beautiful woman in his arms.

He knew he was not bedding a virgin and it didn't matter. She knew the art of making love to a man and Kirby had never experienced such pleasure as he did with Gabriella. She was like no other woman he'd ever made love to — her passion was as fierce as his. Her eager surrender made him feel total ecstasy.

This had to be paradise, Kirby thought, as he felt himself consumed by this woman. He knew that he'd like to stay in this state of rapture forever. He also knew something else: if Gabriella couldn't share the rest of his life then he'd go it alone. He was spoiled now—no other woman could ever take her place.

Gabriella had never known such a sweet, tender lover—but there was also a power and force in Kirby that thrilled and stirred her wildly.

Maybe she'd never experience a moment of splendor like this again in her life but she'd have tonight to remember as long as she lived. No one could take this away!

For the longest time the two of them lay there silently in one another's arms. Kirby had intended to slip out and go to his pa's room but he fell exhaustedly to sleep.

So it was with Gabriella as her eyes grew heavy. They both fell asleep before they knew it.

Old Tom Murphy had heard the two young people enter the house and try to move quietly toward Kirby's bedroom. So he had not expected his son to share his bed tonight. Old Tom would have considered him a damned fool if he had!

The truth was Tom was surprised it hadn't happened sooner!

Chapter Forty-one

As soon as she had dressed and eaten a hasty breakfast, Angelique told her mother she was going over to the Benoit's to see Nicole.

"Mercy, you two girls are keeping the path between our houses beaten down," she laughed. But she was truly glad they were such dear, close friends.

Angelique smiled. "Aren't we! Nicole has a new gown that she wants me to see, Momma," she lied. Later she was to realize how easy it was for her to do that now. A few months ago she would not have thought of lying to her mother.

But there were times when you just could not tell the truth, she thought, justifying her action. This seemed to soothe her conscience.

All the time she rode through the countryside toward the Benoits', she prayed that everything had gone as Nicole had hoped.

When she arrived at the front entrance, she turned her horse over to the young stable boy who happened to be sitting on the front steps.

A servant opened the door and invited her to come in. Angelique asked to see Nicole and the young servant girl ushered her into the parlor.

"This way, mademoiselle. I will take your message upstairs."

Angelique could not explain it but something about the servant's manner made her feel uneasy. She knew why when, a few minutes later, Madame Benoit came into the parlor.

"Good morning, Angelique. I—I'm so sorry you've ridden over this morning for nothing. Nicole is not here."

Angelique protested gently that Nicole had told her to come over this morning.

"She didn't know she would be leaving bright and early this morning when she was with you yesterday. Everything came up quite suddenly late yesterday afternoon—she left to go to her Aunt Pricilla, who is ill. Nicole is going to stay with her in Baton Rouge for a few weeks."

"I see," Angelique murmured. For the second time today she had lied for she didn't understand her friend's sudden disappearance.

Nicole's mother noticed the disturbed look on Angelique's face and she wondered if she was questioning what she'd just told her. Madame Benoit knew how close the two girls were.

"I'll—I'll tell Nicole to write to you, Angelique, if her stay in Baton Rouge is to be a long one," she said. Madame Benoit was feeling very ill at ease.

"Oh, please do, Madame Benoit," Angelique replied as she rose to leave. She tried to hide her feelings as she bade Nicole's mother a fond farewell, but she did not believe her. Madame Benoit was lying. Angelique decided to seek out Mark

Terhune, so it was not toward her home that she rode out of the Benoit drive but in the opposite direction.

For Nicole to be so hastily whisked off to Baton Rouge, Angelique knew that all had not gone well when she'd confronted Mark with the news that she was pregnant. If he had not offered to do the honorable thing, she knew that Nicole must have been in a panic when she had returned home.

It was less than a fifteen-minute ride and she had no trouble spotting the handsome trainer in the corral training one of the thoroughbreds. She rode up to the fence and addressed him, "Good morning, Mark!"

"Well, good morning, Angelique! What a nice surprise this is! What a beautiful sight you are!" His trim figure moved across the grounds to where she had reined her horse.

Angelique found him far too glib and smooth-tongued for a man who'd caused her good friend so much heartache. He certainly did not act like a man feeling any remorse. In fact, she saw a devious glint in his eyes.

She wasted no time asking him if he knew that Nicole had suddenly left for Baton Rouge.

"No, I didn't but then I have no control of what the Benoits do, now do I?" There was an arrogant look on his finely-chiseled features that Angelique did not like.

Angelique looked at Mark intensely, her dark eyes flashing. "Did Nicole come to see you yesterday?"

338

"She did," he shot back with a snap to his voice.

"And?"

"And what, Angelique? Let's not parry with each other," he declared indignantly.

"So you were told she was pregnant and you did nothing to help her, Mark?"

"Nicole knew the chance she was taking and she knew from the first that I could not offer her marriage. I told her that."

"But that didn't keep you from taking your pleasure with her, did it? You're a liar, Mark Terhune!"

He laughed huskily. "Oh, Angelique—don't be so naive. A man always takes his pleasure with a beautiful lady when he can and it doesn't mean that he'd marry her. The truth is I've a wife and a son back in Ireland."

A rage erupted in Angelique for she knew that Nicole did not know this and she could imagine how such a revelation would have devastated her friend yesterday if he finally confessed.

"Oh, Mark—you're the lowest bastard on the face of the earth! I hope you burn in hell!" she hissed as she turned her horse around. As she rode away she wondered what she could do to destroy this vicious man who'd so sorely used her friend. She wanted him to hurt as Nicole was hurting.

She could not dismiss some of the things he'd said about how a man always took his pleasure with a beautiful girl when he could. She could not believe that of Scott O'Roarke. He wasn't like

Mark. She had to believe he wasn't. He would not have been so heartless and cruel if she had gone to him as Nicole had gone to Mark to tell him she was carrying his child.

That evening Angelique left the parlor early after the dinner hour to go to her bedroom for she had a letter to write. It was to Mark's employer — she had no intention of signing it but she was going to inform him of the philanderer his trainer was and that he violated all the conventions of proper French Creole morals. He had taken advantage of the daughter of a very prominent family. Her letter stated that to preserve the fine name of her family, it would be in his best interests to take this letter seriously and investigate the trainer.

She knew of no way to help Nicole other than to seek revenge. The next day she sent the letter but she carefully avoided mentioning any name.

She also had to face her mother that afternoon when she returned — she'd told her about Nicole's sudden departure. Simone did not question her, for which Angelique was grateful.

The week seemed long to Angelique since that Monday morning when she'd gone to see Nicole and found her gone. Scott had not made an appearance since he'd brought her home from the party out on the bayou. By the end of the week Angelique found that time was hanging heavily on her hands and she yearned to seek out Gabriella. But she knew she should not from what Scott had told her. If Francois was back in New Orleans and stalking her as he had in the past, she could lead him to Gabriella. This was the last thing in the world she wanted to do.

When they were coming back to New Orleans after the party, he had told her what Kirby had confided to him and what Gabriella was yet to learn because he did not want to dampen her high spirits before the party.

He'd cautiously admonished her to be careful. She'd promised that she would but Angelique also knew that she couldn't be a hermit.

That is why she took her letter to post it on Tuesday after her visit to the Benoits Monday morning. She also had lunch at the Gardens where she and Nicole had enjoyed such a lovely time a few short weeks ago. But it was not the same without the vivacious Nicole to share the laughter and chatter so she ordered Zachariah to take her home.

Old Zachariah sensed that Mademoiselle Angelique was not happy and he wondered what was troubling her. He thought to himself as they were going homeward that this young lady he'd known all her life had lived a lifetime in the last few months. The old man could see how those experiences had made very definite changes in her personality.

She was more beautiful than ever, old Zachariah thought as he looked at her delicate features. He'd seen this little lady bud and blossom into the sensuous lady he was driving around — he took her moods very seriously for he wanted only happiness for her. He also took his job as her driver very seriously, knowing what had happened to her so recently.

But he saw something about her that troubled him since she'd returned home. There was a recklessness and a daring about her that made him very nervous when he was driving her around New Orleans. He would have expected her to be more cautious, but she wasn't!

He was always relieved when she gave him the order to take her home. As far as Mademoiselle Angelique was concerned it seemed to Zachariah that she feared no one anymore! This scared the old black man.

It would have scared Angelique if she had known who saw her as she rode down Dumaine Street. She made a most fetching sight in her blue-green gown and matching chapeau. Zachariah had brought the carriage to a halt and it was enough time for Francois LaTour to savor all the loveliness that had drawn him to the edge of madness to possess her. God, she was the most exquisite woman he'd ever seen! He still felt that way but he also hated her with a passion for all the trouble she'd caused.

Sitting in his carriage quietly looking at her, he thought that to possess such a woman even once would be worth the cost. Suddenly, he was filled with as much ardor as he had been many weeks ago.

If he ever dared to take her again he would do it himself as he had when he was a pirate under Lafitte's command. He was still the man he was back then. Nothing had really changed except that he'd decided to be a businessman; in truth, there wasn't a lot of difference. He still used the same tactics even though he applied them differently. It was his nature to be ruthless, regardless of his occupation.

But if he should ever take her again there would be no stopping him from having his way with her this time. Gabriella had stopped him when they were at Pointe a la Hache and now he questioned her motives.

This time there would be no gallant airs about him, no Gabriella with her cunning ways and devious plots.

He'd had many women after he'd no longer taken Gabriella to his bed and she had not turned against him. He had no doubt that the two of them had schemed against him but he was still puzzled as to why!

Chapter Forty-two

Desmond knew that Francois was displeased after he'd reported for the second time that he still had no clues about the missing Gabriella. It was beginning to rile him as he took it personally that Gabriella was outsmarting him as well as La-Tour.

He'd even checked out the docks daily and trailed that young Irish fisherman when he'd left the docks. He and a friend had gone up and down the bayou where O'Roarke lived to see if she might be hiding out there. Desmond had spent an entire afternoon asking questions of people living along the bayou but they'd told him nothing.

When that failed, he began dogging the jaunts Angelique Dupree took with her black driver. There were occasional trips to boutiques and shops, but she did not leave her home that much.

Desmond never thought of trailing little Nat, who could have given him the most important clue to finding Gabriella. It never dawned on him that this little black boy held the secret.

Nat's eyes and ears were always observing

everything that went on in the palatial mansion. He was always sneaking around the grounds and the kitchen door to overhear the gossip of the servants.

None of them paid any attention to him as he sat on the back steps. He knew by the end of the week that Desmond was still trying to find and kill Gabriella.

He'd heard two of the servants talking that morning. "That Desmond was here again. Wouldn't want to be in Gabriella's shoes when he finds her!"

The other one retorted, "Ain't going to find her after all this time. She gone. It's been too long. That gal was smart, Cleo! Maybe you didn't know her as long as I did. She smart, I tell you. They ain't going to find her or that Desmond would have already done it."

"Oh, I pray they don't! Hope you right, Dorie."

"Know I'm right, Cleo."

Little Nat prayed that Dorie was right too for he liked Gabriella very much. He knew that when or if he ever went to see Kirby again he was going to be looking back over his shoulder.

Had Angelique known she was being trailed by Desmond, she would have been glad she had resisted the temptation to go to Kirby's smitty shop. The urge to see Angelique was just as great for Gabriella by the end of the week. But it was a desolate strip out on Old Cypress Road and had she encountered Desmond and his pals, she would have been no match. So she contented herself with the thought that this could not last forever.

In the meanwhile she made herself useful around the cottage tending to Kirby's father during the day and savoring the few brief hours she shared with Kirby in the evening after he got home from the shop.

This was enough to keep her happy but she still was not as free as she wished to be. She tried not to be impatient, for she had waited a long time for this much freedom.

One thing was troubling her and that was her primitive instinct. It was not a foreboding about her own safety but that of Angelique. She yearned to warn her of the persistent feeling that she was in danger.

That night she could no longer keep her fears to herself. "Oh, I know I can't risk going to see her, but Kirby, these feelings are so strong."

"Don't you worry so much about this, Gabriella. I'll take care of it."

It was a wonderful feeling to have Kirby caring so much and loving her as he did. Never had she expected to experience the bliss she felt in this little cottage. Maybe it could all end tomorrow but as long as it lasted she was going to enjoy it to the fullest.

Kirby did not think about getting word to Angelique immediately as Gabriella was consuming his thoughts. But the next morning after he got to the shop he thought about the wisest way he could get Gabriella's message of warning to Angelique.

He did not wish to go out to the Duprees for that could connect him with them and this was what he wished to avoid. He finally decided it should be Scott he talked to so he sent a young lad down to the docks to see if he could spot Scott's boat.

"If you see him pulling in, stay there until he gets up on the wharf and tell him to come here, Billy."

For the price of a few coins, the lad went down on the docks to watch for the *Bayou Queen*.

Kirby worked steadily and hoped that Billy made contact with O'Roarke. As he worked he found himself recalling the concerned look on Gabriella's face and he knew that her fears were real to her.

When he was just about to give up and it was almost time to close the shop, Scott came rushing in.

"Kirby — something wrong? Nothing has happened to Angelique or Gabriella, I hope," Scott inquired with a look of concern. Scott looked as weary from his full day of fishing as Kirby knew he must look right now.

"It may be nothing, Scott, but Gabriella has apparently been worried for a few days that something bad was going to happen to Angelique — she told me about her premonition last night. I promised her I'd see that Angelique was told, but I didn't want to go out there. I don't want LaTour's attention drawn to me for Gabriella's sake. You can understand that, I'm sure."

Scott assured him that he understood and promised Kirby he would see that Angelique was warned.

"Well, you know where my mare is whenever you want to use it, Scott."

"Thanks, Kirby. I can't ride out there tonight 'cause I got to get home. Pa's ailing and I've got medicine for him. I figure Angelique is safe for tonight knowing how strict her parents are. I'll ride out first thing in the morning before me and Justin pull out to go fishing. It's the afternoons that she ventures away from home from what she's told me."

"Well, I'll leave that in your hands. I just didn't want Gabriella going out there and she's promised me she wouldn't," Kirby declared protectively.

A twinkle came to Scott's blue eyes. "Well, I'll be damned! Kirby, you're in love with her, aren't you?"

Kirby did not hesitate to confess that he was very much in love with Gabriella. "I've never felt about any woman the way I feel about her and it doesn't matter to me that she's a quadroon, Scott."

"That's your business, Kirby. It may not be an easy boat to row, as you must know," Scott said softly.

"I'll row the boat. I'd do anything to keep her, Scott, and she feels the same way about me."

"Well, she's one special lady and I'm happy for

the two of you, Kirby. You know you've got my blessing and I suspect that Angelique would feel the same way."

Scott told Kirby goodbye and Kirby turned his attention to the closing of his shop. It was a good feeling to be going to the cottage to find Gabriella there, greeting him with a warm smile and a kiss. How different it was now in the evenings when he got home.

But it wasn't just his life that had changed drastically. His father seemed to have found a new zest for living since Gabriella had come. No longer did he lie in bed most of the day—he even strolled around the yard occasionally. The old man had one hell of an appetite and slept like a baby so it was obvious to Kirby he was a far piece from death's door, and Kirby gave Gabriella the credit.

Kirby closed the doors and locked them as he started up the slight incline to his cottage.

He had no inkling that he was being watched by a mountain of a man sitting on a horse. It was a huge black stallion the man sat astraddle, but then it would take a powerful horse to carry this man.

Fate played into Kirby's hands but he was not aware of it. He did not go directly to his cottage—Desmond could have tracked him there. Instead he went to purchase tobacco for his father and cheroots for himself. When he was preparing to leave the tobacco shop, a sudden distraction outside was enough to keep him from being seen as he was leaving. The observer was also unable to see the direction he took due to a runaway team of horses and flat-bedded wagon surging wildly down the street. The owner and several bystanders went rushing down the street to try to stop the animals. In the melee, Desmond lost sight of his prey.

Kirby was lost up in the rushing group as he sauntered toward his cottage, completly unaware that he was the target of the feared Desmond.

Once he entered the cottage and was greeted by his Gabriella, the rest of the world was shut out. His cottage had become his paradise and haven of happiness.

Kirby had never expected to find this kind of serenity and now that it had happened he did not intend to lose it at any price. The way his father had accepted the woman he loved was so very pleasing to him. He could have objected to a third person sharing their cottage but Gabriella had won his heart as well as Kirby's.

He sought to ease her mind about Angelique, so he told her that Scott had come to the shop. "I told him of your foreboding and he will go to her, Gabriella. Now you can rest easy."

Her dark eyes looked up at him and she smiled warmly, "I'll not rest easy, *mon cher,* until this feeling is swept away. I can't explain it to you but I know. I've had this many times in my life."

Kirby's eyes searched her face before he spoke. "I want to know more about you someday, Gabriella. You must tell me about your life before we met."

"It won't be such a nice story, Kirby."

"That's all right. When you love a woman like I love you, you want to know about her. I want to know everything!"

"And I shall tell you everything, Kirby," she promised.

Kirby's adoring eyes swept over her as he vowed, "Nothing you'd tell me could make me stop loving you as I do, Gabriella, I can assure you."

Her dark eyes searched his face anxiously. "There cannot be anything but honesty between us, Kirby, so as sordid as my tale is you shall hear it all."

What she did not say was that she was praying that he would still love her as he had said he would! She had to pray that he would!

Chapter Forty-three

A slow pelting rain fell on the city of New Orleans and it seemed to hint that autumn had arrived for the air was cooler. Little Nat felt so lazy that he curled up in one of the stalls for a nap even though it wasn't yet mid-day.

The nip in the air made him reach for his ragged sweater hanging on the wood peg. He was sleeping quite soundly when he felt the toe of a boot kicking his rump. He leaped up hastily. "Yes sir! Yes sir," he stammered as he instantly came alive.

"Get the buggy ready, Nat, and move that lazy butt of yours," Francois demanded, his black eyes glaring down at the lad.

Nat tried to move hastily but his fingers fumbled when he was frightened and this man always frightened him.

When Nat finally had the bay harnessed and the buggy ready to go, Francois told him, "Now you can get busy getting some dry wood carried in the house so the cook will have it for her stove if this rain keeps up all day."

"Yes sir, I'll get cook some wood," Nat answered as he scampered out of the stable, more than glad to be gone from there.

He carried wood to fill the bin next to the cookstove and then stacked a good supply on the back porch, too. Monsieur LaTour could not say he had not carried out his orders.

But he did not dare to go back to the stable and try to nap again even though he knew of no chores that needed his attention.

Francois guided his carriage toward the offices of one of his old friends. Knowing that LaTour was in a touchy predicament the last few weeks, the businessman had made him an offer for some of the goods in his warehouse. He happened to know that LaTour had not been attending to his import company regularly.

Another article the man wished to buy from Francois was a strand of exquisite pearls. When he found out that Francois still had them he made an offer which Francois accepted. Neglecting his business affairs, as he'd done ever since the escapade with Angelique, had cost him dearly. Coupled with Gabriella taking the gold in his safe, it was enough to make him jump at Samuel Ellis' offer.

He shied away from the busier areas of the city and was glad that Ellis' office was on a side street. He didn't want Paulo accompanying him this morning so he'd told him to go down to the dock to check with old Joseph. "We may be leaving for Pointe a la Hache very soon," he'd told Paulo.

He pulled his buggy up to the office door and

picked up the velvet case containing the pearls and slipped it in the pocket of his coat. He made his way up the dark stairway to Ellis' office, which seemed even darker this morning with the weather so dismal.

As he climbed the steps, he was thinking that Ellis certainly didn't have a very plush office even though he'd always been under the impression that he was a wealthy businessman.

Not that any of this mattered. An hour later he came back down the steps with several thousand dollars tucked in the inside pocket of his coat. He got into the buggy and started for the docks, taking the back streets again.

A light rain was still falling as he guided the buggy toward the docks. He'd had Joseph moor his boat away from the busy section of the wharf in a small, secluded cove. He knew that despite the weather the wharf would be a busy place today with all the fishing boats there to sell their fish.

Somewhere down there would be the bastard who'd invaded his place at Pointe a la Hache to get Angelique. But he was also certain now that he did it with the help of Gabriella. It would not have happened otherwise.

For a moment, he slowed down and let his eyes scan the flotilla. Which one was O'Roarke's? They were too far away for him to make out the names.

But then he caught sight of a small figure stepping aboard one of the boats — it told him all he wanted to know. He recognized that petite figure immediately as Angelique Dupree. She'd come to see her lover this rainy morning, it would seem. Francois lingered a little longer to watch the two of them.

A light wool cape was draped over her shoulders, the hood pulled over her head. Her waist-long black hair was flung to one side outside the cape.

He watched her rush into the arms of her lover and a snarl came to Francois' face for this had been the fantasy he'd envisioned for himself. He saw them kisisng and seethed with envy; all the time she was with him, he had not received one kiss!

What a damned fool he had been not to have taken what he desired when he had the opportunity! But as he'd had time to take stock of everything about that period he knew what had stopped him—that little bitch, Gabriella.

Why had he listened to her? Well, now he knew the answer to that, too! Gabriella had more power over him than he'd realized. How it had happened or when, he couldn't say.

There was no denying there was an essence of mystery and intrigue about the woman. Gabriella had cast a spell on him with her beguiling charm.

Francois could no longer see Angelique or O'Roarke for they had moved to another spot on the boat so he urged the bay on to the cove where his boat was.

Joseph and Paulo were passing the rainy morning playing dominoes and drinking coffee.

"Boat ready for leaving this evening, Joseph?" Francois asked as he sauntered up.

"Yes, Monsieur LaTour. What time will you be wanting to leave?" Joseph asked.

"As soon as it gets dark."

"Am I to stay here with Joseph or return to the house with you, Monsieur LaTour?" Paulo inquired. He had not found Francois LaTour the most pleasant man to be around lately. If he had a choice he preferred to stay here with old Joseph and play dominoes than to return to the house.

It pleased him when he was told that he could just stay on the boat. "I've no need of your services this afternoon, Paulo."

Francois left the two of them and went to board his buggy to go back to his house. But he could not resist stopping at the spot where he had the perfect view of O'Roarke's fishing boat.

The rains seemed to be coming down a little harder and it had made the crowd hurry to purchase fish and leave the wharf.

Carriages were not lining the roadway as they had earlier. He wondered if the Dupree carriage was still waiting for Angelique to return from her little rendezvous.

When Angelique left the carriage she told Zachariah, "I won't be long but don't you stay up there getting wet. Sit inside the carriage, you hear me?"

He had obeyed and once he was inside, got so cozy in the plush seat that he went to sleep. The light rain resounding against the top of the carriage was a soothing sound.

She felt rather guilty asking Zachariah to drive her to the docks but she wanted so desperately to see Scott. What had happened with Nicole kept plaguing her. When she woke up to see this dark, dismal day outside her bedroom window, she felt even more depressed. She knew the only tonic was to go to the wharf and since this was Friday, Scott and Justin would be there.

So once again she conjured up a little lie to tell her mother and ordered the carriage brought to the front entrance.

When she was dressed in a bottle green frock with the matching short cape flung over her arm, she dashed down the stairs. Simone was puzzled as her daughter gave her a hastily mumbled reason for going out on such a foul day.

But before Simone could voice any kind of protest, Angelique was already out the door. So Simone helplessly shook her head and went into the parlor, still in her dressing gown, to enjoy her cup of hot tea.

On days like this Simone did not make any effort to be dressed. She enjoyed lounging around for hours in her dressing gown. She was going to do that until late afternoon, she decided. Maurice would be gone until then and, obviously, Angelique would not be home to keep her company.

It was good to feel Scott's strong arms around her as she boarded the *Bayou Queen* and it didn't matter that Justin was watching them with a smile on his bronzed face. After they finally

357

broke the embrace and Scott kissed her, he looked at her with a pleased grin. "This is a nice surprise, little angel! I hope it's because you just couldn't bear it without seeing me."

"That's the truth. I wanted desperately to see you, Scott," she declared as she bent her head back to look up into his blue eyes. His arms continued to hold her and she clung to him. He loved her honest confession. He thought she looked so adorable with the deep green hood framing her face. He swore no girl could have thicker or longer eyelashes than Angelique's.

He moved her to the other side of the boat, wanting to be sure that nothing was wrong. After what Kirby had told him, he was more and more concerned about Angelique. LaTour was a man who'd have his revenge one way or the other. He must surely feel the same fury for Angelique as he did for Gabriella.

But she assured him that everything was fine. "It's my friend, Nicole, I'm upset about. She came to see me Sunday and was going to meet Mark. She's pregnant with Mark's child!"

"But that isn't the end of the world, Angelique. She and Mark will just have to have a very quick wedding. Surely Mark would be agreeable."

"No, that's not what happened." She told him that the next day when she went to see Nicole she had suddenly left for Baton Rouge. "I knew something had gone wrong when she'd left me the day before to go to talk to Mark. So I rode over to see him. That bastard never had any intention of marrying Nicole. He's already has a wife back in Ireland."

There was a fire and fury about her that Scott found tremendously exciting with her black eyes flashing as they were right now. It was obvious what she thought about Mark!

"So he confessed this when you spoke to him about Nicole?" Scott asked.

"He did and I told him I thought he was the lowest bastard on the face of the earth!"

Scott could not repress his laughter as he took her into his arms again. "What a little spitfire you are, Angelique Dupree! You're just as beautiful when you're mad as you are when you're cool and calm. I'll love you even when we're fussing after we're married."

"And when is that to be, Scott O'Roarke?" she boldly inquired with her eyes staring up at him.

"Any time you say, my beautiful Angelique!" he said smiling down at her. "You only have to name the day!"

Later as she was leaving the boat she thought it was a strange proposal, but he did ask her to marry him. He wasn't Mark's kind of man!

As the rain was coming down harder, she pulled the hood over her head as she walked down the wharf toward the carriage. Just seeing Scott for those few brief moments was enough to lift the gloomy mood she'd been in for a couple of days.

The hood covered both sides of her face but that didn't matter to Angelique as long as she could see straight ahead. But if she had not had the hood pulled so far over her head she might have seen the awesome figure approaching behind her.

The road was almost deserted and Francois saw his opportunity and didn't hesitate to take it. This time it would not fail, for he would carry out his own plans!

Without knowing what was happening, Angelique felt herself grabbed and swung violently around. Before she could scream for help a blow assaulted her face like the mighty fury of a hurricane.

All the hate and indignation he had harbored against her was in the force of his clenched fist as he swung it against the side of her head. She immediately went limp.

Like a wilted flower, she sank in his arms as he carried her toward his buggy. As soon as he propped her on the seat, he hastily urged the bay into motion.

He should have handled it this way the first time, Francois thought to himself as he traveled swiftly toward his house!

Chapter Forty-four

With the rain coming down heavier and the hearty lunch the cook had given him, little Nat could no longer resist curling up in the stables to take a nap. His sleep was deep and he'd not heard the arrival of Francois' buggy. But as La-Tour carried the limp figure out of the buggy to the house, Nat did rouse enough to see a woman's long black hair.

She wasn't Gabriella, but Nat knew something wasn't right. The lady was in some kind of helpless state.

He rushed out of the stable to slip in the front door. Down the dark hallway, he watched Francois LaTour as he climbed the steps with the lady in his arms.

Nat stood in the empty hall until Francois had reached the second landing. That was the longest hair little Nat had ever seen on any woman. He wondered who she might be. He wished he had Gabriella to tell but he couldn't do that. He didn't know what to do so he slipped out the door to go back to the stable. Maybe he'd think of something.

* * *

Old Zachariah had no idea of how long he'd slept when he woke up in the carriage but he did see that the rains were coming down harder. Of course, his first thoughts were about Angelique. Pulling out his pocket watch he saw that it had been over three hours since she'd left and he also quickly noticed that there were no other carriages around now.

The old man became upset and moved as fast as his body would allow to get out of the carriage. His concern mounted when he saw that all the fishing boats had already moved out earlier than they usually did on a Friday.

Mademoiselle Angelique's young man, Scott O'Roarke, had also left but she would not have left with him. Zachariah, like little Nat, didn't know what to do. After he'd walked the length of the wharf he went back to the carriage and sat for a minute to think.

He knew nothing to do but go home, so he urged the horses into action. A heavy burden of guilt was on his shoulders—he blamed himself for sleeping so long.

He knew that the Duprees would hold him responsible and he felt like he was, too. He dreaded facing them.

Long before Simone saw the carriage rolling up the drive, she had been pacing the floor wondering why Angelique was gone so long on such a miserable rainy day. When she watched old Zachariah rush to the front door and there was no sight of Angelique getting out of the carriage, her worst fears were realized.

She rushed to the front door. The agony was etched there on her face when she opened the door. "What is it, Zachariah? Angelique—where is she?"

"Don't know, ma'am. Let her out of the carriage to go down on the dock to see that young fisherman. Saw her safely board his fishing boat and then I napped. She told me she'd not be long." A mist gathered on old Zachariah's eyes as he told her, "Never forgive myself for sleeping so sound as I did, Madame. But I did and I'll not lie."

Simone patted his humped shoulder and told him to calm himself. "It was nothing you did, Zachariah. I'm sure of that. What happened next?"

"Well, I woke up and couldn't believe that I'd done slept two hours so I rushes down to the wharf to see all the boats gone and the carriages along the road, too. By now the rains were coming down real good. I walk over all the wharf and as I said this Mister Scott's boat was gone like the rest of them. But I know Mademoiselle Angelique would not have left with him without telling me. She wouldn't have done that."

"No, she wouldn't, Zachariah. She's not with Scott. I'm sure of that," Simone said softly. She dismissed him to take care of the carriage and, seeing how upset he was, told him to get to his quarters and rest.

"Yes ma'am. I guess I better do just that," Zachariah said, for he was not feeling well. Every-

363

thing that had happened had drained the old man.

Dejectedly, Simone went back to the parlor to wait for Maurice. Dear God, the madness was to start all over again!

Simone cupped her face in her hands as she broke into tears. Somehow, she'd felt that the nightmare was not over even after Angelique had returned home. There was a heaviness in her heart each time her daughter left home. There was that new independent, reckless attitude Angelique had that concerned Simone, especially since she knew that the authorities had not arrested Francois LaTour.

She knew instinctively, as mothers often do, that the wicked hand of LaTour had touched her daughter's life once again.

Little Nat sat in the stable for only a short time before he darted out into the rain and ran as fast as he could to the smitty shop before it closed. He didn't know why he had to talk to Kirby about this, he just knew.

He was drenched by the time he rushed through the shop's doors as Kirby was about to close. Breathlessly, he told Kirby about what he'd seen.

"Why did you come to me, Nat?" Kirby asked, realizing immediately who the woman was. All Nat had to do was talk about that long black hair for Kirby to know that LaTour had once again taken Angelique prisoner.

"I've got no one but you, Kirby, now that Gabriella is gone."

"Well, we're going to help that lady, Nat, and we all have you to thank for what you've done." The big-hearted Irishman knew that he was going to do, what he'd wanted to do for a long time since the little black boy had been coming around his shop. He planned to take this kid under his wing.

"Come on, Nat—we're going home," he said. He looked at his rain-soaked clothes and saw him still panting from the long run and Kirby could not turn his back on him. He wanted to take care of this mite of a boy who was braver than most grown men he knew and had a lot more guts.

"I—I better get back before monsieur finds me missing, Kirby," Nat stammered.

"To hell with monsieur! You're coming to live with me and I'll not let monsieur do nothing to you or he'll have to crawl over me, Nat," he said, patting the boy's small shoulder.

By the time Kirby had gone back into the shop to grab an old blanket to drape around Nat's shoulder and was preparing to lock up, he chanced to glance down at the lad's face. Kirby would never forget the look of wonder and worship in his eyes. He couldn't be happier, knowing that he didn't have to return to that place.

The husky smitty and his little companion draped in an old ragged blanket marched up the incline to Kirby's cottage.

When they arrived, Kirby allowed little Nat and

Gabriella to have a brief happy reunion before he told her, "LaTour's got Angelique again and I've got to get to Scott. Little Nat's staying here. I'm not letting him go back to that devil. Tell Pa what I'm up to, Gabriella." He gave her a kiss before he dashed out the front door.

Before Gabriella could stop him or say anything, he was gone so she turned her attention to Nat. She urged him to make himself comfortable as she explained what had happened to old Tom. She was concerned about Kirby going into the bayou on a rainy night like this—now she knew her foreboding had substance.

At least, it helped to have old Tom and Nat for company while Kirby was gone. She found it impossible to eat the dinner she'd prepared but neither Tom nor little Nat seemed to be having trouble.

Nat had never known such a wonderful evening as he sat at the table and ate Gabriella's good food. For once, he had all the milk he could drink as she constantly filled his empty glass.

When the hour grew late and it was time for the young boy to go to sleep, she folded quilts and made him a bed in the room where she slept.

The soft pallet was the best bed he'd ever known. He fell asleep immediately for he had no reason to fear for his safety now that he was with Gabriella again.

Tom stayed up as long as he could, knowing that Gabriella was gravely concerned about Kirby as well as her friend, but he had to give up to get to bed. "We'll have to leave it all in God's hands, I guess," he told her.

She nodded. "Go and get your rest. There's nothing either of us can do but wait."

After he had gone she sat in the parlor to wait for Kirby. Each minute seemed like an hour as she agonized, wondering what was happening to Angelique alone with Francois.

She could only guess how long she'd been at his mercy—from the time Nat had come to the smitty shop to what the hands of the clock indicated now. Four or five hours could be an eternity!

Kirby had never stroked the oars of a canoe as fast as he did this late afternoon. He knew he had surely set a record. When he arrived at the O'Roarke cottage as they were about to sit down to dinner and told Scott the bad news, he knew he'd never forget the look on his friend's face as long as he lived.

Kate O'Roarke had moaned, "Oh, mercy lord!" Her husband cussed the sonofabitch LaTour but Scott said nothing for a moment or two. Quickly, he leaped out of the chair ready to leave with Kirby. As they traveled back up the bayou Scott was silent and thoughtful, his face like granite.

Kirby did not seek to engage him in conversation for he knew it was not the time. When they were nearing New Orleans Scott finally broke the long silence, "I've got to kill him, Kirby. It's the only way Angelique will be free."

Kirby said nothing but he understood. He wondered what weapon Scott would use since he'd leaped up from the kitchen table so fast back at the cottage. He'd not noticed the vicious-looking scaling knife on Scott's belt.

When they arrived at the docks in New Orleans, Scott was like a man Kirby had never seen before. He insisted that Kirby go home. "The rest of this night is up to me. You just take care of little Nat and Gabriella."

Kirby wanted desperately to go with him but he saw the look on Scott's face and knew he had to let him have his way. He knew one thing, though: before the midnight hour Francois LaTour or Scott O'Roarke would be dead. Kirby could only pray that it would be LaTour.

The two Irishmen walked together from the wharf until they came to the street which would take Kirby in one direction and Scott in another. Kirby's face was serious as he said, "God go with you, pal!"

In the darkness, he saw Scott's head nod.

Kirby walked on toward his house but his thoughts were with Scott, who walked in the other direction.

From the moment the brutal blow hit the side of her face, Angelique felt herself sinking into an abyss of blackness. She had not seen her attacker and she didn't know how much time had gone by as she started to regain consciousness. Her vision was foggy and her eyelashes began to flutter open.

It took several minutes of lying there, allowing her eyes to open, before she knew she was in a strange place. Her first thought was frightening — this was not a bad dream!

Francois LaTour had kidnapped her again!

Chapter Forty-five

For a moment she lay there trembling, then she moaned aloud as a sharp pain shot around her jaw and the side of her face, reminding her of the harsh blow. Whoever had carried her to this room had apparently just flung her unconscious body on the bed. Her damp cape was still around her shoulders.

If this was Francois' house, it wasn't the same room. Now that she'd had time to look around, she saw that it wasn't furnished as nicely as the other one. But at least she was alone and she welcomed that. There were a couple of windows so her next thought was to check them out—there was no Gabriella to help her this time.

It was a struggle to sit up. For a second her head whirled and her face throbbed horribly. Had there been a mirror she knew she would see angry redness and swelling.

Hope surged when she saw that one window wasn't locked, but then she glanced down to see how far it was to the ground below. Quietly, she lowered the window and moved back to the bed. How could she manage to lower herself down the side of the house? Her eyes scoured the room for something she might use. The coverlet divided in strips might do if only she had a way to cut it. So again she moved off the bed to search the chest and nightstand but there was nothing in the drawers. Obviously, this room had been unoccupied for a long time judging from the cobwebs and dust.

On top of a highboy she found a piece of a broken looking glass. She knew it probably wouldn't work but she had to try it. After she had worked and worked on one end of the coverlet, she saw it was futile.

Another idea came to her as she flung the coverlet aside. She tucked the broken glass under the pillow and lay back, pulling the coverlet up over her shoulders.

She remembered Gabriella's words about how Francois could not stand anyone who was ailing. It had worked before so she might have to try it again.

When Francois had rushed into his house carrying Angelique, he did not place her in one of his lavishly furnished guest rooms as he had before. He'd taken her to a small room once used by a servant and flung her roughly on the bed. He locked the door before he marched down the dark hallway to his own quarters to rid himself of his damp clothing. He would have more than enough time to change before she came to, he figured. The blow he'd given her had more force than he'd realized for he saw the ugly mark on her face when he took her limp body out of his buggy to carry her into the house.

He'd give her no tender touches this time for he did not feel about her as he once had. This time he would take pleasure in punishing her for all the misery she'd caused him. What gratification that was going to be!

When he was dressed, he started down the hallway to that little secluded room. No Gabriella would outfox him this time!

Angelique heard the door open and lay very still. She knew without looking that Francois was moving closer and closer to her bed. She tried not to flutter her lashes as she felt his evil heat leaning over her.

His dark eyes had already spotted her cape on the foot on the bed and since he'd left it on her, he knew she was not asleep. He laughed wickedly. "Wake up, Sleeping Beauty. You're a little faker but it isn't going to work this time." His hands reached for the coverlet and flung it aside. Angelique had been lying on her side but his hand grasped her shoulder, forcing her to lie on her back.

She moaned in protest against his roughness, but he merely laughed. "Oh, I tried the gentle way and ended up the fool, my little minx. You'll find no gentleness about me now."

His hands took hold of her wrists in a vise-like grip and his head bent down so that his lips could capture hers. Fiercely, he'd taken her lips and she felt a sickening feeling engulf her. When he finally removed his mouth from hers the pain from her face and the brutal assault on her mouth made her moan in anguish. She stammered, "I—I feel like I'm going to retch. Get off of me, you animal!"

"Oh, no—that little ploy isn't going to work this time, Mademoiselle Dupree. I *shall* be an animal before I get my fill of you this rainy afternoon. There's nothing you or anyone can do to stop it."

The truth was she was suffering from a consuming queasy feeling that she was not faking. She *did* feel like she was about to retch. The feeling mounted as his busy fingers opened the front of her bodice and began to fondle the tip of her breast. She tried to push him away but he flung her hand aside and she slipped it beneath the pillow.

She flinched as she found the keen edge of the broken glass. Her fingers took a firm hold on it before she slowly slipped her hand out from under the pillow. She knew that she must make her first attempt a perfect blow as she endured Francois's fondling for a second or two, even though it repulsed her.

He was so engrossed in his own lust, he didn't see her swing her hand up to bring the jagged edge of the mirror down the side of his face.

An animal-like sound echoed through the room as bright red blood poured profusely from the jagged cut. A look of panic flashed in his eyes as he screamed and leaped from the bed.

With his hand pressed to his face, he rushed out of the room and grabbed a cloth to hold against the wound. He vowed that as soon as he tended to his face he'd return to that bitch and kill her.

When he walked over to the mirror and took the damp cloth away, he looked like a hog that had been butchered. The blood was still flowing so he had to get a new cloth to press against the cut.

Angelique knew she had merely delayed his wicked plans and was also feeling desperate panic as Francois fled from the room.

She dashed to the door and gave a frantic pull on the door—much to her surprise Francois had failed to lock it! There was only one way she could go—down that long dark hall until she came to the top of the stairs.

Without any hesitation, she crept down the steps, praying she'd encounter no servants and certainly not the angry LaTour. She would never forget the savage fury in his eyes.

Fate or Lady Luck was with her as she moved toward the front door. Once outside the rain was coming down even harder than it was when she left Scott on the docks earlier. But this didn't bother her. Nor was she concerned that the front of her bodice was still unfastened and her breasts partially exposed.

Like a gazelle, she ran swiftly down the drive toward the iron gate. She didn't intend to stop until she was outside that gate even though she was gasping for breath.

Once she was on the other side, she hesitated a moment to take a deep breath and sigh deeply when she suddenly found herself enclosed by two strong arms. When she turned to look up at the towering figure holding her, she broke into tears. "Oh, Scott—thank God! Thank God, it's you!"

Never had she seen such a fierce look in Scott's eyes as they danced over the open front of her frock and saw the ugly redness on her face. "That bastard hurt you!"

"He tried but I ended up hurting him before he could carry out his wicked intentions. I found a broken mirror in the room and ran it down his face—it may never look the same again. Lucky for me he rushed out of the room without locking the door."

He took off his dark blue jacket and put it around her shoulders. "You stay right here, Angelique! I've a score to settle with that bastard once and for all. I won't be long." He gave her a hasty kiss and ran through the gate.

He didn't wait for anyone to admit him but bolted in like a predatory cat, moving up the stairway to the second landing. He had no trouble finding LaTour.

He was still administering to himself when the tall Irishman entered the room. "Who the hell are you?" he roared. As he took away the cloth, which had been blurring his vision, he recognized O'Roarke.

Francois knew he was looking at a man eager for revenge. "Know me now, LaTour. Take a very good look at this face. It may be the last face you ever see."

Francois began to move toward the nightstand

where he kept a pistol. "Think so, O'Roarke? The likes of you don't scare me."

Scott saw him move and suspected he was going for a weapon. Boldly, he kept moving directly toward LaTour and could see for himself the wicked looking cut Angelique had given him. Just too bad it wasn't his throat, Scott thought!

Francois surveyed the formidable figure getting closer and closer. He made a quick move toward the nightstand, but the drawer slipped to the floor as Scott grabbed him by the collar and flung him around.

His strong fist dealt a vicious blow to Francois' bloody face. Francois moaned as he reeled back from the force but he chanced to fall near the side of the bed. In the drawer with the pistol, he also kept the prized dagger Lafitte had given him years ago. His hand swept down to grab the dagger but Scott's keen eyes saw him. He leaped to cover Francois' body and once again his clenched fist slammed against Francois' face but the dagger was already positioned and Francois thrust it rapidly upward. It barely missed Scott's side as he quickly shifted his body. There was no question in Scott's mind that one of them was not leaving this room alive as they wrestled back and forth.

Scott felt the pressure of his scaling knife as he rolled and tossed on the floor. The piercing prick of Francois' dagger had made marks on his arm as he'd only been using his fists. Scott realized instantly that LaTour was an expert at using that vicious dagger. While he could hold his own in a fist fight, he saw that he was at a disadvantage battling against the weapon.

Flinging himself away from LaTour, Scott grabbed the scaling knife from his belt. He could tell by the look on Francois' face that he was feeling smug as Scott backed away from him. A few moments later that look was to change when he saw that the fisherman's hand held an odd-looking knife.

"Now I'll give you a more even fight, LaTour. Not as fancy as your dagger but it's just as sharp. Cuts real fine as it's sharpened every night," Scott taunted, a bright fire in his eyes.

Francois moved with a little more caution as he slowly circled Scott to find that one split second to thrust the dagger.

When he thought the time was right, he made his move —but Francois missed! That proved to be the advantage Scott needed to surge forward and stab Francois right below the ribs.

With a startled look Francois suddenly froze and glared at his assailant. Scott sensed that his blow had been fatal from the look in LaTour's eyes as he slumped to the floor.

In that last fleeting second of life Francois La-Tour thought about his earlier role as a pirate; he'd seen many a comrade die from the evil stab of a knife. He'd had many close calls but luck had been with him. Today, Lady Luck was not riding on his shoulder. He knew he was a dead man as he felt himself go limp.

Jean Lafitte had been right; he had played himself for a fool!

Scott knew he was dead when he turned to leave the room. Wiping his knife clean, he fastened it back to his belt. It had been a fair fight and he felt no remorse.

At least, Angelique or Gabriella would never have to live in fear of what he might do to them ever again.

He walked into the dark hallway and down the steps. The house seemed deserted—he encountered no one as he made his departure out the front entranceway. Rain was still falling as he went down the steps.

The beautiful but frightened lady he loved with all his heart was waiting just outside the gate and that was enough to make him run hastily across the grounds.

Chapter Forty-six

Every minute Angelique sat on the damp ground waiting for Scott seemed like an eternity. Her legs were too weak to stand, but she had finally been able to breathe more easily.

When she heard the sound of boots plowing down the path, she almost stopped breathing. It might not be Scott—it could be Francois! She was just too drained to get up.

But it *was* Scott coming through the gate and a wonderful sight he was!

With a broad grin, he spotted her on the wet ground looking like a bedraggled little girl with damp black hair all around her shoulders.

"Come on, honey—we're going home," he said, taking her hands to lift her.

They were quite a sight as they walked from La-Tour's house toward Kirby's cottage. "Got to let them know we're both safe before we leave here," Scott murmured against her cheek.

By now Angelique had seen the three or four spots of blood on Scott's shirt. "Are you injured, Scott? Francois hurt you!"

"I've a few cuts but not as bad as the one I gave him. He won't trouble you or Gabriella anymore."

"You — you mean you killed him?" she said with a startled look.

"I mean just that. It was a fair fight. He had his knife and I had mine. I hardly think the authorities will do anything to me after what that man tried to do to you. I'm not concerned so don't worry." He pulled her closer.

By the time Kirby's cottage came in sight, the rains suddenly ceased. The two of them looked like ragamuffins as they came up the steps and walked across the porch.

Gabriella opened the door and screamed with delight. Her arms went around them and by this time Kirby had also joined in the rejoicing.

Gabriella warmed up food as the two of them sat draped in blankets, their clothes hung over chairs by the cookstove.

While Gabriella talked with Angelique, Kirby tended to the bloody scratches on Scott's arm. He was gently arguing with Scott that they should remain overnight. But Scott was stubborn. "I'm taking her home with me. I don't give a damn what the Duprees think! Little Nat can take a message to them that she's in safe hands."

Kirby could not help but admire Scott's boldness for he knew how his friend felt. Once again he'd rescued her, and this time he'd killed the bastard. Could any man do more to prove his love?

As the two men talked in the kitchen, Little Nat sat with old Tom on the front porch. The little boy had already proved to be great company for Kirby's dad.

Angelique and Gabriella were in the parlor and Gabriella had to admit she was surprised that

Angelique was going to the bayou with Scott.

"I want to be with him."

"But what will your parents think, Angelique?"

"They'll be shocked at first but perhaps it's the only way I can make them accept him."

Gabriella nodded. "You must do as your heart tells you as I, too, have done by staying here with Kirby."

"I'm going to," she said firmly.

"Well, if it's your plan to start for the bayou tonight I suggest you come with me. I've a dress you can wear for your clothes will never be dry." Angelique followed her back to the bedroom but when Gabriella took the scissors out of the drawer and began to shorten the dress, Angelique protested.

"That's one thing I've got plenty of, Angelique. Little Nat managed to get all my things. Kirby and I live a very simple life so there's no reason to have so many gowns like this one. At least, you'll have something dry to wear. Now, get changed," she said smiling.

She left Angelique and she went into the kitchen to suggest to Kirby that he find some clothing for Scott as well.

"Since these two are determined to go on to the bayou I think you better supply a change of clothes for Scott. Theirs won't be dry until tomorrow," she pointed out.

A half hour later, Angelique and Scott headed for the docks. She was wearing Gabriella's cut-off dress with a shawl draped around her shoulders and Scott wore Kirby's oversized pants and shirt.

The rain and thick clouds had moved out of New Orleans. A gleam of moonlight was beginning to show against the dark sky. Scott thought it was a good omen as he began to paddle the canoe toward the bayou.

After all the harrowing events of the day that should have left Angelique shaken to the core, a peace and calm consumed her as they moved through the water. It was nice to see the bright moonlight and a few stars twinkling above.

Although it was dark, Angelique was beginning to see the familiar bend along the bayou. Soon they would pass Justin's pier and the next one would be the O'Roarke's.

The night sounds of the bayou intrigued Angelique and seemed to set it apart from the rest of the world. All the frightening tales she had heard just weren't true.

She was listening so intensely to the calling of the night birds and inhaling the sweet fragrance of the night-blooming flowers that she didn't realize they were already approaching the pier. Scott's voice drew her attention. "We're home, Angelique!"

She saw the lamplight reflecting from the front window and the strangest feeling swept over her: she felt she was coming home.

Happiness swelled in her like none she'd never known!

Little Nat delivered the message as he'd been told but he did not linger for the stern, sober face of Maurice Dupree frightened the young boy. The lady standing with him read the message and sank down in the chair and sighed, "Oh, thank God! Thank God! Tell me, young fellow, did you see Angelique?"

"Sure did and she's just fine. Now, Mister Scott—he got a few cuts but he's fine, too, ma'am."

"Oh, Maurice!" she declared exuberantly, feeling so happy that no harm had come to their daughter. But he stood there expressionless.

The little black boy was dismissed by Maurice Dupree and Nat was more than ready to take his leave. As he went back toward Kirby's cottage he couldn't quite figure out that man back there but the lady seemed very nice. He liked her.

But if little Nat was feeling perplexed about Maurice Dupree, so was his wife. She sat for a moment just watching him pace back and forth. In a faltering voice, she dared to remark, "You—you didn't even thank the young lad who brought us such wonderful news, Maurice. She's alive and well! Doesn't that mean anything to you?"

He replied gruffly, "Oh, of course it does, Simone. Why must you be so silly?"

"Silly, Maurice? You dare to call me silly? It is you who are acting silly and stupid!"

He turned around to look at her furiously. "Now, wait just a minute, Simone! You mean to tell me you don't find it strange that our daughter didn't have O'Roarke bring her home instead of going to that bayou with him? I find that unacceptable. I—I just don't understand Angelique any more."

"Whether you do or I do, Maurice, it doesn't matter now and it hasn't since Angelique got back home the first time. Perhaps she's trying to tell us if we can't accept Scott O'Roarke then we can't have her either. Don't you understand, Maurice?

383

Angelique is in love with Scott. What you think or feel isn't going to change that." She got up to leave. It was best that she leave him there alone to think.

Simone went to her bedroom to be alone for a while. She knew that when Angelique wished to come back and face them she would and until that time they would have to be patient.

She found herself wishing that her life had been more like that of her grandmother, Delphine, or her daughter, Angelique. Both of them had experienced an excitement and ecstasy she'd never known. Like her mother, she had married the young man whom her family chose. It was not that Maurice had not been a good husband; he certainly provided a very luxurious life but now Simone knew that something had always been missing. If only Maurice had not been so stern and rigid all the time, she wondered if she could not have been a different woman. But it was too late for that now. However, it wasn't too late to let him know that his lordly ways were not going to rule this house or his family's lives. He would have to accept that whether he liked it or not.

As she always did, Kate O'Roarke had kept her vigil the night before until Angelique and Scott arrived. After they had told their tale, they all retired with the same sleeping arrangements as they had when Angelique had stayed at their cottage before. She had taken Scott's bedroom and Scott had bunked on the daybed in the kitchen. Kate would have allowed nothing else under her roof.

The next morning after the four of them shared

breakfast, Scott announced, "I'm going back to New Orleans to the authorities to tell them what happened. I hope you understand, Angelique. Otherwise, we can't go on with our lives. I want it all behind us."

"I understand, Scott. But I don't want you put in jail."

"I won't be, love. Believe me, I won't be," he said reassuringly.

She wanted to believe him as he kissed her goodbye to go down to the pier, promising to be back before the sun set.

When he arrived in New Orleans, he gave way to the impulse to call on the Duprees before he went to the authorities. He knew that little Nat had gotten the message to them but he was man enough to face them. It didn't matter if they didn't greet him with warmth. He wanted to make the effort to speak to them.

When he arrived at the house, he found only Madame Dupree at home. He told her everything that had happened and that he was going directly to the authorities when he left.

"I've never killed a man before but I did yesterday and I feel no remorse. It's not the O'Roarke's way not to face the music, as my mother says."

"The man deserved to die," Simone Dupree said fervently. She added that she was going to accompany him to confirm the facts.

When Scott tried to protest, she insisted. "That's precious little after what you've done for Angelique and this family. Yes, the word of the Dupree family might prove to be to your advantage, my boy. I don't want you to go to jail when my confirmation could save you. I'm going!"

Simone Dupree was absolutely right for when she appeared by Scott's side to back him up, the authorities did not detain him. There had always been questions about the elusive Francois LaTour and his activities in the city of New Orleans. Madame Dupree's statement was all the officer needed to hear. When they walked out into the street and Scott knew that he was a free man, he turned to Simone and thanked her. "I promised Angelique I would be back before sundown and, thanks to you, I will, Madame Dupree. I will be forever grateful for what you did today."

"Give her my love, Scott, and tell her if she stays too long I might just have to come there," Simone said smiling. She had not felt so happy in a long time for she knew she'd done the right thing by coming with this young man. He was good and she knew it. She'd always known it. It was not difficult to see why Angelique had lost her heart to him.

"The O'Roarke family would be delighted if you would come. We bayou people are a proud breed, Madame Dupree." With a boyish grin, he confessed that his mother was always in the parlor waiting up for him regardless of the hour he returned.

Simone laughed heartily, "All mothers are the same whether we be French Creole or Irish, I guess."

By the time he had escorted her back to the house and prepared to leave, Scott was feeling a warm bond with Simone Dupree. Never would the same bond be felt with Maurice Dupree but he was glad that he and Angelique's mother could share this friendly warmth.

As he prepared to depart, he bent down to plant a kiss on her cheek and thanked her again.

His candid blue eyes looked deep into hers as he said, "The name of Angelique Dupree will never be sullied because she's on the bayou, madame. My mother is a very strict, strait-laced lady. I sleep on a daybed in the kitchen and Angelique has taken over my bedroom. I just wanted you to know."

"Thank you, Scott, for caring so much that you would tell me. I admire your honesty. I always have!"

It had been a very long time since Simone had felt so at peace. She went inside after she and Scott had said their goodbyes on the porch.

Her beautiful Angelique was going to know a world of blissful happiness that she had never known and for that she was a very grateful woman!

Chapter Forty-seven

Angelique watched Scott's boat until it went around the bend and she could no longer see it. Then she turned to go back to the cottage where Kate O'Roarke puttered about in her kitchen.

The day was going to be endless, worrying if Scott would be coming back this afternoon or if he would end up in a cell at the Cabildo.

Kate wasn't feeling as cheerful as she appeared to be. She was plenty worried and that was why she was keeping herself busy in the kitchen.

"Why don't you take a stroll around the grounds, dear? You've not had a good look at our little place in the daylight. You'll have no cause to worry about anything harming you out here, I assure you," Kate declared. Angelique had tried to help with the chores, but Kate wouldn't hear of it.

"Then I will take a stroll, if you think it would be all right," Angelique said, as Kate stuck her bonnet atop her head and prepared to go to the backyard to feed her chickens.

After she left, Angelique went out the door to roam at will down the little pathway. Huge magnolia trees lined either side all the way down to the pier. But she did not go out on the pier and turned to walk along the side of the stream. The Spanish moss in the oak trees was so long it kept entrapping locks of her hair. Willows and palmettoes grew thick along the banks.

She caught the sight of a heron perched on the huge, jutting roots of an old cypress tree. As she looked all around her, Angelique thought this had to be the most serene place she'd ever seen. No wonder the people here loved the quiet and peace.

Just when she thought she was the only one anywhere around, she heard the sound of a canoe moving through the water and strained to see who was coming upstream. To her delight, it was Mimi so she rushed back to the pier to greet her. Angelique quickly noticed how she paddled the canoe with as much ease as Justin or Scott.

Angelique was waiting for her when Mimi urged the canoe toward one of the wide posts supporting the pier.

"Ah, Angelique—so good to see you! Scott stopped by the cottage this morning on his way to the city to tell us everything that happened. So Justin took the fishing boat on out by himself," she told Angelique as she mounted the wooden steps after the canoe was secured.

As Mimi stepped onto the pier, they embraced and Mimi told her how glad she was to know that she was safe once again. "I'm—I'm glad Scott brought you back here to the bayou."

"So am I. It's where I wanted to come, Mimi."

Mimi suggested that the two of them sit on the pier to chat a while for she knew that Kate was busy doing her chores at this time of day.

"Yes, I'd like to sit and have a talk with you,

Mimi. It's so wonderfully quiet." She followed Mimi's lead and sank down on the pier. She laughed as she noticed Mimi's eyes surveying the cutoff skirt.

"Scott and I were both drenched by the time we got to Kirby's cottage so Gabriella insisted I change into one of her dresses. As you'll recall, Gabriella is taller than I am."

Mimi smiled and nodded, reaching over to pat Angelique's hand as she said, "Well, you won't have to go through any of this again, Angelique. Scott said he took care of that once and for all."

"It's — it's like a heavy burden lifted. Finally maybe the nightmares of so many nights when I relived that first time I was abducted will cease now. I pray they do."

"They will," Mimi assured her.

Angelique thought maybe it was because she was looking across the rippling waters of the stream, but she began to have a strange sensation while she and Mimi sat and talked. Yesterday, she'd blamed that terrible queasy feeling on the obnoxious Francois but she knew it was not Mimi's nearness making her feel that way now. She suddenly felt so sick to her stomach, and it couldn't be Kate's delicious cooking!

Mimi noticed her sudden quietness and the paleness of her face. "You ailing, dear?"

"Feel sick at my stomach, Mimi — just all of a sudden," Angelique muttered.

"Probably just nerves over yesterday. That could easily cause it," Mimi said, trying to comfort her.

"Guess that could be," Angelique remarked.

Mimi sat with her until the feeling began to fade

before she announced she needed to be getting back home. "I just had to come to say hello after Scott told us you were here. Tell Kate I'll see her before too long. You're feeling better now, aren't you, dear?"

Angelique assured her that she was. Mimi prepared to move down the wooden steps to board her canoe.

Angelique walked back up the pathway to the cottage. When Kate offered her some lunch she politely refused, saying she'd eaten too much breakfast.

Instead, she sought the comfort of Scott's bed. She felt very weary after her roam around the grounds and long chat on the pier with Mimi.

Kate thought nothing about finding Angelique in the bedroom sleeping soundly as she peered through the open door. Poor little thing was still exhausted from the ordeal, Kate figured.

She quietly closed the door so she and Timothy would not disturb her as they moved around the house. Kate knew that time was hanging heavily for Angelique as she was waiting for Scott to return from New Orleans. She, too, was feeling weary from waiting.

The thought of her son being put in jail petrified her but she had put up a brave front all morning. For Timothy's sake she'd had to put on this act.

The afternoon was one of endless solitude for Kate once she finally managed to rest a while in her rocking chair. Her Tim was in their room taking his usual afternoon nap and Angelique was sleeping. She rocked and waited for the sight of Scott coming through the door.

* * *

Scott O'Roarke was probably the happiest man in New Orleans that early afternoon as he went down Canal Street to get to the docks and start for home. The past was behind him and Angelique and he was encouraged now that he had a champion in Simone Dupree. It meant a lot that she had supported him today. Maurice Dupree could surely be won over in time when he saw that his daughter was loved so devotedly, Scott told himself.

He would get home much earlier than usual and he was so happy that he didn't even feel guilty that Justin would probably not get home for anther two hours. But he could make that up to him by letting him take an entire day off.

Scott O'Roarke might have been a happy man but such was not the case with Maurice Dupree as he went toward his house at the end of the day. All the old gossip and rumors had flared up again after the news of Francois' death broke. Maurice could not abide the scandal attached to his family as the news traveled like wildfire around the city.

He'd witnessed the side glances the gentlemen had given him as he'd dined at the hotel. The entire day had been so disturbing that he decided to call it a day and go home early. But when he arrived he found his wife in a lighthearted, happy mood which only tended to vex him more.

He immediately marched over to the liquor chest to pour himself a generous drink. He felt the urgent need of something to calm his frayed nerves. "Dear God—I wonder how long it will take for this new scandal to fade! That's all I've heard about all day. Now, I'm faced with these curious questions about our Angelique all over again."

Simone strolled over to help herself to a glass of sherry from the cut crystal decanter. "It will soon fade. LaTour is dead and thank God for that. I went with Scott this morning to help him clear himself of any charges with the authorities. I confirmed everything he told them about what LaTour had done to our daughter and that it was for her honor and his own defense that he was forced to kill Francois LaTour."

"You—you did what? You went with him?" Maurice roared. Now his wife was sashaying around with this Irishman!

"I think you heard me, Maurice. I went with him and I'm glad. The young man is free of any charges. He's probably back in the bayou right now."

Maurice could not believe the madness that had taken over his family and his life in a few months time. What had happened since the springtime and the autumn? More than the seasons had changed. Everything had changed!

He left the room without another word but all she had to do was look at his flushed face to know that he was so furious he was about to explode.

She knew it was bound to happen when she told him about what she had done so it was best that he be alone. She remained in the parlor to sip her sherry and let his fury subside.

She finished her drink and poured herself another before she decided to go up to her bedroom.

During dinner Maurice and his wife sat at their long dining table as remote as strangers. So it remained for the rest of the evening and the next few days. Maurice was feeling betrayed by his daughter and his wife.

All Kate O'Roarke could say as she leaped up out of her rocker when she saw her son coming up the path was, "Thank God! He's home!"

She was at the door with her arms stretched out as he got there to pick her up and swing her around. "Everything is fine, Momma! Everything is just wonderful. There will be no charges against me."

"Oh, son—son! I'm the happiest mother alive!"

"And I'm one happy Irishman. Let's celebrate tonight! Angelique—where is she?" His eyes looked around the parlor and kitchen.

"She sleeps, son. I think the poor little thing was more tuckered out than she realized when she got up this morning. Guess everything that happened yesterday is telling on her today. She walked around the grounds and was ready to take a nap—and there she's been for about three hours now."

"Yesterday was a cruel day for her, Momma. We'll let her sleep as long as she needs to," he said as he urged his mother to sit down for he had something else to tell her.

Kate sat in her rocking chair with a curious look. "What is it you have to tell me?"

A smug look came to his tanned face and a prideful glint was in his brilliant blue eyes as he told her he had gone to the Dupree house before he made his report to the authorities. "Madame Dupree insisted on going with me to back me up.

She didn't have to do that but she wanted to. But for her, I don't know that I would be a free man tonight!"

"She did that for you, Scott?"

"She did!"

"Then she's a very nice lady that I'm very grateful to her. Oh, Scott—we surely do have something to celebrate tonight! While your pretty Angelique sleeps, why don't you clean some fish and we'll have ourselves a fine feast tonight," she declared with the same brilliant gleam in her blue eyes.

Scott immediately jumped up to do as his mother had requested. But when he was out on the back porch cleaning fish he looked at his scaling kinfe, thinking about that moment of struggle when he didn't know whether he was going to live or die. He thanked God that he'd been the one to survive.

Fate had been kind to him!

Chapter Forty-eight

The sound of Scott's husky laughter was what Angelique heard upon awakening from her long nap. He was home! He wasn't put in jail for killing Francois. She sat up in the bed with a smile on her face and happiness swelling within her. Nothing else mattered, for Scott was not going to pay a price for what he did. It was a just punishment for Francois LaTour.

She gave her hair a few quick strokes with the brush before she rushed out to find him and his mother in the kitchen. When he looked up to see her, he leaped from the chair and grabbed her up in his arms to swing her around. Teasing her, he murmured in her ear, "Hello, sleepyhead. Here I was anticipating you down here to greet me and you were sleeping."

She smiled. "I needed my beauty sleep."

"And you surely got it for you sure look beautiful to me. Don't she, Momma?"

"She sure does," Kate agreed as she looked over at Angelique's glowing face. She knew that part of that radiance was because Scott was back home. Kate O'Roarke figured there better be a wedding soon for everyone's best interest. The passionate flame of youth, which she knew her Scott and Angelique were feeling, was impossible to control.

Timothy joined the gathering in the kitchen and when he smelled the wonderful aroma of fish frying in cast iron skillets his appetite was whetted.

A short time later, the four of them shared the meal, enjoying a festive evening in the O'Roarke's small kitchen. Timothy was a little tipsy as he poured plenty of his favorite Irish whiskey, which he usually tried to ration out to himself and Scott. But tonight was a special night—his son was not only alive but a free man!

As soon as Kate and Angelique had the kitchen in order, Scott announced that he was going to turn in early. "I'm getting up early so I can get over to Justin's to let him know he has an entire day off in return for what he did for me today."

He lingered only long enough to take a brief stroll around the yard with Angelique. It was the only chance he'd had to be alone with her. He had to have one of her kisses before he said goodnight. As they were walking, he grinned, "You know this arrangement can't go on much longer or I'll be a crazy man. Having you right here under my roof and not being able to make love to you is asking too much."

She laughed softly. "Then shall we have a hasty wedding, Scott?"

"Oh, love—I'd like that! And it's our own little nest I'd want and I know a place I can get if only you'll say the word."

"What have you found for our little nest?"

"It's the little place we come by just before we get to Justin's pier. It isn't too big but it's well built and the fellow who lived there for years died about two months ago. I've thought about buying it for weeks now."

"Could I see it, Scott?"

"Sure you could. Want to go there tomorrow after I come home?"

"I'd love to!"

"All right, we'll do it. Now do I have any hope of getting you to marry me quickly?" His blue eyes danced over her face adoringly.

"Whenever you wish, Scott, and I want us to be married right here in the bayou," she declared. This came as a shock to Scott for he knew that it wouldn't sit well with the Dupree family. They would never break down Maurice's barrier of resentment. But he couldn't refuse if this was what she wished.

"It shall be a bayou wedding if that's what you want, my angel," he promised as he began to guide her back toward the house.

He gave her one last lingering kiss before they went back. Then he said goodnight to her and his parents.

Everyone was still asleep when Scott left the next morning for Justin's pier where the *Bayou Queen* had docked the evening before.

Justin and Mimi were delighted to see their young friend and hear his good news. Justin naturally welcomed an entire day to be home with his family when Scott told him he'd take full charge of the *Bayou Queen* for the day. By the time he left their cottage and boarded the fishing boat the dawn was just breaking. Everything in the bayou was just rousing from the night's rest. The birds were singing a happy morning song and the little critters of the wooded area could be seen scampering on the banks. He saw a couple of raccoons having a playful romp along a fallen log and a trio of squirrels raced one another up one of the oaks. He spotted a couple of huge alligators sliding down from the bank to splash in the water. The way the fish were jumping up in the stream he felt certain there would be good fishing in Lake Pontchartrain today.

Very soon he was out of the bayou and moving into the waters of the lake. By the noon hour, he had made a good morning catch and Scott was sure that life would be calmer and more pleasant for a change.

He worked vigorously to fill his bins. Two hours before the sun was beginning to set, he had a fine day's catch so he guided his boat toward the wharf.

By the time he left the wharf he had enough to buy the four acres of land where the little cottage stood vacant where the old bachelor, Paul Carisse, had lived for as long as he could remember. It would be his wedding present to Angelique as she had said she wanted to marry in the bayou. He had to believe she was telling him she wished to live there, too.

Tomorrow, he was going to take the money he'd saved to purchase the little cottage and land for his beautiful bride-to-be.

When he arrived back home in the late afternoon, Angelique was there to greet him as the *Bayou Queen* neared the pier. She was exceedingly happy—he could tell by the look on her face—as she greeted him with the news that her mother had sent her two valises of clothing.

"Oh, Scott, she understands and that means so much to me!"

Scott felt like a fool—he had told his mother about how Simone had supported him but he'd failed to tell Angelique. He quickly told her and praised the dear lady for what she'd done.

"I'll never forget that, Angelique. Now all I've got to do is win your father's favor. I fear I'll have a harder time doing that, but I'll damned well try."

What Scott had told her and the arrival of the clothing told Angelique that her mother was defying her father's wishes. It was long overdue, for her father had been lording it over his wife for far too long.

Hand in hand they walked back toward the cottage. There was a certain magic Angelique found in the bayou that she'd never known in the palatial home she'd always lived in. There were things she did miss like her little pup and old Zachariah. But it was the relaxed, peaceful atmosphere and the people who'd become very dear to her that appealed to her.

There was no dressing for dinner or sitting down at an elegant table as she was used to. Kate O'Roarke came to the table wearing the simple cotton frock she'd worn all day to do her chores. Timothy came to the table in his cotton shirt and wrinkled twill pants. But there was laughter in that small kitchen and a happy look on their faces that Angelique did not often see around their candlelit dining table. She knew that wealth did not buy happiness. It was love that gave happiness and contentment, which was what she wanted. This was why she wanted her wedding to be in the bayou where life was simple and sweet!

After they had enjoyed the evening meal, Scott urged her to come with him. "We've only got an hour before the sun goes down. You want to see that place I was telling you about?"

"You know I do!" she declared, taking his hand.

Timothy gave his wife a quizzical look as the young couple rushed out but Kate explained that Scott was taking her up to the Carisse cottage. "Guess our son is thinking about that place for his honeymoon cottage, Timothy."

A broad smile spread over his face. "Hope you're right, Kate. They'd be close by and it sure would be nice to see the beautiful grandkids those two would have."

She roared with laughter. "We sound like a couple of sentimental old fools, Timothy."

"And what's wrong with that, Kate? That's what we're supposed to be at this age," he said with a grin.

Looking out the window, Kate figured that the young people wouldn't have much time to look over the cottage as the sun was going down quickly. It was hardly the kind of house that Angelique had been used to and she wondered how she would feel about that.

When Scott and Angelique arrived at the Carisse cottage, the path to the front door was overgrown and the grounds neglected. "Old Carisse once had all this looking beautiful. He loved to putter around the yard when he wasn't shrimping in his boat," Scott remarked.

The door wasn't locked so they walked right in.

There was no woman's touch in the cottage, Angelique quickly noticed, but things were orderly. A thick layer of dust covered everything, but it was neat with no clutter in any of the rooms.

"He was a bachelor—no family as far as I ever knew." Scott led her into the bedroom. Carisse's bed was neatly made, as he'd left it that morning when he'd gone out on his ill-fated boat trip. He was caught in a furious storm that hit the coast and wrecked his boat, killing him.

The cottage had a magnificent cypress floor which could be beautiful again once it was polished; Angelique could easily envision how she could make this place a perfect little cottage. None of the rooms was large, nor would they accommodate large scale furnishings like those back at her home in New Orleans. Bright colors could do wonders instead of the dull ones in it now.

Scott saw her eyes dancing over the parlor and enjoyed watching the excitement on her face.

"What do you see, my angel, if this were our cottage?"

"I see a huge rug in front of the hearth and two comfortable chairs on either side of the fireplace so we could sit and watch a fire burning. Maybe a bright floral-covered settee on that solid wall with curtains to match."

"I can see that," he said, trying to be very serious.

"I see my ladies' desk and chair over there in the corner so I could enjoy the bright sunshine—and a huge pot of greenery there, too, which would love all the bright light.

So he took her into the kitchen so she could tell him her ideas. "Oh, white and blue curtains for this room—that would be perfect."

Once again he agreed with her. Then they went back to the front bedroom. She was so very serious as she went over each little detail. "My dressing table would go over there by the window and my pink satin coverlet with all the little pillows on the bed. Your chest would go against that wall and my chest would be over here. A wicker rocker would be perfect there to sit in and enjoy the scenery."

"Well, that leaves the one back bedroom and we've just about enough time to go over it before it's too dark to see. Come on," he urged.

"Pastel curtains at the window, for this would be our nursery. A baby's bed over there away from the window and a chest here. Of course, there has to be a rocker in here, too," she added as she whirled around suddenly to look at him

403

with an impish smile. Scott looked at her adoringly for she hardly looked old enough to be a mother. He had never given that any thought at all. She looked so delicate and tiny, but then he also knew she was hardly helpless or frail.

"Well, I think we better buy this place so you can turn it into our enchanted cottage, Angelique Dupree."

"Really, Scott — you are going to buy it for us?"

"I am the first thing in the morning," he declared, pulling her into his arms. "My wedding gift to you!"

Because he wanted the cottage to be just exactly as she'd described, his next words were to stun Angelique. "I'm taking you back to New Orleans in the morning, Angelique."

She pulled away with a frown. "You're — you're what?"

"I'm taking you back to your folks tomorrow. Now, wait until I tell you why. When we get married I don't want to be living with my folks. I want us to come directly here to our own home, exactly as you pictured it. We'll have our wedding as you want it here in the bayou but if you're home for two weeks while I get this cottage ready you can make peace with your father. I know you want your parents to be here with us when we get married, don't you?"

"Well, yes," she muttered.

"Don't worry, honey, 'cause I'm coming to see you before the two weeks are over. Besides, during that time you can pack the things you want to bring out here. And you can visit with Gabriella and Kirby and invite them to our wedding. I want it to be a day and time we'll remember forever."

She stood on tiptoe to kiss him. "I didn't realize what a sentimental man you are, Scott O'Roarke, and it makes me love you even more. So I guess I must suffer for two weeks then."

He threw back his head and laughed. "Ah, but love, think what a honeymoon we can anticipate after those two weeks of being apart."

By the time they left the cottage darkness had closed in so Scott picked her up and carried her down the bank to the boat.

As it had surprised Angelique when Scott announced he was taking her back to New Orleans, it shocked his parents until he explained why.

Kate quickly remarked, "Well, I guess we can endure two weeks but that's all, Scott O'Roarke. That cottage will be cleaned and in order when I round up all my friends."

Scott grinned, for he'd seen her go into action before and he knew what bayou people could accomplish when they gathered together.

Angelique would learn this, too, once she'd lived there for a while.

Chapter Forty-nine

Three days after Scott had taken Angelique back to her parents' home and he and Justin were coming from their daily run, he glanced over to see activity around his newly-acquired property.

"That's the Gayarre boys, Scott," Justin grinned as they moved downstream. Later, after Scott had let Justin off and gone on home to eat supper, he rowed back to see what those four husky fellows had been up to. To his amazement he walked up a path no longer hidden by knee-high weeds and grass. All the grounds were manicured and the shrubs pruned. A coat of fresh paint gleamed on the steps and front door.

Inside he saw that Kate had been busy seeing that the house had been emptied of all furnishings except for the kitchen table, four chairs, and two long chests in the front room.

Like busy little leprechauns, his bayou friends worked while he and Justin were out on their fishing boat. Mimi made curtains for all the rooms according to Kate's instructions. Pink ones were hung in the front bedroom and blue ones covered the back bedroom windows. In the kitchen they were blue and white checked. The kitchen table and chairs had been given a new look with a coat of paint and the cupboards were clean and ready for pots and pans. The cypress floors were scrubbed and polished to a high sheen.

Angelique's enchanted cottage was coming along much faster than Scott had imagined. He only hoped that the time was passing as quickly for her as it was for him.

At the end of the week, Scott went to New Orleans to see his bride-to-be and purchase the gold wedding band he'd place on her finger in one week. He was eager to tell her about the transformation that had taken place since she'd left.

He'd always known about the generosity of his bayou friends but the Beauvoirs' gift of the exquisite bed with its high headboard astonished him. His mother told him it had come all the way from France. She smiled with pride when she told him that almost everything that Angelique had envisioned for the cottage had been accomplished.

After Scott arrived in New Orleans the next day and made his purchase of the wedding band, he headed down Old Cypress Road.

When he rode up the long drive of the Dupree estate and walked jauntily up to the front door he'd never been happier. As if she expected him at that exact moment, Angelique opened the door and flung herself into his arms. His lips captured hers in a long, hungry kiss. When they finally broke their embrace and strolled into the parlor, he told her with boyish enthusiasm about the magic happening at their little cottage. Simone happened to be at the top of the stairs observing the young couple.

She could not help thinking what a wonderful time this was for the two of them as she descended the stairs. She stood in the archway listening to Scott tell her that all that was lacking was her pink satin coverlet, her desk, and dressing table.

"Oh Scott, I can't believe this," Angelique exclaimed.

"Told you bayou people pitch in to help one another," he said, grinning down at her.

Simone found herself envying them. All week since Angelique had returned home and they'd been packing, she had been more and more agitated with her unbending and difficult husband. But it had been a marvelous week! She had shared these days with her daughter and they had shopped for a simple wedding gown, since that is what Angelique wanted.

Together they had visited Kirby's cottage and spent a pleasant two hours with Gabriella. Simone had a chance to get to know Gabriella and found her utterly charming. If the truth were told, most young quadroons like Gabriella were more beautiful than French Creoles. Simone had to admit secretly that Gabriella was almost as fair as Angelique. It was understandable that wealthy New Orleans gentlemen often took quadroons as mistresses.

She stood for a moment listening to Scott's exciting news before she made an entrance. She knew one thing for certain: she was going to her daughter's wedding even if Maurice flatly refused to go.

"Your parlor will be furnished, Scott and Angelique, and that will be my wedding gift," she declared as she walked into the room. "It will all be brought down to the bayou before the end of the week — I will see to it. Your house will be complete by the time of the wedding."

Angelique jumped up from the settee. "Did you hear all the wonderful things these people have been doing?"

"I did — and you may have all the things from this house that you wish to have in your new home before you marry. I shall bring my daughter to you on her wedding day, Scott, but I would like to have her here until that time. Can you understand this, Scott?"

"I certainly can, Madame Dupree." He was reluctant to leave Angelique but if he was to make this wedding as wonderful as he wanted it to be there were still many things to accomplish.

When he prepared to take his leave, he took Simone's hand and smiled at her warmly. "I'll be anticipating you bringing my bride to me in a week, madame."

"I will, Scott," she promised. She excused herself to allow the young lovers a private farewell. As she mounted the stairs she found herself wondering why Maurice could possibly object to such a nice young man.

He was hard-working and certainly honorable.

He was far more handsome than any young French Creole she'd ever met in their little clique.

After Angelique had said goodbye and come back into the house, she went to seek out her mother. For all the discomfort her father had made her feel this last week her mother had more than made up for it. She would be grateful to her forever for that and the warmth she'd shown to Scott.

The next morning, Angelique had an unexpected visitor. When she came downstairs she saw Nicole Benoit sitting in the parlor and she was elated. "Nicole! Oh, what a wonderful surprise!" To her great delight, her little friend looked as perky and vivacious as she used to and there were certainly no signs of the advanced pregnancy she would have expected to see.

But Nicole explained that. "God granted me a blessing and I miscarried, Angelique. I heard that there is to be a wedding in the bayou. May I come?"

"Of course, you can! Oh, Nicole, it's good to have you back!"

"I'm not back for long, Angelique. I'll leave shortly after your wedding is over—I'm going to Paris for a year. My parents have agreed to this and I shall see if I have any talent as an artist. I'll be living with my Tante Fifi, my mother's younger sister, but I'll keep in touch with you."

"You better or I'll never forgive you."

"Oh, I will and I'll bring you a canvas I did just recently in Baton Rouge. It's my wedding gift to you and Scott so if one day I become famous you can say you have an original Nicole Benoit painting," she added, laughing infectiously.

By the time Nicole left and Angelique climbed the stairs to her bedroom, she could not have been happier for the people she loved so dearly were all going to be at her wedding. Nicole, Kirby, and Gabriella would be there and little Nat was going to stay at the house with Tom. Simone had already told her that her father was proving to be very stubborn about attending with her.

"But nothing is going to stop me from coming, Angelique, and I'll have Zachariah accompany me if I have to come without your father," she'd told Angelique.

"Oh, I'd love for Zachariah to come. Please bring him, Momma," she urged.

"I will, Angelique. I promise."

From the minute Maurice Dupree arrived in the late afternoon a shroud of gloom seemed to fall over the house. It had been that way every evening since Angelique had come home so it seemed normal as the three of them dined together.

Once again she sought to make a feeble attempt to spur some interest in her father about her approaching wedding by telling him of Scott's visit.

"So it's a week from today you'll be marrying Scott, eh?"

"Yes, Poppa. I guess I'm just about the happiest lady alive."

411

He gave her a weak smile and forced himself to say, "I'm glad to know you're so happy, Angelique."

As he had been doing every evening after the meal was finished, he excused himself from the table and went for a stroll in the garden.

Angelique saw the distressed look on her mother's face and so Simone would not feel she had to put on a brave front, announced she was going up to bed.

But what Angelique did not know was that Simone did not linger in the parlor. She, too, mounted the stairs and did not wait for Maurice to come in from the garden.

For the next few days Simone threw herself into keeping her promise to Scott. All of Angelique's belongings, along with a newly-purchased settee and two matching chairs, were loaded aboard a flat boat to be taken into the bayou. But when the wagon came to pick up the items, without Maurice's approval she sent several bottles of his finest wine to the bayou cottage.

After all, this was their one and only daughter's wedding!

Not even Angelique had realized the change in her mother and the authoritative air she'd assumed recently. Had she sensed it, she would have applauded her. The insanity of it all was that it took what had happened to her daughter to make Simone realize what a strong woman she was. It was Maurice who wanted to make her think she was weak and helpless! Suddenly, she realized she wasn't and she began to assert herself. This did not please her husband.

Nothing had been the same since the first night Angelique was abducted. Simone had wondered if it ever would be the same. She honestly doubted it for she would never be the same woman. If Maurice could not accept that, then so be it. Neither could he accept the young woman his beautiful daughter had become. But that was his failing and not hers or Angelique's!

Never in her life had Simone had a more complete understanding of herself and the way she wanted to live her life, so she slept peacefully. She did not know when Maurice came to bed.

Each day became harder for Maurice Dupree and he woke up the next morning feeling as exhausted as he'd felt when he'd gone to bed.

He went through the routine of his usual working day but his heart was no longer in his business when he went to the city or took an inspection trip around his sugar cane crop. In part, Simone was right about his displeasure with his wife and daughter becoming stubbornly independent. But neither of them had any inkling of the real torment gnawing away at him — or what had sparked it.

He was like a volcano that had been peaceful and calm then suddenly erupted with fire and fury. A door he'd closed long ago and never expected to see again had been opened. For the last few months one door seemed to jar another open. He didn't know how to close them.

He left the house long before anyone else woke up. Simone was up and dressed before Angelique finally joined her downstairs. "Good morning, dear. I trust you slept well." She laughed as she commented that little Cuddles must still be sleepy from the way she was yawning.

Taking a sip of her hot tea she asked Angelique to be sure she had chosen all the things she wished to be taken to her cottage. "I have a man coming to load them on his wagon this afternoon."

Angelique named the various items again and Simone jotted them down. She told Angelique she should pay a visit to Nicole or Gabriella for it was going to be a very busy day.

"Well, I think I might go over to see Gabriella this afternoon," she told her mother as she turned to leave the parlor.

Now that she had the list of things her daughter wished to take she went to summon Zachariah.

When the elderly black man came to the house she told him to go to see Elmer Murdock and tell him she wanted him to do a job for her.

An hour later Murdock and one of his hired men were at the house and began to carry the desk and chair, along with the other items from upstairs, to his flat bed wagon.

When Angelique returned from Gabriella's and found the vacant corner of her bedroom and the wicker rocker missing by her bedroom window, it looked strange. The pink satin coverlet was also gone from her bed. Rushing down the stairs she looked for her mother but she could not find her anywhere. But then she spied her out in the garden picking some beautiful asters, so she went through the door and joined her mother, who was bent over cutting a cluster of golden blossoms.

"Momma, my — my room looks so different," she declared.

Simone straightened up and laughed. "It's all on the way to your new home, *ma petite*. I also included that lovely floral settee we had in one of the extra bedrooms. You'll also find two very comfortable chairs for your little parlor."

Angelique flung her arms around her mother in a warm embrace. "Oh, Momma — you've been so wonderful about everything. I love you for that!"

"Oh, my darling — I'm delighted for you. I want you and Scott to be happy."

"We will. I'm sure we will be. I — I just wish that Poppa could be like you but I can't let that stop me from marrying Scott."

"And you shouldn't, Angelique. You'd regret that the rest of your life." Seeing that she had her basket filled she started toward the house with Angelique trailing beside her.

Simone smiled as she inquired about the pup romping around the grounds. "You'll be taking Cuddles with you, won't you, dear?"

"Oh, I could never leave her behind."

Maurice stood in his study looking out the window at the two of them coming toward the veranda. They seemed so happy. He knew that

Angelique would never forgive him for not going to her wedding but he could not go.

But then Simone would never forgive him, either!

Chapter Fifty

For three days before the wedding Mimi helped Kate bake and cook for the feast. The little honeymoon cottage was ready—Scott was more than pleased when he toured the place after the things had arrived from New Orleans.

The cupboards were even stocked with necessities as Angelique and Scott began their lives in their little home. He felt pride that she would have her enchanted cottage, but he knew he never could have done it alone. His heart swelled with gratitude to all his family and friends.

He had never expected to be the nervous groom-to-be but damned if he wasn't now that the time was growing near.

All he had to do was hope that the weather would cooperate as it was to be a twilight wedding with dinner served afterwards on the grounds of his parents' home. It was the bayou people's way when there was a big gathering for none of the little cottages could accommodate such a crowd. There were no spacious dining rooms or parlors like those in the homes of Angelique or Nicole.

With all she'd done Kate had made herself a

new frock and new shirts for Timothy and Scott. But Scott knew she had stayed up late several nights to do so. He adored her for all that she'd done for him and Angelique.

The day before the wedding Scott made a last trip into New Orleans. His restless heart had to know his bride-to-be was really coming to the bayou tomorrow to marry him. He knew he wouldn't sleep if he didn't see her one more time before they were married. This last week had been endless—there was no denying he was getting impatient.

Angelique had to laugh when he confessed all this. "Nothing would stop me from coming to you tomorrow, Scott O'Roarke. Don't you know that?"

"Guess I'm just nervous, love."

He told her of the arrangements he'd made with Justin to come in the *Bayou Queen* to get her and her family as well as Gabriella and Kirby.

"Oh, I've got some exciting news, Scott! Nicole is back and she's coming. She's going to Paris to live with her aunt and study art."

"But what about—about the baby?"

"She said God blessed her by allowing her to miscarry. She was happy about it. She's just fine."

"Perhaps it was a blessing since Mark proved to be such a bastard."

He gathered her in his arms for one last kiss until the next day when there would be no more parting for the two of them.

As he slowly moved back to leave her, he murmured softly with a flaming fire in his blue eyes, "Until tomorrow, my angel! Then never again will we be apart."

"Tomorrow, my love!" she responded, blowing him a kiss as he finally turned to leave.

All she could think about after he left was that in a matter of hours she would be the wife of Scott O'Roarke. Nothing could have made her happier!

Maybe he wasn't wealthy but how rich she was going to be with a man so devoted and loving!

Angelique's wedding gown was not traditional but then this was not a fancy New Orleans wedding with all her parents' French Creole friends. This was a bayou wedding and she had picked out a pink satin gown with a ruffled flounce. The sleeves were gathered with lace trim and the low scooped neckline was edged with lace. Atop her head she would wear no veil but some dainty pink velvet flowers attached to a comb. Her bouquet was the last lovely rosebuds of pink and white from her mother's garden.

She planned to wear her mother's pearls and, Simone's special gift — a pair of magnificent pearl earrings. Gabriella had given her an exquisite lace-bordered handkerchief and a fancy blue satin garter.

When Angelique went to bed she had no inkling of all the wonderful things happening in the bayou to make her wedding the most wonderful occasion. Nicole had hired a boatman to take her to the O'Roarkes and with her she took the painting she wanted to present to Angelique and Scott as their wedding gift. She and Kate had gone to the cottage and laboriously worked to place it over the mantel in the small parlor. Kate exclaimed, "Mercy! That's Scott and Angelique sitting on that grassy knoll!"

"Yes, Madame O'Roarke—it is. I did this when I needed to capture a happy time in my life and I remembered a day that I'd shared with Scott and Angelique."

"Oh, dear, what a talent you have! How wonderful to be able to do something like that! What a glorious gift God gave to you!" Kate declared as she stood there admiring the painting. How thrilled her son and Angelique would be to see this when they entered the cottage.

"Well, I'm going to find out how good I am, Madame O'Roarke. I'm going to Paris to study," Nicole added.

"You take my word for it, young lady. You're good! Look at my Scott's face and you've even captured his crooked grin."

"Oh, thank you, madame."

Kate figured that with a French Creole daughter-in-law she'd get used to being called madame but for now she still found it strange.

Nicole left for New Orleans and Kate returned to her own cottage down the stream. There were still many things she had to attend to before her head could hit the pillow.

It was also late when old Zachariah finally went to bed for he was putting the finishing touches on the wooden cradle he'd purchased a week ago in the market place. This was going to be his wedding gift to the young couple for he knew they would surely be needing it soon.

By the time the last stroke was done he was well pleased with the gift he would proudly present to them tomorrow. He even purchased a new hat for the occasion and brushed his best pair of pants and old coat. A mending job had been necessary on his one good white shirt. When all this was done and he was prepared to meet tomorrow, he finally sat down on his cot and dimmed the lamp.

Scott was upset when he woke to a cloudy sky. Fate could not play such a cruel trick! But there was no denying it when he looked out the window and saw the heavy, dark clouds. But his mother kept telling him that those clouds were going to lift and the sun would come shining through.

Irish optimism never ceased to amaze him and he prayed that she was right. But by midday the heavy clouds still shrouded the bayou.

At the appointed hour that Justin was due to leave the bayou to pick up the wedding party in New Orleans, the clouds were still there. Kate watched her son fuss as he paced the floor. "There's nothing you can do to change it, Scott. Best you go get yourself ready to greet your bride."

He'd not told his mother or father about the fine attire he'd purchased a week ago. He'd never liked the idea of dressing in fine tailored pants or coat, but for a bride that would look as beautiful as Angelique he wanted to look handsome. So he'd spent what he'd considered a tremendous price for a pair of deep grey pants and a slate-colored coat. For the first time in his life he planned to wear a fine white linen shirt. But his mother gave him the new shirt she'd spent many hours working on, so it was hers that he wore when he got dressed.

The sun did come out as Kate had predicted it would and all the clouds rolled away. As the sun began to set, she declared smugly, "Scott, I told you so!" She also took the time to survey him in his elegant new clothes. "Well now, aren't you a handsome one!" Motherly pride gleamed on her face and she was in a frivolous mood as she called out to her husband, "Would you look at this son of ours, Timothy? Is he a real gent or not?"

"I'd say he's a real dandy," Timothy laughed.

There was a very festive air around the O'Roarke cottage this autumn evening. In her new dress with all her food prepared, Kate was ready to greet her guests.

The entourage from New Orleans arrived at the appointed time and came from the pier up to the cottage. To Scott's dismay he saw that Maurice Dupree was not among them and he knew how disappointed Angelique must be. Her face did not reflect it — he'd never seen her looking more radiant.

She and her mother were followed by Zachariah

carrying the cradle. Kirby and Gabriella followed carrying their wedding gifts.

Scott knew that as long as he lived he'd never forget this special moment. She had come back to him and now he knew nothing was going to stop him from marrying her. Twice he'd lost her and the fear was still there that something could have happened.

No bride could have been more beautiful than Angelique in her lovely pink gown with the velvet flowers in her long black hair. He told her that as soon as he took her hand in his and led her and her mother over to introduce Simone to his parents.

"Well, Mrs. Dupree, it's a pleasure to meet you," Kate said as she shook her hand.

"A pleasure for me, Madame O'Roarke, as well. It's a glorious evening for the wedding," Simone said with a warm smile. She was glad she'd worn one of her simpler gowns. Her only jewelry worn was a cameo brooch.

Outside the cottage in Kate's small garden where people would be sitting on long makeshift benches, Justin and Mimi were greeting guests as the neighbors began to arrive.

After the parish priest had come, Kate suggested that she and Simone go out to the garden to sit with Timothy.

It was a brief ceremony with Kirby by Scott's side and Gabriella with Angelique. Old Zachariah walked Angelique out of the cottage—it was a grand moment for the old black man who found it difficult to understand how Maurice Dupree could be so hardhearted. More than ever he knew what truly gracious ladies Simone and Angelique were.

It was a beautiful twilight time when the priest declared Scott and Angelique man and wife. Her new husband held her lovingly and kissed her as the twenty guests looked on, blissfully happy for the couple. They made a very striking pair with Scott in his fine grey attire and Angelique in her pink wedding gown.

They were immediately swamped by guests wishing them well. Simone and Kate gave way to tears, feeling very sentimental and happy about the touching moment they'd shared.

Timothy and Zachariah exchanged understanding smiles and Timothy whispered that it was a shame that Angelique's father had denied himself such a special memory. "Sure hate it that he didn't come," Timothy said.

"Fears he'll regret it someday," Zachariah told him, shaking his head dejectedly.

The bayou rang with laughter and gaiety for the next few hours as they ate Kate's food and drank the fine wine Nicole had brought to the O'Roarkes.

There seemed to be a reluctance for the neighbors to board their canoes to go home and the hour grew very late before the first guests pulled away from the pier.

Kindhearted Kate suggested to Simone that she and Zachariah spend the night instead of making the long trip back to New Orleans.

"You may have Scott's room and I've a daybed

Zachariah could use. Then Justin could get you home the first thing in the morning. We'd love to have you stay, Mrs. Dupree."

At first, Simone was going to refuse but she was a little weary after all the excitement of the wedding and the merrymaking so she did accept the invitation. Besides, it would serve Maurice right if she didn't return home tonight. Let him stew and fume!

Hearing Kate and Simone talking, Mimi knew Nicole would want to get back to New Orleans and she also knew how much Justin had done to see that Scott's wedding was perfect. So she immediately urged Nicole to spend the night with them. This way poor Justin could get home and go to bed as he was probably ready to do.

Nicole eagerly accepted Mimi's offer. "Oh, you're an angel! My head is slightly whirling — too much wine." In her hand she had the bride's bouquet which she'd caught when Angelique tossed it as she and Scott stood at the pier ready to go to their honeymoon cottage.

"Think there's any truth to the fable that I'll be the next to be married, Mimi?" she giggled.

"I believe it because it happened to me when I caught my friend's wedding bouquet. I got married about three months later," Mimi declared.

"Well, I hope my wedding is just as beautiful as Angelique's. I'm so very happy for them!"

Justin was delighted to hear that there would be no trip to make tonight.

"Getting your friends married can really tax

you," he sighed, and the three of them began to laugh.

All of them were ready to take their leave and go to Justin's cottage to seek the sweet comfort of sleep.

Chapter Fifty-one

It seemed to Angelique that their friends had thought of everything to make their wedding perfect. Neighbors had made garlands of flowers to decorate the canoe they boarded to get to their cottage. The first thing she noticed as Scott carried her through the door was Nicole's painting over their mantel. "Dear God, Scott—look!"

At first he thought something was wrong until his eyes glanced upward. "That Nicole! How darn sweet of her to capture that afternoon on canvas for us forever!"

"Oh, Scott—I'm so very happy and I couldn't have possibly had a more wonderful wedding."

"Nor I, Angelique," he smiled taking her hand in his. A glint came to his blue eyes as he looked at the gold wedding band on her finger. "I'm also happy to see that band on your finger and know you're truly my wife."

"It took no wedding band to make me yours, Scott O'Roarke."

"Well, just the same it makes me feel better," he teased. Remembering that Nicole had whispered that they'd find a bottle of champagne she'd left when she and his mother had hung the painting, Scott suggested they have some.

Angelique laughed softly. "I feel like I've already had enough wine but since I'm with my husband I guess it's all right."

"You're in good hands, love," he whispered, leading her by the hand into the kitchen. He found the champagne and poured it as Angelique stood observing her little kitchen and the newly-painted furniture. As they sipped their champagne, he took her on a tour of the cottage. Her pink satin coverlet was neatly placed across the bed and her wicker rocker was by the window.

Everything was exactly as she'd imagined it could look. They even strolled into the vacant bedroom to see the blue curtains that Mimi had made hanging at the window. In a matter of fact tone, she told him, "Zachariah's cradle will go in this room."

Mischief twinkled in his eyes as he teased her. "The little fellow's going to be awfully lonely in here all by himself."

"So it's to be a boy?" she asked as she whirled around to face him.

"The first one but then the next one will be a darling little daughter with long black hair like her Momma's."

"Sounds like you've got it all planned out, Scott."

"Oh, I have. I've got all kinds of plans for us that I've not had time to tell you about, Angelique. But right now I think I better take that glass. It's tilting, and that dress is too beautiful to spoil with dripping champagne." He noticed

428

that his beautiful bride was feeling a bit tipsy.

A few minutes later he had the devil's own time helping her out of the gown, cussing the dressmaker who'd made the task so complicated. She giggled as she felt him fumbling and he swore he'd make her pay for making fun of him.

"Enough to drive a man crazy!" he mumbled as he finally got the job accomplished and Angelique sank down on the bed.

She was a sensuous sight as her lacy undergarments displayed much of her satiny flesh. His eyes flashed with fire as he looked down at her and in a husky voice he murmured, "God, Angelique—you're the most beautiful thing I've ever seen!"

His eyes were still devouring her as he started to remove his shirt. He sat down beside her, his bare chest pressed against her, and took her lips in a tender kiss. As his strong arms enclosed her, she felt the fierce pounding in his chest. Her heart also beat faster as the thrill of passion surged within her.

Once again, his fingers started to fumble as he began to remove her undergarments. He was impatient to have nothing between him and her silken skin.

With a couple of hasty moves, he removed his pants and lay by her side.

Unhurriedly but ardently he made love to her, sensing that her passion was soaring as fervently and wildly as his. Her small body swayed and arched against him, sending a mounting sensation through his body.

Angelique felt the blazing heat of him consuming her as his lips and hands as well as his body caressed and filled her so completely. She moaned softly with pleasure as he carried her to each level of ecstasy. She hoped the moment would never end although she knew it must. She gasped breathlessly as she felt his mighty shudder.

They lay there in sweet exhausted languor with no need to speak. Several minutes later Scott tried to untangle his arm from her long mane of hair.

"Got a feeling that Zachariah's cradle will be occupied in nine months," he whispered in her ear.

"I love you, Scott O'Roarke," she murmured softly in a sleepy voice. But there was a smug smile on her face for she was almost sure that the cradle would be occupied in another seven months. But she had had enough excitement for tonight. She would enlighten him about that tomorrow, she decided.

Right now, she wanted to lie in her husband's arms and sleep!

The morning after the wedding, Simone and Zachariah sat at the table with Scott's parents to enjoy a hearty breakfast before they boarded the *Bayou Queen* for New Orleans. Simone could see why her daughter had come to love the people of the bayou—she could not remember when she'd enjoyed herself as much as she had the last twenty-four hours.

They made her feel so welcome in their humble little cottage and she found herself thoroughly enjoying the lively company of Kate O'Roarke. She really felt they were dear friends by the time they embraced and she boarded the *Bayou Queen*.

"You come back to see us and soon," Kate called out as she waved goodbye.

"And you must come to see me, Kate," Simone replied. In truth, she was reluctant to invite her, not knowing how Maurice would react.

It was a very happy trio that disembarked at the dock in New Orleans. Nicole had also had a wonderful time staying overnight with Mimi and Justin.

When she told Simone goodbye, she said, "I'll not be seeing you for a time, Madame Dupree. I'm leaving New Orleans day after tomorrow to sail for France. But I'm sure taking some wonderful memories with me. I wouldn't have missed Angelique's wedding for anything in the world. She's a very happy woman, madame."

Simone gave her a kiss on the cheek and wished her well. "I know she is, Nicole, and I hope you will be, too."

All the way home Simone and Zachariah talked about the wonderful time they'd had. Zachariah said, "They are mighty fine folks—those O'Roarkes. Mademoiselle Nicole is right. Your little Angelique is a happy lady."

When they pulled into the long drive Simone wondered why Maurice's buggy wasn't there to get him to his office—then it dawned on her that it was Sunday.

She got out of the carriage and bid Zachariah farewell. Once she had taken off her bonnet she walked into the dining room expecting to find Maurice but he wasn't there.

There were no servants scurrying around the hallway or dining room but she heard them chattering in the kitchen. She did not wish to seek any of them outright so she turned to mount the stairs.

There was a strange quiet on the second landing as well. Their bedroom was as neat and undisturbed as she'd left it late yesterday afternoon when she'd gone to the bayou.

Feminine instinct told her that something was not right; perhaps she should have come home last night.

Something told her to go to the study. In the hall she encountered her servant, Dicie, and instructed her to bring a pot of tea.

She then proceeded down the dark hallway toward Maurice's study. As she went through the carved door, the room seemed so dark she went over immediately to pull back the drapes and allow the bright sunshine to enter the room. She sat alone for a while wondering where her husband could be. By this time Dicie had brought her a tray with the pot of tea and she asked if the servant had seen monsieur.

"No, madame, I've not seen him this morning. Come to think of it, I don't think Monsieur Dupree dined at home last night."

"Thank you, Dicie. That will be all," Simone said, dismissing her. Taking her tea, she roamed

432

around the room for a moment before going over to Maurice's desk where she saw a thick letter addressed to her. Slowly she sat down in his black leather chair. She had only to read the first three lines to know why there was no sign of him. He was gone!

His letter stated that he was catching a boat last evening to go to Mobile and he went on to explain that it was from Mobile that his family had migrated to New Orleans. 'I had two choices as I saw it, Simone,' his letter stated. 'I could leave without facing you and Angelique, or I could put a pistol to my head. I chose the cowardly way out, as I didn't have the guts to kill myself.'

Simone wondered if this was some kind of nightmare. This could not really be happening — but she had the letter in her hand and there it was in Maurice's own hand.

So she read on. He explained that she would understand everything by the time she finished the letter. She found that hard to believe from a solid family man and respected citizen of the community.

He wrote that she would have no financial worries, as their sugar cane business was in the capable hands of his foreman and an expert bookkeeper. There were ample funds in the bank for her to live comfortably the rest of her life.

"It was strange that all this madness happened at such a happy time for us — when Scott rescued Angelique from Pointe a la Hache. She spoke to us about what had happened and sang the praises of this young quadroon woman, Gabriella, he wrote. Simone laid the letter down on the desk. Was Maurice going to tell her he had a quadroon mistress as most French Creole gentlemen did? Had it been the exotically beautiful Gabriella? It would literally crush Angelique if it were true. Perhaps he did not attend the wedding because he knew he would have to face her.

There was no turning back and Simone knew it so she poured herself another cup of tea. Going back over to the desk, she sank down into the chair and picked up the letter again.

His revelation went back some twenty-odd years to when they were first married and the long time it took before she finally conceived Angelique. He spoke about the past and how he was always thought of as the nice Dupree and his brother, Jean Gabriel, was considered the scoundrel. Maurice did not deny that Jean Gabriel paid regular visits to the section of what was called shanty town on the levee. But he confessed that one night when he and Jean Gabriel had been drinking heavily, he went along. He'd spent that night and other nights after that with a young black woman named Cornelia. She was fairer than most of the black women there. In her own way, he wrote, she was very beautiful.

She gave birth to a baby daughter, Maurice continued, who grew into a darling toddler he continued to visit at the shanty where Cornelia lived.

'I closed the door on that part of my life after Angelique was born and never went back again,'

434

he stated. Years went by and he never thought about that episode in his life until Angelique returned home and spoke about Gabriella. That was the name Cornelia had given her daughter.

It was enough to make him recall that part of his past—then he chanced to be riding in from the sugar cane fields the day Gabriella came to the house. He knew she had to be Cornelia's daughter because of the sharp resemblance, despite her lighter skin. Her features and the way she wore that kerchief tied around her head had so reminded him of Cornelia that he was stunned with shock.

He knew in his own mind she was his daughter—Angelique's half-sister. The burden grew heavier and heavier as their lives seemed to tangle more and more with the past. There was no way to shut the doors as he once had and he knew it.

In the last paragraph of his letter he wrote, 'I decided to be my own executioner to pay for my sins of long ago. I thought about blowing my brains out but I didn't want that scandal for you and Angelique. So I decided to disappear, which is what I will do while you are with our daughter at her wedding. It will be your decision whether Angelique reads this. I suddenly realized the last few months that you were a far wiser woman than I'd ever realized.

Slowly Simone folded the letter and left the study to go to her bedroom. There was no question about allowing Angelique to read the letter—she wouldn't keep the truth from her daughter as Maurice had kept it from her all these years.

There could never be true happiness if it was built on lies. Angelique had a right to know the truth, as did Gabriella. As far as she was concerned, Simone did not figure it really mattered for she had lived most of her life. But by the time she reached her bedroom door she was thinking about her precious Angelique. How happy she was that her daughter had followed her heart's desire and married the man she loved! She could not help but wonder how different her own life might have been if she'd defied her parents and married the young man she loved when she was seventeen.

It didn't matter, Simone told herself. All that was past. Today was almost gone now so she was not going to dwell on this; there was always tomorrow and she was looking forward to a new day and a new dawn.

She was already anticipating her next trip to the bayou to see her daughter and her new-found friends.

She had some good years left to enjoy life and that was exactly what she intended to do!

Chapter Fifty-two

Simone was in no hurry to announce to anyone that her husband had left her. But the servants were a gossipy lot and the word did spread that Maurice Dupree was not at home and no longer in the city.

The only ones that Simone did tell, because necessity demanded it, were the foreman and the bookkeeper. As she had expected, their response was the assurance they'd help her. Each had told her she could rely on them to do for her what they'd done for Monsieur Dupree.

For almost a week, she went about her usual daily routine but she knew that very soon she had to make a trip to the bayou to tell Angelique. At least she could have a wonderful week or two before her mother brought this news.

Little Nat, whose eyes and ears were always open and alert, had been down by the wharf when he heard two gentlemen talking. One remarked that he'd seen Maurice Dupree boarding the *Delta Star* for Mobile, Alabama, a few nights previous. Nat had rushed home to convey all he'd heard to Gabriella and when Kirby came home from his smitty shop she told him.

"Think we should pay a visit over there tonight, Gabriella. I found her a very nice lady and felt a bit sorry for her when her husband didn't show up for the wedding," Kirby declared.

The two of them got in the buggy to head out on Old Cypress Road as soon as the evening meal was over. Little Nat and Tom were left in charge of cleaning up the kitchen.

When they arrived one of the servants ushered them into the parlor where Simone sat with Angelique's pup keeping her company. She greeted them warmly. "I've still got to get this little lady out to Angelique," Simone said. "She's a handful for me and misses her mistress terribly."

She seemed in a very pleasant mood and Gabriella wondered if little Nat had heard wrong. She and Kirby took a seat but they politely refused the offer of refreshments.

"You're looking quite well, madame," Gabriella remarked. "I trust Monsieur Dupree is fine?"

Simone realized the reason for their unexpected visit. It was obvious that the rumors and gossip had them over the last week. They were concerned, which endeared them to her.

So she decided that while she'd not planned it this way, she would allow Gabriella to read Maurice's letter before she let Angelique read it.

In a calm, cool voice Simone informed them of Maurice's departure on the evening of Angelique's wedding. "Please excuse me for a moment. I've something to show you." Her slender figure rose from the chair and shortly she returned with the letter, handing it to Gabriella. "Read it, my dear, and then I've no need to say more."

As she was asked to do, Gabriella began to read. Kirby saw her expressive face run a gamut of emotions as she perused the pages. Instinctively, he knew that there was something in those pages that involved her.

He had never seen Gabriella cry in all the time they'd been together, but when she finished the letter there were tears in her lovely almond-shaped eyes. She handed the letter to Kirby, knowing he had to share this.

Gabriella's hand reached out to take Simone's.

"Oh, madame—my—my heart goes out to you and I can only pray that Angelique will not hate me. That would break my heart. Now I understand why I was so drawn to her at Pointe a la Hache. I wondered about that so often. I just knew that if I could prevent it Francois was not going to use that beautiful girl. Now I know why."

Simone patted her hand and assured her, "Angelique will not hate you, Gabriella. This I know. I think she'll be pleased to know that you're her sister. Oh, no, it will not be you she will hate."

By now, Kirby had finished reading the letter. All he could do was mutter, "Dear God! Dear God!"

Simone assured Gabriella that her heart went out to her, too. "But it makes me feel very happy that both you and Angelique seem to have found happiness." Simone assured them both that she was going to be fine.

Gabriella could see from the look on her face that she truly meant it. Simone Dupree was a very strong lady and she now understood where Angelique had gathered her strength during that terrible time at Pointe a la Hache.

"We'll say goodnight madame, but any time you should need us you only have to let us know and we'll be here. When you see Angelique, give her our love," Gabriella said as she urged Kirby toward the door.

As they traveled back to their cottage, Kirby knew his beautiful Gabriella was in a state of shock. She sat so quiet and thoughtful by him in the buggy that he didn't try to talk.

When she did finally speak it was about her fears that things could never be the same. "Once she reads that letter, Kirby, I just know she'll never want to see me again," she lamented.

He put his arm around her and pulled her closer. "I'll bet you're wrong. I got more faith in Angelique Dupree than that. Isn't to say that she ain't going to be as stunned as you were but after that passes she'll realize why you were such instant friends. Just wait and see."

She wanted so to believe him and she knew he was right—she would just have to wait and see.

Maurice Dupree had been gone almost three weeks before Simone finally decided to go to the bayou and visit with the O'Roarkes. It was late on a Friday afternoon that she had Zachariah take her down to the dock so she could catch

Scott's *Bayou Queen*. She mentioned nothing as she traveled with him and Justin over the lake toward the bayou.

It was good to see that her son-in-law was obviously still in such a state of bliss. In that happy-go-lucky way of his he was telling Simone how Angelique's cooking was improving. "It's not to say that a lot of things haven't got burned," he laughed.

"I never thought about that but it's true. She's never cooked in her life. I'm sure you've helped her though," she said, smiling up at him.

"Well, I think I did know more than she did and Momma and Mimi have been very good about bringing some stuff over."

"So you haven't gone hungry?"

"Oh, no ma'am. You know you couldn't have come on a better evening. We're going over to the folks' for a fish fry."

"Sounds wonderful. I'll stay the night over there since your mother invited me. I know you have no bedroom except your own."

"Just Zachariah's cradle right now," he admitted, a gleam of mischief in his eyes.

As they reached the bayou Scott noticed that his mother-in-law's mood grew very quiet when she'd been so gay only a moment ago. "Something wrong, Mrs. Dupree?"

"I fear there is and it just dawned on me there is something I must do. I've a letter for Angelique to read. Perhaps I should let you read it first before we get to your cottage. Then you can advise me what to do."

Scott lingered at Justin's wharf after Justin left as Simone handed him the letter. Compassion was etched on his tanned face as he finally handed the letter back to her. "Why didn't you come to us sooner instead of bearing all this alone for almost three weeks? You needed to be with your family."

"No, Scott, dear. I needed to be by myself but it's very sweet of you to feel that way. Why should I have spoiled the most wonderful occasion in your lives?"

Scott nodded that he understood. "You're quite a grand lady, Mrs. Dupree. Now I know why Angelique loves and admires you so. She said a dozen times how glad she was that you and Zachariah came to our wedding even though her father wouldn't. Tell her before we go over to my folks for supper. She's a pretty brave lady, too, so it will be all right. There's no reason to delay it as I see it."

"I'll do as you say then." Simone could see the next fishing pier jutting out in front of a giant cypress. She knew they were coming to Scott's cottage.

Angelique had been sitting on the front step as she often did lately to watch for the *Bayou Queen*. Tonight she did not have to cook supper, for Kate had invited them over for a fish fry and that sounded good. Cooking had proved to be an ordeal but she knew that one day it would become easier. She was determined to cook as good as Kate O'Roarke did but she didn't fool herself that it was going to take time.

Her black eyes flashed with excitement when she saw the petite figure of her mother walking along beside her husband. They were laughing and talking as they came toward the pathway.

Leaping up from the steps, she dashed down to greet them. Hugging her mother warmly, she exclaimed, "What a marvelous surprise!"

It pleased Simone very much to see that her daughter was overjoyed by her unexpected visit. She was only sorry that she had to bring such news.

Angelique took pride in taking her mother around the house as soon as they entered the cottage. She pointed out the wedding gift Nicole had given them and from there she was led into the bright, cheerful kitchen.

When they were in the bedroom, Angelique told her if she wished to refresh herself before they went to the O'Roarkes she could use their bedroom. "Recognize my little dressing table and stool?" she asked smiling.

"Of course I do, dear. You look so very happy, Angelique!"

"I am deliriously happy, Momma! Is everything fine with you and Poppa? You look wonderful! Maybe one of these days we can get that stubborn father of mine out here," she murmured with a soft little laugh.

It was difficult to know where to begin, so Simone decided to do as Scott had suggested. She asked Angelique to sit on the bed because she had something to tell her.

"It's Poppa, isn't it, Momma?" Angelique asked

as she sat down. "Is he sick?"

"Angelique, when I got home from your wedding Poppa was gone and I found this on his desk. Rather than me telling you I'll let you read the letter—then you'll understand everything." With that said, she handed Angelique the letter.

As she'd watched Gabriella, Simone observed the many emotions on her daughter's face. She saw the frown and Angelique shaking her head as though she was finding the letter hard to believe. She wiped away a tear or two from her eyes. When the last page was read, she slowly folded the letter and collapsed into her mother's arms. "Now we know the devil tormenting Poppa for all those many weeks, don't we, Momma? But it was not our curse."

"No, Angelique, it was not our curse." She wanted no secrets between her and her daughter so she told her that she had let Gabriella read the letter when she and Kirby had come by the house a few nights ago.

As Gabriella had done, Angelique dejectedly sighed. "Oh, I hope this won't destroy our friendship."

"That was her concern but I tried to assure her you wouldn't hate her," Simone said.

"Hate her? Oh, dear God, that's the one good thing in that letter: she and I are half-sisters! Nothing could have pleased me more! I love Gabriella! I always have!"

Scott had made a point of giving the two of them privacy but when he heard Angelique's voice a smile came to his face. He knew she would be fine and she was!

"I also let Scott read it, Angelique, for I didn't know whether to do it before we went over to the O'Roarkes or afterward. But then I remembered I was spending the night over there as I could hardly get in that cradle Zachariah made for you." The two of them embraced and laughed. Each knew the other was going to be just fine as their laughter mingled with their tears.

In fact an hour later it was a jovial trio that boarded the boat to travel the short distance to Scott's folks' cottage.

Kate was elated to hear that Simone was staying with them for the weekend. The fish were fried outside as a golden autumn moon glowed over the grounds surrounding the cottage. Simone stuffed herself on Kate's cornbread cakes and roasted potatoes.

Her toes tapped to the lively music Timothy played on his fiddle. Kate had a fine singing voice, and they all joined her.

She had missed so much, Simone thought, by not having someone to share the simple joys of life and loving. Poor Maurice!

The hour was late when Scott and Angelique left for their cottage—it had been such a glorious evening for everyone.

No sadness consumed Angelique as they traveled in the boat toward home. She was filled with too much happiness as she anticipated the future.

When they approached the pier her soft voice declared in a very positive tone, "Our first son

445

will be called Gabriel, Scott. He shall be named Scott Gabriel O'Roarke."

A loving smile came to Scott's face as he guided the boat to the pier. He worshipped her so much that there was nothing he'd deny her if it was within his power to give.

"Sounds like a fine name to me, love."

Once again, she was to know Scott's all-consuming love. She always knew the rapture of fulfillment when she lay in his strong arms.

"That ought to make little Gabriel get on his way," her Irish husband teased her, still holding her close.

She wore an impish smile as she lay there in the dark. Tonight was the night to tell him something she'd been intending to tell him since their wedding night.

"Oh, little Gabriel is well on his way, my husband. He's been on the way for over two months. I've just kept it my little secret." She laughed lightheartedly as she felt his firm body stiffen.

"You—you little vixen! How did I ever think you were such an angel?"

Her soft body wiggled close to him and she kissed his flushed cheek as she softly murmured, "Because you love me, Scott O'Roarke, and you always will."

He couldn't argue with her about that. He would love her forever!

Chapter Fifty-three

Maurice Dupree never returned to the city of New Orleans and after five years, Simone Dupree didn't expect to see him again. Perhaps it was just as well for had he returned he would not have liked the woman she'd become. Five years of being friends with the people of the bayou had had a tremendous impact on her, so he would not have liked this simple woman with her simple tastes.

He would not have taken any pride in the life her daughter lived with her husband and children. But Simone was so proud of Angelique and the name the people out there called her. She was known as the Queen of the Bayou and was held in high esteem.

She had learned to cook. Pies and cakes from her kitchen were taken all over the bayou to the sick and elderly. Baskets of her homemade bread and kettles of soup and broth were taken to grateful families in dire need. Those people called the lovely young lady with her waist-long hair an angel for her kind and generous heart.

The longer she lived in the bayou the people saw that her beauty went much deeper for she was just as lovely within her heart and soul.

Her first baby was a son named Scott Gabriel O'Roarke but as he grew into a tot and tagged along with his mother around the bayou he became known as Gabe. A handsome young lad he was with his mother's jet black hair and his father's brilliant blue eyes. There was a bit of the Irish devilment in him and the people couldn't help adoring him.

His Tante Gabriella worshipped him from the minute he was born and she had helped in his delivery. She knew why Angelique had named him Gabriel. She also knew that nothing could ever destroy the love between the two of them. The years had brought them even closer.

When her daughter was born, Angelique named her Delphine and she was the apple of her father's eye. As he'd told Angelique, a daughter must look exactly like her — and little Delphine had silky black hair and onyx eyes.

Some might have looked upon Scott O'Roarke as an ordinary fisherman but he saw himself as a king. He envied no man for he had everything he had ever wanted in life. He had the most beautiful woman in the world for his wife and two adorable children.

His chest swelled with pride when he heard Angelique called the Queen of the Bayou, but she had always been his queen in their little enchanted cottage where they lived and loved!